BLAC

GEOFFREY DAVID WEST

For Olga with love

This novel is entirely a work of fiction. Real events are referred to, but related matters described here that are not in the public domain are completely fictitious and bear no relation to anything that has actually happened and are not in any way intended to suggest that the facts known about the real events are incorrect in any way whatsoever. Likewise, real people are referred to in passing, but no fictional character is intended to bear any resemblance to anyone, living or dead, and if there are any accidental similarities these are entirely coincidental.

Also by Geoffrey David West

Sean Delaney Mystery #2

The Irish Goodbye

The Jack Lockwood Mystery Series:

Rock 'n' Roll Suicide
Doppellganger
Sheer Fear
Jack Lockwood Diaries (short stories)

And regular free short stories/podcasts at:

www.geoffreydavidwest.com

ONE

August 2012, the Lazenby Estate, Brixton, South London

"Christ, Sean, he's gonna use it!"

The tall man had his gun arm raised, the weapon aimed directly at us.

I fired by instinct. The sharp *crack snap* rang out as unexpectedly as a snarled expletive in church, shattering the purity of that hot, blue-skied summer's morning.

Instinct had made me flip off the safety of my Heckler & Koch MP5 semi-automatic carbine and raise it up to aim, firing the second that the red dot above the vertical post of the front sight aligned with his forehead.

It did the job sure enough.

Trevor Goodbody's head exploded into red, he stumbled, and then dropped forwards across the low wall of the landing. Then he toppled over, headfirst, tumbling like a rag doll down to the concrete three storeys below.

"You had no alternative, Sean, you had to take him down," reassured my friend, tall blonde WPC Molly McGivven, who put a reassuring hand on my arm. "He was going to kill us."

"Oh sweet Jesus! Oh fuck!" was all I could manage.

I had the overwhelming urge to start repeating a 'Hail Mary' to myself. An Irish Catholic upbringing comes to the fore in the most unlikely circumstances.

We had been stationed in the opposite landing of the huge block of council flats, watching the armed drugs dealer who was trying to evade capture from my colleagues who weren't far behind him. None of us were expecting it when he turned and aimed his gun across at us instead.

I unclipped the carbine's strap and handed the discharged weapon to my friend Molly, who passed it across to an officer behind us, so it could be given to the investigating team, who would scrutinise every single action we had taken that morning. All of us in The Specialist Criminal and Operational Specialist Firearms Command Unit of the Metropolitan Police's armed response unit, SCO19, knew that in cases of discharged police weapons causing injury and death an inquiry is always instigated, and the authorities come down hard on anyone who hasn't followed procedure to the letter. A detailed report has to be made for each shot fired, and the weapon has to be forensically examined. I would be facing fierce interrogations and debriefings, the like of which I couldn't even begin to imagine. It is inculcated in us from our earliest training that the European Convention of Human Rights only allows 'use of force which is no more than absolutely necessary', and we are only allowed to discharge a weapon 'to stop an imminent threat to life'.

Still shaking from the shock, I let the others run down to look at the body, as I followed them to the stairwell more slowly, horrified by what I'd done. The weirdness of the morning crept on like a bad dream. It had started with 'the shout' received at the station, directing us to the notorious Lazenby Estate, where reportedly shots had been fired by drug dealer Trevor Goodbody, who was on the run from the local, unarmed officers.

Surprisingly, as I followed the others helter-skeltering down the concrete steps of the cramped stairwell, all I could think about was the rank smell of urine, and the absurd whiteness of a thread of cotton on the back of WPC McGivven's blue stab-vest as she charged down in front of me. We all knew that taking someone's life was sometimes necessary, but nothing prepares you for the enormity of it. Believe me, killing someone – even someone decidedly evil – doesn't make you feel excited, exultant or triumphant. You just feel empty, shocked, stunned. You feel like shit. It's the *worst* feeling in the world.

"Fuck me rigid! Looks like it's only a replica!" someone shouted from the yard where the mangled blood-spattered body of the black man was spreadeagled on the ground. The kneeling policeman was pointing to the dead man's fist, which was still clutched tightly around what looked like a large-calibre revolver.

Another kneeling officer, his head even closer to the dead man's arm, was staring hard at the 'gun' still clutched in the man's hand. He looked up at us and his face said it all. "Yup, it's a very good replica. Sorry, mate."

"Don't worry, Sean, you did the only thing you could have done." Molly put her arm around my shoulders, giving me a reassuring squeeze. "It's going to be okay. Anyone would have done what you did, we all thought the same as you. We were here, we all saw what happened. You followed procedure to the letter."

"So it wasn't a real gun he was aiming at us?" I repeated like an idiot, incredulous, my heart pounding.

"No, mate, I'm very sorry, it wasn't." Molly McGivven shook her head sadly, her arm still around me. "But listen to me, Sean. The lads could only see it was a replica when they were within feet – we were twenty yards away across on the opposite landing. No one could have known from that distance. Anyone would have done the same as you. You're in the clear. They'll mount a full enquiry, the IPCC will probably get involved, but you've got nothing to worry about. We've got your back."

*

Penton **Feverill, Wiltshire, 10 December 2014**

River water closed over my head and Penton Feverill's high street Christmas lights were the last thing I saw. Sights and sounds dissolved into a world of green and black. Panic was a heartbeat away.

The river was deeper than I had realised, and I felt the powerful tug of its tide, sucking me down.

Fighting my way up to the surface, I saw the foam of swirling water ahead and swam towards the drowning dog. I grabbed him around the chest and hauled his face above the water. Eventually, in a welter of struggling, fighting animal, wildly kicking legs and sheer brute force, I somehow managed to get us both back to the riverbank.

The woman and the two children were there, reaching out to pull up their struggling canine, and I managed to haul myself clear of the river. It had been sheer serendipity that as I'd been driving though the village I had seen the dog racing after the duck and then flailing in the water. I had braked my car to a halt, leapt out, kicked off my shoes and dived in.

"You were wonderful!" said the woman, her arms around the quivering golden-haired Labrador as the little girl was stroking the dog's face and pressing her cheek against his wet fur. "But you'll catch your death in those soaking clothes. Will you come back to our house and get changed?"

"Thanks, but I'd much sooner you just take him straight to a vet, quick as you can," I advised, shivering in my soaking shirt and jeans in the freezing December wind. "He's not out of danger – the water could still be in his lungs."

"You're very tall, aren't you?" said the little boy, who still had a hand on the dog's fur as he turned towards me, staring up at me through his little round spectacles, displaying a calmness beyond his years. "Why do you talk funny?"

"I guess it's because I'm Irish."

"And you were very brave to save Roger."

"A dog like Roger saved my life once, when I was a policeman. So you see I was just returning the favour. Besides," I told him, kneeling down so I was on his level. "I felt like going for a swim."

The woman turned towards me, tears running down her cheeks. "I can't thank you enough for what you did. Everything happened so fast that even if I could swim I'd never have made it in time. And the river's deeper than it looks, there's a dangerous undertow. I just wish there was something I could do to repay you. . ."

"Seeing that wagging tail is all the repayment I want." I smiled as I touched her hand. "I grew up on a farm in Galway. Dogs were always part of my life. . ."

"We'll never forget you."

After the woman's car had gone, the deserted road meant that I was able to swiftly strip off my soaking clothes to my underwear and use one of the dustsheets to dry myself as best I could, shivering in the chill air of the snowy afternoon. I'd packed quite a few spare garments in my old

Land Rover Discovery, along with the paintbrushes, dustsheets and other assorted decorators' equipment I was going to need for the weeks I was planning to spend working in the West Country. Once I'd put on some dry clothes, I sat in the front with the engine running and the heater going full pelt to try to warm up, aware of that cosy kind of self-sufficiency feeling when you've got everything you could possibly need to survive packed in the car behind you: spare clothes, books to read, biscuits, flask of coffee and sandwiches. I turned off the music radio station because I couldn't stand hearing again 'Rock and Rolling Christmas', by the band Nightingale Green, the jaunty perennial oldie that gets played in supermarkets and radio stations ad infinitum for the pre-Christmas weeks every year.

Was my near-drowning a bad omen, I wondered?

Coming to Wiltshire all the way from my home in Whitstable, Kent, had been a rash decision, just like jumping into the river to rescue the drowning dog had been.

It was hard to think that it was barely nine months ago since I had come here to paint the portrait of ex-rock star Adrian Dark at his home, Netherwold Hall. The cheerless wretched place had been cold, dark and unwelcoming, but I had found *'Just call me Adie, mate'* to be an exuberant, lively old rock-and-roller who had a leathery face chock full of wrinkles, a store of fanciful tales, a beguiling smile and a penchant for hard drink and white powder. During his endless chatter, when I'd actually rather he'd kept his hard-to-capture-with-paint mouth motionless, he had bemoaned the fact that writing his autobiography was much harder than he had realised. Suggesting that my journalist wife should help him had seemed a good idea at the time. And it would have been, except that after their initial first few meetings, in September, Adrian died in a freak accident, and a week later, Jodie was dead too.

Coincidence? I certainly didn't think so, and as an ex-policeman myself I knew the score more than most. But the police were convinced that my wife had missed her footing on a crowded Underground train platform and slipped down in front of a speeding train. Nor were they interested in the coincidence that a week earlier an inebriated Adrian Dark had tripped and fallen downstairs in the night and broken his neck. No one had been willing to follow up the circumstances of her death, and after doing everything I could think of to investigate things myself I had finally run out of options. Coming here today was my last throw of the dice to try to assuage the guilt at my responsibility for her death that gnawed away at me like a disease.

I missed our laughs together, our arguments, our rough-and-tumble conversations, her perpetual restlessness before she embarked on one of her assignments, while I struggled to earn money wherever I could, painting people's portraits when I was lucky enough to be commissioned, as well as painting and decorating people's houses. It was all a far cry from the security of regular income of a constable in the Metropolitan Police, but the political fallout after mistakenly shooting the unarmed man meant that, despite being cleared by the enquiry, I was encouraged to leave the force, because my reputation followed me wherever I went.

Jodie had been more accomplished than me, had earnt good money. Jodie had been the clever, successful half of the partnership, leaving me as the struggling idiot freelancer.

Mind, our marriage had been no idyllic love story. Over the years we had drifted apart in many ways: the early passion had dissipated, giving way to a firm friendship, which faltered when I found out she had been having an affair. In fact, Jodie had been incredibly ambitious and driven in her work, almost as if that took precedence over her personal relationships, certainly her relationship with me. Maybe a lack of any kind of romance in my life for so long was why the thought of meeting my old girlfriend, Mairéad O'Shaughnessy, was so appealing.

The offer of a decorating job from Mairéad had come out of the blue. The estate agency branch of the firm she worked for were selling a house in one of Bath's lesser known rows of terraced houses. Mairéad had advised the vendors – who lived abroad and had inherited the house from a distant relative – that the expense of sprucing it up would achieve an appreciably higher price than the makeover would cost, and they had agreed to fund the work, especially as putting it on the market in spring would make more sense than marketing it so soon before Christmas. Was I prepared to come down and live there rent free and do the place up over the Christmas period, she had asked?

The work was welcome of course, but the real reason I was coming was because Mairéad had told me that her company, Landseer's Auctioneers and Estate Agents, were holding an auction of Adrian Dark's property as part of the sale of his estate, based at his home, Netherwold Hall. The chance of seeing the place again, and perhaps gleaning a few facts that might solve the mystery of my wife's death, was really why I had come.

Professional ethics had always precluded Jodie from talking about her projects until they were done and dusted, so I had no idea what other projects she had been working on, or who else she might have upset. And all her records, computers and papers had been lost in a fire shortly after her death. I was sure she had been murdered. But I was less certain that her death was necessarily linked to that of Adrian Dark.

But for the past few weeks I had reached the point where I wondered if I was becoming obsessed. I had kept Jodie's phone, continuing to pay the monthly charge in the hope of hearing from one of her contacts who might be unaware of her death. I had phoned everyone in her prodigious contacts list, but no one had any ideas. There'd been slews of calls from people who weren't in her contact list but, so far, none of them had been helpful.

"You keep me grounded," she used to say in that calm kind voice that was such a contrast to the hard, cold, surgically invasive tone she adopted when she was conducting a particularly bruising interview on TV or radio. She always told me that I provided a safe haven after her wild adventures – the reporting in war-torn African states, or her poker-faced fact-gathering in the aftermath of tsunamis and earthquakes. If it took me the rest of my life I would eventually prove that her death had not been accidental, as the police had insisted.

Kendal Abbey, as it had originally been known, had been in Adrian Dark's family for generations, but the Dark dynasty had apparently all but fizzled out, with childless fortyish Vernon Dark, Adrian's middle-aged, wayward son, being the end of the line. Vernon had inherited pretty much everything, so I understood. In our chats, Adrian had made no bones about his opinion of his son as a disappointment, a chancer, indeed an out and out 'ducker and diver', who had spent several years in jail, and whose criminal expertise spanned a panoply of murky activities.

Why on earth had Mairéad contacted me out of the blue after all this time, I wondered? Sure, it was true that once we'd been more than close, but the years had made us strangers now. And what was the meaning of her enigmatic remarks in the phone call of: "*Come along to the auction at the big house, because I've got another great idea for you."*

A great idea for me?

Only later on would I find out what a mistake it had been to go back to wretched Netherwold Hall, that ramshackle old manor house that oozed misery from its very core. But by the time I found out my error it would be much too late to back out.

*

The last of the minimal winter sunlight had drained from the sky as the nose of my trusty old car lined up with the crown of the slope. The weather was getting colder and I felt the car slither now and again on what I presumed was the black ice predicted in the forecast. Even the name makes you shiver, something black and skulking and deadly under your tyres that you don't know is there until you crash and die.

As I drove I couldn't resist peeking at the sheer drop to my right, where beneath me in the valley, the fields, trees and villages seemed to smile up at me, occasional lonely lights blinking on in the wild panoply of darkness. To the left, down below, were the bright dazzling lights of Bath, which was only a few miles away according to the map.

Just as I often do in retrospective moments like that I tried to picture the scene as I would present it on canvas. Though I'm principally a portraitist, I paint and sketch all kinds of other things, and I specially enjoy painting night scenes, for I love the effect of light against darkness. Contrast is one of the most exciting concepts we have in life, I reckon: truth against lies, life against death, good against bad. Maybe that was why I originally went into law enforcement – because I like correcting the balance between right and wrong. And I'd say I'm surely a great observer of places and people – the primary function of both a painter and a policeman is to see *everything* and remember it. Lost in my reverie and concentration, I almost missed the turning, and then followed the winding narrow road for four miles, until I saw the turn-off. The track was bumpy, and when I reached the huge black wrought-iron gates, my spirits sank as I heard the ring of my mobile when I halted the car. Sure enough, when I answered I could see it was an unknown number.

"You're going to die, you bastard! You deserve to die because you murdered Trevor!"

TWO

"Who is this? How did you get my number?"

Silence.

"You're going to die! You won't know where and you won't know when. . ."

And then there was, as always, a wild burst of hysterical laughter before the line went dead.

I thought back to two years ago when, as a police officer within SCO19, I had mistakenly shot nineteen-year-old Trevor Goodbody, a drug dealer on the run, because the replica firearm he was aiming at us looked real. The nutcase who had somehow got hold of my phone number had called me many times before, making all kinds of wild threats and promises, and there was nothing I could do about it – I had blocked him repeatedly, but he'd always ring again using a new number, and the inconvenience of changing my phone number simply wasn't worth the hassle. The death threats had so far amounted to nothing, so all I could do was trust that he was a harmless weirdo. Nevertheless, nowadays I always avoided dark alleys at night, and generally kept my wits about me.

I'd met Mairéad O'Shaughnessy at art school when we were both eighteen. In those far-off days we'd been kindred spirits: Irish renegades in the cosmopolitan milieu of St

Martin's School of Art in London. Our peers were mostly polite, well-spoken English teenagers from the Home Counties, and we'd both been outsiders, wild-spirited country bumpkins, brought up in rural Ireland, full of joie de vivre, yet naively impressed by this grand sexy metropolis that everyone else took for granted. We'd become lovers, never out of each other's company.

But we had fallen out of touch years ago, after that final row that I had never really understood.

Sure, it was true that in the years since our explosive parting our paths had diverged even more, as each of us followed our dreams. After getting her degree, Mairéad had landed a trainee job in the fine art department of Landseer's, a firm of upmarket auctioneers and estate agents, while I had taken up a hard-won scholarship for a postgraduate degree in portrait painting, after which I'd taken the hard road of the lonely artist. I'd struggled on, honing my craft, gaining recognition here and there, but gathering precious little financial security. Accepting that my art was never going to give me a decent living, I'd then joined the police and after ten years I was a lowly constable in SCO19, keeping my painting strictly to my leisure hours, until everything in my life had fallen apart. And now here I was in my mid-thirties, slap back down to square one. Struggling artist and painter and decorator, when I was at an age when I should have had a proper career. It was also pretty humiliating to admit that my social life was so pathetic that I had nothing better to do during the Christmas break than to slog away alone, many miles from home, decorating someone else's house, partly because I'd sooner do that than be on my own.

The auction at Netherwold was part of Mairéad's company's responsibility, on the orders of the solicitor administering Dark's estate. She had explained that Vernon

Dark had been forced to realise some of his father's assets, in order to pay the inheritance tax before probate could be granted.

Recently I'd read that Adrian Dark's grip on sanity had been tenuous, and he'd apparently even been diagnosed once as having a 'severe personality disorder', but when I had met him a year ago there'd been no evidence of that. Adie (as he was colloquially known) had been a musician all his working life, and had led a band called Nightingale Green for a long time, which had broken up in 1987. Since then I couldn't name a single song he'd had success with. But somehow I assumed that he'd straddled that nebulous wave that so many ex-pop music professionals seem to ride. Years after their last hit these pop Peter Pans like Adrian still often seemed to be as rich as Croesus, presumably living off the proceeds of their back-catalogue royalties, doing occasional gigs, writing songs for other people, or going into management or production roles.

The Adrian Dark I had painted I remembered as a bald, fat-headed, bleary-eyed lecher whose face boasted more lines than an elephant's backside. Whilst in a low mood he had told me that he was mortally ill: the doctors had given him only a few months to live.

His appearance had been a far cry from the old television clips of the young handsome rocker whose shoulder-length black hair danced around his face as he bucked and dived to his songs. I remember he had specialised in a kind of 'duck walk' where he paced perpetually forwards and backwards, his head jutting backwards and forwards like a chicken.

I got out of the car and looked around, aware of the powerful night aromas of the trees, vying with the scent of newly-mown grass. The countryside smells took me back to my parents' farm in rural Ireland, the taste of home baked bread, the keen scent of burning peat and new-mown hay. But beyond the gates there was a huge manor house, reminding me of Rabson Court, where some years ago now I'd been tearing away some wooden wall panels and ceilings whilst searching for illegal substances, when I'd been a member of the Serious and Organised Crime Command (Middle Market Drugs Partnership division), which is now part of M07.

After leaving the force, on Jodie's advice and with her help, I had written a book about a string of cases I had been involved in. Writing the book had been cathartic, and to my surprise I had enjoyed it. It had sold enough copies to bring in a tiny income, but they'd fizzled out a while ago now.

For some reason I thought of one of the eulogies at Jodie's funeral: *Jodie Whittaker-Delaney was bright, perceptive, clever and fearless. . .*

All too often she had also been arrogant, bigoted and downright cruel. Sometimes I had hated her. For much of our time together we had argued – my Irish quick temper and Jodie's mercurial personality frequently clashed. But the truth of it was, this was the first Christmas after her death, and spending holiday time alone in my cottage on the seafront in Whitstable was something I really didn't want to face.

I got back into the car, closed my eyes and shook my head to clear away my thoughts, and called Mairéad O'Shaughnessy's number on my mobile.

"Good evening, Landseer's Auctioneers, how can I help?"

"Is that you, Mairéad?"

I knew it was. I'd recognise her voice anywhere.

"Sean. I'm so glad you came."

She told me she could open the gates electronically, and I was to drive up to the front of the house. A couple of times already I'd felt the car slew sideways, succumbing to the ice on the road that the weather forecast had warned about.

Kendal Abbey had been built as one of the large abbeys in the Middle Ages. During Henry VIII's reign it was sacked and largely destroyed at the hands of Thomas Cromwell's iconoclasts, who smashed and looted the centuries-old relics and tore down the guts of the building. However, the shell of it remained, and the ruined husk was bought in 1815 by Sir Netherwold D'arque, who had rebuilt the abbey so drastically that little of the original building remained, apart from some of the original external stone walls. Henceforth it had been renamed Netherwold Hall, and the name had stuck.

When Adrian Dark senior died and left the abbey to his eponymous son, the younger Adrian had been a newly successful pop star aged twenty-two. He had used his wealth to renovate the place, installed a recording studio there and used Netherwold as his English base to offer hospitality to musicians and friends from all over the world. When Nightingale Green weren't touring, Netherwold was a centre for constant partying. Indeed, music and partying had made the place legendary in the late 1960s, and the likes of George Harrison, Eric Clapton and John Martyn had been regular visitors and guests.

As I rounded the final bend I drew up in the semi-circular front drive, it struck me that it was possibly one of the most beautiful buildings I had ever seen, like a fairy-tale castle, illuminated by the exterior lamps which shot beams dramatically across the fine stone façade, illuminating the fine carved stonework and the grand upper turrets and castellations. Behind the mansion, spreading up Holywell Hill, I could see rolling woodland. I parked and got out.

Either side of the main entrance portico of the mansion were two large stone plinths, on one of which was a bronze life-size model of a Cavalier soldier of the Civil War, brandishing a sword; unfortunately his head had been removed. The plinth on the other side was host to an oversized bronze effigy of a dog, curled up and sleeping.

Mairéad came out of the main entrance to meet me, long black hair caught in the wind blowing across her features, making her look more than ever like a wild Irish princess from centuries past. But she was no longer the carefree jeans-and-tee shirt-wearing easy-going rebel that I remembered. The wisps of grey hair above her ears added to her allure, and the dark grey business suit and smart white shirt and tasteful earrings and necklace, smacked of a style and sophistication I never knew she had. Her crunching heels on the gravel sounded loud and fast, just like my heartbeat.

Then she was in my arms and I hugged her close, the years we'd been apart vanishing like dew in sunlight. In the past she had rarely smelt of fine perfume, neither had she worn this faultless make-up that had to be hiding those freckles I used to adore. I noticed that even her eyebrows were finely plucked, swooping and dark, setting off the topaz coloured eyes that had a way of staring right into your soul. Her body was toned and fit, with not a spare ounce of flesh.

"Sean! Jeez, you look just the same, so you do!"

"You don't," I told her. "You look rich."

"Get away with you!" She laughed as she pulled away from me. "You're selling your paintings, are ye not? I read that you had an exhibition of your work in Bristol last year."

"A combined exhibition with four other artists, and I hardly sold anything. I'm best at painting portraits, and commissions are non-existent right now."

"And you're a writer."

"One book, Mairéad, and sales have stalled. I had a lot of help writing it, from Jodie. Mind, the publisher said they'd consider any other ideas I had."

"Which is the real reason why I invited you here." She moved closer again, beaming with that wall-to-wall smile I remembered so well. "Adrian Dark's personal diaries are going to be in the auction. I've had a wee flick through them. There's plenty of action, sex, references to wild parties and the musical hierarchy of the old days, details of the songs he wrote, his life on tour. I'm thinking they'd form the basis for a cracking book."

But could I write a cracking book, I wondered? I wouldn't be getting any professional help with this one.

"And there's something else. Masses of photos from all kinds of sources like magazines and newspapers that obviously can't be used without permission, and buying permission from the copyright holders would be prohibitively expensive. Whereas a good artist like you could copy those photographs as paintings, and bypass the copyright laws."

"But what's the betting these diaries will be out of my price range?"

"Aye well, you've got a friend in high places. The auctioneer, Hugo, is my boyfriend. He's on our side."

"Thanks, I really appreciate the thought," I told her, feeling a surge of disappointment, a flash of bitter jealousy towards the unknown Hugo. "Did you know my wife Jodie was helping Adrian Dark to write his autobiography? When

I came up here to paint his portrait, he told me he'd made a start on it, but got stuck – I suggested he spoke to Jodie, and then he wanted her to be his ghost writer. Then he died. And she died about a week later."

"But he fell down stairs and broke his neck – the police were satisfied it was an accident, weren't they?"

"Sure they were."

"And Jodie tripped and fell in front of a Tube train."

"Or she was pushed."

"Come on, Sean! It happened in daytime, with witnesses around, yet no one saw anything strange. It was rush hour, the platform was crowded. She was tired, standing too close to the platform's edge and she had a terrible accident."

"So you followed the case?"

"I read about it in the paper. But just because two people died in accidents a week apart and they happened to know each other, it doesn't mean a thing. Coincidences happen."

"Or they were both murdered to stop him revealing some secret in his autobiography that the killer wanted suppressed. If I can get those diaries, or even the part of his biography he's begun, I might find out about why someone wanted to shut him up."

"You're imagining things. Why would anyone care about a rock star's memoirs, when most of his rock-and-roller years were a sight more than forty years ago?"

"I have no idea. But if I can get hold of his diaries maybe I can find out."

"See here, Sean, I don't want to be giving you any false hopes now. If you can get a bit of writing work that's all well and good, but I warn you if you're looking for any hidden motives for Jodie's apparent murder, you're going to be disappointed."

"I'll risk it. And thanks for giving me this chance, Mairéad. I appreciate it."

"You've had it tough, Sean. First being kicked out of the police through no fault of your own, and I'd guess that trying to make it as an artist is pretty difficult. I want to help you."

"But why? We've been out of touch for years now. I never thought I'd hear from you again. After all the things you said to me in our final row."

"Oh sure, Sean, our final row. When we were stupid, flighty and young, and thought we had it all in front of us. Maybe it was because I suddenly realised after all these years what a fool I was to lose touch with one of my oldest friends." She came close and stared into my eyes. "If you want the truth, I read about Jodie's death and I felt sorry for you. And then I just woke up one morning and thought, why on earth did I let that sexy Sean Delaney slip through my fingers?" She leaned closer. "Breaking up with you was one of the hardest things I ever had to do. Don't you realise that you were the love of my life?"

I remembered her words long after the trouble started. But by then it was too late.

I was in too deep.

THREE

We drove in convoy back into Bath town centre, then skirted the town to the south side, crossing Churchill Bridge and turning right onto the Lower Bristol Road, and finally taking a left. It was like several of the roads of Regency terraced houses in Bath, but unlike the famous Royal Crescent it wasn't built in a semicircle, just a standard straight line.

Number 46 was a small house but it had character – I felt the interesting atmosphere as soon as I stepped into the dank, dark cavern-like hallway. The place smelt damp and musty, redolent of years of cat pee and dirty carpets. I pictured an elderly lady, eking out her days here alone, save for a number of feline friends. Nevertheless, I felt that thrill of anticipation I always got at the start of a decorating project.

"We'd like you to rip out the carpets, give it a bit of a clean and blitz the place from top to bottom. The surfaces are pretty sound, so a few coats of magnolia emulsion on the walls and white for the gloss work should set it off a treat."

"No problem."

"Sorry, but you'll have to rough it, living here," Mairéad apologised. "But the electric is on, all the kitchen appliances are working fine and we've left you a lot of plug-in fan heaters for the cold winter evenings." Mairéad switched on the hall light, but the weak dribble of yellowness barely pierced the gloom. "But I'm thinking you'll need to fit a few new bulbs. You can phone our works department in town, and they'll let you have them and all the ladders and scaffold boards and equipment you'll be needing, and I'll give you our credit card for the local builders' centre for the paint and bits and pieces."

"I have my own brushes and rollers."

"I thought you would have." She nodded. "I also asked them to sort out a comfy bed and some sheets and bedding for you, I don't know if it's okay. The phone line and the broadband connection are active, so you can work on any projects here if you've a mind to. There's food in the freezer and frig and a telly and DVD player for the evenings when you're not out on the town, having a high old time."

"A low old time is more my style these days, Mairéad. I found I had a grey hair the other day. Thirty-five is almost middle-aged."

"You? Middle-aged?" She smiled that thousand-megawatt smile. "You'll be climbing mountains when you're ninety."

"Anyway, don't worry, Mairéad," I told her. "I've happily bedded down on bare boards in my time. I like this house, and I appreciate the change of scenery and I surely need the money. I wanted to get away for a while. . ."

She nodded. "Christmas is an awful time to be on your own, especially now, when it's not long since. . ." Her words petered out. "Sure, I can understand why you just want to get stuck into some work and ignore it. And believe me, I'm truly sorry about what happened to Jodie."

"I don't like to talk about it."

"Course you don't, I'm not prying. If you ever want to talk I'm always here. But of course you never shared your secrets, did you, Sean? You were always moody, contemplative, you always built walls around yourself. Always the one to want to know everyone else's business, but you never liked to talk about yourself. But remember, Sean, I'm your friend. Maybe now we're both a wee bit older you'll not be so secretive."

"Me? Secretive?"

"None of us ever knew what was going on behind those deep blue eyes. You were always a bit of a mystery."

I stretched and yawned, the weariness of the long drive catching up with me. "Mairéad, I really appreciate all this you're doing for me. This was going to be my first Christmas on my own, and I wasn't looking forward to it."

"You plan to stay here all the time, working?"

"The best therapy for loneliness is hard work. And you know me, I do like a challenge. But I mean it, Mairéad. I really appreciate this."

"Have you forgotten, Sean? At one time we were close."

"Now we're different people."

"But sometimes I think back to those days." She stared up into my eyes and dared me to look away. In those moments the years seemed to disappear.

And then she was in my arms and I was kissing her.

"Hold on there," I whispered as we broke apart. "You said that the auctioneer fella, Hugo, is your boyfriend?"

"So he is."

"And yet—"

"He doesn't have to know, does he? God, Hugo is so *English,* he's so, I don't know. .." She was staring into my eyes. "And we have a nice wee love nest here, do we not?"

"Sorry, Mairéad," I told her, stepping away. "With me, it's all or nothing."

"Sure, I might have known, the honourable Sean Delaney." She laughed self-consciously. "I guess you're right, you can't turn the clock back. Well, I'll leave you to settle in. Be at the big house at ten in the morning if you can for the auction – we're starting at 10.30 sharp."

*

When she'd gone, I investigated my new home as I pondered what she had said to me. She had made it clear that she wasn't available, then she had laid herself on the line. What did it mean? The day I understand women is surely going to be when hell freezes over.

There was a pervasive smell of damp and mildew in the bathroom and kitchen, but the other rooms seemed comfortable enough, the bareness and lack of furniture making it seem lifeless and spartan. In the downstairs front room, a knackered sofa squatted on the wall opposite the telly, and I was in professional mode as I anticipated having to rip up all the filthy ruined carpets before scrubbing the walls. As I took a quick recce I was glad to note that the wall surfaces seemed in good order, none of the woodchip paper you often find that's holding together cracked and splintering plasterwork. The yellowing ceilings and walls suggested that a smoker had lived here.

I looked at my watch, noticing it was around 8pm. Sylvia, my editor at Charngate Publishing, was likely to be at home, and I dialled her number, hoping that she was in a good mood.

"Sylvia, does your firm ever publish biographies of rock musicians?"

"Oh yeah!" She coughed her usual smoker's cough.

"They're quite a lucrative line actually. Yeah, yeah, yeah, they are, they are. Pop stars' and footballers' biographies sell well as a rule, depending on the name."

"Would you consider a biography of a musician who's just died? A biography without a whole heap of text, but plenty of good illustrations, copies of original photos of band members."

"Who is it?"

"Adrian Dark."

"The old rocker? Didn't he have a band at one time?"

"Yes." I was winging it, trying to trawl my memory. I had managed to google him on my laptop as I was talking, and just in time the Wikipedia page filled my screen. "They were called Nightingale Green, active in the seventies and eighties. Then Adrian went into production and songwriting."

"Yeah, yeah, yeah." Speaking in duplicate or triplicate was a very 'Sylvia' way of talking. "He died about two months ago, didn't he? About two months, yeah?"

"Yes."

"Um, well then he is still well-known enough to be remembered," she went on. "Well known, yeah. Okay, Sean, I'm not promising, but I'll suggest it tomorrow. Well illustrated, you say?"

"Yes, my own paintings of photographs, so no copyright issues."

"Hm, yeah, sounds like a goodie. As it goes, we're having a management meeting at nine, and I can see what the big cheeses think of the idea. I think they'll like it. Yeah, yeah. I think they'll like it."

"Can you let me know as soon as possible?"

"Sure thing. Sure thing. Soon as the meeting's over I'll tip you the wink. What's happened then? Have you been researching Adie's career for years and years and decided to cash in on it now he's snuffed it?"

"I've always been interested in him."

"But you have done a lot of research already? And you've got full access to his contacts? His family, his friends, they're all willing to give you interviews?"

"Sure they are." Lying was easier on the phone than face-to-face.

"Well I'll give you a bell, yeah? Give you a bell? In the morning."

"Sweet."

"I know I am."

I heard the smash of breaking glass downstairs as I cut the call.

Flying down the stairs, I ran into the kitchen and the intruder spun around.

FOUR

The man who'd come to kill me was a tattooed, black-whiskered hulk, whose muscles bulged under the straining filthy tee-shirt.

A stench of stale sweat and alcohol hit as he dived towards me.

Instinct kicked in as I landed a right hook, straight to the jaw. Although the angle hadn't been the knockout shot I'd hoped for, it slowed him. He blinked in shock.

Until he smashed a left to my eye. I ducked and gave him a pile-driver to the guts. His knee came up and crashed my balls and I fell back. But then, instead of consolidating his win, he ran. I managed to stumble after him. But by the time I reached the broken window, he'd already vaulted up onto the sill, screamed in pain as a jagged shard of frame-held glass tore a gash in his arm, and ran down the garden, blood pulsing and spurting.

My head spun, taking me back to my amateur boxing days, reminding me of those seconds in the ring where you get blurry vision, the brain fuzz, the instant muzzy blur. My groin was agony and my face was on fire.

There was one comfort: no killer would have arrived without a weapon. My intruder had been unkempt and down-at-heel, devoid of the fast reactions or decisiveness of a trained assassin. And the instant look of surprise when he'd seen me was genuine: he didn't even know I was going to be there. Judging by his appearance he was just a desperate chancer, perhaps a drug addict, an opportunistic burglar hoping for rich pickings in an obviously empty house, or even a potential squatter.

I hadn't got any materials with me for boarding up the window, and besides, the long drive and the adrenalin rush of facing the intruder had taken the last of my reserves. All that had happened made me long for sleep, especially as I was going to have to get up early tomorrow to be at Netherwold by 10am. I went back upstairs, lay down in my clothes on the bed and fell fast asleep.

*

Run and run. Push yourself.

That's what I always tell myself when I'm running, forcing myself on even when I'm practically exhausted. Make myself go that wee bit extra, and have my chest heaving, that's the way to do it, so it is.

The stresses and strains of yesterday had made me want to vent my frustration in physical activity, and I sailed across the Churchill Bridge, along Green Park Road, and headed along Charles Street, trying to get a glimpse of the Bath that I remembered. I took a right along Monmouth Street, with the Theatre Royal on the left, then down Westgate Street and Cheap Street. On the right was the vast frontage of Bath Abbey, with its huge soaring central section, reminding me of Paris's Notre-Dame. In front of the abbey was the large square, where a busker was playing a violin to the crowd, and I went down High Street to Bridge Street, then on to Grand Parade, where you can lean on a low stone wall and watch the swirling waters of Pulteney Weir far below you. To the left there's a fine view of the shops and buildings on Pulteney Bridge, that straddles the wide waterway.

I find that thinking while you're running is a very special time. See, your mind is in neutral, open and receptive, and the stress on your body and the wind in your hair, or indeed the drizzle in your face like today, kicks alive new thoughts and ideas.

I had reported last night's break-in to Landseer's Estate Agency department, explaining the circumstances, and that the window needed replacing, and I'd also reported it to the police, but they weren't interested enough to pay me a visit. Now that the burglar, or potential squatter, knew the place was occupied it was unlikely he'd come back.

Running also reinforces the sad fact that I often reflect on. That we are all alone. Alone in our struggle with the world, with life and death and illness. Running reinforces that essential loneliness, but it also affirms your strength, strength that no one can take away from you.

"Why do you spend all those hours on just one painting?" Jodie had said to me one morning. "I mean, how much will you get paid if you sell it? How much would that make you per hour?"

Any artist will tell you that quantifying your creative work, trying to assess how much you can earn in a given time, is a nonsensical exercise. You might paint a picture in ten minutes that takes someone's fancy, or else spend hours and hours perfecting a landscape that no one wants. There are no hard and fast rules, what counts is the passion you feel that drives you to record what you see onto canvas. I like painting buildings, mainly old castles, and landscapes, and also seascapes. An artist has to see everything, and maybe that's what originally attracted me to police work.

Portraiture is my main love, and if I see a face just once, then it's in my brain for evermore. In the police I was what was known as a 'super recogniser', a quirky group of officers who could instantly remember a face, even if they'd only seen it once.

After my run, back at Number 46 I stood naked in front of the full-length bathroom mirror, in the mouldy-walled cramped old-fashioned bathroom. The dinky little scar on my chin was always noticeable to me, a bit like an old friend: a reminder not to argue with a man holding a machete. Now I had a large black circle around my bloodshot right eye, as a result of my encounter last night. Black hair that needed a trim topped a face that had always struck me as neither handsome or ugly – the mouth was a wee bit too big, a few more lines on my forehead than I'd have liked, and a jaw that was more often than not covered in raft of lazy man's stubble. But various girlfriends had called me good-looking, so what do I know? I've still got a six-pack – largely due to the regular five-mile runs and workouts in the gym. I'd given up amateur boxing years ago, but I'd done pretty well at it in my day. Nobody tells you this, but Jeez, how easy it is to get used to the buzzing feeling each time you take a hit to the head, it's part of the toughening up process, the 'not being a wuss' camp of thought. Witnessing post-mortems where you can see the brain swimming in fluid makes you kind of nervous of shaking it up too much, and boxing had taken a back seat in my life years ago now.

I thought hard about my memories of Netherworld, for the last time I had been there, I really had not liked the place. It was like one of those rotten apples that have a fine exterior, but cut the skin and you see the brown and decaying flesh. There was something oppressive in the atmosphere of the place, a deep sense of gloom. I had read that Adrian Dark had spent his last months there more or less as a recluse, unable or unwilling to often leave the place which had been his home for more than forty years. While reputably being a typically hedonistic and party-loving rock star in his youth, he'd apparently matured into an enthusiastic collector. He had an eye for fine antique furniture, valuable paintings, antiquarian books and had a large collection of valuable china, so that when I last saw Netherwold it had become like a stuffy museum of gloom.

What had Adrian *really* been like, I wondered? While he sat for his portrait for many hours, he had been quite loquacious and friendly – I had liked him. However, I also remembered seeing him being interviewed by Alan Yentob for a television documentary. Yentob, the veteran broadcaster, as a rule is brilliant at drawing out the best of his subjects by his skilful and self-denigrating interviews. His talents had elucidated that jovial 'man of the people' quality that I had noticed when I met Adie, the friendly raconteur who liked nothing more than a good natter. However, Adrian Dark had also been surprisingly touchy. Alan Yentob's careful questions about Adrian's self-confessed bouts of schizophrenia had been met with sullen anger and monosyllabic answers. Adie wasn't about to talk at length about his weaknesses, would much rather switch the conversation back to his music and his past successes, particularly his solo album *Fields of the Mind*, made after the break-up of his band in 1987. *Fields* had actually failed to garner much acclaim, and Adrian had pronounced it as 'ahead of its time'. The probing questions about the sudden and abrupt break-up of Nightingale Green, on the day after the night of the Great Storm, 16 October 1987, had been met with an equally evasive response.

*

The day of the auction stands out in my memory as one of those make-or-break snapshots in time, when a little seed of trouble gets stuck to the core of your life, and slowly, relentlessly, gathers momentum. The spirit of the approaching Christmas holidays was in the air, seeping out amongst the gathered people as over-enthusiastic laughter, and fake bonhomie shot through with that peculiar air of suppressed excitement people get when they're anticipating getting inebriated in good company. A tiny silver decorated Christmas tree squatted in embarrassment in the corner of the room, wishing it was somewhere else.

The Great Hall, which had been adapted into a makeshift auction room, smelt of the soothing perfumes of well-groomed professional people, combined with that lovely furniture-polish-and-old-stone aroma that truly ancient buildings can never quite outgrow. The ceiling had grand white sculptured plasterwork and hosted magnificent chandeliers, and the neat rows of padded chairs had the same oval logo on their backs as the large auctioneer's podium on the dais had on its front: *Landseer's, Auctioneers, Estate Agents and Valuers, est. 1789.* Ahead of us several platinum and gold records in glass cases were mounted on the dark wooden wainscoting of the walls, and the trio of custom-made Gretch guitars, with the ubiquitous *Adrian Dark* signature emblazoned on their stocks, were set up in a grand display stand.

The less music-orientated sales items were the standard fare of antique dealers' auction houses around the country: a plethora of valuable china, a few old masters' paintings, lots of fine furniture plus, and what turned out to be the magnet of my morning, several large antiquarian books. The woman standing at the book table didn't even see me, for her excitement at poring over the ancient tome in front of her seemed all-consuming. I gazed critically at my portrait on the wall of a rather uncharacteristically severe-looking Adrian Dark that I had done nine months ago, now in a grand gilt frame that had probably cost more than I had charged. My portraits are always oils on canvas, I love the textural, almost 3D effect you can get with thickly applied oil paint, following in the style of two of my all-time heroes, Frans Hals and Rembrandt.

And then I caught my first sight of Laura's face. A slightly myopic, slender, blonde-haired woman, who was so wrapped up in what she was doing she didn't even notice me. She was standing at the table, totally absorbed in studying a large, ancient volume.

When I looked again, her face fell into my subconscious puzzle-box of starts – I usually begin by drawing or painting one feature on a face and work outwards from there. Would it be her full red lips that I'd begin with? Or the slightly retroussé nose below the massive black-framed spectacles balanced precariously on its tip? Her blonde hair was scrunched up into a short bouncy ponytail and she wore a fluffy Fair Isle jersey, whose black-and-white zigzag pattern went well with the skinny jeans and Ugg boots. I was put in mind of an eccentric Scandinavian holidaymaker absorbed in a museum exhibit. She wasn't conventionally beautiful at all, which somehow made her even more interesting.

"Are you a dealer?" I asked, moving beside her, almost hesitant to interrupt her white-gloved inspection of the huge opened leather-bound volume on the table, with its ancient yellowing parchment, the old print a scrawling, flamboyant swirl.

"Yes, but that's not really why I'm here." She turned to face me.

"Oh?"

"Adrian Dark was my father."

"I'm very sorry for your loss."

"Don't waste your sympathy. I didn't even know him. I've been an orphan since I was five and only found out I had a father who acknowledged me because his solicitor wrote to tell me he'd left me something. Now I've seen Adrian Dark's home and all this, frankly I'm pretty disgusted." She gestured around the room. "I'm feeling pretty *shit* at the moment, to tell you the truth. And it's not just the money – growing up in children's homes, not knowing if either of your parents are alive or dead is a bloody awful existence."

"What about your mother?" I asked her. "Didn't she tell you who your father was?"

"No." She shook her head and smiled peremptorily, as if to push away a hateful memory. "My mother disappeared. She abandoned me when I was five years old."

"I'm sorry."

"Don't keep apologising, for God's sake!" she snapped, then she shook her head and gave that twitchy-lipped smile again. "Sorry, I shouldn't have bitten your head off like that. It's just that it's a long story, and I hate talking about it. It upsets me to even think about it. And I don't need anyone's sympathy." She reverentially closed the book and removed the special white gloves, laying them on the table and turning towards me.

"I'll leave you in peace then." I turned to go, reflecting that her rancid personality hardly matched her fascinating face.

But as she removed the right glove, something took my attention, changing my mind. To my astonishment I saw a very small extra finger, attached to the side of her little finger.

FIVE

"It's called polydactyly," she told me, having noticed my stare.

"I'm sorry, I didn't mean to—"

"—Stare? Why not? Everyone else does when they first see me. I call it the 'sixth finger shiver' of revulsion people shoot me with. And no, I've heard all the clever remarks. I can't use a computer super-fast, or play the piano like a prodigy, because of the extra finger, because the damned thing is pretty much useless. They tell me Henry VIII's second wife Ann Boleyn had six fingers, which was why they thought she was a witch – it's supposed to be a sign of the devil. Just imagine, I wouldn't have been welcome in this place when it was a monastery in the 1400s, would I? Do you know that this was one of the richest monasteries in the south of England before that old bastard Henry destroyed everything inside it, and thieved the rest? They say that 90 per cent of the ancient artworks and books that were held in monasteries were destroyed. *Ancient even in those days.* Think of it. All that wonderful knowledge destroyed. What these walls must have seen."

"And in the seventies and eighties I heard it was a mecca for the elite in the world of rock music. The spiritual home of Adrian Dark's band Nightingale Green and all their friends and hangers-on."

"So it's quite an honour to see the place, isn't it?" she said, aiming a lopsided grin at me. "And yet, you know something?" She moved closer to me, talking in a hushed conspiratorial way as she clutched my sleeve, almost like a child looking for succour. "I have the weirdest feeling that I must have been here before, as a child. There's just *something* about this place that's familiar but I can't place it. Could be something I recognise or even a smell, you know? The memory is tantalising close, close enough to touch, kind of like a lost dream."

"A lost dream?"

She nodded. "Haven't you ever had a lovely dream that you longed to recapture but you never can? And you long and long to get into it again but it's disappeared?"

"Reminds me of an old Irish word *Aisling*. It means a dream or a vision, used in poetry of the 1800s."

"I love those old celtic words. Had an Irish boyfriend once, he used to call me *Cuchla Macree*, he told me it means 'beat of my heart'. Don't you think that's so romantic?"

"*Cushla Macree*, I'd almost forgotten." I instantly thought back to my great grandmother's words crooned to me when I was a toddler.

"And to think, the man I never knew was my father, ended up falling downstairs and landing somewhere right here, near to where we're standing." She changed the subject abruptly. "Makes you shiver to think about it, doesn't it?"

"Sure it does."

"Do you think his death was an accident, like they say?" she asked.

"The police must have checked everything at the time."

"That's not an answer."

"It's all I'm saying." Playing devil's advocate seemed like a useful way of slapping down her arrogance. "But then, it's a mighty long staircase. He missed his footing, or tripped, and hitting your head on a marble floor would surely do the trick. And they say he'd had a few drinks that night."

"But it's very sad to think that he had a riotous life for all those years, and yet he died alone, because of a ridiculous accident. I wish I'd known him. I wish I could have *talked* to him."

"Sure you do. All those questions that'll never be answered."

"Hey, look, see that man over there?" She wasn't listening to me as she indicated a short, powerful thick-set bald man in a dark suit, who was talking to the auctioneer. "That's Vernon Dark, the brother I never knew I had until last week. Or rather the half-brother. He's inherited this place, all the money, *everything.*"

"Have you spoken to him?" I asked her.

"I've tried to, but he can barely bring himself to be civil. I'm an embarrassment to the family. Or rather to Vernon. He's all the legitimate family that's left, apparently. *The last surviving Dark.* Bloody nerve that he's ashamed of me! Someone told me he's a criminal, a drug dealer or something, based in London or Leeds, can't remember which. Look at the way he walks. He looks about as comfortable in a suit as a tame gorilla. He's been in prison, you know, more than once."

She watched him as he walked away from the auctioneer in our direction, studiously avoiding her eye as he passed within a few inches of us.

"Well, fuck you, Vernon my *dear older brother!*" she muttered to his back, loud enough for him to hear. "What do I care? Anyway, I'm sorry, why should you be interested in my freaky family, who don't want to know me?" She paused for a moment, regarding me quizzically. "So what *are* you doing here? Don't tell me, let me guess. Blue jeans, scuffed trainers, a battered leather jacket, too much hair and a day's black stubble. And judging by that black eye, you were in a fight recently. You certainly don't look like a dealer."

"More like a tramp or a troublemaker?" I began to move away from her, regretting that I'd not done so before now.

"No, no, please, I didn't mean that, honestly. You look nice. Comfy. I don't know, kind of like, yeah, I know! You look like a singer at a music festival, or a gorgeously handsome poet maybe? Yeah you look like a singer or a poet, especially with that lovely Irish accent." Her gaze was pleasantly appraising. "So who hit you? And why *are* you here?"

"I knew him slightly." I pointed across to where my portrait was hanging on the wall. "I'm an artist. A portrait painter. I painted Adrian Dark's portrait almost a year ago."

"A portrait painter?" She stared at me, then across to the painting. "Oh boy, you've captured him sure enough. It's almost creepy – it's as if he's actually here, in the room with us."

"Painting someone's portrait is always a balance between flattery and reality. I guess flattery got the upper hand a wee bit in his case."

"He was an ugly old bugger, wasn't he? I saw him on telly once, and he looked *awful.* All his youthful good looks gone to seed." She looked around. "So are you curious about his possessions? Is that why you're here?"

"No. An old friend tipped me the wink that some of

your father's diaries are in the sale. I'm hoping to get them."

"What for?"

"To use as research in order to write his biography."

"I thought you said you were an artist?"

"I am. But I'm a wee bit of a writer as well."

"A 'wee bit of a writer', eh?" She mimicked my accent, irritating me even more. "I'd have thought that learning to be a writer was every bit as hard as training to be a portrait painter. Surely you can't write a book, just like that, can you?"

"I was in the police. I wrote my memoirs. My wife was an investigative journalist, and she helped me a lot."

"Is she here?"

"No, no, she died."

"It's my turn to say sorry."

"And it's my turn to say I don't like talking about it," I snapped back, but she seemed oblivious to my tone.

She nodded, frowning. "Hmm. Well, who would have thought it? A portrait painter who's writing a biography. Don't you think that's rather tacky?" She looked at the floor for a moment. "I mean isn't it a rather despicable thing to do? For heaven's sake, nosing into someone's life and just setting it all out for all the world to see? It seems like, I don't know, poking into someone else's business without their permission."

She'd hit my Achilles heel dead on. For sure, I did have serious reservations about whether I had the moral right to consider the project. Which made me dislike her all the more. "I don't see what's wrong with cataloguing someone's life."

"Come on! You'll be poking and prying and trying to dig up nasty secrets."

"Well I'm sorry you find me so despicable, I'll leave

you in peace!" I turned my back on her and walked away briskly.

"Please, please, I'm sorry."

She had followed me right across the room, ignoring the irritated glances of the well-heeled men and women whom she pushed aside in her haste to reach me. Her hand was on my arm again, pulling gently. When I turned back towards her, there was the glint of tears in her eyes and a blush to her cheeks. The big spectacles were practically dislodged as she hurriedly pushed them back up her nose.

Why oh why didn't I obey my instincts right then and ditch her then, as I should have done?

For the indications of what was wrong with her were there, right from the start, but I deliberately ignored them.

SIX

I later found out that she wallowed in balancing on a knife-edge of emotion, the lightning-fast interplays between joy and despair that are the outward signposts of people with serious mental issues.

"For heaven's sake, please, please don't rush off like that. I've been an absolute bitch, and I'm *really really* sorry, I don't know what's got into me. You see I've had a pretty hard time recently, and I went through hell psyching myself up to come here. I'm all alone, and I'm nervous and uptight with all these snooty people who don't even look at me, unless it's to stare at my hand, so that they can make me feel like a freak. That shit Vernon has made it plain that he hates me, and I was on the point of packing it in and going home when you arrived. I keep feeling as if I just want to burst into tears, and I'm so nervous I say things I don't mean. And it was so nice when you stopped to talk to me, and I so wanted to sit with you in the auction and get to know you more, but now I've gone and spoilt everything by my ridiculous tactless remarks. I'm insensitive, I'm stupid and I'm sorry! *Please, please,* can we just turn back time and start again?"

She blinked away the almost-tears, and I wondered why she was talking so fast, and apparently so on edge. "Are you always so ruthlessly honest?"

"No, not always. You see all it is, as soon as I met you I felt we had this connection. For some reason I just felt totally relaxed, I felt as if I'd known you ages, as if I could say pretty much anything to you, and it wouldn't matter – just like you can open up to an old friend, who'll just tell you to fuck off if he's offended."

"Fuck off then."

She smiled. "I really am truly sorry. I'm Laura Kaplan."

The handshake seemed overly formal, but somehow necessary, a peace offering. I expected her hand to feel cold, but her palm was warm. "Sean Delaney."

"So, Sean, you're a biographer as well as a portrait painter?"

"Heavens no! I trained as an artist, tried my hand at getting portrait commissions, but I couldn't get enough work, so I then joined the police because I needed a regular income. After I left the force I wrote a true-life crime book that I managed to get published and I'm thinking I can maybe persuade my publisher into letting me do this. I'm really down here to do some decorating work on a house in Bath."

"A man of many talents."

"A man who doesn't want to starve."

"Being an artist doesn't pay?"

"Only when you're famous."

"Listen, what I said about digging up nasty secrets, it's not always true anyway when you think about it, is it? Lots of biographers write sensitive, flattering accounts of their subjects, don't they? Blimey almost nauseatingly sycophantic, some of them, especially when they're about royalty."

"Sycophantic or prying and disgusting? Oh boy, Laura, you really do have a way with words."

"Look, Oh Lord, I'm sorry, Sean, I didn't mean—"

But I laughed, and she joined in.

"And what happened to your eye?" she asked.

"I interrupted a burglary last night, and the guy got a lucky punch."

"Does it hurt?"

I shook my head, enjoying the way she was staring at my injury. "Tell me, Laura, have we met somewhere before? There's something about you – I don't know what it is, but just like you said, I feel like I already know you."

"Well, you may have wandered into my bookshop in Stukely Street in town – it's called *Novelicious*. Even though I stock every type of book under the sun, people always tend to think of most books as novels, don't they? So I pondered for ages and came up with a catchy name, but sometimes I wonder if it's a bit yukky, you know? Mainly because we don't sell mostly novels, and it's not delicious at all, to be honest it's a bit of a bear-pit of a place really. *Please, please* do come along and see me there. But I warn you, it's a mess. Books spilling out all over the pavement, chaos inside. A bit like my life really."

"Never seen Novelicious, I'm afraid. I've only been to Bath once before."

"And you only had time to see the Roman baths and the cathedral? And the Roman baths—

"*—Were a let-down.*"

"*—Were a let-down!*"

We finished saying the words at exactly the same time, and our embryonic relationship was sealed with laughter.

"Ladies and gentlemen, take your seats, the auction is about to begin," came the announcement from behind us as the plummy-voiced auctioneer took his place behind the podium. Mairéad had introduced me to her boyfriend earlier on, the very English, very posh, Hugo. To be fair he'd seemed a nice, friendly, agreeable kind of fella.

I was nervous and excited at the same time, mainly because Laura was sitting next to me, but also because I'd never been to an auction before now, and wasn't sure what to do. She was clutching her special numbered paddle, as I was, and we waited for proceedings to start.

Hugo was a real showman, a tall, powerful, blond-haired man with the poise, grace and confidence of an Eton education, and the panache to carry off the stylish dark pinstriped suit and crisp white shirt and colourful tie. Vernon, Adrian Dark's corpulent son, had no such air of aristocratic good humour or grace. Even his dark suit, blue shirt and dark-blue tie couldn't make him look like the self-assured man of the world he obviously thought he was, for Vernon was one of those men who belong to the racing track or a backstreet pub. The suit didn't seem to fit, the collar looked too large, and his ham-like hands with their stubby chewed fingernails nestled half-in half-out of his overlong sleeves were like nervous actors hiding in the wings. He strode across to the front of the room and sat, perched there watchfully, alert to what was happening, piggy eyes scanning the room as his foot twitched rhythmically and he revealed too much hairy ankle above his sock.

"Let's make a start," began the smooth and charming Hugo, once he'd taken his seat at the podium.

The action proceeded slowly, most items reaching and breaching their reserve prices, Hugo's clattering hammer brisk and business-like. There was antique furniture, extremely valuable paintings and a number of guitars that had belonged to Adrian, in addition to his awards from the music industry, gold discs or whatever they were called. There were also some handwritten music scores of several of his hits, including the famous 'Down by the Merrydown Shore'.

As I usually do when I'm at a loose end, I took the small sketchpad I always carry around with me and did sketches of the scene around me. A few quick studies of the more interesting faces: a jowly old frowning man on the other side of the room. A hatchet-faced lady with perfectly coiffed blonde hair, whose eyes looked like those of a hawk seeking prey. Then I did a quick sketch of Vernon, his fat bald head and hunched shoulders, the brutish expression. Laura looked down at my efforts, smiling and laughing to herself, clutching my arm in delight. I felt a thrill run through me.

The morning wore on and soon they came to Lot 32, the antiquarian books.

Each rare volume was held up reverentially by the Landseer's man. But before they began, Laura abruptly got up, all eyes upon her. Unperturbed, she walked up to the front of the room and spoke quietly to one of the assistants.

"Ladies and gentlemen," Hugo said, after having a brief chat with his colleagues and examining one of the large volumes, with a lot of head scratching. "It has been brought to my notice that there's damage to several pages of this volume, something that, regrettably, our rigorous pre-auction checks failed to discover and mention in the catalogue description."

The assistant gravely opened the pages to display several loose pages, coming away from the binding.

"So accordingly, we have lowered the reserve price for this particular volume."

I held my breath when Laura bid for the very same book, and she got it.

She gleefully whispered in my ear. "No one saw me rip those pages out – what a coup eh? I could never have afforded the full price. I'm a bookbinder, so I can repair it easily."

"That's a terrible thing to do!"

She laughed. "Sorry, Sean, I do believe I've shocked you." She went on giggling for a long time, completely unaware of the distaste I felt for her action.

It was my first of my many shocks about Laura.

Shortly after that she looked at her watch and told me she had to get back to her shop, asking me to call in when I could. I agreed, slightly bemused, as I watched her leave.

Much later came Item 64, the diaries and assorted personal papers.

"What am I bid for these personal diaries, photographs and a partial memoir of Adrian Dark, from 1970 to 1987?" Hugo asked imperiously, sweeping his autocratic gaze around the room.

Silence.

I waited.

"Shall we start at one hundred?" He looked around. "One hundred pounds, anyone?"

I held up my paddle.

"Thank you, sir." I probably imagined the extra scintilla of warmth in Hugo's smile as he looked into my eyes. I'd liked him when we'd met earlier, and it seemed that the feeling was reciprocated. "Any advance on one hundred? One hundred and twenty, anyone?"

Someone on the other side of the room held up their paddle.

It went back and forth a few times, until it reached three-eighty. Four hundred was my absolute tops, so I made my final bid.

"Thank you, sir. Any advance on four hundred?"

The man on the other side of the room swallowed,

then agreed to four hundred and twenty.

I looked across at him and something made me feel reckless.

My rival in the bid was a sour looking and weedy elderly man with a mingy white beard and sparse hair, who looked like a badly nourished garden gnome. He was talking on the phone, wrapped up in the call, seemingly unaware that his bid could still be topped. I was determined now. Those diaries represented possible work for me, and my curiosity into Adrian's intriguing life had been piqued. More important than anything else, they just might hold the clue to my wife's untimely death.

See, I wanted those diaries.

And I was determined to have them.

"Four hundred and forty?" Hugo called across to me, locking eyes across the room.

I nodded.

"Thank you, sir." I picked up on the almost-wink that Hugo directed at me.

"All done?" He glanced across at the gnome, who was still distracted, talking into his phone, seemingly unaware of my latest bid, or the auctioneer's question.

"Right, no other bids?" Hugo snapped out in double-quick time, taking advantage of the gnome's inattention. "All done at four hundred and forty. Going once, going twice!" He rattled off his spiel. Then speedily banged his gavel on the desk, smiling warmly in my direction, while out of the corner of my eye I could see the gnome beginning to shout something.

"To you, sir," Hugo said smoothly. "Now the next item—"

"Now see here, fella!" yelled the gnome, now standing up and red in the face. "I was going to make another bid."

"House rules are sacrosanct, I'm afraid, sir." Hugo's poker face was icy as he went on talking firmly and decisively. "When the gavel goes down, that means that bidding has closed."

"But this is a—"

"The next item is Lot 65, an engraved Stratocaster Starburst guitar. Shall we start at—"

But he stopped talking because the gnome was shouting loudly, demanding attention, waving his arms about. Hugo waited a moment, then nodded at a couple of large men at the other side of the room who moved across and, one either side of him, managed to march the small man out of the room.

*

Later, after I had collected the large cardboard box, which appeared to contain a number of small black diaries, loose photographs and sheaves of papers covered in spidery handwriting, and packed it into the boot of my battered Land Rover Discovery, I looked back at Netherwold, wondering what to make of Laura Kaplan. I tried to remember her face, anxious to sketch it from memory, yet aware that I'd never be able to catch it properly.

Back inside the hall I was looking around for Mairéad to thank her and to say goodbye. To my surprise, I looked up to see the big man who looked so ill-at-ease in his suit, Vernon Dark, Adrian Dark's only son. He was walking across to talk to me.

"Hi, I'm Vernon," he introduced himself. His handshake was firm and genuine, as he smiled into my eyes. "Mairéad told me you're a writer and I see you've bought my dad's diaries, with a view to writing a biography of his life," he said.

"That's right."

"Well I'm delighted he'll be honoured that way. We didn't always see eye to eye, but when all's said and done, I only had one father, and if he had his faults he certainly had his virtues."

"I've heard a lot about him. And I got to know him slightly when I painted his portrait last year."

"And a very fine portrait it is," he enthused, staring across at it. "I'm not selling that to anyone, by the way, Mr Delaney. It's a masterpiece, that's taking pride of place in my house. You've really captured his personality on the canvas. And I'm sure you'll do the same on paper. Listen, Sean, can I call you Sean?"

"Of course."

He leaned closer, and I had the feeling I'd initially misjudged him. "I've got to shoot off in a moment but I wanted a quick word, which was to tell you that anything you need, I mean it, *anything*, you just ask me and I'll do whatever I can to help. I know quite a few anecdotes about Dad's life and I'm the sort of bloke who can chatter away till kingdom come."

"Really? That's great news. The diaries could only be a basis for the book, I was planning on lots of interviews from friends and family."

"I can certainly help you there then, pal," he said enthusiastically. "Gimme your email, and I'll send you over a list and contact details. Plus you can always reach me on my mobile – I'm always up for a quick natter – there's nothing I'd like more than to do everything I can to help."

"It's very kind of you."

"No, my friend, it's kind of you to try and make my dad immortal. Mairéad told me that I can trust you not to do one of those bitchy hatchet jobs, that you're too nice a bloke to go digging around for scandal and dirt."

"That's certainly not my intention."

"Because he wasn't a bastard and a shit, like some of his jealous rivals might say. Nor was he out of his mind, as those who latch on to his mental troubles later in life carry on about. As I say, he had his faults, but underneath it all he was a nice bloke, a kind guy who trusted people. That was his downfall really, trusting people too much."

"I met your half-sister."

"My half-sister?" His friendly expression degenerated into a frown.

"Laura Kaplan. The woman I was sitting next to. It must be a wonderful surprise to find out you've got a sister you never knew you had."

"Surprise?" He glared at me with fury in his eyes. "I tell you this, Sean mate, my father made a lot of mistakes in his life," he muttered angrily. "Impregnating Laura's mother was one of them."

"I like Laura."

"Then you don't know her!" he snapped, then moved closer, spitting the words out in a hiss of hatred: "And if you've got any sense you'll keep well clear. When my solicitor traced her he made a few enquiries about Miss Laura Kaplan, and I can tell you she's not someone I'd want to have anything to do with."

"Why not? What's wrong with her?"

"My father kept well clear of her in his lifetime. There were very good reasons for that."

"What reasons?"

He said nothing, just shook his head, glaring into the distance.

"Look, Sean." He was suddenly back to his smiling self again. "Let's stay friends. Here are my contact details. I can talk to you anytime, just call me." He handed over his business card. "Cheers."

After all Laura's warnings about what a bastard Vernon Dark was, he'd certainly been nice to me, until I'd mentioned her name. What did he know about her that I didn't?

Strangely enough, after weeks of worry I finally had some paid work and an interesting project all set up and I should have been excited to get cracking with it, yet something was keeping my enthusiasm in check, ever since the early morning call from Sylvia telling me that the 'big cheeses' at Charngate Publishing wanted me to go ahead. Maybe I was scared of blagging my way into writing this book, when I knew I wasn't a real writer and knew next to nothing about my subject.

I'd be glad to get away from Netherwold, for I found that I disliked the place intensely. What's more I had the sinking feeling that this idea of a biography of Adrian Dark might turn out to be a non-starter. 'Rock Biogs', as they're known in the trade, are usually ghost-written memoirs, chock full of scandal, sex, drugs, more scandals and more sex. So the question remained, would there be enough such details in the diaries? And if there was, who was to say that spinning a life story from the diaries and interviews wouldn't be stultifying boring? Sure, I could underpin it with lots of interviews, and make copies in paintings of the photos to illustrate it lavishly, but would there be enough people around to help me, even if they were willing?

Outside in the car park, I was just about to get into my car when I looked up to see the gnome man, my bidding rival from the auction, approaching me.

"Hi there." He smiled, revealing yellowing teeth. "Allow me to congratulate you on winning the bid. I'm James Patterson."

"Like the novelist."

"Indeed yes, but alas I'm not that James Patterson. But I sure wish I had his money and success. No, for my sins I'm a more humble kind of writer, a professional biographer."

I told him my name.

"Gee, I'm sorry about that bit of trouble in there." He had an American accent, and the words were clipped and decisive, as if he was used to giving orders. "That asshole of an auctioneer should have waited for me, 'cause I was prepared to bid higher, *considerably* higher. But hey, these things happen. And it looks like his mistake is your lucky day."

"Why's that?"

"Because I'll take them off of your hands. I'll give you five hundred and fifty. So there you are, Mr Delaney, you've made a neat little profit for carrying a box the few yards to your car." He took notes out of his pocket, counting them into his hand as he beamed with pleasure. "As I said, it surely is your lucky day."

"Well 'tis rare good of you to offer so much, and I appreciate it," I told him agreeably, overplaying my Irishness to confuse him. "But I'm not after wanting to sell them."

"You're kidding me!" He sounded baffled, then gave a snort of laughter. "Okay then, point taken. I respect a good businessman. Let's say seven hundred then."

"Did you not hear me the first time? No."

"A thousand."

"I'm not selling."

"Excuse me, fella, but you *are* selling!" He coughed, shaking his head, looking astounded. "Understand this, Mr Delaney, I don't kid around. I get what I want. I've *got to have* those diaries." He moved closer, his expression suddenly tight, hard and vicious. "See here, I heard about you. You're just some guy who's written one crappy book and figures he can be a biographer. Believe me, my friend, it takes years to write a compelling memoir, and that's when you've already got a solid grounding in your subject, which I have. How much do you know about Adrian's life? I've been studying the guy for years, and, unlike you, I'm a professional biographer and I've already set up a deal with my publisher in the States. I'm in a much better position to write a book about him than you are. You surely see that."

"Is that so?"

"You don't know me, but let me tell you, my friend, people generally do as I tell them."

"Do they?"

"Sure, my friend, they do." He paused. "If they know what's good for them."

That's where he lost out. If he'd been a nice agreeable guy who'd approached me in a courteous manner I might have reconsidered, but his attitude rubbed me up the wrong way.

"Nobody tells me what to do," I told him. "So, if you'll excuse me, I'm busy."

He clicked his fingers. Suddenly a large man who had been loitering nearby appeared by his side, staring at me impassively. "See here, Delaney, I'm trying to be fair and reasonable. I'll give you a thousand pounds for those diaries. And I won't take no for an answer."

"That's a mighty shame, so it is, because it's the only answer you're getting." I turned away once again.

"Listen," he said angrily. "Do you have any idea of who I am?"

I turned back to him. "I'd say at a rough guess that

you're an obnoxious little twat."

After receiving a nod from the gnome, the big man took a swing at my face. I parried the blow easily, doing a couple of quick jabs to his guts, causing him to double over in pain. He came at me again, but I slammed my fist into his mouth, regretting it instantly as pain shot up my arm, and I wondered if I'd damaged my knuckles. But he fell backwards, blood pouring from his lip.

"And now, both of you, *fuck off!*" I told them.

Patterson glared at me, clenching and unclenching his fists. "*I'm getting those diaries!*"

"Over my dead body."

"That can be arranged."

"You'll need a man, not Cinderella here." I glared across at the big man, who was holding a handkerchief against his bleeding mouth.

"Fuck you, Sean Delaney! You've just made a big mistake!"

"You have a really nice day Mr Patterson. It's been good not doing business with you. Let's hope we never meet again."

SEVEN

Jodie was standing in the distance, yelling at me, wanting me to understand what she was saying. But she was talking in French, using her hands to emphasise her words, and try as I might, my schoolboy grasp of the language wasn't up to following her speed of delivery. I was running towards her, but as I got closer she moved backwards, always maintaining the distance, and as I ran I was sinking in a kind of treacly bog. There was a foul stench of putrefaction. And as I tried to get nearer to her, I found that something was dragging me back, someone's hands were around my throat and choking me. Then Mairéad appeared nearby, telling me that she loved me, that everything had been a misunderstanding. Yet she wouldn't help me, just watched me as I was being slowly strangled to death. Then she came closer. And as I looked at Mairéad's face I saw she had a huge raw fresh scar running from her forehead to under her chin, and it was oozing blood. Her fingers then clamped across my mouth, cutting off my breath, even as I felt my strangulation intensifying. I tried to yell and scream, but my throat had closed and no breath would come. Jodie appeared again, moving closer this time, shouting and shouting something in French, angry with me. Eventually she yelled in English.

"Don't die, you bastard! Don't die!"

The chime of my mobile phone broke into my dream, thankfully waking me up with a start.

"Yes?"

"*Sean, you know I'm going to kill you, don't you? Trevor didn't deserve to die, but you do.*"

"Go and fuck yourself!"

"Am I getting under your skin, Sean? Am I really upsetting you? Oh I am going to enjoy killing you… "Then the maniacal laughter, and, as always the call cut off abruptly.

I blinked away sleep, drenched in sweat and thankful that my mind's eye images before the phone call from hell had only been a dream.

Moonlight outside the window spilled out onto my bed, liquid and mesmeric, as my heartbeat began to ease off. I closed my eyes again, hoping to wash away the horror with the oblivion of some dreamless sleep. But it was no good: something of the horror and terror lived on, and I couldn't rid myself of the ghastly oppressive feeling that had come over me ever since setting foot in Netherwold Hall once more.

I lay back down, and the next thing I knew, there was sunlight streaming through my bedroom window. I tried to evaluate all that had happened in the past few days.

I'd gone from having no paid work at all to the prospect of many days of hard slog, preparing the walls of this slum-like dwelling and then doing all the filling, finishing and painting. In addition I had the prospect of a new project in the pipeline, a biography of a rock star I barely knew anything about, and against my better judgement I had blagged my way into persuading my editor that I was some kind of fan. Would I be able to make a decent job of writing such a book from the diaries alone?

Would I be able to find enough people to give me interviews to give it life? Right now, pessimism filled me to the brim, and I sank back into gloom.

My thoughts turned to the enigmatic Laura Kaplan, whom for some reason I found so hard to forget. The sketch I had made of her yesterday from memory was far from accurate, for it had been impossible to capture her properly.

An hour later, in the living room of Number 46 where the only furniture was the battered ancient sofa, I tipped out the diaries and other papers and the many photographs that had been in the cardboard box, and began to look through them. Had I wasted a lot of money, I was wondering? Simply reproducing his diary would make for quite a dull read, but on skimming through the pages various celebrity names stood out: 'the two Erics' – Eric Clapton and Eric Burdon, the brilliant late great John Martyn, and Martyn's friend, the iconic poet and songwriter Nick Drake, who had sadly died far too young. Was he one of the 'Twenty-sevens', I wondered? The band of pop stars who had died in their twenty-eighth year? Jimi Hendrix and Amy Winehouse were in that ghoulish fraternity certainly.

Many of the songs he'd written and recorded over the years were mentioned, the lyrics of many of them included, so I had the idea of starting each chapter with the lyrics of one of these songs, as a form of introduction, a way of weaving his disparate day-to-day ramblings into a whole.

The rough draft of Adrian's partial autobiography was more interesting, and I noticed an entire chapter devoted to Jimi Hendrix's death. In an ideal world I would be able to gather a number of people who might give me interviews to add to the text, but not many of Adrian's contemporaries were around anymore. However, I knew that at least one other member of Nightingale Green was still alive. Roger

Bracken was living on a farm not far away from here, according to Vernon, whom I had phoned first thing to ask a few preliminary questions.

I hated Jimi, was how the opening chapter of the book went on, after describing the circumstances of the musician's untimely death. He went on to describe how he, Adrian, had taken a girlfriend to a party, where she caught the eye of Jimi Hendrix, and she had promptly abandoned Adie. He went on to elaborate on dirty tricks that Hendrix had done to others in the business, and how badly he was thought of, even saying that his musical ability had been overrated. This was intriguing and controversial, and an adverse view of such a revered musician as Hendrix might well give the book a unique selling advantage.

Coincidentally I had read a lot about Jimi Hendrix, from a variety of authors. Probably the most comprehensive is *Room Full of Mirrors*, by Charles R. Cross. While the rock star was obviously no saint, Cross paints a picture of an extremely talented musician, who was also generally well liked. Sharon Lawrence, a journalist who was a close personal friend of Jimi's, presents in her book much the same kind of person: totally crazy, obeying no one's rules and living a life of wild excesses. But essentially a nice man, happy to help others and even teach them some of his tricks on the guitar, a man who was devoid of jealousy or meanness to the extent that he was almost naive. He had no morals regarding sex, maybe, but he was a rock star and those were the permissive sixties.

A roadie called Tappy Wright who mentions him in his memoirs, also seemed to like him a lot. I remembered Tappy Wright stating that Mike Jeffrey, Jimi's now-deceased agent, had drunkenly confessed to him that he had murdered Hendrix, because his client was 'getting out of control', and threatening to leave his agency, and because Jeffrey was in money difficulties and relying on his most famous star's earning power, and that was supposed to be his motive. The reasoning behind this spurious tale was that Jeffrey had a lot of recorded video and music that could be produced for sale after Jimi's death, guaranteeing a healthy income for his agent for years. Which turned out to be true. But, to my mind squaring the circle of Jeffrey's success after Jimi's death, and saying he had predicted this and therefore was his motive, was not convincing at all.

Aside from Tappy Wright's tale, every one of the other accounts of Jimi's death, plus the official findings I've read, state a far less dramatic end for poor Hendrix, and they all have the ring of truth. Unable to sleep he had taken nine Vesparax tablets – a German sleeping pill supplied by Monika Danneman, his sometime girlfriend and companion of the night – plus other drugs, and he had also drunk a lot of red wine. The coroner's verdict was that death was accidental, caused by suffocation when he vomited up the drug-and-wine mixture, which entered his airways. Unconscious, and thus unaware of his plight, he had simply died as result of this accident. Indeed, a former girlfriend had stated that when with him she had helped him through a similar ordeal, clearing his airway when he was unconscious and in difficulties.

But on the night in question, it seemed that Monika was fast asleep and unaware of what was going on. Monika herself had never got over the trauma of being unable to save Jimi's life, and killed herself several years later after writing a book about her relationship with him, and appearing in court cases relating to her account of what had happened. Jimi's death being as a result of suicide had been hinted at, but this was vehemently refuted by Jimi's friends and acquaintances, and furthermore made no sense.

However, it seemed as if Adrian Dark had another take on things, and this was the dramatic opening of his memoirs:

I was there. And I know absolutely what happened.

On the day Jimi died he had been going through a bad patch in his life. All the accounts refer to him being upset and off-colour, not turning up for the jam session organised by Eric Burdon that last evening. I can reveal the reason why he was so upset.

Jimi had been having an affair with a married woman who I'm not going to name, as it would not be fair on her family. This was nothing new: he thought nothing of going with the wives of friends or acquaintances, but this was different. Her husband was a musician who had always liked Jimi, they had been good friends for several years. For a long time, this man and his wife had been trying for a baby, without success.

On the 16th of September, 1970, the wife told her husband that she was pregnant. At first, he was over the moon, thinking that at last luck had been on their side. But then, knowing she couldn't get away with lying when the baby was born, she confessed to him that she had been having an affair with Jimi Hendrix, and the baby was his.

I know what happened then because I was there. On the evening of the 16 September I was at Ronnie Scott's club and listening to Eric Burdon and his band War, and Jimi was playing along with them, none too successfully in fact at first, but he got better. Afterwards I heard that he spent time with Daniel Secunda, Devon Wilson, Alan Douglas and his wife Stella, and he spent the night with the last three. Jimi had been having a lot of trouble with his agent of that time, Mike Jeffrey, and he was planning to sack Mike and appoint Alan Douglas as his agent. Alan flew back in the morning, to set things in motion, full of plans for their future partnership.

Next day, 17 September, he spent largely in the company of a girlfriend, Monika Danneman. He arranged with his friend and fellow Jimi Hendrix Experience band member, Mitch Mitchell, to meet him at the Speakeasy Club at midnight to have a jamming session, also in the company of a musician called Sly Stone, who was flying into London that night.

He never turned up.

Nobody else knows what happened during the early hours of the 18 September 1970.

But I do. I had gone to see Jimi, having heard that he hadn't turned up at the Speakeasy. I knew he was staying at the Samarkand Hotel, with Monika.

When I arrived there, the door wasn't completely closed, and I heard loud voices. Monika was nowhere in sight, but the husband of the woman Jimi Hendrix had made pregnant was standing over Jimi. He had a bottle of red wine in his hand, and he'd been pouring it down Jimi's throat, but Jimi had vomited. When I came in, Jimi was motionless, his eyes closed, vomit all over the place.

This killer then attacked me, hitting me hard in the face, and I was spark out for I don't know how long. When I woke up, I was alone with Jimi, but he was in the same prone position he'd been in when I'd first come into the room. I think he had been dead all that time.

I went across to look at Jimi, but he wasn't breathing, he wasn't moving, and I could see that he was dead.

I left the room, knowing there was nothing I could do. When I looked at my watch it was 2am.

Afterwards, later that day, I heard about his death, and I knew what had happened. What was true and what was not.

Why didn't I tell anyone at the time?

I was afraid. I was only just starting out in the music business, and I didn't want to make enemies. Besides, at the time Jimi's killer had a reputation as a tough guy – he had associations with some dangerous characters, and I knew that a word in the wrong ear and at best I might have my fingers smashed so I could never play an instrument again, or at worst I'd be found floating in the river.

But after all these years I think the truth should be told. The killer and his wife are both dead. I think the son is still alive, and maybe he deserves to know the truth about his father. Of course his real father was murdered by the man he grew up with, who told him he was his father. This man was dark-skinned, so the son's appearance didn't immediately alert you to his having African blood. Also, by a quirk of fate, he had inherited his mother's non-wavy hair and European features.

This man, who I have decided not to name, should be known as the man who killed arguably the best rock musician of the twentieth century.

The story seem wildly far-fetched and unlikely, and it stuck me that Adrian Dark was likely to be a liar. It wouldn't be the first time that someone tried to enliven an otherwise boring biography by injecting an exciting, sexy, but apocryphal story.

Which meant that writing his biography was going to be fraught with difficulties.

I didn't know it at the time but taking it on was one of the biggest mistakes of my life.

EIGHT

Novelicious was in the middle of a run-down row of shops, adjacent to a fish-and-chip shop. Books of all kinds were stacked up high on the pavement in untidy piles and heaps. Finding a path through the mounds of them wasn't easy and once past the shop's threshold it was like entering a tomb, such was the darkness and gloom. Everywhere there was mess and untidiness, teetering piles of volumes blocking the way at every turn, and shelves crammed full right up to the ceiling.

Once I was fully inside, the stodgy cloying aroma of old paper and cardboard and dampness seemed to permeate everywhere. There were a couple of scruffy looking middle-aged men frowning as they peered at books on shelves and the man nearest me reached for what looked like a giant atlas, a huge volume that he could hardly lift. Another man in a raincoat was skulking in a corner, hands poised near his crotch and looking for all the world like he was the archetypical flasher, keen to sample some exotic pornography. The place was oddly reminiscent of those TV programmes about hoarders, where items are so densely packed into a space that it's hard to move, and you have to carefully negotiate a passage through. The darkness and gloom created a morbid fetid atmosphere, and I had a claustrophobic urge to turn round and go back outside.

As I walked further into the shop the chaos got even worse. I passed an open door leading to a flight of stairs that apparently led up to a void of pitch darkness. Ahead I could see a stepladder leaning up against the far wall. Laura was perched at its top, reaching precariously across a long row of books on an upper shelf, just beyond her reach. She was wearing a tight-fitting yellow jersey and faded blue jeans with fashionable slashes at the knees, exposing glimpses of flesh. I picked up the faint odour of a flowery perfume, and noticed her fast and neat athletic movements.

Her left jean-clad leg was projecting outwards in mid-air to allow herself to get even further and the ladder rocked sideways, one of its feet coming right off the floor. She saw me and climbed down, clutching a huge old tome in her arms.

"Thanks for coming, Sean," she told me as she came closer. "I was so glad you called me. It's lucky you did – I've got to go up north on business later on today. An avid book collector died in York, and I'm making an offer for part of his collection."

A diminutive black woman with a curtain of frizzy hair and a friendly smile came up beside her, pointing to the IPad she held in her hands.

"Sean, this is my friend Barbara. We manage the shop together, and she holds the fort while I'm upstairs in my workshop. I couldn't do it without her."

"No she couldn't," Barbara replied, smiling. "She's a useless, idle cow, don't know why I put up with her!"

They laughed, then heads together over the IPad in Barbara's hand they discussed something before Barbara turned towards me as she left and said, "Good to meet you, Sean. Hope you enjoy your stay in Bath."

"We can talk upstairs in my workshop," Laura told me, leading the way.

The room was up two flights of stairs, cramped awkward flights with uncomfortable narrow turns.

It was a long room with the ceiling sloping in different planes, and had clearly once been the attic area and it had an abundance of natural daylight. Like the downstairs shop area, the place smelt of dampness and paper, but here there was the odour of oils and adhesives and the bright sharp tang of new leather.

"This used to be the loft area," she explained as we walked along, passing the racks of chisels on the wall and a large metal press of some kind. Books in various stages of completion were on the long workbench. In the centre of the bench was a vice: two large wooden jaws held apart by a screw device, in which a book was held.

"Tell me about bookbinding," I asked her. "I know nothing about it."

"Ever since I was young, I always loved books with a passion. Growing up in a children's home, books were my escape, they were my lovers, they were my opening into different worlds. I love everything about old books, the feel of them, the smell of them, the idea of wondering how many people have handled them over the years. See this?" she asked me, leading me to the workbench, and turning the handle of the vice, releasing the huge leather-bound volume that had been held in its jaws. She lifted it across and laid it down carefully on a threadbare blanket that was on the workbench's timber surface. "It's a sixteenth-century family Bible. One of the few remaining examples that are still in existence. This was rescued from an old barn, would you believe? Fortunately it had been locked up in a metal box, otherwise the mice would have eaten it years earlier. God, it's so exciting to hold it, feel your hands on something that was made all those years ago. If I ever got some serious money I'd buy more books like this for myself, I can spend hours playing around with them. I could even open up a book museum – that's a dream I've always had."

"How do you restore a fragile thing like this?"

"First of all, you have to decide what can be saved and what can't. For instance this leather covering is just too far gone. But look inside!"

The Bible was heavy for her to lift, and when she carefully opened it up the amazing illustration and the colours were astounding.

"The guiding principle we always follow is whatever repairs we make, have to be reversible, because with technology coming on in leaps and bounds, for all we know there might soon be a better technique developed for making repairs, so we have to be careful that everything we do can be undone without causing further damage to the original. The original is sacrosanct."

She fussed about at a tiny sink and worktop in the corner, then brought two mugs of coffee across and handed one to me, and took a sip from the other. "Christ, this is awful!" she said, making a face as she picked up her mug and took mine, tipping their contents down the sink. "How about wine? I've got an opened red here somewhere, I only hope it hasn't gone off."

"Thanks."

She rummaged in a cupboard and produced a half empty bottle, pouring us both a generous measure in the mugs. After she'd given me mine, she sat beside me on the sofa.

"So, what are your plans, Sean?" she asked.

"I want to make a start on the book. In the meantime

I'll get cracking on the house."

"Is it a big job?"

"Not too bad. The walls are sound, all I have to do is strip away the floor coverings, then get going on the main surfaces. It's a lot of work."

"So you're going to be around here for the Christmas holidays?"

"For sure."

"Won't your family mind you being away at Christmas?"

"I don't have a family. As I told you, my wife died, and there's no one else."

"I see." She gave me a sympathetic nod.

"By the way, I may as well tell you what I really think about her death. I don't believe Adrian Dark or my wife died as a result of accidents. I think they were both murdered, so as to prevent the release of some revelation in his diaries or his partial biography."

"But you told me that the diaries only go up to 1987, the break-up of Nightingale Green. Who would care about things that happened more than thirty-five years ago?

"That's what I'm hoping to find out."

There was a pause.

"How about you?"

"Me?"

"What?"

"Do you have any relatives you like to spend time with at Christmas?" I asked.

"No. No parents as you know, no siblings apart from bloody Vernon. No boyfriend at the moment. I'm pretty much on my own."

"Flying solo has its advantages."

"Does it?" She stared at me for a moment. "Do you

know something, Sean? Meeting you has helped me make a decision."

"What decision?"

"It was seeing Netherwold, and wanting to find that *Aisling* you know? That forgotten memory."

"Aisling doesn't quite mean that. It means—"

"Shut up and don't be so pedantic, Sean! Look, I've read about psychiatrists who can hypnotise you into remembering things, who can help you to access forgotten memories. I found one in Harley Street, in London, and he's agreed to see me."

"Why have you done that?"

"Remember I told you I had this feeling that I'd been at Netherwold before, that the place seemed familiar? Well, as I told you, my mum went missing, and it's all a long story which I don't want to go into now, but I reckon that everything in my past could be connected somehow."

"Connected? How?"

"Okay." She shook her head, staring at me. "My mother disappeared and I have no idea what happened to her. All I know is that I was abandoned as a child of four and was found wandering alone in the village of Penton Feverill, which is the closest village to Netherwold. I was wandering on my own and I wouldn't tell anyone about what happened that day – they reckon I was traumatised or something. But that was the same time that my mother disappeared. Something happened that day, and I have to find out what it was. Everyone told me that she was a rubbish, terrible mother, who simply abandoned me, fled to the Netherlands with the circus that had been working in the area, and the police couldn't trace her. But now that I know my father was Adrian Dark, it's obvious that she must have come to Netherwold to see him, maybe to ask for money or something. And then she disappeared. Maybe Adrian Dark got rid of her? Maybe he killed her and hid her body?"

"It's guesswork."

"'Course it is. That's why I want to see a psychiatrist who can hypnotise me and take me back to that time. . ."

"It's a shame." I told her. "I've only just come down here, and now you're going away. I'd hoped to get to know you better."

"And I want to get to know you too, Sean, I really really want to." She stared into my eyes. Put her hand to my face and traced a finger along my lips. "I'll be back in a few days – before Christmas certainly. If you're not doing anything on Christmas day, maybe we could spend it together? Do you know something, Sean? Ever since I saw you. . ."

"Yes?"

"It doesn't matter."

"It matters to me."

She looked into my eyes. The moment seemed right. I pulled her into my arms and kissed her.

For a second everything was fine. Then, suddenly, she started to struggle and pushed me away. And as she did so, without warning, her fist smashed into my mouth, knocking me backwards, so that I fell to the floor.

I could taste blood.

"Don't you dare touch me!" she yelled at me, standing, glaring down at me as I struggled to my feet. "Don't you dare. ."

I didn't hear the rest of what she said as I ran down the stairs and out of the shop.

NINE

As I drove back to 46 Latimer Terrace, I felt a deep weariness.

In the short space of time in which I'd got to know Laura I had first of all disliked her, then found her fascinating, and finally admitted to myself that she was incredibly attractive.

However, what had happened just now was like some weird kind of nightmare. I obviously didn't know Laura at all.

What had I done wrong? I was beyond certain that she had wanted me to kiss her, then she had changed abruptly, reacting with fear and extreme aggression. The *volte face* was as unexpected as it had been scaring.

What's more it triggered off something in my mind, from a long time ago.

I pulled into a lay-by, parked and concentrated hard. Scanned through my 'face recognition memory', that had never let me down during my days in the force, when colleagues had asked me to try to put a name to a face.

Because I now realised that the reason Laura had interested me from the start was that I thought I already knew her face from somewhere. Then it clicked.

On my phone, I googled around from the fragments I could remember.

Child abuse. A big case that had blown up about twenty years ago. A children's home, Harper's Dyke House, and the key whistle-blower, 'Laura McKechnie', aged fifteen, her real identity protected, who had given evidence in court against several members of staff, who had subsequently received substantial custodial terms for years of systematic sexual exploitation of children in their care. While her identity had been secret, it seemed that one of the tabloid newspapers had got a picture of her, which they had published. The face on my screen was that of a much younger Laura.

I'm no psychiatrist, but I could well imagine that if you associate having sex with fear and pain and disgust, it might explain her reaction towards me. But, if that was the case, why had she led me on?

Vernon Dark had warned me that there was something odd about her, and he was right. I could still remember the sheer undiluted hatred she had directed at me when she stared at me for the last time.

Oh well, it definitely *would* be the last time. One more disappointment in my love life to chalk up with all the rest.

Fortunately I had more than enough work to do in the next few weeks, without getting tied up with a madwoman. Perhaps I had been lucky to have found out about her early on, before I had got more involved with her?

Ten minutes later I drove down the narrow alley between the rows of houses, and onto my parking space, at the rear of the property. That's when I saw that the back door was open.

The rear gardens were long, and with any luck the intruder had not seen me arrive.

I parked and got out of the car, walking slowly and carefully up to the rear of the house.

Another break-in?

Or had the man who wanted to kill me in revenge for shooting Trevor Goodbody managed to trace me to here?

From the outside, it was pretty clear that the house was unoccupied and in a bad state of repair. And the Landseer's *For Sale* sign outside would most likely deter squatters.

As I got closer, I moved fast and got into the back kitchen, straining to hear any noises. Silence.

And then, as I concentrated I could hear something upstairs.

I tiptoed up the stairs, then inched along the corridor to where there was an open door.

"What's your game?" I yelled at the man in the balaclava and dark tracksuit, who was searching through my cases.

He spun round and flew at me. He landed a punch to my chin, I went down. As we struggled on the floor, he pulled out of my grasp and, as I tried to pull him down, he kicked me in the face.

I struggled to my feet, catching up with him and caught him around the waist and he dragged me out onto the landing. For a long time we struggled together, landing punches as best we could. Until we crashed against the banister at the top of the stairs. There was a splintering sound as it gave way.

He had fallen from the top landing to the hall floor, landing awkwardly. But as I went downstairs I easily caught up with him hobbling towards the front door, one foot dragging badly, as if his ankle was broken or strained.

When he swung the big tin of paint into my head.

I woke up much later on, wondering who he had been

and what he had wanted to find.

It was not the same man as before – this one was altogether slimmer and taller.

He had been searching through my stuff. I remembered James Patterson warning me that he was determined to get the diaries. Had this man been searching for them?

If so, what was in them that he was so keen to find?

*

Laura Kaplan in Sheffield

Go higher! Go higher!"

And she did.

My mother climbed higher and higher with me on her back, my four-year-old arms locked around her neck, my knees clutching her chest as I giggled in delight. The world below us was getting further and further away and my horizons were splendidly filled with exciting new things. Sights, sounds, even the air tasted sweeter, and everything was thrilling, from the bird that flew past my ear to the shimmer of sunlight on glass. Her trainer-clad feet were twisting and turning, cramped toes clinging, as she clambered on windowsills and brickwork, and we moved up into the sky. My mum was taking us where no one else was going. We were together up in the sky where no one could touch us or hurt us, ever again. As a circus acrobat she was used to walking the trapeze, she could glide through the air like a bird and she could *climb anything!*

I yearn for those days. That's why I climb on my own now, thirty years later, even though I haven't got her amazing skills. Climbing up buildings where no one else can go seems like a way of getting back to that amazing rapturous feeling that I can never quite recapture except in my dreams.

When I climb I am Sarah. Laura goes away. Sarah is free, wild, empowered, courageous, daring, *sexy*.

A million miles away from boring Laura.

Doing what I do is dangerous, illegal, and a world away from my respectable life. But when the adrenalin courses through my veins I'm higher than any drug taker on her first trip of heroin, sexier than a nymphomaniac riding her umpteenth orgasm.

Going up and up and up forever. Reaching for the sky. It's all I've ever wanted to do. And to look down on the world from on high and to never have to go back down to all the darkness and the misery and the loneliness. The camcorder in my helmet records the wonderful panorama below and all around, the sheer view of the streets and fields below, my toes on windowsills over the edge of a fall like a beckoning eternity. Tonight @SarahintheSky will have another video to post online to my Twitter followers and to share on my Facebook page.

No one knows the real identity of Sarah in the Sky.

As I crammed my toe into the next foothold I looked down on the city of Sheffield, now emerging from the haze of cold morning mist.

I remembered Paris, and meeting Emil Hervé. And what had happened to him.

Everything seemed to somehow spin out of control.

Until there was the horror as I watched him fall.

Emil's face seems to fill my nightmares. . .

And now, I can't stop thinking about Sean.

I have to see him again and explain what went wrong.

I have to talk to him again.

I have to hold him in my arms. . .

*

Laura Kaplan in London, January 2015

The man is tearing Mummy's clothes off – ripping them. But she's fighting with him, kicking, slapping, biting him. But he's just laughing, hitting her back. Now he's torn her top off, and pulling her jeans and pants to her feet. The other men are joining in and slapping her, touching her tummy and chest. All of the men are naked now. They're kicking her legs, pinching and slapping her, and now they've dragged her down onto the floor. Two of them are holding her down while she's struggling and fighting. Another is on top of her, crushing her. She's screaming out in pain! They've pulled her legs apart. The men are laughing. Shouting. Hitting her with great slaps. There's a crack as someone grabs her by the hair and smashes her head backwards onto the hard floor. She's stopped screaming. There's lots of blood. . .

"Stop! We're ending this session."

I heard his voice from a long, long way away, its slightly altered tone alerting me to my real self, like a plaintiff whistle inside a dream.

"Laura, listen to me! When I snap my fingers you'll be in the here and now, in my Consulting rooms in London."

And I was.

Back to the cosy smell of the hard leather couch, the crackling of the roaring log fire in the grate, the bright Impressionist paintings on the velvety green walls, the soft lighting. I was lying on the couch, feeling woozy, tired, confused. Dr Fanshaw was sitting beside me, holding my hand. He's so kind and gentle, with his sweet soft voice and silver hair and comforting smile, that it wasn't scaring to go into the trance. In fact, to be honest, even though this was only our second session, I'd come to rely on him more than I should. They say that patients sometimes fall in love with their psychiatrist, don't they?

"Did I say anything during the session?" I asked him, remembering fragments of an awful dream, shot through with disturbing horrible images.

"Yes, you did." He played the recording back to me from the beginning, and we both listened in silence.

Now I can see the big old house. It's magic, like a castle in a fairy tale. Mummy's leading me across the grass, past the cars, through the grand front door. There's a funny old-woody smell and a whiff of boiled cabbage. Mummy's holding my hand, making me walk fast.

"And?" Dr Fanshaw asked.

Walking along way along the long room. Getting closer to the noises, the crash of a drum, the whine of a guitar. So loud it hurt my ears. And Mummy is making me walk faster and faster. She's dragging me!

There are funny smells everywhere. Burning smell, like in that church we once went to.

We're in the big room. I look up at the high ceiling. The funny carvings, the mouldy stink of the walls. And the up-and-down clangs of a guitar. The slap-crash-slosh of a drum.

Nobody sees me. Mummy's not looking at me now. I hide under the sofa and huddle up to keep warm. It's fun to watch and wait and see what's going to happen.

More men have come into the room. They're all crowding around Mummy, shouting at her and laughing. She's trying to get away. She's screaming. Now the man is tearing Mummy's clothes off. . .

The quietness afterwards was like a soft blanket of silk cocooned around us.

"So that was the last time I ever saw my mother," I said, breaking the silence. "And it's the first time I remembered what happened that day."

"I'm very sorry, Laura."

"But I saw my mother being attacked. Why didn't I call out to try and stop them?"

"You were five years old and you were beyond terrified. It's called a catatonic trance. You were literally paralysed with fear. You were witnessing something you couldn't understand but you did realise that your mother, who had always been your sole protector, was being attacked. Your mind shut down, and I think at some point you fainted. Then, when you woke up, you were alone and you couldn't find her. So you ran away, ending up in the village high street."

"But afterwards? Why didn't I tell someone what happened?"

"Your mind locked it into your subconscious, what's called traumatic amnesia. Soldiers can get it after particularly horrifying combat experiences."

"Yet I remembered under hypnosis."

"With my help and guidance. I've helped people suffering from post-traumatic stress disorder, which is one way of describing what happened to you."

"So now I know that my mother didn't just abandon me, as everyone said at the time. As I told you, they found me wandering around Penton Feverill in the middle of the night. There was a huge manhunt for my mother, so I was told, but there were no sightings, and everyone assumed she'd just abandoned me."

"And afterwards you were taken into care?"

"Yes."

"And you were unhappy?"

"I've told you part of what happened at Harper's Dyke. I hate to think about it."

Dr Fanshaw nodded gravely.

"There was a Dutch circus in the village of Penton Feverill that was leaving that day, and everyone assumed that my mother must have gone away with them, even though they denied it. I had no idea that she took me to the big manor house."

"Until you went there recently and found that the owner, Adrian Dark, was your father?"

"Yes."

"It must have been a terrible shock to find out who your father was after all these years."

"Yes. Worst of all was to realise that when I was alone, and I really needed someone to care for me, he didn't care a damn. Yet he goes and leaves me money in his will."

"Ultimately he must have realised how badly he'd behaved."

"And finally after all this time I'm getting some answers. He must have known what happened to my mother, all along."

"I'm sorry, Laura." His lined gentle face was troubled.

"So what should I do now?" I asked him.

"Go to the police and tell them your story. Even though it's thirty years too late, they have a duty to investigate what happened." He paused. "Of course you realise what you've described?"

I nodded. "I witnessed my mother being raped and possibly murdered."

"How vivid was your recollection of these men? Would you recognise them again?"

"I don't think so. I didn't see them properly." I closed my eyes, straining to remember. The memory wasn't really there, it had all been more like a dream. But if I concentrated hard I could almost get back to it, but it was blurred, fuzzy, diminishing by the second, a dying dream in daylight. "But from the pictures I've seen of Adrian Dark as a young man, I don't think he was one of her attackers. I think it was the members of his band."

We sat in silence for a few minutes.

"I almost wish I could un-remember it."

"Never wish that. Because, Laura, today has been a breakthrough. Right now you're *remembering* and to get more details, I suggest that next we try a technique that I've used successfully with a number of patients suffering from PTSD. It's called Eye Movement Desensitization and Reprocessing, EMDR. I will ask you to recall the images you've just recounted to me while I do repetitive hand-tapping movements. The idea is that the repetitive movements can reduce the stress associated with these events, and possibly help you to remember more details."

"Honestly. Seeing something as awful as that and my mind blocking it out, it seems so strange. Am I mentally ill?"

"Not at all. A child's mind is more complicated than you might think. But a child's reactions can be primitive and protective. You have various issues that we're working through, that's all."

I shook my head, to try and clear the insistent throbbing headache. "I can't stop thinking about my mum. Everyone was convinced she'd just done a bunk, yet they never found any trace of her, or evidence that she was living somewhere else. On that day in 1987 she simply vanished. They never even suspected foul play."

"Now they'll have to."

"All my life," I pondered, sliding off the couch and onto my feet, the headache growing stronger every second. "All my life I thought my mother had just abandoned me, gone abroad to join another circus. Everyone told me how worthless she was to abandon me like that. I've grown up hating her. Hating her for abandoning me. And now I know she didn't."

I wept quietly for a few moments.

I thought about a few days ago, when I went to Netherwold and met the handsome Irishman and everything in my life had changed.

Did he still like me, or had I ruined everything?

Would I ever see him again?

And if I did get close to Sean Delaney, what about Emil Hervé, and what happened to him? What about the others?

Oh, Sean, where are you now?

I need you.

TEN

Laura

"I'm very sorry, Miss Kaplan," said the plainclothes policeman who sat across the desk from me in the interview room in Bath's Lido Road Police Station. At first another detective had started talking to me, but he'd soon been replaced by this character, who seemed a lot less amenable than the first guy had been. "As I say, I'm very sorry, but all this sounds very vague."

"Vague? Look, my mother went missing in 1987 and I'm telling you that a psychiatrist has helped me to recover my memory of what happened to her. She was attacked by a group of men, I saw it happening in front of my own eyes, when I was five! Then she disappeared. She was attacked, and afterwards she disappeared – there were extensive police searches at the time. She must have been murdered!"

Detective Constable Steven Cope was a chunky, shortish man with dark hair and a Mediterranean complexion, looking as if he ought to be called Giuseppe, and have a pronounced Italian accent. But his voice was Estuary English, and he had a restless air, constantly tapping his foot or drumming his fat fingers on the table, occasionally tugging at his pendulous lower lip. His cool stare was disquieting, but not unexpected after my unlikely tale.

"Have you any idea of the number of people there are who've undergone hypnosis treatment and suddenly claim that they've only just realised that something nefarious happened in their past?" he went on. "Usually that they were sexually molested by their parents?"

"This is totally different."

"Is it? Sorry, Miss Kaplan, but I've been on the wrong end of one of those investigations. A poor old bloke of seventy-five, whose forty-five-year-old daughter told us she'd suddenly remembered that he'd molested her when she was six. At the time, she said she never told anyone because she was afraid of him, and had no recollection of it happening until she'd seen a 'hypnotherapist'—"

As he said it, DC Cope actually held up two fingers either side of his face in that irritating 'inverted commas' gesture.

"—Then, lo and behold, she remembered every detail of all the times he raped her when she was a child. The man was shattered, the stress of the whole mess killed his poor wife, who didn't believe he was telling the truth. Not long afterwards we found out that the same hypnotherapist had produced five more patients who had allegedly remembered being sexually abused by their own fathers. One of whom had been impotent since the child was born."

"But this is not the same thing."

"Is it not? I have a degree in psychology myself, by the way, and I'm very interested in the workings of the mind. Haven't you ever thought you remembered something happening, being absolutely *certain* of it, and then suddenly realised you were wrong? I happens to us all. And memory implantation is actually a recognised technique used in cognitive psychology to investigate human memory. When you trust a therapist, you're relaxed, you go into a trance. Things can be suggested, suggested so convincingly that you genuinely believe them."

"Come on, Detective Constable! Why would a psychiatrist, who doesn't even know me, invent a scenario and feed it to me and then try to make me believe it?"

"I'm not saying that's the way it happens in every case," he replied. "And incidentally I've heard of Dr Fanshaw's work, I've got a lot of respect for him, and I accept that he wouldn't do anything unethical deliberately. He's helped a lot of ex-soldiers with PTSD. I'd go further, in fact I think he's a sincere, well intentioned professional man. How long have you been seeing him?"

"Three weeks. Ten sessions."

"Long enough to establish a rapport then. I'm not saying a man like Dr Fanshaw would deliberately plant a memory, far from it. But I think he lulled you into a state of consciousness where you created things, you made things up just as you create a dream, and afterwards you genuinely believed they happened. All your life you've longed to know what happened to your mother, to know why she abandoned you as she did. Look, you were honest with me, you've already told me all about the terrible experiences you've had in your childhood. The sexual abuse you suffered while you were in the care home, of course this was real, this really happened, of course it did.

"But I think it's eminently possible that these terrible actual experiences became a part of your living memory, transposed onto your mother. And while you were under hypnosis the experiences fed into your imagination, and you constructed this scenario just as we create a dream, and then watched it unfold. Rather like these tales of so-called experiences of former lives under hypnosis being held up supposedly as evidence of reincarnation. The mind is essentially creative, that's why you have dreams and see them as if you're watching a film. The subliminal mind is extraordinary. It can invent a scenario, it can manufacture an entire situation and afterwards you can sincerely believe it happened."

"You're wrong. *It happened.* When I was a child of five, I hid under some furniture at Netherwold Hall and watched as my mother was raped in front of my eyes."

"What happened afterwards?"

"What do you mean?"

"What did this man do to your mother after he raped her and bashed her head against the floor?"

"I don't know. I think I must have fainted. When I woke up I was alone."

"Okay. Now these men. Can you describe any of them?"

"I don't know. They were big."

"All of them?"

"Not all of them. The main one was big. The one who was on top of my mother."

"Okay, let's concentrate on this one man. Was he big meaning tall? Or a fat bloke with duck's disease like me?"

"I'm not sure."

"Old? Young?"

"I don't know."

"Skin colour?"

"White."

"Hair colour? Or was he bald?"

"Black hair I think."

"You think?"

"I'm not sure."

"Do you think you'd recognise him again?"

"Possibly. I've looked at pictures on the net of Adrian Dark's band, Nightingale Green, in their heyday. And I think the man who raped her was Roger Bracken. And one of the ones who held her down was Paul Cotter."

He sat in silence, shaking his head slowly.

"I'm very sorry, Miss Kaplan, but in order to investigate a crime, first we have to be convinced that a crime has been committed. And in this case there is no evidence whatsoever."

"But it happened! I saw it happening!"

"No. You think it happened, I accept that. You're certain that twenty-eight years ago, you saw your mother being raped and attacked in a room at the country house that belonged to your father. You don't know who did it, and you couldn't identity him or any of the others for certain."

"My mother vanished. No one could find her. I think she was murdered, and they got rid of her body."

"That's a supposition. Have you any idea how many people vanish in the world every single day? Only a small percentage of them have been murdered. There are thousands of ways of staying under the radar if you want to. Using a false name, getting forged papers, stealing someone else's identity, or even just plain living outside the system: no employment details, no credit card traces, doing a job for cash. And if she went abroad she'd be a needle in a haystack, especially if she used a false name. I'm very sorry, Ms Kaplan, but there's absolutely no reason to suppose that your mother was raped or murdered."

"So you're not going to help me find the man who did this?"

"I can't. This is an impossible situation. Miss Kaplan, I'm sorry. Look, I understand you run a bookshop and that you're a highly skilled bookbinder."

"Why is that relevant?"

"Because being a demonstrably intelligent person, you can surely see things from my point of view, can't you? You must realise that there's nothing on earth I can do to help you?"

"But if the police won't take things further, what can I do?"

"Nothing. It's all in the past. Please, Miss Kaplan, I know that losing your mother was the most awful thing that's ever happened to you. Being taken into care at such a young age was a terrible calamitous thing for you too, especially in the light of the abuse you suffered during those years. And to find out all this time later that you had a father who never even bothered to help you when you were on your own must be very hard to accept. But you've done well, you've made a success of your life. Why go delving into the past?"

I glared at him.

"It's quite understandable why you long to know what happened to your mother and why she went out of your life, especially when you've been told that she abandoned you. I agree, she might well have been murdered, but, equally, she might well have abandoned you. But you have to accept that with the best will in the world, we never will know what happened to her, however much we would like to find out. Please, Miss Kaplan, take my advice. You're a successful and personable young woman with everything to live for. Go home and forget about all this."

*

That night, asleep in my flat above Novelicious, I had the dream again. The dream that wasn't really a dream, but a mental re-enactment of the day Mr Carey died.

It's just him and me, walking together in the woods. I was Laura, poor little helpless eleven-year-old Laura. The girl who was a timid little mouse, scared of her own shadow. Who'd been petrified when he stopped in the cluster of trees, then lifted her skirt and touched her and started to try to do all those awful thing, the things he'd done all those times before. The things that made her retreat into her own world to get away from what was happening.

But this time, for some reason, it was different.

I changed.

Laura was a scared little mouse. But the new Laura was afraid of nothing.

I invented a kind of game, a game where I was a loudmouth yob, a troublemaker, the sort of girl who gets into fights and spits and swears at everyone:

Me? Afraid? Get a fucking grip! I ain't afraid of what they tell us. That the staff here are on God's side, and that if we tell anyone what happens, we'd be cast into the flames of eternal hell. I ain't letting them maul me about, I ain't afraid of telling anyone what happens in this place. Nor am I scared of the spiders. The spiders that listen to your words: that would overhear you if you told any outsider the home's secrets and would report your words back to the chosen ones.

The Devil! The Devil! That's why you have six fingers on your hand, because you are the spawn of the devil!

They told me that again and again.

And I ain't afraid of The Chosen Ones themselves, those faceless worshippers at church, the ones who prayed aloud and sang and clapped and swayed to the music…

And that was when I pushed Mr Carey away, so he sprawled out on the grass in front of a tree. Then I ran across and trod on his throat, and stamped down hard on it again and again, the wellington boots unpleasantly soft and squidgy, unable to do the damage that I *really* wanted to inflict, but hurting him badly, nonetheless, so that he struggled and squirmed, his mouth opening and closing like a dying fish. . . . .

Then I'm kneeling on his chest and putting my hands around his throat and squeezing. I stop after a while. But then, when he starts coughing and choking and swearing, his eyes are bulging as he tries to sit up. Then he falls back down again. He is fighting for breath, coughing, spluttering. Gasping for air. He thrashes about, his eyes popping from his head, making an awful croaking sound.

And I watch. And I smile and I wait. I watch as he thrashes around less and less. As I watch the light goes out in his eyes and that glazed look takes over. I glory in that wonderful moment. That exquisite crossing over time between life and death.

I run back to the house to tell them what has happened, crying and terrified.

Pretending to be sorry.

ELEVEN

Sean, mid-January 2015

Done!

I was at home in my house in Whitstable, Kent. It had taken four long weeks of slog and a massive amount of phone interviewing, but at last I had emailed the final copy of the MS for *Adrian Dark, Keeping on Rocking* to Sylvia. Vernon Dark had lived up to his promise and been particularly helpful, and I'd got some good copy from the erstwhile band Nightingale Green's one surviving member, Roger Bracken, as well as from sundry friends and relatives.

Even though I'd done my best to produce an actual biography, all I'd actually slammed together was a hotch-potch description of his tours, as detailed in the diaries, plus the lyrics for songs he'd written over the years, coupled with the paintings and drawings I'd made of the photographs that couldn't be reproduced directly for reasons of copyright. The interview parts fleshed out the book a bit, but on the whole I wasn't confident that my writing skills were up to par. I was also worried that the diaries ended in 1987, the year that Nightingale Green had disbanded. Were the publishers going to say they needed more details of what Adrian had done in the twenty-eight years since that date? If they did, it was going to be hard for me to get any information. What's more, my understanding was that apart from suffering from debilitating bouts of mental illness, Adrian Dark had done very little in the last few years, certainly nothing interesting enough to entertain readers with.

Although I had reported the second break-in at Number 46 Latimer Terrace to the police, they were not hopeful of finding who was responsible. Nothing had been taken – I had clearly disturbed him and he'd knocked me out and left, not wanting to risk me waking up and calling the police. Just like the previous break-in this man, who was a different height and build to the first burglar, appeared to have been an opportunist thief unless he had been sent by James Patterson to steal the diaries, a scenario which did seem unlikely.

Landseer's had inspected the damage to the banisters, and agreed to have them repaired, so I had decided there and then to go back home to Kent, so as to get cracking on writing the book, since it was my top priority, and Charngate Publishing had given me a near impossible deadline to meet. Although I had promised to decorate Number 46 over the Christmas holidays, Mairéad had agreed to hold the job over and she was happy for me to put off the decorating work until after I'd written the book.

Now that I had finished reading and extrapolating all Adie's diaries and notes, to my great disappointment, I had not found anything that might have been a revelation that anyone would have cared about, let alone considered it was worth murdering two people to suppress. So my main reason for going to Bath had been to try and throw light on any possible reason for my wife Jodie being murdered, and

I had failed. Mairéad had been right: who on earth would care about reminiscences from thirty to fifty years ago? It seemed as if either Jodie really had been the victim of an accident or her murder had been connected to one of the other stories she had been working on at the time of her death.

And Laura? I should have forgotten all about Laura, but I had not. I missed her all the time. The weird connection I had felt was still there, at the back of my mind, despite what had happened. The realisation that she had been abused by men since she was six years old was sobering and depressing, and went a long way to explaining why she had attacked me when I started kissing her.

I had begun a painting of her, from memory. And one of the greatest pleasures of my days during those cold miserable weeks while I was writing up the diaries, was to work on that portrait as a way of keeping her alive in my head.

Laura had texted me the same night we had parted, apologising for how she had behaved, begging to see me again, and wanting me to forgive her. At the time I had been wary of replying, but the following day I gave in. I had texted her back, saying that I understood, that I'd like to see her again, but had to go back to Kent to work non-stop on the book, and that I would be in touch in a few weeks.

I wanted to see her again, was already making excuses for why she had behaved in such a bizarre fashion. I hardly knew her, yet I was missing her, missing her all the time.

In my phone chats to Vernon, he had warned me that there was something wrong with Laura, that she was, in his opinion 'raving mad'. Of course I had not told Vernon about the fiasco of my experience with her, that was too embarrassing, and I would never tell a soul.

Next day Sylvia called me, to my huge relief and surprise, telling me that she had taken a quick preparatory look at my work and it was acceptable. She was putting it out to the copy editor, and finally the proofreader, and the designer had already been booked for a month's time, so that a publication date could be envisaged, and according to her 'the sooner the better'.

Did I tell you that I still had Jodie's phone, still paid the provider's bill every month, just in case someone who didn't know she was dead tried to call? I got the phone call on her phone at about 11 o'clock at night.

"Hello?" I said, heart beating in anticipation as it always did when I had the tantalising hope I would learn something new about Jodie's life.

"Who are you?" The male voice sounded wary, guarded.

"I'm Jodie's husband."

"Can I speak to her?"

"No. I'm sorry." I cleared my throat, willing my words to come, trying to calm down. "I'm afraid that she died six months ago."

"Died? Oh shit, man, I'm so sorry."

There was a pause.

"Please, don't hang up, whoever you are," I begged into the silence. "Look. I think she was murdered, but the police insist she had an accident. She was involved with different projects when she died, and I think one of them might have upset someone enough to make them shut her up permanently. But all her notes and phones and computers were destroyed in a fire, and I've reached a dead end. If you were in touch with her in her final weeks, *please* talk to me."

"I'm sorry." After a long while the man went on: "I

liked Jodie, she was good to me. So okay, if I can help you of course I will. My name is Brian Coulter, and I used to be a roadie for several pop bands in the 1980s, and I was working with her on a story, connected with the guy who died not long ago – Adrian Dark. I've been in prison – only just got out. Jodie came to visit me, and we talked there. She was murdered, you say?"

"Yes, I think so."

"God, I'm so sorry. Look, I'd very much like to talk to you, but when they let me out of prison I came straight out here, to my wife in Amsterdam. Money's a bit short—"

"No problem, please, really, I'll come to you," I told him. "*Please*. I'm desperate to follow up any lead."

"Well, I can tell you she was working on something pretty big, and I was helping her with information, but whether it has anything to do with what happened to her, I have no idea. Can you really come here? It would be helpful actually because I've got some stuff here that I'd like to show you. . ."

"Give me your address and I'll get on the first plane."

*

On the plane, mercifully I had a dreamless sleep, and when the big aircraft touched down at Schiphol Airport, I was wide awake and prepared for whatever might lie ahead.

I caught the train to Central Station, and found a hotel nearby where I booked in. That evening I wandered along the old part of town, with its narrow streets and canals that follow the core of the old city. My hotel was in a road leading off the Damrak, a broad partially-filled canal in the centre of town, running between Amsterdam Centraal in the north and Dam Square in the south. It was a broad, nondescript road, lined with a number of restaurants and bars. Along Prins Henrikkade I found the Basilica of St Nicolas, a large Catholic church, and nearby the Schreierstoren, a large piece of the medieval wall. I walked down further and found myself in De Wallen, the red-light district. The place filled me with a deep sense of depression and returning to the hotel I fell into a bone-weary sleep.

In the morning I bought a street map, and was relieved that most people I came across spoke English. The address that Brian had given me was in what's known as The Bijlmermeer part of the borough of Amsterdam Zuidoost, quite a way from where I was. At the station taxi rank, when I showed the address to the driver, he made a face, and looked depressed. He spoke English, and when I asked if it was far, he said in an American accent, "Oh the Bijlmer. It's quite a way." He looked at me warily. "Are you sure you've got the right address?"

"Yes, absolutely."

He nodded to himself. "Well, I'll give you a tip, my friend: keep your money safe if you're going down there. And stay away after dark."

"What do you mean?"

"You're English, right? Let's just say it isn't exactly a tourist area. It's one of the places we won't go after dark. You won't find any cabs hanging around there either, so here's my card if you want collecting."

We stopped outside one of the tall concrete high-rise blocks that seemed to make up this area. This one was distinguished by garish and graffiti-covered walls, and broken glass on the pavement, with balconies on the upper levels. My taxi driver had explained how the neighbourhood had been built as a single project, a series of nearly identical high-rise buildings laid out in a hexagonal grid. The few people around walked fast with their heads down. As I got out of the cab, the sound of loud reggae music took over the street. I phoned Brian, and he told me to come straight up.

The main entrance to the block was wide open: the door appeared to have been smashed off, and there was broken glass on the pavement. According to the map on the wall, Number 48 was on the fourth floor. I walked up the urine-smelling concrete stairs, wondering just what kind of person Brian Coulter might be. I passed a couple of black guys who were speaking quietly, swapping packages and money, and I took care to move fast and look in the other direction.

Outside Number 48, I double checked the address and then rang the bell. I waited quite a while until I heard movement from inside: footsteps. The door opened a few inches.

"Sean?"

"Yes. Brian?"

"Come in, mate." The door opened wide and he stepped back and let me in. He was a large bald man in his fifties, with a sizeable belly, and plenty of tattoos on his bare arms below the tee-shirt sleeves. What, I wondered, might Jodie and this man have had to discuss?

The small living room was surprisingly neat and clean, with a leather three-piece suite and a blue carpet. There were vases of flowers on the windowsill and an old music centre on the chest of drawers in the corner. Brian asked if I'd like coffee, tea or something stronger. When I asked for coffee he returned shortly afterwards with two mugs, handing one to me as he sat opposite me on the armchair, while I took the sofa.

"I was a roadie for Nightingale Green, from 1981 until 1987, when they disbanded," he began, leaning back in the chair. "Jodie came to see me when I was in prison because she'd been talking to Adrian Dark about writing his autobiography. She had been listening to his stories, looking at his old diaries. But there was one aspect of his life with the band that did not make sense, and that bothered Jodie. She was determined to find out about it."

"What?" I asked.

"The reason why the band broke up forever on the sixteenth of October, 1987. She asked him why it had happened, and he wouldn't say, just rabbited on about differences of musical opinion. But you know Jodie, once she was onto a story nothing could hold her back, it just made her all the more determined. She tracked me down, and asked for my help. I happened to know the guys in that band in those days. Now, there's only one of them still alive, old Roger. But I happened to know that after Nightingale Green split up, each of the members had a tidy sum to invest. Roger Bracken bought a farm, Paul Cotter opened up a chain of lighting shops, and Duncan Forrester had enough money to move to LA and blow a fortune on high living. It was a mystery. The band split up, yet each of them had a huge wad of money."

"But Nightingale Green was successful, wasn't it?" I asked. "Wouldn't that explain the money?"

"No. Because at the time they broke up they'd had several lousy years, and Paul, for one, I know was thinking about declaring himself bankrupt. No. I never knew what happened until a few years ago when I visited Duncan Forrester, who had some awful disease and was dying. He wanted to talk to me, to tell me all about what happened on that night, told me he wanted to get it off his conscience."

"And?"

"Of course you're a young man, but think back to what

you know about recent history. What have you heard about the night of the fifteenth and sixteenth of October, 1987?"

Suddenly I remembered why the date was important. "The night of the Great Storm?"

"Yes. Most of the damage was in the South East of England, the Home Counties, but it landed in Cornwall and on its way across to the Wash there were quite a few other places that were also affected. One of them was around Penton Feverill. A huge old tree was uprooted in the grounds of Netherwold Hall during the night. The boys in the band had been staying at the manor, but Adrian was away. As I said, one of the oldest trees on the estate was uprooted. When they looked at the hole, they saw what looked like an old metal trunk, a fair way down. They broke it open and found it was full of old gemstones, icons made of gold, goblets encrusted with jewels, all kinds of stuff, and all *really, really* old. When Adrian arrived and saw it, he explained that during the time of the Dissolution of the Monasteries, when Kendal Abbey was the largest monastery for miles around, all the most valuable items belonging to the order were buried so that Henry's people who were sacking the monasteries couldn't get hold of it. It had been lost ever since, but now, clearly it had been found. By accident."

"So Adrian was suddenly very rich?"

"No. it wasn't as simple as that. That treasure had originally belonged to the order of monks who owned Kendal Abbey in the fifteenth century, before it was dissolved. Much later, Adrian's ancestors bought the ruins of what had been the abbey and they rebuilt and added to it. But they couldn't buy all rights to the land and what was in it, that was specifically mentioned in the deeds of sale, because even at that time it was suspected that the treasure could be somewhere on the premises. The treasure still belonged to the monks, and their order still exists, so, in law, Adrian would have had to hand it over to them. So four of them knew about the treasure, any one of them could have told the order of monks, to whom they'd have had to hand it over."

"Tricky."

"So all they could do was dispose of it illegally, to fences who'd give them much less than the market value, and then divide the spoils between them. Which is what happened."

There was a long silence. "So was that the story that you discussed with Jodie?"

"That was part of it. But there was more. Much more."

The light outside was fading fast, and jetlag was catching up with me. While he'd been talking the room had become dark and dismal.

Sensing this, Brian stood up and switched the light on. "Hang on a minute."

He went outside and returned a moment later carrying one of those old fashioned cassette tape players and put it on the table.

"Before he died, Duncan gave me a tape recording of what Pieter van Dries, a friend of the band who was there that night, said had happened during the afternoon of the fifteenth of October. You see, Sean, *this* was the real reason why the band broke up. It's fairly unpleasant, I can tell you that. Adrian claimed to know nothing about it until years later, and he certainly never intended Jodie to know about it. In fact he contacted me, furious, telling me that she was a damned nuisance, and had no authority to poke and pry into his affairs as she had, and that he wished he'd never asked her to help him with his autobiography. He was angry, very angry, threatening all sorts.

"However, I know that Jodie listened to this tape, and she was determined to act on it. If she was murdered, perhaps it was because Adrian himself wanted to shut her up? He certainly wouldn't have wanted any of this coming out."

"But that's not possible. Adrian died before she did."

"Did he? Well, Sean, here we go. See what you think."

TWELVE

"My name is Pieter van Dries and this is my confession," the recording began.

It was a man's voice, deep and mellifluous, with a heavy American accent, like that of many Dutch people whose second language is English.

"The date is the seventeenth October 1987. Two days ago I watched a woman being raped and attacked and I did nothing to help her. I'm recording this because the truth has to be told."

I felt the hairs at the back of my neck rise as I closed my eyes to concentrate.

"What can I say about yesterday afternoon at Netherwold? Everyone remembers that the night of the fifteenth of October 1987 was the time of the Great Storm. But what happened on the afternoon of the fifteenth was much more important to me.

"The three members of the band – Roger, Duncan and Paul, were all high on this and that – mostly acid and Charlie and booze. There'd been some chicks here, we'd been partying hard. Everyone had gone home, except the four of us. We were arguing about something, things were at a low point between us, we were arguing more often than usual, yeah arguing big time. Well, in the middle of it all, this girl turns up. I can hardly remember what she looked like now. Just one of the groupies, or so we thought – there were so many, you see. This girl turned up and she started asking about Adie, telling us that he had to face up to his responsibilities, or something like that. By that time I was out of it really, drifting in and out of sleep, I hardly knew what was going on. Adie wasn't there when she arrived, he'd been delayed in Paris and was supposed to be coming on later. They kept telling her he wasn't there, but she wouldn't believe us. Kept on pestering us to find him, but none of us knew where the fuck he was.

"She kept going on about a child she had who was five now – that he hadn't bothered to give her any money or support for months. Adie had never even officially acknowledged the child as his. And she'd reached the end of the road she said, demanding that he gave her some help. I was in and out of sleep for most of the time, but she kept going on about 'Adie's child' and that she needed help and support and money. They told her again and again that he wasn't there, but she wouldn't go. And then. . ."

There was a long silence.

"As I said, we was all stoned in one way or another. I was half asleep, lying around, like in a dream, barely aware of what was going on. But Roger wasn't. The gear had affected him badly. Released something inside him, something really nasty you know? Roger was a bit of a bastard anyway, but that afternoon he was lively, horny, angry, like a wild beast. This girl, she kept yelling at him and she just wouldn't shut up. I remember she grabbed his arm, and he pushed her off. And then he started pulling at her clothes. Going on about teaching her a lesson, how she should shut up and go or take what was coming, some shit like that. Paul saw what was happening and came over to watch, with this big smirk on his face, you know? Roger pulled her top off, and her breasts were swinging around and free? And then, I dunno it all seemed to happen at once. She was fighting, squirming, kicking and screaming, but that made them start laughing, behaving even worse. They were excited, *enjoying it,* you know? Tossing her around, from one to the other, stripping off her clothes, ripping and tearing them, slapping her around. And laughing. In the end they ripped off all her clothes. She started to cry and plead with them. I thought at that point it would all stop, you know? I got up and walked across, I tried to stop them…

"I can't think about it without crying."

His words became choked and barely audible as he broke down. Then they were barely above a whisper.

"Paul and Duncan were holding her down, while Roger did the business."

I felt a sick chill in my stomach as I pictured the scene.

"I did nothing. To my eternal fucking shame, I did *nothing,* I kept clear, I didn't even try to interfere. As I said, Paul and Duncan held her down, and then Roger started, you know. .. I wanted to do something to stop it, I tried to stop them, I swear I did, but there was something stopping me, you know? It was like a dream. It wasn't real. And it was all happening so fast."

Another long silence.

"When it started I just wanted to tear them to pieces, but I couldn't move, you know? The drugs I guess, sort of made me lethargic, I couldn't move, I could barely think. Part of me wanted her just to stop yelling, anything that stopped her yelling suited me if I'm honest.

"I was a coward and a shit. I did nothing to help her. I could make all kinds of excuses, like I didn't realise what was happening until it was too late, or I thought they would stop, or she didn't really mind. But the truth is, I was too spaced out on acid to hardly move, I was only partly aware of what was happening. And I was afraid to go up against the three of them. Plus I told myself that she wasn't really objecting, you know? I kind of kidded myself that maybe she was up for it, and just making a fuss? It all happened so fast and I couldn't take it all in.

"That was it. I was out of it by then and I never saw the girl again. What happened to her? I never knew, and no one would ever tell me. They got rid of her somehow, that's all I know. I fell asleep with her screams in my ears and when I woke up she was gone.

"A couple of days later I heard that the woman's little girl was found wandering alone in the nearby village, and there was an almighty manhunt for her mother. My blood ran cold when I thought about the possibility that the poor kid might have been there all the time, might have seen what happened to her mother! But we never saw her, and if she'd seen anything, she'd have told someone, surely? But why didn't she tell the police that her mum had visited Netherwold? I never knew, I never understood. But I'm kidding myself really. What's more I cannot face the prospect of never knowing when there's going to be a knock on the door...

"I made this recording of my own free will in case by some fluke, the others all get away with it. Someone has to know the truth. I wasn't innocent, because I should have intervened. But I wasn't as guilty as the others."

The voice ended.

"And a few days after that, Pieter van Ries topped himself. Jumped from the roof of a multi-storey car park," said Brian Coulter, his head in his hands.

I sat there for a long time, realising the ramifications of what I had just heard.

Laura Kaplan had told me that she had a dim recollection of being at Netherwold as a child, and knew that she had been found wandering around the local village alone, having been abandoned by her mother, after which she had been taken into care. Now it seemed that I knew what had happened to her mother. Of course I had to share the news with her.

Was this the reason why Jodie had been murdered? To hush up this terrible incident? These men had raped Angela Kaplan and she had gone missing. Had they murdered her, to shut her up about the rape? Had they accidentally killed her while they were attacking her? Or had Jodie found out about the theft of Adrian Dark's family treasure and was threatening to tell people about it?

All the other band members but one were now dead. The only one alive was Roger Bracken, the man who had allegedly raped Angela. If the truth came out he might be charged with rape, assuming it could be proved. If the police reopened their investigation into Angela's disappearance, they might even find that she had been murdered, if they could find where the body had been hidden.

If Adrian Dark had indeed not known about the attack on Angela Kaplan at the time, perhaps when Jodie told him about it, this had been a shocking revelation. Roger Bracken had apparently been the rapist, so maybe Adrian had gone to see Roger to confront him, and Roger Bracken had killed him to keep him quiet. And since Jodie had known about it too, he had been forced to kill her as well.

A man in his sixties, charged with a twenty-eight-year-old rape and possibly murder? If it could be proved it would mean humiliation and disgrace, a horrific court case and spending the rest of his life in jail.

Suppressing such information was certainly a motive for murder.

THIRTEEN

The interview room at Bath's Lido Road Police Station was spartan and airless, but DC Cope struck me as the kind of copper who was good at his job. Short and chubby, with receding black hair, he had a number of disquieting habits, such as tapping his front teeth with a pen, rocking his heels up and down while he was talking and drumming his fingers on the desk. He had listened patiently to Pieter van Dries's recording and made notes, while his face remained inscrutable.

Yesterday's reunion with Laura had been all I could have hoped for. She had apologised again and again for lashing out at me, and I in turn explained that I had found out about the terrible things that had happened in her life, and fully understood why she had reacted as she had. I had explained about the testimony of Pieter van Dries, and she had told me all about the recovered memories that Dr Julian Fanshaw had helped her to uncover.

"God, how I've missed you," I whispered into her ear as I held her tight.

"Oh, Sean, I just kept hoping and hoping I'd see you again. I was afraid I'd lost you, I was so afraid. . ."

In all kinds of ways, Laura appeared to be a complete mystery, and although I was falling in love with her I was scared. What did I really know about her, except for the fact that she kept her past a closeted secret, apart from this obsession about her mother, that now seemed to be taking over her life?

"So this man, Pieter van Dries," DC Cope began, looking across at me and Laura. "What do you know about him?"

"According to research I did while I was writing a book about Adrian Dark's band, Nightingale Green, Pieter was one of their roadies for a long period, and also was a close friend of all the members of the group," I told him, while Laura watched us, staying silent.

"So this account we've just listened to is credible, in your view?"

"Yes," I told him. "And it precisely matches Laura's recovered memory."

"Did you ever meet Mr van Dries?"

"Of course not. I was seven years old when he died."

"And he died shortly after making this tape?"

"So I was told."

"Can anyone testify that he made this recording? This man in Amsterdam, Brian Coulter, claims an old friend who was dying gave him this tape, alleging it was genuine?"

"Yes."

As I spoke I was aware of Cope's cynical stare.

"And, Mr Delaney, it's your contention that your wife was murdered because she stumbled upon this crime. Or because she found out about the discovery of this so-called 'Kendal Treasure', and its wrongful appropriation?"

"Yes."

"Well I agree with you. Unlike Ms Kaplan's recovered memories, the fact that someone has gone on record to state that this thing happened is an important development. But unfortunately the person who made the recording is dead, so he can't attest that he made it. Nor can anyone else. There's no way of knowing who recorded this statement, and for it to be legally valid it would have to stand up in a court of law. I'm sorry, but you tell me a man told you, that *another* man told *him*, that this tape was made by Pieter van Dries, now deceased. Anyone could have made this recording."

"For God's sake!" Laura yelled, "just what does it take to try and get some *fucking justice?*"

"*Fucking evidence*, Ms Kaplan," he replied, immune to her anger, his face impassive. "*Evidence.* Look, hear me out. Let me present this business as it appears to me." He sat back in his seat, looking at each of us in turn before his gaze settled on me. "The pair of you come to see me, all fired up with this theory, alleging that you now have evidence that this terrible crime took place. Mr Delaney, you are convinced that your wife was murdered to keep her silent about something she found out, but the official verdict on her death is an accident. You stumbled on this recording, and now you're accepting it at face value."

"Why would Pieter van Dries make up something like that?"

"I don't know. But consider this. Someone who didn't know you, or who disliked you, might conclude that you've formed a relationship with Ms Kaplan here, you're convinced by her dubious story of this recovered memory, and so you made this recording yourself, as an attempt to make her testimony credible."

"I didn't!" I said angrily.

He held up his hand, palm upwards. "Of course you didn't! I know that, but I'm playing devil's advocate here. But if this case was taken up officially that's precisely what you're going to be accused of, because there's no way on earth anyone can prove who made that recording, or when. Make no mistake, you two are alleging that an elderly, respectable person, Roger Bracken, raped a woman, and that other people were complicit in this attack, possibly including the late Mr Dark, because presumably he must have known about it, yet he didn't report the crime. These are serious accusations and anyone accused of these crimes would fight tooth and nail to deny them, and would also accuse you of slander."

"The four members of the band stopped working together on the sixteenth of October 1987, and according to my checks, none of them continued a career in music after that time," I pointed out. "Yet at the point when they effectively retired from the music industry, Roger Bracken bought a farm, Paul Cotter established a chain of lighting retailers and Duncan Forrester, who is also dead, allegedly lived the high life in Los Angeles for many years. I've learnt from Adrian Dark's diaries that Nightingale Green had no hits and no tours from 1984 onwards. Yet at the time they stopped working in 1987, each of them had a massive amount of capital to invest."

"The band, Nightingale Green. Was it very successful before that time?"

"I think so."

"There you are then. They could have been prudent and saved the money they made in their glory days."

"All three of them? Rock stars aren't noted for living frugally and saving their money for a rainy day."

"That's conjecture, not fact. Besides, why do you care about establishing that they found this treasure and nicked it?"

"Because it might have some bearing on my wife's murder."

"Your wife died in an accident, Mr Delaney."

"Whatever."

"I understood that the two of you are most concerned about this alleged rape, and the disappearance of Angela Kaplan."

"We are," Laura agreed.

"Couldn't you at least confront Roger Bracken, the man named in this tape?" I asked him. "At least see what he has to say about it?"

I looked across at Laura. She was getting more and more angry, staring at Cope as if her life depended on it.

He shook his head slowly. "No, Mr Delaney, that's the last thing I would want to do. Think about it. If there is any truth to this story, do you really want to forewarn him? This is an elderly retired man, and if this accusation is true and can be proved, then he's facing a sixteen-year sentence, meaning possibly jail for the remainder of his life. Even if it's true this man will fight tooth and nail to refute it, so what's the point of going off at half cock so he can prepare a defence? Our only possible course of action would be to find proof that, as you suggest, Ms Angela Kaplan never in fact left Netherwold Hall. Your supposition is that she disappeared because she was murdered by the people who raped her, so as to shut her up. At the time of her disappearance, police searched for a body and none was found, but the search did not include Netherwold Hall or its grounds. If someone *were* to find a body, and it was proved to be that of your mother, then we could start an investigation."

Laura glared at him furiously. "So nothing's changed?"

"I didn't say that," he told her. "Wait there."

He was gone a few minutes and when he returned he had two large manila files in his hands, that he laid down on the desk, opening one of them.

"Ms Kaplan, after you last came to see me I was very upset and moved by what you told me, despite what you may think. I spent a lot of time trying to find out what I could about your mother's disappearance." He laid out some photographs on the desk. "There was a comprehensive enquiry at the time, involving a lot of manpower and many, many hours. We took statements from all the villagers who found you wandering around, we questioned people in the vicinity. Unfortunately it was in the days before CCTV cameras being all over the place, but officers did knock on doors of all the nearby houses, including questioning the people living near Netherwold. It seems. . ." He riffled through the papers and picked one out and laid it in front of us. "Here we are. A Mrs Doris Lovecraft, who lived in one of the cottages near the village green where the Dutch circus was set up, she says she saw a young woman arrive on the village green with her daughter at approximately 3.30pm. Another sighting we have of this pair is them being seen walking off in the direction of Yaddlethorpe Hill, the steep hill road that leads up to Netherwold. This would be at around 5pm. She wasn't seen again."

"But," Laura stuttered, "I don't understand. Last time you told me to forget about it. You virtually threw me out of here."

"No, Ms Kaplan, I didn't throw you out, I talked to you realistically because I didn't want to raise your hopes unnecessarily. I tried to make you realise the situation as it is. But I wanted to help you, *of course* I wanted to help you. And, please believe me, I want to help you now, if I can."

He tapped his front teeth with the pencil for a few moments. "I'm sure you realise that I'm not allowed to divulge anything in these files to members of the public."

He leaned back and looked at his watch. "But it just so happens that I have to pop out for ten minutes, and if I happen to leave these files on the desk, then it's not my fault if someone sees the contents, is it? I see you've both got mobile phones. Who would like coffee or tea?"

When we thanked him for getting coffee, he stood up and gave us a broad wink as he left us alone, pointedly shutting the door behind him.

Ten minutes was long enough for us both to take a file each and photograph all the useful looking pages, with the names of the interviewees and other information that looked important. I concentrated on the photos, trying to remember the images.

When he came back he put the Styrofoam cups of coffee on the table and sat down again, opening one of the files.

"Okay, now let's re-examine precisely what happened on the 15th and 16th of October 1987, the day of the Great Storm, that devastated other parts of the country. I've put together a timeline of events as we've perceived them. Your mother, Mrs Angela Kaplan, and you arrived at the station at 3pm, we think you got the midday train from London's Paddington Station. The bus driver remembers you both on his bus at 3.10, and getting off in the village of Penton Feverill. You were seen by Joyce Whittingdale walking up the Stoats Nest Road towards Yaddlethorpe Hill, which as you know leads to Netherwold Hall. There was only one more sighting of your mother after that time, but of course we weren't able to speak to any of the circus people, who were packing up their equipment on the village green, because on the late afternoon of that same day, they left the area en route for the Netherlands. So if your mother had gone to see them, she might have gone away with them, which was the assumption at the time." He paused, again tapping his teeth with the pen. "Resources were stretched to the limit because, even though our area wasn't too badly affected by the storm's devastation, our officers were loaned to the affected areas from all over the country, leaving us very short of manpower. Everyone in the vicinity was questioned, but no one there had seen Angela Kaplan after Mrs Whittingdale saw her and her daughter going up Yaddlethorpe Hill. The official conclusion of the investigation was that your mother had most likely been offered a job with the circus, leaving you behind. Indeed there's one witness that claims she saw your mother in conversation with the person in charge of the acrobatic troupe. We assume she was discussing the possibility of joining the circus as a trapeze artist, and this was on the afternoon of the fifteenth." He laid the pen down on the desk. "But that doesn't ring true to me. In all my years in this job I've never heard of a mother just abandoning her child. Leaving her with a friend, relative or neighbour? Yes. Even taking her to social services and doing a vanishing act? Yes. But just leaving her alone? No. But at the time, the police looked into all other avenues of possibility, of course foul play came to mind, but we found no body, and no suggestion of any crime happening."

"So we're stuck," I said.

"No, there is one interesting thing I happened to find out. During that particular week, British Gas replaced the mains gas pipe to Netherwold, and in doing so they had to excavate part of the floor of the chapel in the grounds. I just checked with British Gas engineers, and they were able to confirm that they did install a gas service to Netherwold Hall on that date. The job lasted one week, and they did fill in the hole, which stretched from the boundary of the property, through the chapel and into the house, but they couldn't make it good until the following week, because of all the fallout from the Great Storm, the damage caused to gas equipment all over the country. They filled in the hole on the following Monday week. If anyone had wanted to conceal a body at Netherwold, at that time, it would have been an ideal opportunity to do so. They simply had to dig down a bit deeper, beside the gas pipe, cover over everything and rest assured that the Gas Board would cover everything."

"So that's good?" I suggested.

"Possibly."

"So what can we do?" asked Laura.

"Nothing. With no body, and no evidence of a crime being committed, we're stuck." He looked at the table for a few moments. "Who owns Netherwold Hall now?"

"The owner is Adrian Dark's son, Vernon Dark," Laura told him. "Whether probate has gone through, and he's now actually taken possession, I don't know."

"The best thing you can do then, is appeal to Mr Dark, and ask him if he'll agree to the floor of the chapel being dug up in order to search for a body."

"He'd never agree to that," Laura told him. "After all, if they find a body, and it can be proved to be my mother, then Vernon's father would be implicated in her death. Why would he want that to happen?"

"I'm sorry. But on this evidence we wouldn't be able to get a court order to dig up the chapel floor, so if the owner of the property doesn't agree, then there's nothing we can do."

*

In the back room of Novelicious, we were discussing what to do next. Laura was in a strange, truculent mood, blaming

DC Cope for everything, and depressed that it seemed as if nothing could be done. Her friend Barbara came in, and Laura had to leave for a moment, apologising.

Laura's smartphone was on the table, and I heard it ring. So I picked it up, but by the time I'd answered it the caller had rung off.

Curiosity got the better of me, and, making sure she was still out of the room, I clicked on her internet history. The last item she'd looked at was the Twitter page of @SarahintheSky.

At the top of her page was a photograph of a girl in a mask to protect her identity.

Yet something about her was familiar.

Her bio described how Sarah was a 'buildings warrior', who climbed up the side of buildings and, using the camcorder in her helmet, recorded the amazing panoramic sights she could see from on high. I flicked down the tweets, seeing dates on several successive weekends, with jokey messages about her latest climb. There was even one where in a heart-stopping moment, the camera picked up her wobbling view as she did a back-flip: judging from the scenes before, during and after, she seemed to stand still, then somersault backwards to land back on her feet on the narrow ledge. The successful exercise resulted in paroxysms of her excited laughter.

And as I looked at the tweets and the videos, I knew beyond doubt that @SarahintheSky and Laura were one and the same person.

Yet Laura had told me she was a bookworm. Quiet, unadventurous, not sporty in any way.

Exactly who was she?

In that moment I was scared. Having thought that I had got close to Laura, she was suddenly once more a complete and utter mystery to me.

If she could keep that part of her life secret, what else had she not told me about herself?

When she came back into the room and I confronted her with what I'd seen on her phone, something about Laura scared me, just like it had done the first time I'd come to her shop.

Did I really know her at all?

"It's my life, and if I want to climb buildings at weekends and post my climbs on Facebook and Twitter, why shouldn't I do it?" she demanded.

"Because it's illegal, for a start," I told her.

"For God's sake, don't be such a pussy, Sean! Getting past a few barriers? Trespassing on private property? What harm am I doing?"

"You never told me you did this. That you had this *secret life.*"

"You never told me you shot an unarmed man and got thrown out of the police."

There was a stunned silence.

"I couldn't stop thinking about you, Sean. I wanted to know everything about you. And you wouldn't tell me why you left the police, so I googled around and it wasn't hard to find," she went on, sounding desperate. "Don't you see, Sean? You've got your secrets, why shouldn't I have mine?" She stared at me, then burst into tears. "*Well, say something, Sean, for God's sake...*"

I didn't hear the rest of what she said as I walked away.

FOURTEEN

Robin Villiers, vicar in an outlying parish near Whitstable, is my best friend. I had gone home to Whitstable and popped round to see him at the vicarage, and I had told him everything that had been happening to me in the last few days.

My mind was all over the place. While my instinct was to go and see Roger Bracken, and if necessary beat the truth out of him, it would have been stupid. He would obviously deny the rape of Laura's mother, and any involvement in Jodie's death, plus it would put him on his guard for any subsequent action I might be able to take, as DC Cope had warned.

Robin's home was an old rambling Victorian stone-built villa, originally intended for a large family, and suited Robin and Caroline, his wife, perfectly, even though Robin voiced concerns and guilt, feeling that they didn't deserve the spare bedrooms, the big old draughty bathrooms or the huge room that was referred to as 'the pantry' when they first moved in, but which was now indisputably his workshop. Robin was an accomplished woodworker and model-maker and his hobby was making elaborate architectural models, facsimiles of actual buildings that those not in the know might mistakenly refer to as 'dolls' houses'. He had told me at length about his small band of fellow craftsmen who described themselves as 'miniaturists'.

We sat together at his woodwork bench, and I marvelled at the beginning stages of the Houses of Parliament, his latest project. The outer shell was almost complete, the familiar façade of Big Ben, all the windows painstakingly cut out and the decorative stonework recreated on the high density MDF board by the application of a sculptured kind of plasterwork, something he referred to as a modern form of 'gesso', which had been the material used by the old craftsmen for decorating picture frames.

This workshop was no amateurish den, but a professional place, with the big bandsaw table in the corner and a laser cutter beside it, next to the router. Racks of hand tools were along the walls: chisels, handsaws, screwdrivers, and other shaping and chiselling implements. An entire rack was filled with tiny air-driven hand-held drills, akin to a dental surgeon's tools, for the construction of tiny scale-model furniture to go into his miniature rooms. I had once marvelled at the way he could make a mahogany chest of drawers three inches high, using a magnifying glass to craft each individual drawer so that it slid in and out perfectly.

Tall thin Robin had a face that had stepped out of the 1950s: clean-cut, clean shaven, prone to friendly smiles. His most noticeable feature was a long, aquiline nose, tailor made for staring down when he was concerned about something. Dressed as he normally was when not 'on duty', in ancient jeans and a tee-shirt, you'd think he was a jobbing builder rather than an emissary of the church. He held one of his tiny chisels, with its perfectly sharp V-shaped blade, using its ancient wooden handle to stir his mug of tea.

"Seems to me, Sean, as if you're not seeing things

clearly," he began, pushing his spectacles back up his nose. "Right now, your priority is solving the mystery of what happened to Jodie. To automatically assume that this tape recording, and story of rape and assumptions of possible murder that she had allegedly found out about was the reason, could be a big mistake. And I should discount this idea of her being killed to suppress this supposed theft of the 'Kendal Treasure', because it all seems pretty bizarre to me. No one would kill her to suppress that theft, because after all this time no one would care, and it's too late to prove anything anyway."

"Agreed."

"But if Roger Bracken knew that Jodie had found out that he'd raped, and possibly even accidentally killed a woman twenty-eight years ago and there was a chance she could prove it, then, granted, to avoid spending the rest of his life in jail, that could well be a motive for murder. If you can believe it's true."

"Why wouldn't it be true?"

"Sorry, Sean, but you're either deluded or you're lying to yourself." Robin sliced a tiny splinter of timber off the piece of scrap wood he was holding in his other hand, gazing at the up-curl of yellow timber furling up above the blade. "This story about her mother's rape. It doesn't make sense to me."

"Laura's convinced it's what happened. And the tape I found in Amsterdam corroborates her story."

"Yet the police have told you there isn't enough evidence to even open up a murder enquiry. And Pieter van Dries doesn't mention murder, just rape. Besides that, the tape could have been made by anyone."

"Why would someone record a pack of lies?"

"I don't know. But by the same logic, why would they

make a recording like that, yet not report the crime at the time?"

"Maybe because they were scared of the consequences."

"But the man, Pieter van Dries, was supposed to have killed himself soon afterwards, wasn't he? Why would he care about consequences?"

"Maybe he was murdered to shut him up."

He shrugged, half closing his eyes. "I get it, Sean. Laura's attractive, she's lonely, she's in trouble. You're the white knight riding to her rescue."

"I've got to help her."

"Why? Why you?"

"Laura needs to know that Roger Bracken has to pay for what he did all those years ago. And if he thought that Jodie knew his secret, maybe he murdered her too."

"What about Adrian Dark's death? If he was murdered, why would Bracken murder him? And if his death was an accident, why shouldn't Jodie's death have been accidental too, just as the police concluded?"

"Perhaps he did kill Adrian too."

"Maybe? Perhaps? Could be? Couldn't be? Sean, can't you see that you're wading through treacle?"

"But I'm trying to make sense of it all."

"Better to concentrate on the mess you've landed yourself in with this girl."

"Mess?"

"Wake up, Sean! She comes on to you, barely knows you yet she leads you on. When you start kissing her she changes into a banshee. Those are not the acts of a rational person. If the thought of having sex with someone terrifies you, the last thing you would do is encourage it."

"I know," I told him.

"So what does she say about it?"

"She's sorry. She apologised, but she doesn't want to talk about it. It's embarrassing."

"It's embarrassing all right. And when you found out that she is a completely different person at weekends, she starts yelling and screaming at you, telling you to mind your own business."

"She was upset."

"Think on this, mate. What are you going to do if she takes your hand once again and leads you up to the bedroom?"

"I don't know. I haven't thought."

"Don't you think you should talk to her about it?"

"Yes. When the time is right."

"When the hell is the time going to be right?"

"How should I know? I'm not thinking about that right now, I simply want to help her get justice."

"Then you'd better make sure she doesn't approach this man, Roger Bracken. Because I'm telling you straight, that if she does it'll end in disaster. Look, Sean," he said, "what exactly do you know about her?"

"She's clever, interesting. Lonely, I think. She's lively, fun to be with, she talks all the time."

"She tells you she's a bookworm, little Miss Scaredy-Cat who wouldn't say boo to a goose, yet you've found out she's a weekend 'buildings warrior', who illegally climbs tall buildings. Yet she never bothered to tell you about it. And she resented you finding out."

"It's her hobby. It's up to her to tell me what she wants."

"Then she refers to you shooting Trevor Goodbody, when she must have known it was a sore point."

"I left her after that. I didn't want to talk to her."

"I think. . ."

"Go on."

"You don't want to hear it."

"You're my best mate. We don't have secrets."

"Okay. I've had a lot of experience with people. That's my work, that's why I went into the church, because I want to try to understand all types of folk so that hopefully I can help them when they're needing guidance or if they're suffering or in trouble. It's why I spent three years getting a degree in psychology before I was ordained. In my work I've come across all sorts: religious nutters, people who feel terrible guilt about things they've done, and have to confess to someone, people who are distressed to the point of madness through grief. I've done a lot of work with those who have psychiatric disorders, done my best to help them adjust to their illness. And from what you tell me about Laura, she is not normal. She isn't sane."

"She's under a lot of stress."

"Stress of her own making. No one asked her to dig up the past like this."

"When she saw Netherwold she remembered being there. She had to follow it up."

"She's irrational. From what you tell me, it sounds as if she might be suffering from a condition called Dissociative Identity Disorder. It typically happens to children who've been abused, who create a new aggressive personality to counteract the weak person they perceive themselves to be. In the week, Laura is the quiet, shy bookbinder and business owner. At weekends she's tough, sporty Sarah in the Sky, proving to the world that she's afraid of nothing and no one."

I nodded. "You could be right."

"I think that Laura is sucking you into her madness. Besides." He took a swig of tea. "I know you, Sean. You're lonely, you're emotionally vulnerable, having had your life turned upside down when Jodie died, and you've had the added stress of friends and relatives assuming you'd been the ideal couple, when you and I both know that you'd fallen out of love with Jodie for years. This crusade of trying to find out if she was murdered, and who murdered her, is just your way of rationalising your guilt."

"Guilt?"

"Guilt that you weren't broken-hearted when she died, when everyone assumed you were. You're lonely, depressed, and you've fallen in love so hard that you can't see things clearly." He looked down at the bench. "But I'm sorry, Sean. I doubt if Laura reciprocates your feelings. She's just using you."

I took a breath. "What do you mean, using me?"

"She's making a fool of you."

"For God's sake—"

"Just how well do you know her, Sean? Okay, so ostensibly she's a normal person. But she thinks nothing of breaking the law and illegally climbing up buildings and posting her exploits on Twitter, using another name, and hiding her identity. That's not the action of someone normal. You really don't know her at all."

"Everyone has a hobby."

"Breaking the law for no reason? Risking falling to your death? For what?"

"I didn't say I understood her."

"And why is she so close to you all of a sudden? Who did she depend on before the great Sean Delaney walked into her life? She's alone with a difficult problem. You're an ex-policeman, you're resourceful and you can handle yourself in tough situations. Does she know anyone else like that?"

"I don't know."

"So tell me about her friends. Has she got any?"

"There's Barbara, the girl who works with her at the shop. Apart from her she hasn't spoken about her friends. Besides, as far as I can gather, her work is the main thing in her life."

"So your Laura grew up in a children's home, she has no family that she knows of apart from the half-brother Vernon whom she hates, and very few friends, if any. How about exes?"

"She hasn't mentioned anyone."

"No past boyfriends? Girlfriends? Ex-husbands? Lovers?"

"I don't know. She hasn't talked about anyone."

"Well if there aren't any, that's even stranger."

"Why?"

"Because according to you she's an attractive woman, and in my experience attractive women in their twenties and thirties usually have significant others, or a history of one or more failed relationships. There's a mystery in her life and she wants to keep it secret. That's the only explanation. And in my experience, people don't lose their reason overnight. Things happen, events pile up, until eventually their behaviour begins to become abnormal. She claims that when she went to the auction at Netherwold, the place looked familiar to her. And so she went to a psychiatrist to see if he could 'unlock' her memory. She claims that as a child she witnessed this terrible thing happening to her mother, yet she was stuck into a catatonic trance and couldn't move, and conveniently 'traumatic amnesia' set in, so she couldn't tell anyone. I don't believe it. It's rubbish."

Robin sat back on his chair and drank the last of his tea. "My guess is that for years she's probably been on the brink of having some kind of nervous breakdown, and seeing this psychiatrist has sent her over the edge. Frankly, I think she's dangerous. And she's sucking you into her nightmare."

"Shut up!" I told him, storming out of the room.

"You know I'm telling you the truth – you just don't want to hear it."

His words echoed after me as I slammed the door and ran past the grey stone of the old vicarage, and then the squat square church with the blue clock-face and its golden hands. The drunken, haphazardly-angled gravestones were laughing at me as I felt the onset of gloom. I ran on ahead, confused, scared and angry, deciding that a long run was what I needed more than anything.

The weeks since I'd first met Laura at Netherwold before Christmas had been strange ones for me. Most of the time I'd been closeted alone in my cottage, working at my desk, frantically trying to enter into the world of 1970s and 80s music scene. Every few days my mystery caller phoned up, threatening me with death when I least expected it, because of my deadly encounter with Trevor Goodbody.

Before that I'd spent too long alone, either working or brooding about what had happened to Jodie, and why. Meeting Laura and finding out about her problem had been like a rollercoaster ride, and Robin was right, in some strange way she had come to preoccupy me.

There was something much more disquieting about our encounter than simply her volte face. In the seconds after she turned on me I saw viciousness and hatred in her eyes – she looked as if she wanted to murder me.

If looks could kill.

Robin was right. Did Laura and I even have a relationship? All we had ever spoken about was *her* life, *her* problems, *her* difficulties, and apart from her questions when we'd first met, she had not asked a single question about me.

I tried to kid myself that while she was preoccupied with finding out what had happened to her mother she could never have any proper relationship with me, and that would come later. But, as Robin had said, it was weird that she had never mentioned a boyfriend, or indeed any past relationship at all.

Was I making a fool of myself? What exactly did I know about her? I ran and ran, willing the cool breeze to calm me down and the physical excess of the hard run to get my thoughts on an even keel.

All I knew was that I couldn't stop thinking about her.

I missed her.

FIFTEEN

Laura

Why was I doing it?

I could spin out all kinds of lies, reasons, compulsions.

The real reason was that I just couldn't stop myself.

I simply had to do it.

It had been quite easy to find the farm belonging to Roger Bracken, which was near Frome, in Somerset, not too far from my shop in Bath. The small sign indicating the turn-off from the main road announced Bolingbroke Farm, and the rutted lane twisted and turned for a while until the track led to a large gate. I got out and lifted the metal hasp and swung it open so that I could park in front of the large, stone-built house. As I got out and walked up to the front door, I noted the ancient muddy Toyota Land Cruiser, parked front wheels askew as if he'd swept to a halt.

It was wrong. It was stupid. I had promised Sean I'd discuss things with him before tackling the bastard. And DC Cope had warned me not to see him. But despite DC Cope being a nice guy who was obviously trying to help me, in the end I knew that he would be like all the social workers and police I'd encountered in my life.

Unable to do anything.

I knew that ultimately no one was going to stick their neck out on my account. It was true: after twenty-eight years there was no remaining evidence to convict the only living member of Nightingale Green of rape and possibly manslaughter. It was some comfort that the man I thought was the rapist happened to also be the sole survivor.

As DC Cope had pointed out, even if there was some way of charging Roger Bracken with raping my mother, my 'recovered memory' evidence would be ridiculed in court, and the tape-recorded testimony of a dead man carried no weight at all. On the other hand, were there ways of assessing whether a recording had been done at a particular period in time, apart from the type and age of the tape itself, and the quality of the recording? I had no idea, but it was an avenue worth pursuing. If it could be proved that someone made the recording before I had even visited Dr Fanshaw, then that would surely prove something, wouldn't it?

But in spite of all this good reasoning, this morning I had woken up and knew that I couldn't sit around waiting any longer. The old restlessness had returned with a vengeance and I knew I had to do something. I slipped out of the flat during the morning, and I hurriedly left a note for Barbara, telling her that I was visiting a potential client to look at a book collection that was for sale – the client had phoned us yesterday, and I had indeed intended to call on her this afternoon anyway, but had decided against it at the last minute. Barbara would never know what I was planning.

The scene played out over and over again in my mind.

My mother's body, skin against skin of the naked young man who was straddling her. The jiggling of his buttocks during the sex act, the sounds of him grunting and her screaming. Now, twenty-eight years too late, I had to see the monster up close.

But Sean.

God, how I missed Sean. Was there any chance that Sean Delaney could be the one for me, and that by doing this I was wrecking my chances? Every time I was anywhere near Sean I felt strange, obsessed, and I longed to be held in his arms. What would have happened if we'd gone on to have full sex at my flat?

If he hadn't stopped when I told him to, would it have ended up like all the other times? There was no way of knowing.

With a cold bitter shard of horror inside I knew the answer.

I knew that I was only fooling myself to think he could ever love me. When he knew the truth about me, our relationship would end just the same way as all my relationships had ended in the past. I had been a fool to tell him that I knew about his secret, and he had been disgusted that I had not told him about my own secret life. I was kidding myself if I really believed I could bridge the gap between us, even though it was what I wanted more than anything in the world.

It was 4pm, the weather was chilly, the sky grey with drizzle and the last of the daylight fast disappearing. I wondered what sort of reception I would get. Did Roger have a family or live on his own? I realised that I knew virtually nothing about him.

Everything seemed somehow surreal. After all this time I was going to confront the man who had raped and possibly killed my mother, and the mystery of my life would be solved. I had no clue as to what I was going to say, how he would react or indeed anything else at all. I felt sick and scared and on the verge of panic. I was risking everything.

I had to do this thing now, even if it was a mistake.

The man who came to the door looked nothing like I had expected him to be. Short, weedy and stooping, he was also red-faced, overweight and had a drinker's flushed cheeks. He had a thin strip of lifeless white hair caught in up a ponytail that somehow made his otherwise bald pate look pathetic, like an old man clutching at past glories. His small gimlet eyes glinted like blue diamonds and his nostrils flared, exacerbating the redness of their broken veins.

"Can I help you?" he asked me, an impatience in his eyes.

I was clearly an unwelcome intrusion.

I took a breath. "Mr Bracken?"

"Yes."

"Could I come in and talk to you?"

He glared at me, plainly irritated. "I'm afraid I don't buy anything at the door, and I'm not interested in donating to charity." His voice had a prickly edge and a reedy tone, and was delivered in a transatlantic-cum-cockney accent. He was closing the door in my face.

"No, it's nothing like that." I slammed my foot in the crack before it closed completely. "It's a personal matter."

"Personal?"

The door opened slowly, to reveal his face again. Less civilised now, the naked aggression was evident in the twitch to his mouth.

"It's about when you played with the band called Nightingale Green."

"You're the second person who's wanted to know about my time with the band. I've been chatting to an Irish guy who's writing a book about Adrian Dark. Nice guy. Sean, Sean Delaney. Do you know him?"

"Sean is my boyfriend."

"And he asked you to pop over and see me to ask a few

more questions?" he asked hesitantly, his attitude thawing as he opened the door to its full width.

"Something like that." I tried a smile, but my lips couldn't stretch to it.

"Strange. I've never met Sean actually. Is he a shy kind of bloke? We did long phone interviews. Never quite the same to my mind, much better to see the person when you're talking, but he explained what a tight deadline he was on and what with all the travelling problems face-to-face wasn't practical."

"He told me."

"Hard to imagine me as a rocker and roller now, isn't it? But in those days I had it all."

Yes I had seen him before. Age had whittled him down to a husk of the man he'd been. Gone was the confidence, the macho swagger, replaced by a repulsive wary sleaziness.

"Come in then, love, make yourself at home."

Think, think, try and concentrate on what to do now.

He led me along the hall and into a large sitting room, and I fought down the upsurge of nausea that threatened to overtake me. There was a fishy smell that I couldn't place – cooking kitchen-ny smells, plus an underlying aroma of earthiness and dampness, like rotting trees in the forest. I noticed the brown ripple of fungus above the yellowing skirting board, registered the crinkles and bulges in the old paint, as if the timber behind was burgeoning with rot. There were paintings on the walls, abstract art mostly. I recognised a Jackson Pollock and one of the album cover for the Beatles 1968 album *Sergeant Pepper's Lonely Hearts Club*. The last rays of sunshine were lighting up the dust motes in the air as they swirled around the painting of Warhol's cat that hung above the fireplace, where logs were laid in the hearth. I sat on the sofa and he sat in the armchair opposite.

It was very much a man's room, and I noticed the grubby carpet, and weeks' worth of dust on the mismatched scruffy furniture. There were no light touches to the décor, the bright pictures on the walls a heavy-handed concession to a lost generation of artists and pop stars. It looked as if he lived here alone.

And I sat down, I noticed his glance towards my right hand, and his shocked surprise. The expression I was so used to now.

The 'Six finger shiver' in full blown mode. Shock, Revulsion. Surprise. A sort of fascination mixed with distaste.

"Would you like a drink? Tea or coffee? Something stronger?" he asked.

"No thanks."

"As I said, Sean sounded like a really nice guy, we've chatted away for hours on the phone. He's a very good listener, has a talent for it. Have you been together long?"

Together long? What was he talking about?

Of course, I'd told him that Sean and I were together. In a way it was true. Or rather I wish it was. . . If only. . . Oh God, if only!

"Since just before Christmas."

"Long enough to know he's a nice guy then?" His smile was avuncular, encouraging, gappy teeth on display with his eager old-man smile.

I nodded. "This is all very difficult for me, and I hardly know where to begin," I started, unsure, sweating, scared.

The fear had started once again. My heart was beating wildly, my head was pounding, and I felt a hot dark flush spreading across my cheeks. I felt lightheaded, panicked, wishing I was anywhere but here. I closed my eyes. Fought to regain control.

"Are you all right?" he asked, half rising from his chair.

"Sure you wouldn't like a glass of water?"

"No, no, thanks anyway. I've, err, sorry, it's just that I've been ill, but I'm getting over it." I paused. "You see, recently I saw a doctor, who hypnotised me, helping me to remember things that happened to me when I was a child."

He looked confused. "Excuse me, but I thought you were interested in me. In my music career. I gathered that you were here on behalf of Sean, wanting to ask me questions."

"No, you assumed all that. But I do want to ask you questions. About when you were in Nightingale Green."

"Ah, those were the days," he said wistfully. "Chasing my tail all the time, the audiences, the drugs, the parties, the sex, the sheer excitement of it all. I miss it, I really do. To think it was a lifetime ago now, yet to me it's just like yesterday. That's what happens when you get old. Things from your past can be so, so vivid, yet you can forget what happened yesterday. How I've longed for those days again."

"Your band, Nightingale Green. Your friendship and your professional relationship with the others ended quite suddenly, didn't it? It wasn't planned. It wasn't a natural decline."

"We, err, well, we all went our separate ways. As I told Sean, we all agreed to call it a day in our own ways and in our own time. A group decision."

"You all decided at different times?"

"Yes."

"Not according to my sources."

"Your sources?"

"Your break-up happened all at once. On Thursday the sixteenth of October 1987. The day after the night of the Great Storm."

"Did it? I don't remember any particular date, but I

suppose you could say that was the culmination of our group decision."

"On that day you all decided at once that you no longer wanted to work together. Why was that?"

"I've told you. A group decision. *We all decided to call it a day.*"

For the first time, he looked wary.

"Did something happen to make you break up? Did you fall out amongst yourselves? Was there an almighty row that day?"

"I don't remember. Lots of things came into play." I saw a line of sweat break out on his upper lip. "We all wanted to pursue our own separate careers."

"Really? In that case, how come not one of you apart from Adrian ever did any work in the music industry after that date? After 1987, none of you never made a solo record, you never went on tour, not one of you joined forces with another band. After that day you all effectively retired from the music business."

He looked at the floor, shocked, disturbed that my tone of voice was sharp and aggressive.

"Exactly who are you? What do you want from me?" he asked coldly.

"I want the truth. As I told you, I went to see a psychiatrist recently and he hypnotised me. He helped me to remember something that happened at Netherwold Hall, twenty-eight years ago. On the afternoon of the fifteenth of October 1987. The day before Nightingale Green disbanded. A day you must remember very well."

And then, in his anxious stare and furrowed brow I felt the first glimmer of certainty. In so many ways he looked almost totally different to the young man I had seen in my mind's eye, or the strutting rocker in the Wikipedia pictures of Nightingale Green in their heyday.

But then he did it.

I don't know if it was a sideways glance, a glint in his eyes, a minimal movement of his head. Who knows how we recognise people? But there was just *something* I recognised about him, and the shock of it sent me speechless for a few moments. I felt an almost visceral sliver of fear run through my body as I was horribly reminded of what had happened on that night in 1987.

I recognised him from that time.

He was the one!

Why the hell have I come here? Am I going to be safe? After all, if he realises I know the truth he might decide to kill me, to shut me up.

"Look here, I've had enough of this," he said, glaring at me and standing up. "I want you to leave, right now. Shall I call you a cab?" He picked up his mobile from the table.

"I'm not leaving. You have to listen—"

"I don't *have* to do anything! This is my house, and you insisted on coming in here, and now I want you to go! If you have personal issues, I suggest you talk to a doctor or a priest."

"No."

"Then I'll call the police."

"Shut up!" I yelled, standing up and advancing towards him.

Again, the 'sixth finger shiver' as he looked once more at my right hand that I had unconsciously raised in the air.

He backed away slowly, realising that I was serious.

Because I was serious.

Deadly serious.

"My mother left me when I was five years old."

"Your mother?"

"And I remembered under hypnosis that on the last day I saw my mother, she took me to Netherwold Hall. She met some men there and I hid under some furniture while they talked to her. This is a recording of my recovered memory of that night, all those years ago. Listen to it!"

I took out my phone, on which I'd recorded my session and pressed the button and turned it up to its loudest. I listened to my childish under-hypnosis voice recounting what had happened and watched his face all the time:

"*. . . The man was on top of her while the others held her down. They were shouting and laughing and slapping her. . . He was moving, writhing and pushing. . .*"

After the tape ended I switched off the machine and let the silence stretch. I watched the Adam's apple in his throat move up and down.

"And there's another recording, by a man called Pieter van Dries, do you remember him? Your roadie? His account matches mine almost exactly. He named you as the one who raped her."

He was watching me, staring in shocked silence.

"You were the one that raped her. What happened afterwards, Mr Bracken? They never found my mother alive or dead. Did you and the others make sure she was never to tell anyone what happened that day? Did you kill her and bury her body? It's all over for you now, because the police are going to find her body. It's all over for you now," I shouted. "You're going to die in jail!"

SIXTEEN

Sean

I'd driven through the night and much of the morning, encountering traffic jams on the motorway, and my eyes were practically closing by the time I reached the environs of Bath. I longed to get to the derelict house I now called home, climb the stairs and crash out in bed, so I could let the rhythm of the passing miles fade away from my subconscious as my mind slipped into neutral.

My argument with Rob had upset me, principally because I knew I was wrong.

And he was right. I did know virtually nothing about Laura, and all that I did know was unnerving. She was a chatterbox, she was fidgety, she was unpredictable. But she was obsessed, and her obsessive nature made her dangerous. She had convinced herself that her mother had been not only raped by the members of Adrian Dark's band, but that they had murdered her too and, no doubt, buried her body somewhere in the grounds of Netherworld, perhaps in the convenient trench left by the Gas Board engineers. She was full of crazy schemes of trying to find where her body was buried, when it was plainly obvious that no one but Vernon, his solicitor, and certain authorised personnel of Landseer's were allowed to be on the premises, let alone do building excavations.

Most worrying of all, I was certain that despite her denials, she was determined to tackle Roger Bracken, the man she was convinced had raped her mother. She had promised she would not do so, but I was wary of trusting her. It had been Jodie's contact who had provided the evidence from this alleged 'eyewitness', and if Bracken knew Jodie was aware of the accusation against him, he might well have murdered her to shut her up. I wanted to talk to him, but I didn't want to forewarn him. I wanted to be more circumspect than that. If and when I had irrefutable evidence of his guilt, I would tackle him then, once the police had been informed.

Frankly, I wasn't convinced that Laura's therapist had located a 'recovered memory', nor could I be certain that the van Dries tape was genuine.

Something, somehow, just felt wrong.

And the idea of ever having a normal relationship with Laura?

I let the question hang, knowing the answer, but not wanting to admit it to myself. Our relationship was hopeless, impossible, ridiculous.

And yet. . .

As Rob had said, I knew virtually nothing about her, except that she appeared to lead a double life. I also knew that she had been sexually molested as a child, and this had seriously damaged her mentally in ways I could only begin to imagine.

I was overwhelmingly tired and longing to lie on the uncomfortable bed in the attic of the house I was dossing down in. My head was hurting with the concentration of driving, and I was relieved to be getting closer to my current home. I drove down Sebastopol Alley and turned into the narrow lane behind the back gardens of Latimer Row. I moved onto the hard standing, parked and got out of the car, lugging my rucksack from the back seat. Freezing January drizzle had started, and stung my eyes as I strode up the garden.

Opening the back door, I stepped into the kitchen, longing for the oblivion of sleep.

I stopped dead. Through the kitchen door leading to the hallway and stairs I caught a glimpse of movement.

The next thing I knew a line of holes appeared above my head, accompanied by more double-'thocking' sounds.

I saw the muzzle of the Uzi machine pistol pointing at me and dived to the floor. . .

*

Laura

Roger Bracken didn't say anything for a long time. Then he cleared his throat.

"I'm sorry, but whatever you think you know, you're wrong. That description of events." He stared at the floor, lost for words, stumbling, trying to reach for things to say. "If these things happened, I agree, it is absolutely chilling and dreadful. But whatever may have happened I was not involved. I suggest you take this recording to the police."

"I already have done. They don't want to do anything about it. Not yet anyway. Once they start digging up the grounds of Netherwold and find my mother's body, then they'll come and question you."

"Then please, leave me in peace!" He held his hands, palms outwards in denial. "I've told you the truth. If something terrible happened to your mother, I'm very sorry, but it had nothing to do with me. Lots of people came to Netherworld in those days."

"I don't believe you."

"Please will you leave."

"I want some answers first. I want you to confess to the things you've done."

"I've done nothing. And I'm not prepared to listen to your sick fantasies."

"You know I'm telling the truth."

"I know I'm telling you to l-leave, r-right now." He stepped towards me, the stutter betraying his nerves. In spite of his angry bluster, I noticed a tick beginning at the corner of his right eye, the shiver of fear obvious in his voice. Was it the beginning of his realisation that the game was up?

He looked scared. Very scared. He picked up his mobile from the side of the sofa and began to press the keys.

I remembered Mr Carey, the way he'd looked at me, just before I picked up the stone and hit him with it.

Without thinking, I grabbed hold of the heavy table lamp. . .

SEVENTEEN

Sean

It was too soon to grasp what was happening, my head was spinning. He was close, but not close enough to risk charging him.

Ratatatatatatat.

A rip-roaring snarl.

Spitting fire, smoke and bullets ripping towards me. So fast that you couldn't count or even hear the shots individually.

The plaster wall behind me opened up like a suppurating wound, powder raining on my head as I rolled sideways on the floor.

I recognised the blowback-operated submachine pistol. It was an open bolt, mini Uzi 9mm.

And I knew its clip only held enough rounds for a single long burst of fire. Which meant he had to reload.

I leapt up and ran towards him.

"Sean?" Mairéad's voice called out.

As I saw him snap the new clip into place, Mairéad suddenly appeared, throwing the contents of the paint kettle into his face.

I closed the gap between us and grabbed his gun hand, wrestling it upwards. He squeezed off another volley into the ceiling. As I smashed his gun-holding wrist against the wall, Mairéad whacked his hand with the hammer she'd picked up. He dropped the gun.

Then I grabbed the front of his shirt and smashed him into the wall, joyfully slamming my fist into his face several times, effectively pulping the wet paint into his eyes and mouth.

But somehow he twisted out of my grasp, and ran. As I ran after him, I dropped back as I saw him pick up the gun again. Through a daze, I saw him jumping out through a window.

"Leave him, Sean," Mairéad yelled, scrambling to get her phone and dialling. "Police? Yeah. There's just been an intruder at 46 Latimer Row. He's gone. Yeah. He broke in and attacked me and my friend. He's just left the premises. He's armed with a machine gun. Lord, of course I'm sure! He's just been firing it at us!"

"Are you okay, Sean?" Mairéad was beside me now, her arm around my waist.

"Who the hell was he? What did he want?" I asked her, still bemused and shocked at what had happened. "This is the *third fucking time*, for God's sake!"

I looked around the room, noticing for the first time that the drawers of the dressing table and chest of drawers were all gaping open.

"Seems like he was looking for something," Mairéad said. "But did he hurt you, Sean? Do you need an ambulance?"

The pain was subsiding. I could breathe easily.

"No, I think I'm okay. Thanks to you. If you hadn't come when you did..."

Half an hour later, we were giving a statement to the policeman who'd called.

"I just called round on the off-chance," she told me when he'd gone. "I wanted to see how the job was getting on. The front door was hanging open."

"It's lucky you did."

"Who on earth was he?" she asked.

"God knows."

"I'll organise for the locks to be changed again tomorrow," she told me. "Do you think he'll come back?"

"I've got no idea. Look, Mairéad, I've been thinking. It looks as if he's been searching for something. Maybe he's after the diaries? I'm thinking of that guy, James Patterson, the American who tried to buy the diaries at the auction and was so pissed off with me for getting them. Do you think it has something to do with him? He was determined to get them, and he wouldn't know that I took them back home to Whitstable."

"Anything's possible, I suppose."

"But why did he have a gun and use it?" I thought aloud. "He was aiming to kill." I thought of my phantom caller, who was constantly threatening me with death.

If it was him, he had very nearly succeeded.

*

After she had gone I tried to sleep, but it was impossible to switch off my thoughts. As I began to doze off, my mobile rang.

"Sean?"

The name LAURA was on the screen, but I'd have recognised her voice anyway.

"What's happened?"

"I've done something ridiculous. I've ruined everything. I went to see Roger Bracken and I..." She broke down, crying hysterically.

"Where are you?"

She was incomprehensible for a moment, as she babbled hysterically.

"Oh God, Sean," she managed to gasp out. "Everything's gone to shit, I'm in a hell of a mess, I don't know what to do . . . I don't know why I'm ringing you. . . After the way we parted I have no right to expect you to help me. . ."

"Slow down. What's happened?"

"God I'm such a fuck-up! I've wrecked everything! I did what I promised I wouldn't do. I'm sorry, Sean, I'm *really, really* sorry. I know I promised not to go and see Roger Bracken, but I couldn't stop myself." She dissolved into tears for a few moments.

"What happened?"

"When I confronted him, he denied it, and then he said some things. . . I flew at him, we struggled and he overpowered me, and threw me out of the house, saying he was calling the police. He says he'll get me in trouble. He can sue me, apparently, for slander. Oh God, I've ruined everything."

"Calm down, Laura. Listen. Where are you?"

"Sitting in my car. Not far from his house. I drove away, but I realised I lost my glasses in the house and couldn't see properly. This car was coming from the other direction, and I had to swerve to avoid it and I ended up in a ditch. I'm going to have to get a cab or something, but the police might arrest me. I just wanted you to know how sorry I am that I let you down. I'm sorry I'm such a fuck-up!" She burst into tears again. "Sean, whatever happens to me, I love you, I *really, really* love you, and I hope you can forgive me. I've loved you since I first saw you."

"What's the address?"

"What?"

"*The address.* Wait there. I'm coming to get you.

"I'm sorry…." She dissolved into hysterical tears again, then read out the name of the road.

"Wait there. Calm down. Everything's going to be all right."

EIGHTEEN

I broke the speed limit and made it in twenty minutes. Her wrecked car was easy to spot from a distance, perched as it was half-in and half-out of a deep ditch.

She hardly spoke as I helped her to climb out of her car and into mine. Her top was ripped across the front and stained with mud. She had brought a small travelling case with her that she had taken from the back seat.

"I need to call a garage," she said.

"Later. Let's get you away from here, so you can pull yourself together and we can decide what to do."

"How you must hate me," she muttered, almost to herself.

"If I hated you I wouldn't have come, would I?"

"So why did you come?" she asked me finally as we were speeding along the road. "Why?"

"Because I promised to help you." I saw a sign for a Little Chef restaurant, and indicated to pull in, so we could stop and take stock of the situation. "And because ever since I met you I haven't been able to stop thinking about you."

Finally I braked the car to a stop behind a lorry in the car park. I pulled on the handbrake and killed the engine.

"Really?"

"Laura, for God's sake, you promised not to go and see

Roger Bracken, and then you just went ahead and did it!" I snapped. "Christ, Laura, if you won't even keep your word then what's the point? What is the fucking point?"

"The point?"

"Of us having any kind of relationship."

She shook her head, frowning. She started to cry again, grabbing my arm. "Oh, Sean! After what happened, do you still feel anything for me?"

"*Of course I feel something for you!*" I pulled her close and kissed her. Then I whispered in her ear, my heart hammering wildly. "Don't you know, that you're driving me insane? I think about you all the time."

She broke away. "If only that was true."

"I'm not a liar."

"But you don't know me, Sean. You don't know me..."

"I know that you were sexually abused as a child, so it's no wonder you have problems relating to men. You only had to explain that to me, I'd have understood why you're scared of intimacy. I don't understand why you spend your weekends risking your life by climbing buildings just so you can show off on twitter. And I don't know why you went to see Roger Bracken. But I can try to understand. I want to get to know you, if you'll just be honest with me..."

"I'm sorry. Oh, Sean, I'm sorry. I tried to keep my word and not go and see him, I swear I tried. But honestly, something just came over me. Sometimes I feel as if I have no control over what I'm doing."

"That's rubbish. Everybody has control."

She shook her head. "Sorry, Sean. There are things you don't know about me. There are things I don't even know about myself..."

"Listen, Laura. Everyone has things in their past.

Things they've done that they're ashamed of. The important thing is not to dwell on them. To look ahead. Don't you see, *that's* what you've been doing wrong? This obsession with what happened to your mother. It's not healthy. The policeman, DC Cope, was right. We have to play the long game, take things slowly, prepare the ground, not just go crashing in and making accusations. Look, you think your mother was raped at Netherworld Hall, but you don't know for sure. All you know for certain is that she disappeared. There's the possibility that if she was raped, then afterwards she was murdered, and they got rid of her body. So we have to concentrate on somehow trying to find her body. If we can do that, we can take things forward. If there's no way of doing that, I'll think of something else. But just going to see Bracken and confronting him, was a *ridiculous* thing to do. Of course he would deny it, he would have to! Your mother disappeared twenty-eight years ago. Quite possibly she's dead. You have to let it go. She wouldn't want you to be ruining your life on her account. You've got a good life, a successful business. Your mother would be glad that you've become the success that you are. She wouldn't want you to get into trouble with the police, would she?"

"You're right, Sean. I promise, from now on I'll leave it alone."

"So let's get this straight, and for Christ's sake tell me the truth now, or I'm finished with you once and for all."

"Don't say that—"

"*Shut up and listen!* You argued with him, you struggled. He threw you out of the house, and then you drove away. That's all that happened?"

"Yes."

"You swear?"

"Yes."

"You didn't attack him or anything?"

"No. I struggled with him, fought back as he threw me out of the house, but he manhandled me to the front door, and pushed me so that I sprawled onto the ground. Then he slammed the door in my face."

I stared at her.

"Don't you believe me?"

I shook my head, unsure of everything. "Yes. Yes. Of course I believe you. But if you're keeping something back from me, then that's it, Laura, I've had it with you."

"I promised, didn't I?" She began to cry. "Christ, I just don't know what to do now..."

"Shut up, pull yourself together and listen to me!"

She went on crying for a few moments, then she stopped.

"Everything is going to be okay, I promise," I told her, reaching out and holding her hand. "We'll work out what to do. As I say, there's a good chance that he didn't call the police. After all, if he really is guilty of what you think, he isn't going to want the police knowing what you're accusing him of, is he?"

"That's true."

"Have you got any spare glasses?"

"At home, not here."

"Okay. We'll go into this place, you can relax and take a break, while I drive back to your car, phone to get a garage to pick it up and take it to a local garage, or back to your home address. I'll meet you back here."

"Thanks, Sean. I know I'm a coward, but I really can't bear to go back to the car."

"Listen, we have to get things straight. Let's go through it again one last time. You say you struggled. Think hard, because this is important, and if the police arrest you, we need to be sure of the truth. You swear you didn't hit him?"

"I told you, no!" She paused to take stock, closing her eyes and clenching her fists. "Look, Sean, I swear to you, this is what happened. He grabbed my arm, tried to pull me to my feet to throw me out of the house, but I wouldn't go, and we ended up struggling together for bit. I remember he was shaking me by the shoulders as if I was a dog or something! He knocked off my glasses, I started yelling at him, I fell back, knocked some things off the table. Then he took me by the arm and dragged me to the front door and pushed me outside, so that I tripped and fell onto the gravel. As you can see my top is ripped right across. He'd slammed the door. All I could do was pick myself up and get back into the car and drive away, but I didn't get far. I was so upset I wasn't thinking straight, hardly realised I wasn't wearing my glasses and misjudged this car coming towards me."

After leaving her at the table in the Little Chef café, I drove to Roger Bracken's farm. There were no signs of police cars there, so it sounded as if Roger had not reported Laura's visit, and she'd got away with it.

After a bit of careful revving and jerking in first gear, I managed to get Laura's car out of the ditch, and when I examined it I couldn't see that it was damaged at all. Then I parked my own car in a road nearby, and drove Laura's car back to the Little Chef.

I got back to Laura and reassured her that there was no sign of police, and that, with luck, she might have got away with it. I noticed that she had changed her torn top.

"It was just when I was sitting there, looking at him," she told me, "that I was certain he was the one. I recognised his face. He was the one who raped my mother. I'm sure of it."

"Well, there's nothing you can do about it now."

"So what's going to happen?" She was getting hysterical, talking faster and faster.

"With any luck, nothing. We'll work out what to do later. Right now it's damage limitation time. You go home, sit tight, tell no one what you've done. We just try to let everything die down."

As we drove back to Bath, I began to relax, and Laura did too.

"Sean, I don't deserve this," she told me. "I'm so embarrassed about the way I reacted when we were together that time when we almost connected at my shop. Oh God, I've been thinking about it over and over. You must think I'm crazy. Why are you helping me like this, when I keep on letting you down?"

"Because I'm an idiot, I guess…" I swallowed hard. "And because in spite of everything I think you're wonderful."

"Oh God, Sean, I think you're pretty wonderful too, do you know that?"

"Well, swear to me that you'll leave this business alone. Look at it this way. If this doctor actually *did* uncover hidden memories of what happened to your mother when you were a child, then four of the five people who might have been responsible are already dead, aren't they? You say you're convinced Roger Bracken was the one who raped her, yet you tell me you can't fully recapture the memory, you can only access it under hypnosis. So how do you know it's true?"

"Just a feeling. And when I was there, with him, I thought I could remember. It's like it all came back to me."

"Laura, seriously, haven't you read anything about this 'recovered memory' phenomenon? There's a lot of psychiatrists who don't believe it's reliable. It's been proved that people unwittingly invent things and genuinely believe them to be true."

"But there's also the tape you found, of van Dries saying the same thing."

"I agree, we can try to investigate it, but from now on we do it my way. So now, will you give it a rest? Leave it to the police."

"Sean, I'm scared."

"Of what?"

"Of you and me. Of what's going to happen. I've had boyfriends before and it's never worked out. If you want to call it a day, it's up to you—"

"I told you how I feel about you." I squeezed her hand in mine while I held the steering wheel with the other. "I'll take my chances."

"But why would you want to have anything to do with me when you know I'm such a useless crazy fuck-up?"

"Who says I'm not a fuck-up myself? A policeman who got thrown out of the force, an artist who never made it. An eejit who's chasing around the country trying to unravel the mystery of his wife's death."

I heard the police car sirens behind us, then slowed as the car flashed us, indicating that we had to pull in to the side of the road.

When I'd stopped the two policemen got out of the car and walked across to the window.

"Would you and the lady please get out of the car, sir?" he asked politely.

We did as he asked.

"Are you Laura Jane Kaplan?" he asked her.

"Yes."

"Ms Kaplan, I'm arresting you on suspicion of the

attempted murder of Roger Bracken. You do not have to say anything, but if you do . . ."

"This is crazy!" Laura protested, as they took her arm to lead her away. "I ran away from him. When I left he was coming after me. . ."

"And may I ask your name, sir?" the other policeman asked me, as I tried to intervene.

"Sean Delaney."

"And may I ask what relationship Ms Kaplan is to you?"

There was a long pause.

"She's my fiancée."

I saw the gratitude in Laura's eyes as they led her away.

But they were arresting her for murder, and she claimed not to have attacked Roger Bracken.

Someone must have attacked him and nearly killed him.

And they wouldn't be arresting her unless they had some kind of evidence.

Could I believe anything she said from now on?

NINETEEN

"You have to believe me!" Laura pleaded.

In the cramped interview room, Patrick Newby, the young duty solicitor who had agreed to represent Laura, and I were sitting opposite her at the table.

She had been held under suspicion of the attempted murder of Roger Bracken for eighteen hours now. Apparently Bracken had been attacked in his home and had serious head injuries and was currently in a coma in the intensive care unit of the local hospital. It seemed that the injuries had been caused by a heavy table lamp which had her fingerprints on it. Laura had reluctantly admitted that she had picked it up, but insisted that she had not hit him with it.

Under the PACE regulations, the police had to either charge her within the next six hours, release her, or persuade the judge to grant an extension to her detainment. Hearing of all the evidence stacked against her, both her solicitor and I were pretty sure she was going to be charged. Saying I was her fiancé had seemed a good idea at the time, indeed it was the only reason I was allowed to talk to her defence counsel and be here in the police station to support her. But lying to the police is a serious offence, and I was taking a big risk. I felt sick, scared and utterly clueless about what was going on.

Laura looked a wreck. She obviously hadn't slept since her arrest, her eyes were red-rimmed from crying and her hair was wild and uncombed. Yet even now, when she was at her worst, I felt myself pulled towards her, longing to hold her in my arms and tell her everything was going to be all right.

"This is the truth, I swear it," she went on to the solicitor tearfully. "I went to see Roger Bracken. I played him the tape of my recovered memory hypnosis session and told him that I thought that it was him who had raped my mother. He denied it. I got angry. I yelled at him. And yes, I picked up the heavy table lamp. I wanted to hit him with it. But I didn't. I broke down, I was overcome with it all, I just burst into tears, we struggled, I dropped the lamp and he threw me out of the house. When I left him, Bracken was chuntering on, telling me that he was calling the police, that I had no right to accuse him of such terrible things, that I was raving mad and he was going to sue me for slander, and, well, lots of other things. But when I ran out of the house he was standing there, at the door."

Ran out of the house?

I reflected on the account she had given me, straight after it had happened. She had told me that Bracken had physically thrown her out of his house, that she had been sprawled on the ground while he slammed the door. Which version of events was the truth?

A sick feeling of terror was growing inside me.

"Hmm. Look, Laura, I won't lie. This looks very bad for you," Patrick said carefully. "Tell me again. What happened to the top you were wearing?"

"It was ripped, so I changed it in the toilets of the Little Chef restaurant."

"What happened to it?"

"I threw it in the bin."

"The police can't find any trace of it."

"Then I suppose the restaurant had the bin emptied before the police arrived."

"Why did you just happen to have a spare piece of clothing with you, to change into?"

"I, um..." she hesitated, "I had it in mind to go to London afterwards on business and to stay overnight. I had a full change of clothes in the case in the back of the car."

"And in the upset state you were in when Mr Delaney picked you up from outside Mr Bracken's farm, you had the presence of mind to remember the change of clothes to take with you?"

"I was in a mess. I didn't want to look scruffy."

"You cared about looking scruffy in those terrible, upsetting circumstances?"

"Yes," she agreed.

"You realise that they're going to think that this is evidence that this supposed attack on Mr Bracken was premeditated? That you anticipated getting into a confrontation with him, and carried spare clothing to change into afterwards?"

"That's ridiculous."

"Is it? You say that your top was bloodstained, and that's why you got rid of it. From the report they've let me see, he was struck on the head several times at close quarters by that table lamp. His skull was fractured and his nose was broken. There would have been considerable blood spatter. If we could produce that top, and it had no blood on it, or the blood was only yours, then that would have been evidence in your favour."

"They took away my other clothes, my jeans and shoes – there was no blood on them."

"That means nothing. The prosecution could claim that only your top was in range of the blood spatter. Now let's go through the rest of it. The police say that they got a call from Mr Bracken at 4.30pm, telling them that you had called on him, and were accusing him of all kinds of things, and that he had tried to make you leave, but that you wouldn't go."

"Yes. We argued. I think that he called the police while I was there, and then he threw me out."

"Laura, listen to me. You've admitted that you've been under the care of a psychiatrist in London. You've been mentally ill. I believe, in fact I have no doubt, that you are *still* mentally ill. If you tell me the truth now, that you lost control, that indeed you *did* hit Mr Bracken with that table lamp, then it seems reasonable to me to argue that you acted in the heat of the moment, that you acted in what we call a state of diminished responsibility. If you admit to this now, then I promise you things will go easier for you. I don't know about tariffs for this kind of crime, but the first stage is always to cooperate, and I've every belief that if you do, then the police will go easy on you. Honesty is always the best option in a situation when there's no other way out."

"So you don't believe me?" she asked him. Her voice was cracking, as if she was on the verge of tears.

"I'm sorry, Laura. Anyone might lie in your situation, but as things stand it's just ridiculous. There's a raft of evidence against you – your fingerprints on the table lamp, your car on the CCTV, the fact that you tell me you disposed of the clothes you were wearing when you went to see him. You fled the scene. And you have a motive – you blame him for this supposed attack on your mother."

"But I didn't hit him with the table lamp! I've told you! However unlikely it may sound, I'm innocent!"

There was a long pause. "Admitting to the truth is going to go a long way to a reduced sentence. Especially if you acted on the spur of the moment."

"Then if you don't believe me, please leave." She began to cry. "I'll find a solicitor who doesn't think I'm a liar."

Patrick sighed. "Laura, I'm sorry. I promise you that I'm doing my best. You're not going to find many people who are prepared to represent you."

"Then I'll defend myself."

"I can see I'm getting nowhere right now." He glared at her, then stood up, signalling to the waiting policeman that he wanted to leave. "Right now, the police are liaising with the Crown Prosecution Service, and they have more than enough evidence for the CPS to give them the green light to charge you, and after that it's quite likely you won't get bail. Whereas if you make a clean breast of everything, I can make an application for bail and there's a fair chance it'll be granted. If so, then you can go home and take stock of things until the trial. Think about it. I'll come back and see you tomorrow."

He walked out of the room.

There was a long silence. At any moment, I expected the waiting officer to tell me my time was up.

"Sean, thank you. I don't know what I'd do without you." She stared at me, beginning to cry again. "And thanks for agreeing to, you know what."

Now that our interview might be being recorded we had to be careful what was said. I didn't know how illegal it was to pretend to be her fiancé, but I didn't like doing it.

"Why did you get rid of that top?" I asked her.

She looked up at me, and something changed in her eyes. It was a question I couldn't duck, however bad it made me feel for asking it.

I felt as if I was finally waking up from a nightmare.

Falling in love with Laura had blinded me to everything. If she had murdered Roger Bracken, blood splatter would have been evident on her outer clothing. I did remember seeing blood on her top, but I'd also seen that she'd scratched her hand on the gravel and it had been bleeding badly. A DNA test would have proved things one way or another.

And when she disposed of the clothing she would have known that.

"I threw it away because it was ripped and torn." She looked down at the table. "I was in the restaurant. I didn't want people staring at me."

"And that was the only reason?"

"YES! For God's sake, Sean, don't you believe me?"

"Laura, you went to see Roger Bracken, and you took a change of clothes in the car with you. Why did you do that?"

"I told Patrick, for God's sake! I was planning to go away for the weekend afterwards."

"Where?"

"To London."

"Why?"

"To climb up a new hotel in Mayfair."

"You told Patrick you were going to London on business."

"Did I?" she answered.

"Yet now you say you were you planning to go on

another of your climbing expeditions up the side of a building?"

"So?"

"Just another episode in your secret life then?"

"What the fuck is this, Sean? The fucking police are grilling me, and now you're trying to trap me with your questions."

There was a long silence.

"Sean, I have to know. Do you believe me? Do you believe that I did not hit Roger Bracken with that table lamp?"

"Laura, frankly, I'm sorry. I don't know what to believe. I'm in love with you. I can't stop being in love with you, and I'll help you all I can. If you'll only admit the truth I swear I'll stand by you. For goodness sake, you thought he raped your mother and ruined your life. Anyone might have struck out in those circumstances!"

"So you think I'm lying? You think I tried to kill him?"

"I'm not saying that."

"Then just what the fuck are you saying?"

"I don't know. Listen, Laura." I was angry now, furious at the way she was behaving, sick of her stupid games. "You promised me that you wouldn't go and see Roger Bracken, we agreed to wait before tackling him – remember, this isn't just your quarrel – Bracken might have killed my wife if she'd found out any facts that incriminated him, so I want to know if he did. Yet in spite of promising me you wouldn't do it, that we would work out what to do together, you went to see him. If this hadn't happened, you'd have lied to me, told me you hadn't gone to see him, wouldn't you? You went to see him, you argued with him. And I think. . ."

"Go on, say it."

"I think you hit him with that lamp. Maybe you can't

even remember what happened."

"Get out of my sight." She screamed. "Get out of my sight!"

The police officer came across and told me that it was time to go.

But as I left the station, pondering the facts of the case and the impossible situation she was in, I wondered what the hell I had let myself in for.

In my heart of hearts I knew she was guilty.

Yet I was still hopelessly, completely, in love with her.

What the hell else was she guilty of?

TWENTY

The police charged Laura with the attempted murder of Roger Bracken. She was held on remand and bail had been denied.

I had asked to see her again, but been told that she refused to see me. In one way I was relieved. If only I could have switched off my feelings for her, it wouldn't have been so bad. Because in spite of all the facts and evidence pointing to her guilt, there was some part of me that longed to believe that she was telling the truth.

But she had promised not to go and see Roger Bracken, and broken that promise. She had kept her double life as a part-time buildings acrobat secret from me. She had some strange hang-up about sex that had caused her to turn on me viciously, for no apparent reason. While all these things didn't exactly amount to lies, they came pretty close to it, for what is a secret life if it isn't living a lie? She was seeing a psychiatrist, so how could I know if she herself even knew if she was lying or not?

I loved her.

But I really did not know her.

I was talking to Mairéad at the Landseer's offices the next day. She looked worried as she regarded me.

"I'm sorry, Sean, but someone's got to tell you this.

You've got yourself involved with this woman Laura, and no one knows anything about her. All we do know is that she's been charged with attempted murder, and as you know, the CPS don't authorise the police to make charges unless they're pretty sure they'll stick."

"I know that."

"So what do you think happened? That she went to see him, had a row with him, picked up the lamp just for fun, then put it down? And moments after she'd left someone else arrived and picked up the same lamp and used it to hit him so hard that right now he's fighting for his life in intensive care? Do you really think that's likely?"

I took a deep breath. "No, of course not."

"Sean, she's lying to you because you're the only ally she's got. She had to admit to being there, because CCTV had recorded her car being in the vicinity. Forensics found her fingerprints on the weapon. She refused to alter her plea of not guilty, ignoring her solicitor's advice to plead guilty with diminished responsibility."

"I know all that."

"Then I'm sorry, Sean. But I think you're kidding yourself. You're lonely. You've fallen for Laura because this is a low point in your life, and she's given you something to cling on to. And now you're involved with Laura and it's blinded you to the facts. Whether you like it or not, you have to pull yourself together, forget about Laura and get on with your life."

"For God's sake—"

"Listen, Sean, I'm your friend. And I'm not stupid. You're in love with Laura. Which would have been fine if she was a normal person. But she isn't. She *isn't normal.*"

I nodded miserably. "Anyway, I'm making good headway with the house. Hard work is always a good antidote to feeling sorry for yourself."

"Good. Is there any news about the book?"

"The book?"

So much had happened recently that I'd forgotten all about my most recent project. "Sylvia, my editor, phoned a few days ago and she's given it a wee read through, and she reckons it's okay. She especially likes my facsimile paintings of the copyright protected photos – as you thought, being able to get round the copyright laws of the owners of the pics made all the difference. Assuming she doesn't need any rewrites, she'll send it out to the copy editor tomorrow, then the proofreader. Finally the designer will block everything out."

"So how long do you think before it's in print?"

"Oh, I suppose maybe three months. It takes a minimum time but it's nothing like the old days, when six months or even a year was usual. They'll move everything fast because it's topical – won't be long now before Adrian Dark is completely forgotten."

"Well, Sean, you've had a rough time. Why don't you go home and relax? You've made a good start on this place, and you could really do with a change of scene. Give you some perspective."

Just then my mobile rang.

"Mr Delaney?"

"Yes."

"This is Detective Sergeant Jordan. I'm in charge of the investigation into the armed intruder who broke into 46 Latimer Row. Can you come to the Lido Road Police Station, please? There's been a development."

*

When I got there, for once there was some good news. DS

Jordan invited me behind the barrier and took me into the huge office area that he shared with a number of other officers, and I sat opposite his desk, reminded of the camaraderie behind the scenes at a big police station.

"Early this morning, we found what we thought was an abandoned car in a lay-by on the Frome Road," he began. "At first it looked as if the driver had fallen asleep on the back seat, but it turned out that he had shot himself with a semi-automatic weapon – a 9mm Uzi machine pistol to be precise. The same gun that was used in the break-in you reported at your house."

"Really?" I asked him.

"He left a note. The gist of it was that he didn't want to go on living because he had failed to kill ex-police constable Sean Delaney, the man who had shot his partner, Trevor Goodbody. A lot of wild stuff about how now that he'd used a gun there'd be a manhunt for him, and he couldn't face going to jail. He states that he's been phoning you for a while now. I checked up and it seems that we've got a record of you having reported these threatening phone calls."

It was with a huge feeling of relief that I left the police station, knowing that at least one of the problems in my life had been solved once and for all.

As I walked out onto the pavement, a woman in a red miniskirt stepped out in front of me.

"Sean Delaney?" she asked.

The first thing I noticed about her was a dazzling frizzy mass of blond hair with a central blue streak.

"Yes."

"I'm Kate Doyle." The woman pressed her warm palm against mine in an awkward handshake. "I'm a journalist. I knew your wife, Jodie."

"Really?" My heart kicked up a beat.

The dress had been designed to show a lot of thigh, and I noticed her strappy shoes had very high heels. Kate stood there looking up at me, clutching at the strap of her shoulder bag and straining to look taller than her five feet.

"Jodie showed me your picture on her phone. Didn't do you justice."

"You knew Jodie?"

"Yeah."

"Let's find a café."

We found a rough-and-ready snack bar nearby and settled at a table with coffees. The speed at which she chattered away was mesmerising. Kate Doyle could almost be described as ugly, with her somewhat large nose and angular features, and yet the whole effect of her animated face and expressions was somehow mesmerising and decidedly attractive. With her blonde fringe dancing over the forehead, the central blue section falling across her eyes, she reminded me of a chattering jackdaw.

"How did you know Jodie?" I asked her.

"We once worked on a story together." She took a long gulp of coffee and grimaced as if she was in pain. "Sorry, mate, I'm lying. We didn't work on a story together. I never met Jodie, but I read a lot of her work. She was a shit-hot investigator. I admired her. She had more balls than most of the men I know."

"Why did you lie to me?"

"'Cos I wanted your attention, and with all you've got on your plate right now, I wouldn't blame you for telling a pushy, fast-talking tart like me to get stuffed. And I had to talk to you. Truth is, I heard about the shooting and came to the station in the hope of talking to the cop on the case, or at least their press officer. But meeting you means I've hit the jackpot."

"The jackpot? What do you mean?"

"Meeting a sexy guy is always a jackpot for me, mate." She licked her lips as she stared into my eyes. "But seriously, Sean, I've always had a nose for a story – it's how I earn a crust, listening to stories, picking up on what's going on. I heard about Laura Kaplan being arrested for attempted murder," she went on. "Tell me, Sean mate, why did you tell the arresting officers that Ms Kaplan was your fiancée?"

"How do you know she isn't?"

"Gimme a break, I asked around, didn't I? You've only known her since Christmas."

I sighed. "I told them that because I want to help her. And I didn't think they'd let me visit her otherwise."

She nodded. "Look, Sean, I hardly need to remind you that lying to the police is not a good idea."

"I've not had any good ideas for quite a while. What's your excuse for getting involved in this mess? Why are you here?"

"'Cos I'm after a story. But more importantly because you need my help. You may not realise it yet, but you, Sean Delaney, are in deep doo-doo."

"Listen—"

"About Laura. Tell me. What do you actually know about her?"

"Is it any business of yours?"

"My business is to help you dig yourself out of the quicksand that's sucking you down. Okay, mate, cards on the table. I happen to know quite a lot about Laura Kaplan already and that's why I've come to see you. You need to be very careful."

"Careful?"

"One of the children's homes she was resident in had a lot of trouble with the staff investigated for improper relationships with the children. You know she was a high-profile witness in the Harper's Dyke child abuse scandal, back in the nineties? "

"I read about it. She had a terrible time, what with her mother going missing, then being shunted into a children's home, and being at the mercy of bloody perverts."

"I know that. But there's something that didn't make the papers." Kate nibbled a fingernail, looking at the floor, then up at me again. "The director of the home, Harold Carey, died of a heart attack just before the scandal broke, and Laura gave evidence at the trials. When Carey had his fatal attack, she happened to be alone with him at the time."

"So?"

"Questions were asked. Firstly about why a twelve-year-old girl was alone with him. This was strictly against protocol, as you can imagine. She was with him in the woods near the home. What nobody went too deeply into was, how quickly did she raise the alarm, after he had his attack? No one knows. But there was speculation that she did not immediately summon help. Remember, this was one of the men who was convicted of abusing her sexually."

"All you're telling me is that she's had a lot of trouble in her life."

"She certainly has. She was fostered by two families, but couldn't settle in either of the homes, threatening one of the foster fathers with a knife. But she was clever – got herself good A-levels, went to university, did a training course in bookbinding. She managed to open up her own shop a few years ago."

"She did well."

"I'm not denying it. But she was a student, then worked for a bookbinding company in London. And after only two years, she bought her own shop in Bath. How does a young person, with no relatives or rich friends, manage to accrue enough money to buy her own shop, when she's only been working on low wages for a couple of years?"

"What are you suggesting?"

"That she's a liar. I don't know what she's told you, but my guess is that she found out who her father was a long time ago, and she probably remembered her mother visiting him at Netherwold Hall and what happened on that last night. And I think she may have confronted him and blackmailed him into giving her the money to buy that shop."

"That's impossible. She told me that until she heard about Adrian Dark's legacy to her, she had no idea he was her father. And she's been to see a psychiatrist and he's helped her to uncover a hidden memory about when she first came to the big house as a child. Why would she do that if she already knew who her father was?"

"She likes drama. She likes attention. Why else would she climb buildings and post her exploits on Twitter and Facebook? Now that she can no longer blackmail her father, perhaps she wanted to blackmail Roger Bracken, and he told her to get stuffed, and that's why she blew a fuse and attacked him?"

"She says she didn't attack him—"

"And you believe her? Hand on fucking heart, Sean, even though you'd walk through fire for her, can you swear to me, that you really believe she's telling the truth?"

"Yes."

"Okay, Sean, fair enough. But just consider this. What if it's all a pack of lies, and she knew all the time about what happened to her mother, because she *actually did* remember it happening? It's understandable. She might have been afraid to go to the authorities at the time. But years later, when it came to needing money, it suited her to go and see her father and blackmail him into financing her shop."

"I don't believe that."

"Look, she may be telling part of the truth. But she's no fool. When she grew up she might have got to wondering why her mother abandoned her in a village next to the home of a rich songwriter and ex-musician. She might have been told that her mum had been one of those girls who followed pop bands – a groupie. So she puts two and two together, guessing that there was only one logical reason for her mum to have taken her to a village in the West Country. She guessed that Adrian Dark was her father. She might have demanded a paternity test, if he denied all knowledge of her mum, and if he refused she could have threatened to go to the newspapers, and he wouldn't have wanted that."

"If she was a nuisance, blackmailing him, why would he leave her anything in his will?"

"It may not have been blackmail, I'm just guessing. As an older man with only one other child, maybe he was glad to give her money. Things aren't always how they seem. After all, I know you never wanted to shoot Trevor Goodbody, but there'll always be people who reckon you shot him, knowing he was unarmed."

I cringed, hating the thought of her knowing my secret. "You're just guessing."

"Guesswork based on facts. You don't wanna hear what I'm gonna say, but I'm gonna say it anyway. I been sniffing around this story for a long time now."

"What story?"

"*The Laura Kaplan story* of course. You were in the police, so you know that when similar crimes are committed in different localities by the same person, each police force investigates each case independently, frequently duplicating work while not realising it. Indeed there've been a number of high profile cases where it was a long time before different forces realised they were dealing with a single perpetrator, and a joint task force was formed, so that efforts and information could be pooled."

"What sort of crimes are you talking about?"

She shrugged, and I noticed the fast, twitchy way her shoulders moved. "Robberies, rapes. Murders."

"Are you telling me that you suspect that Laura might be responsible for other crimes, in addition to the one she's been charged with?"

"I'm saying that Laura Kaplan is an enigma. If I'm right, she could also be a murderer. . ."

*

Detective Constable Cope

I was late getting to the meeting.

We'd found a new venue – a hall behind the *Shifting Sands* pub, a bit spartan, a bit gloomy. But everyone was there, and I felt the old warmth, the old feeling of comradeship as Buddy called the meeting to order.

Of course, we were all white, many of us were over forty, and we all had the kind of same intrepid determined expressions as we relaxed in the company of our peers. My grandad used to tell me that all England used to be like this, no black faces anywhere, no foreign languages spoken on British streets.

The *Aryans Supreme* movement have a secret code: a bit like the Masons. Don't laugh, but we really do have a special handshake involving extra pressure on the little finger. We have overt signals too, oh yes. And unlike the somewhat embarrassingly obvious 'thumb and index finger circle' held aloft, used to such effect by American white supremacists, our secret signals were much more subtle and nuanced. A scratch to the right side of your mouth, using only the thumb. A closed fist very briefly held over your heart. These were some of the little ways we knew of each other's existence and loyalties. You'd be surprised at the number of politicians and influential powerful people belong to our movement.

We have to provide documentation, birth certificates going back three generations, to prove we're of Caucasian descent. The leader, whom we never name but who we all admire, is of course the driving force behind all our ideas, and we're proud of it. We don't hate the Jews so much, that's the main difference. It's the dark races that we hate. We hate the outlawing of words, the saying of yukky slimy phrases like *the 'n' word*, or *the 'p' word.* We prefer to use the words we know to describe those races, who are rising up everywhere you look and taking control.

Do you know how many mosques they're building now, in our cities? Have you been to Southall recently? Lots of the street names are in Urdu, for heaven's sake. In London!

London, Birmingham, Manchester, every major city in England the dark races are taking over. Rotting young people's lives with drugs, forcing young white girls into prostitution. It makes my blood boil.

We got people in high places, councillors, MPs, all keeping their views hush-hush of course, for the time being, anyway. They tell me they're planning some kind of takeover of the Conservative party, but I don't believe it myself. Even so, those rich Tory boys are too wet to take control of the streets, as someone has got to do eventually.

Okay, I'm not exactly pure British myself, but my mum was Irish, from Galway, where they tell me lots of people have an olive complexion. Dad was rock-solid

English for generations, and Mum's people were all from the Emerald Isle.

"The next operation is going to be in Brixton, London," announced Buddy, from the lectern. "We intercept the next consignment of cocaine and put the word out that one of the rival gangs has done it. That guarantees a war between the two key contenders for control of the area. A few less niggers."

The cheer went up. There were a lot of us.

And we would win in the end.

TWENTY-ONE

Sean

"Laura, a murderer?" I said to Kate. "What are you talking about?"

"Sean, I'm sorry. But Laura isn't the sweet little innocent you think she is. I believe she's killed before."

"What?" It felt as if a chunk of ice was melting in my guts.

"Sorry, Sean, but you gotta know summink about your 'fiancée'. Look at this."

She twisted around and reached into her shoulder bag to get the laptop, which she opened up on the table, pressed some keys, then swivelled the screen round so I could see it.

Mystery of climber's accident in France was the headline, underneath which was the story dated two years ago of a 'boulderer' climber on the famous Le Bas-Cuvier boulder in Fontainebleau, who had apparently lost his footing on the boulder and fallen, hurting himself badly. His companion, known only as 'Rachel' had gone missing after the accident, leaving the man alone for an hour before anyone knew to rescue him. Rachel had apparently abandoned her injured friend, and could not afterwards be traced for questioning.

"And there's this too."

Kate turned the laptop back towards her and touched more buttons.

This time the piece described the death in Paris of a young guy, Emil Hervé, a year ago. His friends had said he had last been seen going off with a woman who said her name was Rachel, and they were going to climb up onto the roof of the three-storey house, for a dare. He fell from the roof and was killed, while Rachel disappeared, and no one could ever trace her. The article placed emphasis on the fact that the victim had exhibited signs of sexual excitement shortly before his death.

"I talked to the guy on the case." She took a sip of coffee. "That last bit means that they found traces of pre-ejaculate on his penis, otherwise known as precum, but, crucially, no semen." She stared at me brazenly, as if daring me to be shocked. "Precum is the clear liquid that sometimes oozes onto the penis head when you get a hard-on. Note the 'pre'. The poor fucker had been sexually aroused but had not come to climax. Meaning that the woman he was with gets her rocks off by turning him on, but stopping at the last minute. She didn't let him have sex."

"So why are you linking Laura with these murders?"

"Two things. In both of these murders, the suspected killer was a proficient climber. The second is polydactyly. Again, in both of them cases the girl involved had an extra tiny digit on her right hand."

I remembered the tiny vestigial finger that sat against Laura's little finger. It had shocked me at first, yet in a way I had found it intriguing.

"As you know, our shy little bookbinder Laura is also the weekend rebel, Sarah in the Sky, of Twitter fame. See, mate, the big clue is she's a climber, and a fucking good climber. You don't just wake up one morning and start climbing up high buildings, you have to become a proficient *conventional* climber first, which means you gotta learn somewhere. Most people join a climbing club and go on mountains. They learn all about safety, how to use ropes and crampons and the correct equipment, it's all about teamwork. But our Laura ain't no team player, she's the archetypal loner, she wants to do everything on her own. So what does she do? She tries a sport called bouldering, which is a different kind of activity altogether. Bouldering is considered to be the macho-macho of climbing, in that they don't use ropes or safety equipment. Boulderers don't bother with safety harnesses, they climb in a completely different way to conventional climbers. Some of them have accidents, but because most of the boulders they climb aren't especially high, and the climbers often put safety mats down to break any possible fall, injuries are rare.

"This climbing accident happened five years ago. The woman accompanying the man who fell is physically very similar to Laura's build. She claims that the man's injury was an accident, but they were climbing alone, and she was the only witness."

"What do the police say about your theory?"

"Nothing can be proved, that it's all guesswork, that the local police concluded it was death by misadventure. But when I heard about the attack on Roger Bracken, I saw the name Laura Kaplan, I got the whole picture. How she grew up in children's homes, where she and others were abused by the staff, and taken away to 'parties', where powerful and influential men did the same."

"But nothing can be proved either way." I was sweating, feeling sick, chilled and horrified.

"Okay, mate, here's the kicker question." She looked

at me, frowning. "Have you had sex with her?"

"What the hell has that got to do with—"

"Penetrative sex?"

"Look, I—"

"Shut up and listen! This is the Kate Doyle theory, and it's a good 'un! She suffered years of abuse in the children's home, right? When she was just a little kid, men forced her to have sex. They used violence on her to get their way. See, Sean, my theory is that shy little Laura turned one day. She stopped being Laura the victim, and became Sarah the fighter. She correlates sex with violence. Soon as someone tries to have sex with her she turns to violence to stop them. She can't help herself. When there's a stiff prick tapping at her door, it triggers off something primeval, deep inside."

"That's just a theory."

"Based on facts, logic and research."

"Are you always this brutal?"

"Yeah, when I want to know something I don't fuck around, I just steam in and ask. I ain't no shrinking violet, Sean, as I told you. Just like your Jodie, I got more balls than most men I know."

"Did anyone ever tell you you're scary?"

She glared at me. "You ain't seen scary yet, mate, I promise you that! So, Sean. Prove me wrong and tell me you had sex with her, yeah? Because if you did, then my theory ain't worth jack shit."

I thought back to the time we had been together the first time and I'd started to kiss her. The weird crazy way she had reacted. Shook my head slightly.

She gave a low whistle. "Then I think you're lucky, Sean. Very lucky indeed."

"But. . ."

"Yeah?"

I remembered the savage expression on her face when she told me to stop kissing her. Of course I had stopped immediately. But what might have happened if I hadn't done so?

"So let's get it straight. You didn't have sex with her, did you?"

"No."

"Then I reckon that's why you're still breathing." She stared at me, nodding in a conclusive, affirmatory way.

My headache was getting worse. "Okay, Kate, your theory is that because Laura has a secret life at weekends, she's got other things to hide. And that Laura deliberately killed two men because they tried to have sex with her. But Roger Bracken didn't do that."

"What's your point?"

"If you're right, and she did these 'sudden impulse' attacks on strangers, it doesn't tie in with a person who kills in cold blood, for a reason. I don't think she attacked Roger Bracken. Because she went to the police and asked for her mother's disappearance to be looked into, making allegations against the man, which they refused to act on. She's not stupid, so she would know that if he was attacked or killed, she would be their prime suspect. She drove her car to his house, knowing it be on CCTV cameras on the approach roads. She made no attempt to hide her identity, and she didn't outright kill him. So if she's guilty, why wouldn't she make sure he couldn't accuse her? Why didn't she finish him off?"

"Well on the balance of probabilities, I reckon that Laura, or Sarah as she calls herself, was responsible for the two climbing accidents. For one climbing partner to slip is unfortunate. For it to happen to two people is too much like a coincidence."

"But the climbs were dangerous, weren't they?" I asked her. "I've heard there's a high rate of mortality amongst climbers."

"Sure there is. But you're talking about conventional climbers, who take huge risks on mountains. Boulderers climb boulders, which aren't that far off the ground, and the incidence of injury is rare. But, on the other hand, chancers who scale high buildings often end up as strawberry jam in a car park. And look at it the other way round. You know the old saying: the first kill is the hardest. After that it gets easier. If she's killed before, number two would be a doddle."

"Fuck."

"Well I've never really investigated the incidents in France, only read about them. Are you up for going over there and making some real enquiries?"

"Yes." I'd come this far. I had no choice now.

"How you fixed for time, then?" She was pressing keys on the laptop.

"I've got a few things to look into for the next couple of days," I told her. "But I'm free after that."

"Yup, me too." As she nodded, the blue fringe took a bow. "I'll email you copies of all these articles, and I'll call you." She turned to smile at me, exposing a small gap between her two front teeth. "I'm glad we met, mate. I'll give you a call in three days. Get your passport."

After she'd gone the revelation that Kate had intimated about Laura had shocked me to the core.

Laura, having been responsible for the death of a man? And, when she was a child, having been responsible for letting a man die because she didn't fetch medical help?

When I got back to my car, I had an idea, and, after searching for Dr Julian Fanshaw on Google, I found contact details for his practice in Harley Street. Without working out what to say I dialled the number.

Obviously, no psychiatrist was going to volunteer information about one of his patients, but I could at least inform the man that his patient had been arrested for attempted murder, and ask if he would just meet me to discuss things, even though I had the feeling that I'd be rejected.

"I'm very sorry, but Dr Fanshaw is on holiday for the next three weeks," apologised his secretary. "But if you'd like to make an appointment to see him for after that, I could certainly do so."

"Thanks, but I'll call back later," I told her.

As I drove back to Whitstable I had an idea, and instead of following the M25 down to where it intercepts with the M20 to Kent, I took the turn-off to central London.

Laura a cold-blooded killer? I couldn't believe it.

But I had to know.

It was a crazy desperate idea. Maybe it was madness to risk so much, but I had to do it.

They say that falling in love is a kind of madness. I couldn't stop thinking about Laura. But was I in love with a killer?

I had to know the truth about her, even if it was bad news.

Even if it meant taking big chances. . .

TWENTY-TWO

I parked the car in a car park in Merton and took the tube to Bond Street Underground station and exited to make my way to Harley Street.

I hadn't really planned what to do, my only idea was to follow my instincts and wing it. I had stopped along the way and bought a rucksack and some tools, as well as a lightweight crutch from a medical supplies company.

Kate Doyle's extraordinary theory that Laura had possibly already killed men in France seemed bizarre in the extreme and I simply could not believe it. But the hard facts were that I didn't know what Laura was capable of.

I was working on the belief that the woman I was in love with must have had long confidential discussions with her psychiatrist, so the chances were that if I could access his notes I would get some insight into what sort of a person she was.

It was five in the evening, and people were walking fast, mostly rushing home, looking neither to right or left. Staying in the middle of the crowds was a good way of making sure my face couldn't be picked out by CCTV, and walking with the crutch ensured that I didn't look my age from a distance, plus I was wearing dark glasses and had a thick scarf wound around the lower part of my face.

Standing at the vestibule of the impressively grand Victorian building, I saw that there were a number of brass plates screwed to the wall. Like most Harley Street addresses, Fanshaw's consulting rooms shared premises with other medical professionals: his neighbours here were a dentist and an osteopath.

Someone went into the main entrance in front of me and I slipped through the door behind them, unnoticed by the woman at the reception desk, who was addressing the newcomer. I quickly stepped down a corridor, and gratefully saw a sign on a door saying 'toilet'. Inside the lavatory there were two cubicles, and I went into one of them, shut the door and sat down and waited.

Time crept by. I had opened the door just a few inches, so that if anyone looked they would think the stall was unoccupied. Sure enough, about a couple of hours later, I heard footsteps approaching, so I climbed onto the seat and squatted, so my feet and head were not in view. I heard the outer door being opened, then someone stepped inside, paused for a moment, then left and switched off the lights.

I gave it another hour in the pitch darkness then slipped out into the corridor, using the torch I had brought with me.

It was easy enough to find the ground floor office with Dr Fanshaw's name on the door. Taking the crowbar from my rucksack, I managed to wedge it between the door and the frame and lever hard so that it broke open. Then I went inside.

An ordinary average-sized room, with the couch, chairs, and a huge desk, behind which was a bank of filing cabinets. Having come this far there was no going back, even though if I was caught I'd be in serious trouble. I tried the first cabinet, which was locked, but my crowbar soon teased it open. The files were stored alphabetically, and in the second drawer down I found the one I wanted, with the name Laura Kaplan on the front. Inside were copious typed notes, and also, nestling at the bottom of the cardboard sleeve, a memory stick.

I took out my phone and took pictures of as many pages as I could. Then, with shaking fingers, took the laptop from my rucksack, switched it on, plugged the flash drive into the USB drive, then copied all the files onto my desktop. Then switched off the machine, packed it away and put everything back in the file and replaced it.

Slipping out of the front door was easy: there was no mortice lock to worry about, just a Yale that I opened from the inside and slammed when I left.

I heard the shout from behind me. Then felt the hand on my shoulder.

*

"Oi you! Stop! I've called the police—"

The man's mistake was to slacken his grip as I spun round. With the rucksack still strapped to my back, my fist smashed into his face, and he fell backwards, staggering slightly before coming at me again. He was reaching forward, grabbing my lapels, attempting to get me into a head lock and failing. All the while he was yelling to anyone passing by to call the police.

With an upward sweep, I broke free of his grip, at the same time as I brought my knee up between his legs, then delivered another right hook, this time catching his chin at the right angle to knock him out cold. A few people were watching, a couple of men coming closer, others talking into their mobiles.

But no one challenged me as I ran. I dodged past

everyone and ran on and on, until I gratefully reached the crowds descending the stairs to the Underground station. I was safe now.

I'd been a prize idiot. I'd come within a whisker of being arrested, meaning that I would have been charged with breaking and entering, and, as things stood, the police would be on the lookout for the burglar who'd just accessed medical records.

As the train pulled out of Bond Street station I began to relax, grimly enjoying the sensation of at last being one step ahead of the game.

*

At home the next day, in the full brightness of the morning, the afternoon and right through into the night, I read and re-read the notes I had photographed. The memory stick that I had copied onto my laptop contained recordings of hypnosis sessions between Laura Kaplan and her psychiatrist Julian Fanshaw.

The initial notes were as follows:

Regarding patient 10005, Laura Kaplan:

Date: 15 January
Conclusions relating to hypnosis session:
This patient came to me asking if I could try the EDMA treatment on her, because she had been abandoned as a child in a village in the West Country, and she believed that immediately prior to being left alone in the village something had happened that she could not remember. Hearing of people suffering from PTSD, who had been helped

by being able to 'relive' memories of terrible occurrences that were currently blocked by traumatic amnesiac barriers, she asked me if I would try the technique on her.

Laura recounted to me that her mother had taken her to a large house in the country that she now recognises as being called Netherwold Hall, the home of Adrian Dark, the recently deceased musician. According to the recorded session she witnessed a horrifying attack on her mother, though at the time she had no memory of having seen such a thing. I believe that the shock of seeing her mother attacked caused her to succumb to a catatonic trance, and when she woke up she had no recollection of the incident at the time because of traumatic amnesia, that effectively locked the memory into her consciousness.

Date: 23 January
This session was not conducted under hypnosis, but was simply a Q and A about her difficult life in the children's home after her mother disappeared.

My conclusion is that her mental issues began as a direct result of Laura suffering serious sexual abuse at the institution, and was also subjected to intimidation and bullying by the senior staff, and also her fellow inmates. To deal with this she developed a number of coping strategies in a way that is typical for abused children. Preliminary conclusions are that she is suffering from a mild version of Dissociative Identity Disorder, such as is typically suffered by child abuse victims. They suffer in silence for a long period, and then eventually find the courage to fight back. When they hit back at their attacker, they assume another distinct personality who behaves in a distinctly more aggressive way than the compliant victim, as indeed Laura did. Laura invented an 'alter' who she calls Sarah. Indeed in some of her recollections she recounts astounding tales, which are clearly apocryphal. Notably the accounts of attack-ing, and even killing people. This alter, Sarah, is the 'other side' of her personality, the brave and fearless climber who is afraid of no one. Whereas her real self, or her primary persona, is Laura Kaplan, the mild-mannered bookbinder and antiquarian book dealer.

I am mildly concerned that Laura has an issue regarding close sexual relations with others, which she finds difficult. The trigger for the imagined violence always seems to be linked to failed sexual en-counters, and she projects the hatred she felt for the men who abused her onto boyfriends. For this reason it seems she has never had a satisfactory sexual relationship, and consequently has no experience of ordinary sexual relations. Sex to her means threats, violence and terror.

*

I stopped to think about what I had just read. I knew that Dissociative Identity Disorder was a condition that used to be known as Multiple Personality Disorder, and had supplied the plot lines for a number of silly TV films, where a character is a 'Jekyll and Hyde', who does many kind, peaceful acts as one person, then abruptly changes into a murderous beast.

According to what I could find out about it on the net, the most common cause of developing such a condition was in children who have been abused, sexually or physically. It's effectively an 'escape mechanism' for a child who is meek and cowed by the abuser. The alter, or secondary, personality is someone strong and assertive, who in effect 'comes to the rescue' and fights back against the bully or attacker, seen in practical terms as the subservient, terrified, bullied person fighting back. Professional opinion is in fact divided about whether the condition actually exists as a mental illness at all, or if the sufferer is in fact imagining everything and subliminally or consciously pretending to have the condition.

I discovered that in the US Kenneth Bianchi, the disgusting and loathsome serial killer who tortured and killed a number of children and young girls, famously pretended to have the condition in an attempt to evade responsibility for his actions. Fortunately, a suspicious psychiatrist had 'deliberately' leaked the information that DID sufferers often have a variety of different alters, rather than just one, and because the very next day Bianchi immediately introduced several more invented personalities, his ruse was uncovered. But prior to that some psychiatrists believed his claims, and the lawyers were beginning to be prepared to take the words of this monster at face value. Legal responsibility for your actions? It's a moot point, and Bianchi and others clearly hoped that a clever lawyer could claim that Bianchi as his primary persona was not responsible for the actions of the 'alter', a bestial vile killer.

But Fanshaw had said that Laura was suffering from a mild form of the illness, hadn't he? Supposing for some people, DID was a kind of mind game, an escape from real life by having the pleasure of 'becoming' another person who exhibits all the attributes that you wish you had?

According to Fanshaw, Laura Kaplan the quiet bookseller was her real self, her primary identity. She had just one so-called 'alter', that of ebullient fearless Sarah in the Sky.

Then the real work began: listening to the recorded hypnosis sessions that were on the laptop.

The earliest of the hypnosis sessions was Laura's voice, and yet it had a child's pitch and timbre. As I heard her speak, shivers went up my spine.

TWENTY-THREE

The sing-song, child's cadence of words had a strange surreal quality:

"Mr Clark wants me to go to the woods again with him. I tell them that I don't want to, but no one listens. I tell Mrs Hardy about him taking his trousers off and lifting my dress and doing those things to me. She hits me and tells me I'm a wicked girl, and I'm lying. One of them tells me that I'm a wicked girl and God will punish me. Three of the grown-ups are in the room with her. They're all shouting at me, hitting me with sticks. They're talking about my six fingers, telling me that the sixth finger is the sign of the devil. They tell me I'm the devil's child. The devil's child."

[There was the sound of her weeping quietly]

Dr F: Why don't you tell someone outside the home about what's happening to you?

Laura: They'd know. And they would kill me. They've killed people before.

Dr F: How would they know?

Laura: They have spies everywhere. Not people. Animals. Spiders especially. Spiders are the messengers who would tell them. They've killed children before. Help!

[Sound of her screaming]

I'm scared!

[A long pause]

[The voice changed into that of an adult, clearly a separate part of the session]

Laura: So what do you think is wrong with me, doctor? Why do I have these blackouts when it's like a dream and I don't know where I've been? Sometimes for days at a time.

Dr F: I think you have a condition called Dissociative Identity Disorder. You suffered abuse as a child, serious sexual abuse, first at the hands of this man, Carey, at the children's home and his colleagues. This is the classic cause of the condition. The usual pattern is a child who's been a victim for many years, subject to abuse of various kinds that she, or he, accepts because she considers herself a weak person. So the child creates another person. Someone strong and combative, who is able to stand up to the bully. It starts off as a means of escape, a desire to actually be that person. Then the person effectively takes on a life of their own. You, Laura, are the real person, or the primary persona. You're a shy, quiet retiring woman. You are thorough, methodical, careful and hard working.

But when I've put you under hypnosis you have sometimes become someone else. This is your alter, the woman you become when you go mountain climbing, Sarah in the Sky. As Sarah you are a tough, dominant female who's afraid of nothing and no one. Sarah hates men for the wicked things they have done to her, or rather what they've done to her alter, Laura.

Listen to this. This is what I recorded when I hypnotised you into becoming your alter:

Dr F: What is your name?

Laura: Sarah.

Dr F: How old are you, Sarah?

Sarah: Thirty-five. What's it to you? [said in an aggressive, edgy tone]

Dr F: Where do you work?

Sarah: I don't work for anyone. I'm a star. I'm famous. I climb up buildings all over the world, I put the videos of my climbs on YouTube and Facebook.

Dr F: What are you afraid of?

Sarah: Nothing. Nothing at all.

Dr F: When you were a child were you ever afraid?

Sarah: I was before.

Dr F: Before what?

Sarah: When I was timid little Laura.

Dr F: But not when you were Sarah?

Sarah: Never. When I was at school a boy tried to kiss me. It reminded me of the men. I pressed his eyes through the lids so hard I tried to blind him. And. . .

Dr F: Go on.

Sarah: ...When I was older I used to climb the electricity pylons with friends. I climbed up to the top of one once, with a boy called Melvyn. He began grabbing me and trying to kiss me. I pushed him. I pushed him hard enough to know that he would fall. He was killed. No one knew that I had been with him. No one knew what I did.

Dr F: So did you hurt anyone else?

Sarah: Yes.

Dr F: Who?

Sarah: Men who've tried to touch me. Men who want to have sex with me.

Dr F: So you can't stand the thought of men touching you?

Sarah: It makes me angry. It makes me want to kill them.

Dr F: And have you ever killed any men?

Sarah: Not lots. Some.

Dr F: What do you mean?

Sarah: I mean I killed some men.

Dr F: Tell me about one of these murders.

Sarah: I can't. When they happen I go into a kind of trance so that afterwards I forget.

*

When Sarah was talking, her voice was harsh and grating, aggressive. Yet Laura was soft and quietly spoken. I opened up the other files and on one of them Sarah was recounting, in detail, the night that she saw her mother attacked at Netherwold.

This 'devil worship' aspect of the sexual attacks she had been subject to at the children's home was new to me. I looked up the details of the court case that I found on the net. There, sure enough, was part of the evidence where one of the victims said that the staff at the home were members of some kind of weird religious cult. That would tie in with Laura's references to 'the devil', and spiders as emissaries, passing messages back to 'their masters'. From what I'd read in the past about paedophile rings, establishing religious groups was par for the course: anything to consolidate power and promote fear.

Finally I found another file, this was entitled 'Discussions with patient'. Dr Fanshaw was talking:

"I promise you, Laura, you have nothing to worry about. The reason why you have these 'gaps' in your life as Sarah, is because for these periods you almost 'become' Sarah. The interesting thing about Dissociative Identity Disorder is that each alter has their own memory bank, a range of experiences and so on, and these are inaccessible to the other alters. These are called amnesiac barriers. The way to treat your condition is to gradually break down these barriers, so that you become aware of what you're doing as Laura when you're Sarah and vice versa. You see, these barriers are not absolute, as you must have guessed. You constructed these barriers as a way of protecting yourself from danger. To live a healthy life as Laura, you have to learn to become completely aware of your alter's life and the things she does, and to completely break down these barriers. We can do this by way of hypnosis – that's the generally accepted way. As Laura becomes more aware of the reality of Sarah, thus Sarah becomes less and less important. Similarly with the experience you had as a child, when you witnessed the terrible things that happened to your mother. You didn't tell anyone because the experience became locked inside your mind. The shock of it caused what we call traumatic amnesia. I would imagine that experience plus the abuse you suffered as a child later on, was what contributed to your DID. What strikes me as strange is the times you recounted to me, under hypnosis as Sarah, that you think you killed people. This is the other aspect of DID. In order to create a completely new person, lying becomes par for the course."

"But I'm afraid that I might be a murderer."

"Don't worry about that, Laura. I can tell you in absolute confidence that you have *not killed anyone.* You talk about a gap in your memory. You talk about a 'dark presence' that comes beside you when these murderous moods come upon you. All this is typical of imagination. I'm absolutely certain you haven't killed anyone, because if you had done, there would be no doubt about it in your mind. You see, essentially, your alter is something you have created. You can do lots of different things as your 'alter', such as climbing buildings, and even behaving in an aggressive daring manner. But I can promise you that you would never ever do anything as Sarah that was totally at odds with what Laura would do. Something as drastic as murder is something that Laura would never ever consider, and therefore nor could Sarah. This 'dark presence' you talk about is a figment of your imagination, but it's a very, very powerful image. I think this is your mind's perception of absolute evil, a 'dark force' that's trying to urge you to do something, which you resist."

"I'm scared."

"There's nothing to be scared of. Your primary persona is Laura Kaplan, and as Laura you are a normal healthy person who would never kill anyone. As Sarah you do daring things, you talk strangely, act in a wild and uninhibited way. These 'killings' you think you did as Sarah are a fantasy, nothing more, nothing less. When you were at an impressionable age, older men forced you to have sex with them. And you hated it. You hated the men so much that you fantasied about killing them. The fantasies entered your subconscious mind, so that years later, when you are in an ostensibly normal, consensual, sexual situation your mindless rage takes control, and the fantasies take over. You have nothing to worry about, because I'm absolutely certain that you didn't kill anyone when you were acting as Sarah. Remember, Sarah lies, she *has to lie,* that's part of her raison d'être. As Sarah you perhaps had the desire to kill certain people, and you daydreamed yourself doing it. . . But I'm quite convinced that you did not do any murders, for the reality of DID is that in essence it's a kind of 'dream state', in which you lie and pretend and wish."

*

Reassuring? Yes, I guess it was, for from what I could gather Dr Fanshaw was a respected expert in his field.

I went back to the file. There were transcripts of other hypnosis sessions with Laura. I glanced through them. A story about learning the sport of bouldering in Fontainebleau in

France, and hitting a fellow climber with a heavy piece of metal equipment, so that he missed his footing and fell. An experience in Paris when she climbed up a building with a man and he tried to have sex with her, and something overcame her, she became angry, and the next thing she knew she was alone on the window ledge, high up above the city. And, more recently, encounters with men in nightclubs, where their sexual attacks were met by brute force.

When I'd examined most of the material I sat back and closed my eyes.

She was not a murderer, according to an eminent doctor who had hypnotised her, who knew her innermost secrets.

And yet.

For Laura to be a murderer was all too credible. Most people don't know that there are many murders, all around the world, where the perpetrator is never caught. The standard rule that 'most murder victims are known to their killer' applies in the majority of cases. However, 'stranger killings' are much harder to crack. And if these 'stranger murders' take place in different places, investigated by different teams of investigators, there's no apparatus to link them all together and pool information.

These are the hardest murder cases of all to solve.

TWENTY-FOUR

Was Laura a killer or not?

Dr Fanshaw's words that he was certain Laura couldn't be a killer were reassuring, and I believed them. But the niggling doubt in my mind was driving me mad. I knew that I had no alternative but to take Kate Doyle up on her offer to accompany her to Paris to investigate the death of the man who had allegedly been climbing with Laura when he died.

The Rue des Olerettes in the Le Marais area of Paris, was a long wide road with a couple of pavement cafés.

They say that falling in love is a kind of madness, and sure enough it was true for me. I couldn't quite believe that I had broken the law, breaking and entering and stealing notes from a doctor's premises. And now, when I should have been getting stuck into an urgent painting and decorating job I had agreed to do, I was spending time and money I could ill afford following up an investigation into a death that even the police weren't interested in. Because I had to know, for my own peace of mind.

I was beginning to think this was going to be another wild goose chase. Kate was good company, but her wild enthusiasms and impulsive behaviour seemed a strange, hit-or-miss approach with which to tackle this complicated problem. And despite her apparent enthusiasm to get to the bottom of things, it was clear that all she cared about was getting a good, saleable story.

I thought back to the transcript of Laura's session with Dr Fanshaw. When she had talked about 'the guy' in Paris, with whom she had climbed up a building, and he had wanted to have sex, and she had a kind of blackout, after which she found herself standing on the window ledge she'd shared with him, but was now alone.

Kate and I went into the café to talk to the locals, and it was fortunate that she seemed pretty much fluent in French. My grasp of the language is fairly minimal, but I try hard. The café owner, a large rotund man who smelt of garlic, nodded several times and seemed entranced by Kate's bi-coloured hair.

As she sat down to the escargots she had ordered, I marvelled and recoiled at the snails on the plate that she was tucking into. I had settled for frites and an odd kind of meat stew that she had recommended.

After having a long discussion with him, she explained what the café owner had said to her. "Emil Hervé – the man who died – was with 'the English woman' and another couple that night, and he's given me their address," she explained. "They live quite close. He especially remembers how the English girl ran away afterwards, how everyone was looking for her, but she'd got clean away."

"Did he recognise the photograph of Laura?"

"He reckons it's her, but he can't be sure."

"Does he think it was an accident?"

"Oh yes. The ledge up there is wide enough to stand, but only just. The general consensus was that they were drunk and went up there and started to have sex, and there wasn't enough room. Just a terrible accident."

"Which it could have been."

"Of course," Kate agreed. "I've still got an open mind. Crucial thing is, if it was an accident, why did she run away? The police did their best to trace her, but all they had was a description, not even a name."

"How did you hear of it?"

"I comb the papers for interesting stories, and came across this 'accidental death in Paris', by chance. It was the six fingers on her right hand that gave me the connection to Laura."

The climb up the fire escape was pretty unpleasant. And the wind was whipping up, making the ascent even harder. Kate was climbing with an air of deep concentration, taking extra care, her long legs moving gracefully. When we reached the narrow ledge the view was pretty panoramic and impressive but my heart was beating wildly with the effort, and all I wanted to do was go down.

"Okay," Kate said. "We keep an open mind. Either Laura came up here with the guy, they started to have sex, and he slipped and it was a terrible accident. Or he started making the preliminary moves, perhaps intending to finish things later, and she reacted with anger, and deliberately pushed him. It's one or the other."

Standing beside her on the narrow ledge I tried to imagine what it must have been like on that winter's night, three years ago.

"However drunk they were, no one but a maniac would try to have sex here," I told her. "And why the hell would anyone want to?"

"Excitement. Danger. Danger could be the real aphrodisiac."

The wind was whipping up her hair. She grabbed hold of my hand.

"Come on then," she said, giggling. "I'm asking in the interests of nailing down the truth. Are you sure it would be impossible to have sex up here?"

"Yes."

"I dunno so much. If you was to stand where I am, your bum pressed up against this window, I reckon I could straddle you quite comfortably. Do you wanna try it?"

"There's no need."

"So he gets turned on," she went on, frowning as she tried to think. "But if he was planning to have sex like that, she would have been in front of him, and she would have been the one likely to fall if it was an accident."

"Unless it was the other way around. Laura had her back to the window and he was in front of her," I suggested. "He's drunk, fumbling about, excited. He could have tried to enter her, push her legs apart, and missed his footing and fallen backwards."

"Yes," she agreed. "Yes, he could have done."

Back on pavement level I was feeling giddy and lightheaded. "I'm thinking back to the transcript of Dr Fanshaw's session with her, when she presumably is describing this incident. She says he tried to have sex with her, and she got angry. But she stops recalling the incident when it gets to this point. Her mind has gone blank for those crucial moments."

"But if it was an accident, why didn't she hang around to talk to the police?" Kate asked.

"Maybe she was scared."

"We don't even know if it was her or not, for sure."

"She looked like Laura, she sounded like Laura, and Laura described what happened to her psychiatrist. And the woman was an expert climber and she had polydactyly. The Americans would call that a slam dunk."

The young couple who the café owner had put us onto lived quite close by, and we walked along several boulevards and up to a large building where renovation work was going on. As we climbed up the stairs, we were assailed by the sweet smell of fresh plaster and timber, and on the third floor we knocked on the pure white door of Apartment 13.

"*Bonjour*," said a young blonde woman who was dressed in paint-spattered jeans and tee-shirt. She opened the door wide and invited us into a long wide room, where dustsheets were on the floor, and a man was up a stepladder, roller in his hand as he turned round and looked our way and descended.

The couple ushered us into another room, a kitchen, where they found seats to go around the large table. Helene, the woman, made coffee and after we were all seated, mugs in hand, the man, Daniel, spoke in hesitant English.

"May I ask who you are?" he began.

"I'm an ex-policeman with an interest in the case, and Kate here is a freelance journalist," I told them. Daniel translated what I'd said to Helene, who nodded thoughtfully.

"Okay, we tell you what happened," Daniel went on, after agreeing that the photo of the woman we showed was indeed the same person he had encountered that night.

"Helene and I had gone out for a meal, and Emil Hervé, a guy I knew slightly from work, came upon us by chance," Daniel went on. "So it was the three of us together for a while, chatting about this and that. Then Emil says he has to go. As he gets up to leave, he sees someone, a woman, whom he calls across to. She looks up and smiles, and comes over to our table."

At that point, Helene interrupted in a long diatribe in French. Daniel listened, then translated: "Helene says that she liked the girl. She was bright and friendly and seemed a genuine person. Emil liked her *very* much. She was English, though her French was pretty good. He called her Rachel. Is that the name you know her by?"

"No, we know her as Laura," Kate said.

"And did she have six fingers on her right hand?" I asked him.

"Yes," he replied. "This looked strange to us, but Rachel, she laughs about it, she makes fun of it. She was in a bright friendly mood. We all liked her very much."

"Did Emil know her well?"

"I don't think so. I think he mentioned that he had met her when he was climbing at Fontainebleau. The English girl, he told us, was like a 'Fly', who can climb so cleverly!"

"So they weren't really close friends?" I asked.

"No, I think not."

Helene then listened to the translation from Daniel of what we'd said. She spoke in French for a long time to Daniel, who nodded as he listened.

"Helene says that the girl sat with them for a bit, but that Emil was flirting with her, and she was happy for this. Emil was keen to show her to the top of the building, he said that as a climber she would appreciate the view from up there."

"So, can you tell us exactly what happened afterwards, please?" Kate asked him.

"We sit there, we wait for them to come back," Daniel said. "Emil, he had this thing." He frowned, looking worried. "How you say? Let me think. Do you know what I talk about when I say the mile-high club?"

"Couples who have sex at high altitudes – normally on a plane?" Kate answered.

"Yes." Daniel's frown cleared. "Emil he was much keen

on this, he thought it very exciting, very daring, and I think that this was on his mind."

"This is important," I interrupted. "Do you think that Rachel knew what he had in mind, I mean having sex, when she went off with him?"

Daniel frowned and held his hand out in front of him, tilting it sideways and shaking his head slightly. "Maybe yes, maybe no. She was bright that night, lively, talking very much, you know? So after they'd gone we waited for a time. And then we heard a loud crash from outside. A girl is screaming in the street, so we go outside to look. And there, in the middle of the road, is his body, twisted, broken."

"And Rachel?" I asked.

"We never saw her again. I can only think that in all the rush and confusion, she managed to run down the fire escape, melt into the crowd and get away."

He translated for Helene, and she spoke back to him, then he told us what she had said.

"Afterwards the police, they come and question us and everyone else. They look for this girl whom you say is Laura, but no one can find her. They talk to us for a long time, but that is it."

"So tell us," Kate went on. "What do you think happened?"

Daniel translated her question to Helene and they spoke in French for a while, then Daniel turned to me.

"We think that they climbed up to that ledge and Emil tried to have sex with her. He missed his footing in his excitement, and he fell."

"What about his clothes?" I asked. "His trousers? Were they unfastened?"

Daniel frowned, trying to remember. "A good point. I hadn't thought about it. To be honest I do not know. He was just a tangle of limbs, you know? Much blood, twisted limbs, it was hard to see things like that."

"Do you think Laura – Rachel – deliberately pushed him off the ledge?" I asked.

Daniel looked me in the eyes. "I cannot know for sure, but my opinion, my firm opinion is no. She wasn't that kind of girl. She was nice, kind, I remember she saw a wasp trapped on the windowsill and she went to a lot of trouble to let it outside. I ask you, is that the action of a woman who could deliberately push someone to their death? Besides, why would she want to kill him? She liked him."

Helene then spoke for a long time to Kate. Kate translated for me.

"There's an old lady who lives opposite the flat, and Helen thinks that she might have seen what happened, for she was well known for spending hours gazing out over the city. But, the same night it happened, she was rushed into hospital with a stroke. She's still in a coma in hospital. It's frustrating, because she might have actually seen what happened and we would know for sure."

As Kate and I walked down the freshly painted stairwell, the lovely odour of wet emulsion paint in the air, I felt a huge sense of relief. Dr Fanshaw was certain that Laura could not have deliberately killed anyone, and now I was convinced that he had been right. She had not killed Emile Hervé. His death had just been a terrible accident.

"Well, Sean, I'm more confused than ever," Kate said, grimly. "Your account of what she said to Dr Fanshaw matches what Daniel and Helene just told us. According to what she said when she was telling him, Emil wanted to have sex with her and she fought him off. Then she says something happened – she had some kind of a blackout – and she saw that he'd fallen to his death, and she panics and runs away. It looks to me as if it was just a terrible accident. But if it was, why didn't she stay and talk to the police?"

"She's scared of authority. She's scared of the situation, so she panics and runs."

"Yeah," she nodded. "Sean, I think you're right. It could have been an accident."

TWENTY-FIVE

That night, as I tried to fall asleep in the cheap hotel, I listened to the traffic outside, the never-ending hum. I tried to picture Laura doing the terrible things she was being accused of. In the end I got up and opened my laptop and looked again at her clip on YouTube, of her doing a backflip on a couple of scaffolding boards at the top of a high-rise building in Cumbria, a year ago.

There on the screen was the wobbling view from her headcam: the rooftops of a city and a long, long way below, cars on roads seemingly as tiny as ants, the view below contrasting strangely with the crags and imperfections of the white concrete edge of the parapet beside where she was standing. Her commentary:

Right, here we go. I'm standing at the end of this narrow platform. It's just two scaffold boards side by side. I reckon there's just enough room for me to do a backflip and be on my feet at the other end. Shit I'm scared. My heart is beating like fuck. But I've gotta to it. Gotta do it…

A pause. Her view, replicated by the headcam on her forehead, wobbling as she steadies herself for the jump.

Here we go!

Then a mad view of crazily flipping clouds and blue sky, a flash of the sun, wild scary maelstrom of shifting sliding madness, before the trembling wobbling view of the world on the platform appears again.

The sound of her laughter, a mad giggling shriek.

I closed the laptop, feeling more depressed than I'd felt for weeks.

Laura was a complete and total mystery to me. A chatterbox, a gifted bookbinder, a collector and lover of antiquarian books, ostensibly a perfectly normal person. Yet she was also a daredevil, a thrill seeker, someone who seemed on the face of it pretty much insane. The illness of Dissociative Identity Disorder, Dr Fanshaw had described it as. And, according to him, her primary persona, Laura Kaplan, was a normal, law-abiding person and her alter was the wild risk-taker, mad Sarah in the Sky. But, he'd assured her, Laura was *not a killer*, and her fears that she might have killed people while she was Sarah were groundless. According to the doctor, a DID sufferer might do various things in his persona as the alter and not remember doing them. But whatever the alter might do, crucially he had said that it could not be anything that was too much out of character of the primary.

Was he right?

*

Kate had managed to locate a group of rock-climbing enthusiasts with whom Laura had once associated. Their leader was willing to introduce us to his group of climbers so that any of them who might remember her could give us their impressions.

So next day, very early in the morning, we hired a car and drove down to Fontainebleau, a densely forested area south of Paris. Kate's contact in the climbing club was Philippe, who turned out to be a tall sixtyish man with a large white beard and clear blue eyes, whom I liked immediately. He had kindly invited us to his home for breakfast. It was an old cottage with low ceilings and small windows, and as we sat at the rough timber kitchen table it felt as if we were in a time warp that hadn't changed since 1900. Philippe was broad and very tall, the biceps below the sleeves of the white tee-shirt bulging dramatically as he pulled pieces of bread from the loaf and smothered them in butter.

"Sarah, she was a strange girl," he told us in his halting English, munching on his breakfast. "Quiet, very, how you say, intense. Although bouldering attracts all kinds of people, on the whole it's more of a man's sport than for women. Though the women who do it often tend to be outstandingly talented."

"Did she make friends here?" I asked him.

He didn't answer immediately, just frowned as if he was trying to decide something. "Her French was not very good. So she could not talk very much. And I had the impression that she was a somewhat cold person. She was absolutely fixated on learning this skill, and that had top priority, not so much making friends."

"Did she have a boyfriend?" Kate asked.

He thought for a while. "Not that I know of. The lads, they liked the look of her, but I don't think she was interested too much. I think she talked of a boyfriend in England."

"I read reports of a man having a climbing accident in this region, in which the woman accompanying him on a climb deliberately pushed him and he fell, narrowly avoiding injury," Kate said. "Have you heard about this?"

He frowned. "Yes, now you mention it, I did hear something about this. But it was someone else, definitely not the woman I knew as Sarah."

"How can you be sure it wasn't her?" Kate pressed.

"Because I knew the woman concerned, and it was not Sarah."

After we'd had coffee with him he drove us in his ancient Land Rover out to the countryside, then the road led into the forest, where he parked in a clearing.

Three young men were standing at the foot of a very strange looking boulder.

I had expected to see large mountain faces, not relatively small blocks of stone. The boulder in front of us was a weird shape, a bit like a mushroom, with a large overhanging top over the main shaft.

"You are surprised, Sean?" Phillipe said.

"Yes."

"Bouldering is not so much about taking huge risks on high mountains. As you see, some of the boulders are relatively small, and here the heights we scale are not that high, and we even lay down foam rubber mattresses in case of falls. We don't use ropes or safety equipment, or even special mountaineering boots or helmets, because if we fall when climbing relatively small individual stones like this, it doesn't matter – we only fall a few feet and that fall is cushioned. This type of bouldering is just for fun, to develop our strengths and our skills, not in order to master great heights or to do conventional mountaineering. Each of these individual rocks is graded according to the difficulty of the climb."

"Jean is going to give you a demonstration," he told us.

One of the climbers took a long pole that had a brush on the end, dipped it into a bucket, then used it to paint something on a crevice on the rock face. That was when I noticed that at intervals the rock face was peppered with areas that looked as if they'd been painted white.

"That is powdered chalk," explained Phillipe. "The climbers dip their fingers into chalk power too. The idea is to allow for resistance and grip on the otherwise smooth rock."

That's when I remembered one of the photos on Twitter, a close up of Laura's fingers, their ends stained white.

"You see his footwear?" Phillippe pointed out. "Trainers, not climbing boots. No safety helmet, no special clothes, most of us wear ordinary stuff. Bouldering is not like regular mountain climbing at all, it is much less regimented, much more relaxed, less rules."

"Do you have many accidents?" Kate asked.

"Very few, I'm glad to say."

The climber, dressed in a white tee-shirt and jeans, stood at the foot of the boulder, the overhang about a foot above his head. He used one hand's chalky fingers to reach up and grip inside one of the white-coloured finger holes, then he hauled himself higher so as to allow his other hand's fingers to reach a higher crevice. When his head met the underside of the overhang, he reached out and up behind him, amazingly clinging on to the underside of the overhang and hauling himself to the edge. Then he reached up and around to haul himself alongside the overhang, finally leaning forward, so that his upper body rested on the topside of the rock. Then, to my amazement, he performed an astonishing manoeuvre, twisting and lifting his leg right up alongside his shoulder to cram the toes of his trainer into a crevice on the side of the overhang. He managed to swing his other leg up too, so that he was up and over, eventually on top of the boulder.

Phillipe then took us in his car to a sheer rock face, where we could see a number of climbers part of the way up, starting to climb higher.

We watched for a while, and then one of the climbers walked back towards us. Phillippe introduced us to Anthony, a tall strong man of about forty, with short blond hair, dressed like all the others. I was already getting used to the odd sight of mountaineers without helmets, ropes, special boots, or indeed any equipment at all.

"Are you aware that Laura, or as you knew her Sarah, now climbs up tall buildings, using the climbing skills she learnt here?" I asked him.

He nodded. "I have seen the videos on YouTube and Twitter."

"What do you think of her doing that?"

"I think she is mad. It is crazy to risk your life like that time and time again. I do this sport myself, I take risks, but not risks like that. You see, I believe we are all born with a certain amount of luck in our lives. The wise person tries to keep plenty of his luck in reserve, does not deliberately use it up at any opportunity. But then that sums up Sarah." He looked at me and nodded to himself. "It was a long time ago that I knew her here, when I was new to the sport myself. Sarah was one of those people you never really get to know. I met her five years ago. I climbed a few of the smaller rocks with her, we were both learning the sport. For a brief time we were close."

"How close?" I asked.

He held his thumb and finger about an inch apart. "I really found her attractive, and I had the impression she liked me too. Little things, like the way she looked at me, smiled at me, giving me little expression of kindness, you know? Laughing at my jokes. One morning we happened to be alone."

He stopped talking for a while. When he started again

his tone was much more subdued.

"I took her arm, I tried to kiss her, you know?" He frowned at the memory. "We kissed, she responded, everything seemed fine. And then, this is difficult for me to say. But I think it is important."

"We appreciate your help," Kate coaxed.

"Everything was fine. I undid the buttons of her jeans. Began to peel them down. I had unfastened my own clothes. I was ready, I was excited, you understand?"

"And?"

"When she see my state of excitement – actually saw my hardness, it was like a switch flipped in her mind. Something came over her, and she pulled away from me. All of a sudden. Right up until that point I could have been sure she had been flirting with me, that she wanted my attention, you know? But she saw me down there, and she reacted badly, violently. She hit me hard in the face. Very hard indeed. When she could see I was bleeding badly, it was as if the sudden switch in her mind flipped back again, as if she was behaving normally once more. She looked at me, hesitated, and then she apologised. She go on and on, telling me how sorry she was, she was upset, tearful. She left to go home without talking to me. I never saw her again."

"When she hit you, were you afraid?" Kate asked. "This is very important. Did you think your life was in danger?"

"No." He smiled. "I was shocked and surprised, yes. But, as I say, when she saw she had hurt me, she was sorry."

"You weren't afraid of her?" I pressed home my point.

He shook his head.

"I was not afraid at all. I was angry, upset, confused. I blamed myself for misreading the signs. But, if you want my opinion, Sarah is not an aggressive person. She would not hurt anyone."

TWENTY-SIX

T*hump, thump. Breathe. Suck it in fast, let it out slow.* Heart pumping fast. The world a joyful panorama of night sky, stars and moonlight.

I enjoy running at night. So at 10 o'clock that evening, five days after I'd got back from France, I was running along beside the seashore from Tankerton Bay, back to my home in Whitstable. Silvery moonlight glinted off the sea to my right and my thoughts returned from neutral, back to all my troubles.

After three days of painting the rooms of the house in Bath, my head was thumping and my body was exhausted. I liked the smell of fresh paint, but you could have too much of it, and I needed to clear my head.

I thought back to a couple of days ago, at 46 Latimer Row, where I'd been working hard. It had been a busy day, but a very rewarding one.

That morning, on one corner of the hallway wall, the only part of the house I hadn't started painting yet, I had found a strange patch of unevenness. Examining the wall more closely, I could see that the surface was bumpy and craggy across an area of about three feet square. I pondered on the possibility of trying to make it good with filler, but when I looked more closely I realised that would be impossible, and the best option would be to hack back the plaster, and make it good by a complete replastering job. Once I had knocked away a few inches of plaster, I found the corner of a buried sheet of hardboard. Ripping this panel away with all its attached plaster, underneath it I found that the wall itself had been chopped back into the brickwork, and in the so-formed cavity were six plastic bags, that were full of white powder.

I phoned Landseer's first, and then the police.

And so, finally, the mystery of my first and second housebreaker was solved.

It was a fair assumption that the men who had broken into Number 46, prior to the break-in of Trevor Goodbody's friend, were not interested in my affairs at all. The police told me unofficially that the grandson of the old lady who had owned the house and who had recently died, was currently in prison. He had been a notorious drug dealer who had finally been caught, and the police reasoned that he had been using his grandmother's house as a storage facility for his drug dealing business.

So it was one huge relief.

It was also a relief that at last I was well on the way to finishing the decorating job, even though the intense sheer hard work had been tiring, although it was a good way of taking my mind off my problems.

For I was still in love with Laura, yet she was still a mystery, and she was still refusing to see me.

Reading Dr Fanshaw's notes on his dealings with her, had given me a unique perspective on her life. I was certain that he was right: Laura was obviously suffering from a mental illness that indeed appeared to be a form of Dissociative Identity Disorder (DID). I was now relieved that it was clear that she was not, indeed *could not be*, a murderer. Going to France with Kate had confirmed my instinctive feeling: it seemed pretty clear to me that Emil Hervé's death had been a terrible accident, and that her attack on the climber, Anthony, was just a display of anger that had no more significance than her outburst when I had almost had sex with her. As for the reported attack on a climber who had been pushed from a rock face, according to Phillippe, it had nothing to do with Laura.

However, my original objective in coming down to Bath, of finding out who had killed Jodie and why, was as elusive as ever, and it didn't seem as if I was even getting close. Although I had completed writing the book about Adrian Dark, just today I had got a depressing email from Sylvia, saying that on looking at the manuscript more closely she'd found that she'd jumped the gun, and in its present state it wasn't suitable for publication – something I had feared all along. They wanted some rewrites done of certain parts, and she was unhappy about some of the lack of content: they wanted more interviews, more material, and at least some details about what Adrian had done in the years between 1987 and now. She had said what I had been afraid of all the time: "It's not too bad, Sean, but it reads like you've just cobbled together a boring collection of entries in a diary, a few lyrics for songs plus some nice illustrations. It needs more ooomph!"

She wanted more ooomph. What the hell did that even mean? I was beginning to realise that maybe I should never have taken the job on.

It was also very embarrassing, since I had told Mairéad that the publishers were perfectly happy with it, and that publication would only be a matter of time.

I had written to Laura in prison, asking her to let me

see her, and she had not replied. Fortunately, Kate Doyle had agreed with me that our trip to France, for her, had been an utter waste of time, and on the flimsy evidence of what we had discovered, she knew she'd be unable to sell any kind of story about Laura to newspapers. But the trip had been good for me: I was finally reassured that the woman I had fallen in love with was not a murderer, which made all the risks I had taken to find out, worth it.

And since I was certain in my mind that Laura could not be a murderer, I was also convinced that she was not a liar, and that she had not attacked Roger Bracken. Nevertheless, who *had* attacked him was a mystery to me.

It was looking more and more likely that Laura had suffered terrible trauma as a child in the care home where she was brought up. As her reminiscences to Dr Fanshaw confirmed, she had been abused by the staff, which presumably had led to the disquieting incident when one of her abusers, Mr Carey, had suffered a heart attack and died whilst alone in her company. She had confessed to Dr Fanshaw that she had done nothing to help him, indeed had watched him suffering in agony without raising the alarm, and that no one had known how long she'd been alone with him – they had assumed she'd reported his condition as soon as she had found him. But it wasn't exactly murder, was it? A terrified child, unsure what to do, hesitating before taking action.

The second incident that she had described to Dr Fanshaw was that of climbing with Emil Hervé in Paris, the circumstances of which Kate and I had just investigated. In the session with her doctor, she claimed that she might have had a kind of mental blackout just before he fell to his death. It seemed certain to me now, that the poor man had simply missed his footing, and the terrible shock of such a thing happening had indeed caused Laura to suffer some kind of blackout so that she genuinely had no idea what had caused the accident.

I thought back to Kate's prurient details of the man's state of sexual arousal when he'd fallen. This would suggest that Laura had led him on, had originally been complicit with the idea of having sex with him, and at some point had changed her mind. This corresponded precisely with the 'flipped switch' that the climber, Anthony, had referred to, the immediate and violent reaction to the sight of an erect penis. But her rejection of my attentions happened when I was simply kissing her, and she wouldn't have known if I'd been aroused.

And what about Jodie's death? The most likely thing was that she had found out about the rape of Angela Kaplan and the theft of the Kendal Treasure, and someone had silenced her. But who? And why?

Now that Roger Bracken was fighting for his life in hospital, I wasn't likely to find out if he had been responsible for Jodie's death anytime soon, if ever.

I was happy to accept Dr Fanshaw's professional opinion that Laura was not now, and could not have ever been, a killer.

And now she was in jail, charged with the attempted murder of Roger Bracken, the man she was convinced had raped her mother.

I took the final downhill part of the journey back home at a fast run, enjoying the sense of freedom, feeling my heart pumping as I breathed hard.

And as I looked towards my old fisherman's cottage, I thought I saw something. I stopped still and stared.

Had I imagined it?

When I'd gone out I knew that I had switched out all

the lights. And yet I saw it again: a split-second's flash of a torch beam in one of the windows.

I ran down the hill as fast as I could.

TWENTY-SEVEN

When I reached my road, there was a Nissan Micra parked near my house, which hadn't been there earlier. I crept up to my own car, doing my best to be silent as I opened the hatch at the back and took out the iron crowbar. I hefted the heavy length of metal in my hand, judging the balance and weight, sure that it would give me a good advantage in any confrontation. I walked slowly back to the house.

The moon was high in the sky as I tiptoed closer, secret-agent style, back against the wall, aware that any movement could alert my intruder.

There!

In the upstairs window I saw the lance of yellow again, the moving torch beam.

I opened the door silently. Padding quietly inside and finding the downstairs empty, I realised that my intruder was apparently alone and in the floor above.

I tiptoed up the stairs.

I found him in the upstairs bedroom. The person had his back to me. A black shadow, his torch aimed at the floor.

"Hands in the air. Then turn around slowly. I've got a gun."

He stood stock still, then dropped the papers in his

hands and raised his hands up in the air as he turned.

I pressed on the light switch.

Then I recognised the wizened features of James Patterson, the elderly American man I had met at the auction at Netherwold last December.

"Okay, Mr Patterson," I told him, balancing the iron bar in my fingers. "Breaking and entering is a crime."

"God sakes," he answered. "Are you gonna whack me with that thing?"

"I'm going to call the police."

His cough turned into a wheeze as we stared at each other. "So what are you waiting for?"

"For you to tell me who sent you."

"No way."

"Are you in this country legally? Have you committed other offences? At your age, I wouldn't want to do jail time."

He stared at me, then his mouth turned down and he shook his head a couple of times.

Something in his manner was completely different from his swagger the last time we had met. Perhaps it was because he was on his own, without his back-up.

"Okay, Mr Delaney, you're a young guy, and I don't fancy my chances if you start swinging that thing. Here's the deal. I was paid to get hold of those diaries you been working on, in any way I can. I wasn't planning on damaging this place, and if I'd wanted to hurt you I'd have brought along some muscle. I just forced the lock on your back door, and tried my luck is all."

"The diaries aren't here."

"Shit. No one told me that." He shrugged in the darkness, moonlight trickling through the window and highlighting the lined contours of his face. I could smell his sweat: foul, pungent and rancid.

"I figured I wouldn't find them. Fact is, you're a smart guy and I'm working for a fool. But this is where my loyalty ends. Mr Delaney, I'm not your enemy. If you can see your way to letting me go, I can pay you towards any inconvenience I caused you. And you'll never see me again."

I shook my head. "I don't want your money, Mr Patterson. I just want to know who sent you."

He said nothing for a while, then let out his breath in a sigh. "Holy shit, what do I care? I'm working for Vernon. Vernon Dark."

"Adrian's son?"

"Yeah."

"So why does he want his father's diaries? He's been nice to me, he was happy for me to have them, he encouraged me to use them to write the book about his father, he even gave me lengthy quotes to use. And if he wanted them, why didn't he just take them himself?"

Patterson shrugged in the darkness. "I figure there's something going on. Remember all that drama after the auction? Me and the heavy guys trying to make you give up the diaries? Vernon put me up to that little scene. Just like I managed to make it look convincing that I screwed up in the bidding process. Vernon said he wanted to test out how keen you were to get those diaries and write the book, so I was supposed to do the heavy act to see if you'd crumble. But you passed our test with flying colours. He was real smiley afterwards. The cat that got the cream."

"So you never wanted the diaries yourself?"

I saw the shake of his head in the moonlight. "They paid me to put on a show, to make out I was some bigshot writer who wanted to outdo you."

"You're not?"

"God sakes. The most I ever wrote was a shopping list."

"I don't understand."

"Me neither. But I tell you this, Mr Delaney. There's something real strange going on. Yesterday, when they called me to discuss using my services again, I arrived early and caught the tail end of the conversation between Vernon and the sexy auctioneer lady, Mairéad O'Shaughnessy. They were discussing the diaries, arguing about them I guess. Moment before I went in the room, I heard her saying, 'Just leave it alone,' and he replies, 'You leave a loose end and it always catches up with you.'"

"What do you think they meant?"

"I guess it's got something to do with you. Something they got on you, maybe? I heard him saying something about 'maybe the Irishman isn't as naïve as you tell me he is, and he might figure it out?' Does that make any sense to you?"

"Not really."

"Well, Mr Delaney, if I was you I'd take a real close look at those diaries. Maybe something will jump out at you? Whatever it is, there's big money at stake. Ask me, I'd say watch your back."

"Watch my back?"

"That Vernon Dark is a real piece of work. He's connected to some dangerous people in London and Leeds. I heard he's involved with people-smuggling, or prostitution, all kindsa stuff. He's a dangerous guy. And the Irish lady who's so sassy and sexy? Who'd a thought they got a thing going, but I guess they have. She's seriously into him, I can tell you that. So what does that make her?"

Seriously into him? Mairéad had told me that she disliked Vernon Dark, that she loathed even being near him, and that her boyfriend was the auctioneer, Hugo.

I thanked Patterson, and he nodded and scuttled away down the stairs.

I heard his car engine start.

My thoughts were spinning out of control as I tried to work it out.

Vernon Dark and Mairéad an item? Plotting something between them?

The Irishman may not be as naïve as you tell me?

What the fuck?

*

"So what the hell is it all about?" asked Robin, flicking through the diaries on the table in my living room. "Why would Vernon pay to get hold of these, when he gave you his blessing to have them as the basis of your book about his father?"

"That's what I've been trying to work out."

"Have you got a list of the characters you interviewed for the book?"

I found the list I had made and passed it across.

He looked down the names. "So, presumably the ones that are ticked mean you managed to contact them?"

"Yes. Two ticks meant they were very helpful, one tick it was like getting blood out of a stone."

"And no tick at all means no luck?"

"Right."

"Phone interviews can't be easy."

"They're usually okay, and they can save a heck of a lot of travelling time. But yes, from my experience in the police, I know you do miss out on seeing reactions, people's facial expressions. You can't show them things they might like to comment on. You can't know for certain if they've been drinking and being helpfully indiscreet."

"Or if they're lying?"

"Phone liars hesitate. Liars in your face can look you straight in the eye and don't blink. But sometimes they sweat."

"Sweat?"

"Just a little bit occasionally. You see a wee sheen on their foreheads. They look away from you too, they smile a tad too much. Talk too fast to compensate."

"What about this fella here?" Robin asked. "No tick against his name, meaning you couldn't get hold of him?"

"Yes. A ringing phone, but no reply and no answerphone."

"And this list, some of the names were given to you by Vernon Dark?"

"Yes. More than half of them actually."

"I tell you what I don't understand. Vernon was keen on you getting hold of the diaries and wanted you to write his father's biography. He was very encouraging, wasn't he?"

"Yes, he was really nice to me, couldn't have done more to help."

"Yet you tell me he's not a nice kind of guy. Not someone who'd try to give a helping hand to a stranger."

"But Mairéad is my friend, who wrote to me specially to ask me down there. Maybe he was doing it for her."

"For her? You just told me that Patterson reckoned that Vernon and Mairéad were an item. So why would he help out the man who used to be romantically linked with his girlfriend? That doesn't sound very likely to me."

"She told me she hated him. I guess I ought to just confront her, ask her what's going on."

"Don't do that," Rob advised. "She'll lie. And you'll

put them on their guard." He stared at the list of names. "Listen, mate, think hard. Mairéad looked you up out of the blue, spun you all kinds of bullshit about missing you, about you once being the love of her life. And using the diaries and partial biography as a basis for a book was all her idea, yeah?"

"It was."

"She even mentioned it on the phone when you called her about the job?"

"Sure."

"She led you on, laid sex on the line, moments after pointing out she had a thing going with the auctioneer while, according to Patterson, she was in a relationship with Vernon. Something isn't right. She's been using you."

"But how? In what way?"

Robin frowned, tapping his teeth. "Tell me again. Which of these guys you interviewed were recommended by Vernon, and which were ones you found on your own?"

"Give it here, and I'll mark them from memory." I did so, and handed the list back.

"If I were you, I would contact all the ones that Vernon *didn't* recommend you to approach. Ask them if they have any idea why Vernon would want to get hold of the diaries."

TWENTY-EIGHT

The second name on the list of people who I'd dug out on my own was Timothy Reason. I dialled the number and waited, not expecting a reply, as I hadn't had one when I tried before. Tim Reason had been a roadie, and I hadn't been able to get in touch with him, there was never any response.

"Hi, this is Tim," came the jaunty voice on the line.

"Hello, my name is Sean Delaney. I'm writing a book about Adrian Dark and I understand you knew him well."

"I did."

"Would you mind if I ask you a few questions?"

"Sure, I'd love to. If you phoned recently I'm sorry I wasn't in. We emigrated to Australia last year, and this number is my old house that I've been letting. You were lucky to catch me on a visit. Yes, Adie and I were good mates, and I'm sure I can give you some useful anecdotes. Well, I'm only here another few days, so how about if we meet up? I've got quite a few bits and pieces, memorabilia I suppose you might call it – tour dates and lists of concerts, stuff like that you might be interested in."

"Thanks very much, sounds excellent news. So where are you staying now?"

"Essex. Where are you?"

"Whitstable, in Kent. Near Canterbury."

"Then let me come down to you. I'm sure you're a busy man, and now that I've retired my time's my own, and I always love visiting Canterbury. Can you bring the diaries? I'd love to see them again."

*

The Cathedral Café, on Burgate beside Canterbury Cathedral, was fairly full with people coming and going all the time.

I recognised Timothy Reason from some of the old photos I'd found of Nightingale Green and their entourage. Unlike a lot of rock stars, Tim had aged well. Still slim, he was a very tall, rangy old man, his hair was pure white and he still had plenty of it. Suntanned and prosperous looking, he was in his seventies, wearing an expensive-looking leather jacket and neatly pressed grey trousers. I waved and we walked to meet each other, and after buying coffee and cakes we found a table in the corner, by the window. One of the most memorable things about his face was the thick white eyebrows over very dark brown eyes. His gaze was honest, easy going and direct.

"You'd love to see the diaries again, you said," I told him, reaching into my backpack, lifting the cardboard box containing the little books out and putting it on the table. "Have you seen them before?"

"Yes. Quite a few years ago I was thinking of doing my own autobiography, so I asked to see Adie's diaries to check up on dates and so on."

"You were their roadie?"

"One of them, for my sins – they had several regular roadies over the years. I had a lot of tales to tell regarding Nightingale Green and a couple of other bands I worked with. But after I got started my enthusiasm kind of fizzled out, you know? Couldn't get going really. Like a lot of people I suppose, you reckon you've got a real cracker of a book inside you, but when it comes to it you've just got a few not very interesting tales that don't stretch to more than twenty pages. Sad really. I could've made a lot of stuff up, exaggerated apocryphal stories, you know? A lot of people do that, but I didn't want to. What would have been the point? It's not as if I need the money."

Tim was a jovial character, like a matey grandad.

"Poor old Adie," he went on, wiping jam from his chin from the doughnut he was eating. "I didn't get to see him much over the last few years. I was told he had mental problems, depression or something. Kept himself to himself. Course he was always a bit stand-offish, old Adrian, not much of a one for people."

He recounted various tales, and I wondered if this was going to be a wasted afternoon, even though I was enjoying his company.

"Can I take a look at the diaries, please, Sean?" he asked.

"Sure." I handed them over.

He produced spectacles from his pocket, put them on and spent a long time, opening each and every one of them, leafing through the pages. While he was doing so, I asked if he wanted more tea and doughnuts and he said yes. So I fetched the food and patiently waited in silence while he opened the little books and read carefully. Then I noticed a strange thing.

He was frowning.

"Well, well, well," he began. "Sean, I don't want to worry you, but I hope you didn't rely too much on these diaries for your book."

"The whole book is based around them."

"Then you're up shit creek, mate. I'm sorry, but someone's been tampering with these."

"What do you mean?"

"See here, for instance?" He swivelled the open diary he was holding so I could read it, and pointed to a paragraph. "They've very cleverly matched the ink and the handwriting, but I know this entry wasn't put there by Adie, because I saw this diary the year after it was written."

I looked at the page. The paragraph he was referring to concerned having completed writing 'Rock and Rolling Christmas' on 3 August 1982, and the band performing it for the first time.

"And see here," Tim went on, opening up one of the other diaries. "Just the same with this one. Claiming that he'd written the songs 'Black Ice', which was the title song for one of their most iconic albums, and 'Slide Along Easy' on 4 March, 1981. I know for a fact that Ken Wheeler, Adrian's writing partner, wrote both of those."

"Wait a minute," I told him, confused. "All through the diaries he's been recording the songs he wrote and the dates they were recorded by his band. That's the framework for the book – I've even used song titles as chapter headings. I thought it gave the book the personal touch."

"Sure, the songs recorded by the band are all there. But let me explain. Adrian and Ken were a songwriting partnership for a short time, like Lennon and McCartney, or Jagger and Richards. But very soon they broke up as a songwriting team, and Adie abandoned songwriting altogether. After that time they were just good friends who each wrote songs separately. And Ken Wheeler was by far the better and more prolific songwriter – his songs are so good, people are still recording them, whereas Adrian only ever wrote a couple of big hits and a few others that sank without trace. The confusion occurs because Nightingale Green performed these songs, but their hits were largely all written by Ken Wheeler. Take this one here, 'Rock and Rolling Christmas', which I know for a fact that Ken wrote. In the diary Adie claims to have written it alone, in 1982."

"But what's the point of claiming Adrian wrote it if he didn't?"

"Who's inherited his back catalogue?"

"You mean the income from royalties, performance rights and so on of Adrian's songs? I imagine that would be Vernon, his son. He's inherited practically everything, as I understand it."

"Well there's your answer. Fact is, most of the people who were around at the time these songs were written are no longer here, or could even be bribed to lie. I gather that Ken Wheeler is very old now, and that he's got early onset Alzheimer's. So if Vernon could establish some claim that his father wrote these six very popular songs that he claims he did, but which I happen to know were written by Ken Wheeler, he'd not only get the ongoing income from his back catalogue, but the income from all the years since then."

"So how much money might be involved?"

"Millions, possibly. 'Rock and Rolling Christmas' alone is played in shops and supermarkets all over the world at Christmastime and every time it's played a royalty is due, same for plays and adverts on TV and radio, and of course record and CD sales and performances by other artists. That's why the people who inherited back catalogues of Jimi Hendrix and Elvis Presley are still rich even all these years after the deaths of those composers. It's like a super-duper pension that doesn't even stop when you die if you've left your back catalogue to someone. Performance rights and royalties can be worth much more than the actual money a songwriter earns in his lifetime."

Then I paused to think. "So if the diaries have been tampered with in order to mislead me, and in turn mislead the public in my book, that would support any legal claim."

"Undoubtedly. And you tell me they tried to steal these diaries? That would make sense too – if I can tell they've been tampered with, any expert would be able to see that too, by comparing the inks, the handwriting, so they'd need to get rid of them in case the court asked to examine them. These things wouldn't stand up to any scrutiny in my opinion, but if you claimed these entries were in his diaries, and the diaries are missing, who's to contradict you?"

"But surely there must be so many people still around who'd testify that Ken wrote those songs, and not Adrian?" I said.

"Not so many now, we're talking many years ago for these particular songs. And think about it. Someone writes a song or a book and until it's published no one knows who wrote it, do they? Adie was notoriously useless at business, so it's conceivable that if he had written songs, Ken might have officially claimed the credit without Adie even realising – trusting his old friend. And the few that do know who actually did write which songs, Vernon could bribe them to keep quiet, couldn't he?"

"That's true."

"But, Sean, I don't understand. Surely you must have checked with other sources about these songs that Adrian claims to have written?" Tim asked. "Some of them are fairly well known, after all."

"I didn't think there was any point. Who would write in their diary that they had written a song if they hadn't done so? Especially when there are plenty of songs in there he claims to have written that he obviously *has* written."

"Well, mate, I'd be very careful if I was you." He leaned closer to me. "I reckon someone has been taking advantage of your good nature. Quite frankly, Adrian Dark's actual back catalogue isn't worth that much, it was Ken who was the master songwriter, it was Ken's songs that were the real successes, and they still are. And it wasn't even a clear-cut partnership like that of Elton John and Bernie Taupin, where one was the musician, the other was a poet who wrote lyrics. Adrian and Ken both wrote songs individually, and also collaboratively. There's always confusion when a couple of songwriters have once formed a songwriting partnership, because if the partnership is still in existence, it can be disputed whether one or other or both of the partners wrote any particular song. I read somewhere that Jagger and Richards each wrote songs individually, but they made a point of always splitting everything fifty-fifty, to avoid arguments later.

"However, in the instances we're looking at, the songwriting partnership between Adrian and Ken had been dissolved, so the songwriter is definitely one or the other of them. I mean, Ken Wheeler is an old guy, a multi-millionaire, but something like this could wipe him out. Someone has gone to a lot trouble of tampering with these diaries in the hope some patsy will give them due credence. I have heard of court cases about copyrights to songs, and they can be very, very complicated, all kinds of evidence gets dragged up. But ultimately the case is likely to be tried before a jury, and subliminally a printed book, even if its origins can be called into question, can hold a lot of sway with people, and if it's in general circulation before the case comes to court, then it's like a fait accompli. People will assume the writer has checked his sources carefully."

"Which I didn't."

"You should have done."

"I know. My God. I'm fucked."

"Yes, mate, you could be royally fucked. Hang on, I've just had a thought." Tim pulled out his phone and pressed some keys, then nodded grimly and passed the phone across for me to see the screen. The article was a piece in one of the popular music newspapers:

Songwriter's son sues for multi-million settlement was the headline, and the story continued:

Vernon Dark, son of Adrian Dark, the recently deceased musician and songwriter, has begun litigation against Ken Wheeler, his father's one-time songwriting partner, for repayment of back royalties and other payments for a number of pop songs that were credited to Mr Wheeler, but which Mr Dark maintains were the brainchild of his father. Vernon Dark claims that his father's health deteriorated in his later years, and this must be why he allowed this state of affairs to continue for so long. Amongst the disputed song titles includes 'Rock and Rolling Christmas' which alone brings in thousands of pounds worth of royalties each year. If successful, this claim against Mr Wheeler could amount to many millions in back payments that will have to be repaid, not to mention ongoing payments for Mr Dark's other disputed back catalogue titles, such as the popular ballad 'Black Ice'...

"So has your book been published yet?" Tim asked.

"No."

"Thank God for that. I can see this has been a bombshell for you, and I'm really, really sorry. But the problem for you is, if this book goes to print, and then Vernon Dark uses your book as evidence during the court case, and the claims in the book are subsequently found to be fraudulent, these incorrect things you claim in the book, which you can't even corroborate if the diaries are missing, could be viewed as deliberate fraud on your part, and criminal proceedings could follow. The law might assume you were in on it from the beginning. You'd be an accessory to fraud. You could get prison time."

"Yes, you're right," I told him. "I just never dreamed of something like this."

"Well, mate, I'm very, very sorry, and I'm on your side. The only way to clear your name is to make a clean breast of it now. Don't let these bloody diaries out of your sight – they're the only thing that might clear your name. I'm perfectly willing to testify in a court of law that these entries to the diaries were not written by Adrian. In fact I want to do it. Ken Wheeler's a lovely old fella, I like him a lot and he's nearly ninety. Why should he have to fight a court case at his age? Why should he risk losing his fortune to some scheming little bastard? And," he went on, looking directly at me, "why should a trusting bloke like you get shafted?"

So at last it all made sense.

Then everything slipped into place. Mairéad's email out of the blue, wanting to re-establish contact, promising me a 'big break' and the chance of lots of material for a new book, to help me make a few quid, even though I wasn't a proper writer. Suddenly I remembered her last words to me, fifteen years ago, standing in the rain and cold outside the gates of art school, on the last day of term. "You're too soft, Sean. You've not got the courage to make it big. In this world you've got to take your chances when you get them."

TWENTY-NINE

By the time I arrived at Landseer's Frome office the following late afternoon it was already getting dark, the fading light a gentle precursor to night.

I was shocked and deeply upset after what I'd found out, but had calmed down a bit on the journey. It was an irony of life, that I had already been aware of the problems with the book that Sylvia had highlighted, and had been deeply concerned that I hadn't got a clue how to put them right. Now I was relieved, knowing that these failures of mine were the only reason why it hadn't gone ahead to the copy editor, on the way to publication: something which would have been catastrophic for me.

The showdown with Mairéad was going to be all the more deadly, now that I'd had several hours and a long drive to clear my thoughts. The big car park at Landseers had a couple of new sleek Jaguars in the neatly marked bays where I parked, the huge glass frontage of the building looking impressive, redolent of money and power. Lights flickered on inside the reception area, bright yellow against the darkness, illuminating the red lettering of *Landseer's* in the window. I strode into reception and asked for Mairéad, and she was in. I was shown to a large office: a neat light room with big picture windows and a long glass table and slender aluminium chairs. A blank, antiseptic room, clearly normally used for corporate meetings.

Mairéad agreed to see me, and I had to wait in the plush office for half an hour before she swept through the door, smelling of fresh perfume and success.

"Oh, Sean, I'm sorry to have kept asking you about the decorating job, I really am. I'd had a bad day and I was taking it out on you. How about coffee? I know you always like it strong and black—"

"I'm going to withdraw the book."

"What?" Her mouth fell open. I saw the full gamut of emotion sweep across her features, from surprise to disbelief, to fear. "You're kidding me."

"I don't joke about money. Nor do I joke about fucking up my chances of any future jobs as a writer."

She sank into a chair.

"They gave you a cut, didn't they?" I asked her. "Whose idea was it to make those additions to the diary entries in preparation for suing Ken Wheeler? Yours?"

"I don't know what you're talking about."

"Maybe it wasn't your plan. But it was your bright idea to rope me in as the patsy, wasn't it? All that stuff about breaking up with me was the hardest thing you ever did, that I had been the love of your life. Stringing me along suited you just fine, didn't it? Whistle for good old Sean, and he'll come running, just like he always used to."

"It wasn't like that."

"Wasn't it? I can just imagine the conversation: 'We'll try and persuade some writer who isn't involved to base a book on these diaries and get it published, that way it'll lend the diaries credibility'. But someone else said, 'But professional writers always check out these things out to cover themselves'. And you said, 'Don't worry, I know a guy who'll help us out without even realising it, he's a bit naïve and trusting. We can rely on him not to do too much checking'."

She shook her head slightly, dumbstruck. "I swear I don't have the least idea what you're talking about."

I looked her in the eyes. Searched for the tremor there, the hint of delay, the jutting out lower lip of self-justification. Instead, I saw the millisecond's glance over my left shoulder, the classic giveaway of a liar.

"You knew," I told her. "By pure chance, an old musician friend of Adrian's had seen the diaries when they were written. He knew which parts were added recently to help your court case. All the mentions of songs he'd written with the dates."

She looked down at the floor, then slowly stared up at me.

"Sean, just hold on now. I know this must have come as a shock. But I think you really need to think about this. It wasn't the way you're saying. I wanted to help you because I knew you needed a break."

"And if you hadn't sent someone to try and nick the diaries it would have worked. You had to get rid of the diaries, otherwise they'd have to be produced in court, and you couldn't risk experts trying to match the ink and paper impression and handwriting or whatever. It was genius really. Get hold of a writer with no vested interest in the songs or who wrote them, get him to put the claims into print, and when the diaries can't be found, it's assumed they've been destroyed in a house fire or something. Ken Wheeler has Alzheimer's, so he lacks credibility, his testimony is called into question.

"The one weak part of the whole plan is that you have to persuade people that Adrian Dark was so naïve that he didn't notice that Ken Wheeler had claimed the copyright of six of his commercially successful songs. But Adrian is dead, and was known to be lackadaisical about business, which he left to his agent to manage, and his agent is also now conveniently dead, so cannot refute the accusation that he was being bribed by Ken Wheeler to deliberately not claim the copyright when the songs were first recorded. So all you have to do then is bribe the few people who were around at the time to lie, and it's down to which way the court case goes. It's clever. What do they always say? What gets you in the end isn't proving the crime, it's exposing the cover-up."

She didn't answer for a long time.

"Look, stop being so bloody high and mighty, Sean, and think for a change." Colour came to her otherwise pale cheeks and her voice was strident now, deeper and arrogant in her own self-belief. "Why would you care who wrote those songs, and why is Ken Wheeler suddenly your new best friend? He's a rich old man, and we don't even know him. And do you have any idea how much money is involved? If this thing pays off, *and it will*, my share is enough for me to retire from this job, and buy a stud farm back home in Ireland, to do what I've wanted to do all my life. Vernon can afford to be generous because he stands to make millions, honest to God, it makes his inheritance seem like a pittance, especially when you take into account the inheritance tax he has to pay. Don't you realise what's involved here? For God's sake, these sums will be an aggregate of the back payments over thirty years, plus an ongoing income for life, for every single play of every song that was written by Adrian, because Vernon owns Adrian's back catalogue. If you'll just keep quiet we can cut you in too, it's only fair really. . ."

I didn't answer for a long time.

"And that was what went wrong with us when we were in our twenties, wasn't it?" I told her sadly. "You were always ambitious. You always had an eye to the main chance."

"God, Sean, don't you find it a wee bit lonely on that cloud cuckoo land where you live, where everyone does the right thing, and no one ever tells a lie? Why do you think you're a failed artist at thirty-five, and you haven't got a pot to piss in? When are you going to join the real world?"

"Your world?" I shook my head.

"Please!" She was standing up now, falling into my arms, banging her fists against my chest. "I'm begging you, *please, please* don't ruin everything, Sean! The work is done now! You've written the bloody book, it's only a question of sitting back and waiting now. And I've told you, I was always going to cut you in on it. I couldn't tell you before, we were going to tell you afterwards, when it was too late for you to back out. That's when we were going to give you your share."

"It's too late." I pushed her away, disgusted to feel her near me. "I'm going to tell the publishers what's happened. They don't want to risk being mixed up in a lawsuit, any more than I fancy being charged as an accessory to fraud."

"You idiot!" she snapped from between clenched teeth. "That won't happen! Don't you understand? *We're home and dry!* Ken Wheeler is an old man, he's in the first stages of Alzheimer's, he won't even be able to remember if he wrote the songs or not! He's got more money than he knows what to do with, and he hasn't even got anyone to leave it to! When he dies it'll all go to charity, so no one's going to lose by this! Do you realise what you're doing?"

"What's the matter, Mairéad?" I asked her, genuinely

intrigued. "Are you afraid of your boyfriend Vernon? Is it more than just the money you're getting? Or has he got some hold over you?"

*

During the drive home, my eyes could barely stay open. I kept replaying the last few hours in my mind. I couldn't stop thinking about how Mairéad must have despised me. Little things came back to me, evidence of her cold-hearted ruthlessness in the past. The time she paid someone to take one of her final exams at art school because she was afraid of failing, the fraudulent whiplash car-crash insurance claim she had made, when other hard-up students would just get a weekend job in Sainsbury's. With respectability, I'd assumed she'd grown some integrity, but it seemed she had merely upped her game. I thought of the cynical way she had talked to me on the first night I'd come to Netherwold, all so as to gain my trust and friendship, when all the time she was hand-in-glove with that scheming criminal shit, Vernon Dark.

What's more, the likelihood was that all the members of the band would know who had really written those songs, and only Roger Bracken still survived. Maybe Roger had been getting greedy, demanding more money in return for not changing his testimony when it came to court. Bracken might have been standing in the way of Vernon's millions, a very good motive for killing him, especially if Roger had phoned him, telling him that a crazy woman had called on him, was threatening him, had picked up the heavy lampstand to hit him with. . .

It was just past junction 18 on the M4 when my eyelids were almost closing and I was wondering whether to go into the next service station for a break and some coffee, that I first became aware of someone on my tail. It was more of a subliminal feeling than anything else, an awareness of headlights coming too close, then backing off, as if my followers were falling back on purpose, then speeding to catch up.

Pulling into the Leigh Delamere Service Station seemed like a good idea. As I found a parking space and turned off the engine, I leaned back and closed my eyes.

I didn't even hear the car door open.

Nor was I aware of the blow to my head.

Oblivion.

*

I woke up, finding myself in my own car's passenger seat, hands tied behind my back, seat belt strapped across tightly, and a man I'd never seen before driving my own car.

"What's happening?" I asked, noticing for the first time that there was another man in the back of the car, staring straight ahead. "Who are you?"

Neither of them spoke.

I struggled. Trying to get free. But I was held securely. I began to panic, wondering what was going to happen, but the whole situation was so surreal and strange that I knew without doubt that there was absolutely nothing I could do. I had the overwhelming urge to pee. But my overriding feeling was that of sheer terror.

We pulled up about twenty minutes later, having turned off a main road and driven across country. It was still night-time, but by the light of the moon I could see that we were in a clearing in a forest, and another vehicle had pulled in behind us.

Then the door beside me opened and I felt strong arms pushing me back down against the seat, as I saw the tube end of a plastic funnel approaching my face, and someone pulling open my mouth and forcing it between my teeth.

I spluttered and gagged as the neat whisky trickled down the tube into my mouth, but when they pinched my nose and poured more whisky down the tube, I had no choice but to swallow, once, twice and then again, before coughing and choking and gagging. Then the whole procedure started again. The last thing I remember before losing consciousness for a second time was the sour smell of aftershave from the man beside me and the aroma of whisky and the growing awareness of my own bitter bubbling vomit.

THIRTY

Laura

It's always the same. More questions. More long-faced arrogant policemen sitting there, trying to trip me up with their questions.

But now this woman, this person who was supposed to be on my side, was sitting here, talking to me as if I was stupid. I almost wondered if it might have been better to stick with my original legal counsel, the bastard Patrick, who didn't believe I was innocent either.

"So, Laura, let's think about what's happened," said Jane Harryman, a tall bespectacled lady with a curtain of grey hair and skeletal hands, whose long red-painted nails drummed gently against the cheap plastic surface of the table. As she sat forward, dressed in her scarlet designer jacket with discreet silver necklace, she looked more like an aggressive politician than the solicitor who had agreed to represent me. "What do you say about this article in the paper?"

"What can I say?"

"Do you deny that Sarah in the Sky is you?"

"I want to."

I had seen the article yesterday and it had brought my

whole world crashing down. The reporter, Kate Doyle, had somehow blown my cover, and published her findings that Sarah in the Sky, who'd been an anonymous Twitter and Facebook sensation for five years, was me. My private life was apparently newsworthy since my arrest on the charge of attempted murder. So my days as quiet self-effacing Laura Kaplan had been finally been compromised, perhaps for ever. True, I always knew it was likely to happen one day, and I could always try denying it – after all, nothing could be proved as far as I knew.

"You've heard of client and solicitor confidentiality?"

"Of course I have," I whispered.

"So tell me the truth. This person who advertises herself as Sarah in the Sky and makes videos for the internet and always keeps her face covered. Is she you?"

"Yes," I muttered quietly.

"So if the police can establish this fact, you are aware that climbing up public buildings is illegal, and you can be charged and prosecuted?"

"Why do you think I wanted to be anonymous? Climbing buildings is my hobby. Up to now I've kept my professional life and my hobby completely separate. It's been like a kind of game, all these years."

"A game?"

"Yes."

"Okay." Her slow nod was ponderous and heavy with meaning. "Okay, I accept you're not a liar, Laura. Though it seems to me that since you invented a persona in order to evade the consequences of your illegal actions, you're not exactly an honest person, are you?"

I nodded miserably.

"But the real question is, are you mentally ill?" she asked.

"What do you mean by that?"

"Okay, I'll make it easier. Have you ever been to see a psychiatrist?"

"Yes."

"Tell me about it."

"As I explained, I first saw Netherwold Hall at the auction, after I discovered that Adrian Dark was my father, and that he'd left me some money. When I was standing in the main hall, the place seemed familiar – as if I had been there before. I just couldn't remember how I came to know the place, I just knew that I'd never visited it to my knowledge. So I went to see a psychiatrist, in the hope he could hypnotise me, to help me remember."

"Did he diagnose you with any kind of mental illness?"

"He thought I might have a mild case of Dissociative Identity Disorder, or possibly schizophrenia. Several people in my father's family have suffered from schizophrenia, and I understand that it can often be hereditary."

"Do you take regular medication to control these schizophrenic episodes?"

"*I don't have schizophrenic episodes.* Dr Fanshaw was just mentioning the possibility that I might be schizophrenic, that's all. You can have elements of mental illnesses without being a full blown sufferer."

"Umm. Schizophrenia. Do you hear voices?"

"No."

"Would you say you have confused thinking?"

"No."

"And this Dissociative Identity Disorder, presumably exemplified by this escape into the Sarah in the Sky character as your 'alter'. Isn't it all part of the same illness? Surely schizophrenia means behaving like another person? Having drastic mood changes?"

"No, that's a fallacy. Schizophrenia is not a 'split personality'. It's completely different."

"And this psychiatrist also helped you unravel these 'rediscovered memories'? These memories you have of members of the band Nightingale Green attacking your mother?"

"Yes."

Again, Jane Harryman spent a long time drumming her nails against the table top.

"Look, Laura, I'm going to be honest with you. These stories about your alter ego, if you like, Sarah in the Sky, have only just surfaced. The police will be looking into them. You engaged me to help you answer the charge of the attempted murder of Roger Bracken. I must warn you that if you're charged with these other crimes, then I'm not sure I can handle those allegations as well. You may have to find someone else."

I nodded grimly.

"However, I do have a suggestion for you as regards this charge that's been made against you, the attempted murder of Roger Bracken, which is what we're concentrating on for now."

"Go on."

"You've seen a psychiatrist, and presumably he'll testify that you have issues regarding your mental health. I know your statement to the police is that you deny the charge of hitting Mr Bracken with the table lamp, and causing his injuries. But right now we do have the chance to change your statement."

"Change my statement?"

"Come now." She paused momentarily, staring at me. "If you continue to plead not guilty, I have to tell you that there's every chance you'll be convicted of this crime. Mr

Bracken's life is hanging in the balance, and at any moment you could be facing a murder charge, which is considerably more serious than attempted murder. Murder quite rightly always incurs a substantial custodial sentence except in rare circumstances, which don't apply to you. Whereas if you plead guilty but make a declaration of diminished responsibility, then it's a very different matter. The presiding judge appreciates your honesty, and the fact you're saving public money and court fees, plus more importantly he officially is allowed to take into account the fact that you're not altogether responsible for your actions. Diminished responsibility, it's a very neat phrase and it means precisely what it says. It's a way of settling your predicament once and for all. There's effectively no trial, all this goes through smoothly, and the chances are you'll get a lighter sentence. Custodial, certainly, but in a special facility, and no doubt for a much shorter period."

"But I didn't do it."

"Maybe you did it, but you had another of those blackouts straight afterwards? What's that interesting phrase you told me that you suffered from as a child? Traumatic amnesia. We can sort out a psychiatric assessment tomorrow."

"No!" I yelled. "I left him standing in his hall. He pushed me out so that I fell and sprawled on the step and he slammed the door after me."

"You picked up that table lamp. Why?"

"He was coming towards me. He was angry. I picked it up in case he hit me. I was defending myself."

"Ah! Now we're getting somewhere. He was coming towards you. You were afraid. So you lashed out to protect yourself?"

"No, it wasn't like that! *I didn't hit him with it.* I just dropped it as I ran out of the front door and drove away. When I left the house he was there, in the hallway, shouting at me."

"I'll see you in the morning, Laura." She gathered her papers together, channelling them into her case, long nails fiery red against the white paper, high-heeled shoes clacking against the floor as she stood up. "Think about what I said."

THIRTY-ONE

Sean

When I opened my eyes, all I could see was a fog of dense smoke. And all I could taste was the swirling sickly mush of burnt gasoline on my tongue. My head was pounding in agony, and my eyes were streaming.

As I took a breath, the foulness of the exhaust fumes choked me once again, and I couldn't stop coughing. Coughing so much that I nearly passed out again. I realised I was in my car and, fumbling in the grey haze that filled the space, I was hardly able to see. Fighting the urge to shut my eyes and fall asleep again, I groped across to find the door. Fumbled along until I found the latch and pulled it outwards. Finally I used an elbow to push the door open wide to let in some grey daylight and rain.

As I leaned out into the howling wind and rain, the droplets kissed my face, soaking my shirt to the skin in seconds. Another coughing fit overtook me, but this time I had it slightly more under control.

I sprawled out into the downpour, falling face down into the grass and soggy earth, and rolled and rolled, taking a huge breaths, before nausea overcame me and I vomited.

Eventually I settled back down, lying on my back, staring up into the tree branches overhead, and catching a glimpse of grey sky. The rain drilling into my face was relentless and savage, and the water streaming down my cheeks made me feel alive. But the fresh air was sent straight from God.

Gradually things began to come back to me. Being overcome by the two men at the service station, knocked unconscious. The car journey, stopping on the waste ground. The foul taste of plastic as the funnel was pushed into my mouth and whisky poured down my throat. My head was pounding in agony, it felt as if it was splitting wide open. My vision was blurred, and the unmistakeable signs of a terrible hangover were better than the previous nauseated longing for sleep.

I was alone. Looking through the rain I could see that the car a few yards away that I'd just tumbled out of was, indeed, my own old Land Rover Discovery. I got up onto my knees, then bent my head right down, tucking it between them, still taking deep breaths, trying to calm down and make sense of things. Shortly afterwards I shuffled across and peered into my car's interior. The key was turned on in its slot, and the ignition lights were alive in the dash, but the engine wasn't running. That was when I noticed the clumsy arrangement of the hose pipe stuffed into the top of the partly opened passenger window, the gap beside it sealed up with tape. The other end of the pipe had been inserted into the car's exhaust, again taped up to seal any gaps.

With relieved amazement I remembered the problem I'd had recently with the car – the engine tended to overheat and cut out in thick traffic after a few minutes of idling. That fault had saved my life. My abductors had obviously poured the whisky down my throat to make me drink until I passed out naturally, then put me in the driver's seat, rigged up the suicide kit, turned on the car's engine to ticking over, and slammed the door. The car would have quickly filled with fumes and in a relatively short period of time I'd be completely overcome, and the air in my lungs would be full of carbon monoxide, which would be transported to my blood, instead of oxygen. Death would have occurred soon afterwards.

Clarity of thought made me realise the danger I was still in. Mairéad had obviously told Vernon Dark what I'd found out and what I was planning to do, and he had arranged this little party as a way of silencing me permanently. It would have worked perfectly: as far as Mairéad knew, the book had been written and was being published, so they simply had to wait for its publication to coincide with the upcoming court case. Of course they were not aware that publication had been delayed for me to make various changes. In the meantime, they would rob my house and get hold of the diaries so as to destroy them, and no one would ever know what I had done with them before I'd died. I was a man alone, no wife or partner, no one to confess my deepest suicidal feelings to. . .

Shakily, I managed to get to my feet. My head was splitting and my vision was still blurred, and I knew I was in no fit state to drive a car. I'd be intoxicated at least for the rest of the day, and I must have ingested quite a bit of carbon monoxide. Was it worth reporting my attack to the police? Should I go to hospital and get myself checked out?

Locating my phone in the car, I took it and walked to the end of the lane.

I clocked on the 'sent' messages, and saw 'my' text that had been sent to Robin Villiers:

Robin, I'm sending this because I can't go on any longer, so I am ending it all.

Robin would have instantly known I hadn't sent it, because I always call him Rob, not Robin. He also knew me well enough to know that I wasn't the kind of person to commit suicide, nor was I in a frame of mind to do so.

This was the cruellest cut of all: only Mairéad knew that Robin was my friend, the person I was most likely to communicate with in times of trouble, I had mentioned my friendship during one of our phone conversations.

Without reading his replies, I pressed 'contacts', and then his number.

"Sean? What's going on?" he answered on the first ring.

"Someone tried to kill me, but I'm okay. Can you get the diaries I lent you?"

"The diaries?"

"It's important. You have to get hold of them now, before someone steals them."

"Okay."

"Then, will you come and get me? And bring the diaries with you. Hang on, I'm just entering a village, I'll ring you back when I find out where I am."

By that time I'd reached a village street and I walked down and went into a pub, the Barley Mow. The barman told me the postcode, which I relayed to Rob when I phoned him back.

"Okay," he replied. "The satnav says I'll be there in a couple of hours, but I'll make it sooner if I can."

"No hurry. I'll be waiting in the pub."

My slurred speech had made the barman wary of me, but I explained that I was actually ill, and had arranged for a friend to pick me up to take me to hospital.

"You look like you died," was Rob's remark as he swept into the bar. "The diaries are in the car. What's this all about?"

Half an hour later I had explained everything and he had reluctantly agreed to help me.

"I still think you should tell the police," he said.

"There's no point. Besides, I want to deal with Vernon Dark and Mairéad in my own way. At the moment they'll think I'm dead, which leaves me free to deal with this situation. I've got a plan."

"Okay. If that's what you really want."

He drove me back to my car and removed all the piping and tape, then started it up and, with the blower going at high speed and all the windows open, he managed to clear the last of the aroma of exhaust gases from the car. He had already made an arrangement with the pub owner to let him leave his car in the car park, so he drove there, walked back and then he drove us away in my Land Rover.

"So right now, they'll think you're dead, so you're safe?" said Rob as he stared hard at the road. "And as soon as you speak out and they know they've failed, there'll be no point in them killing you. How long do you think we've got before they find out you're still alive?"

"My car was in a clearing a long way from the road. It could have remained undiscovered for several days I should think, and even then you'd have to get up close before you could see the hose arrangement."

"Days then. Possibly as much as a week."

"Can you take me to London, to Ken Wheeler's solicitors?"

"Do you think that's a good idea?"

"It's the best I can think of right now."

My head still felt bad but my vision was beginning to get back to normal. Luckily I had researched the court case earlier on, and had remembered the name of Ken Wheeler's solicitors. I'd drunk some water and managed a dry biscuit in the pub, so I was feeling slightly better. "I have to phone the publishers to cancel the book."

He nodded. "But two guys tried to kill you and almost succeeded. I really think you should report it to the police."

"Sure, I ought to. But they'll never get who did it. I guess that Vernon employed people, and they'll have covered their tracks."

"Not necessarily. They'd assume the police would treat your death as suicide, and wouldn't look any further. As it is, they may have left fingerprints or DNA."

"Yeah, but if I tell the police, word gets back to Vernon, and I'd rather he stayed in the dark for a wee while."

"Playing games is what got you into this mess. But you're so damned stubborn there's no point trying to talk sense into you."

I dialled Sylvia's number and held the phone to my ear, wishing this conversation was over.

"Listen, Sylvia, I'm really sorry about this," I concluded, having told her that the book had to be withdrawn.

"Bloody hell! I mean, Sean, bloody hell! I thought you were ringing to say you'd done all that work we were asking for. Bloody hell, you can't fucking do this to me, everything's ready to go! Christ, you promised you'd deliver the extra copy in a week and I've just this minute booked it in with the copy editor, and he's told me he can edit it in a week, then it was due for the proofreader and design. Everything's been set up!"

I sighed. "I'm telling you that I based most of the book on the diaries. And I've only just discovered that the diaries have been tampered with, in order to substantiate a fraudulent attempt to sue another songwriter for millions over the right to songs, claimed in the diary to have been written by Adrian Dark, when in fact, they were written by Ken Wheeler, as is generally accepted anyway."

"You based a book on diaries that have been tampered with by someone? You didn't check the entries with other people?"

"I didn't think I had any reason to."

"But you told me you knew all about Adrian Dark? That you'd been studying his work for years, that you had lots of people lined up to give interviews!"

"I exaggerated a bit."

"You exaggerated so much you pretty well lied, Sean! This really is too much. I don't know what to say. Yeah. I don't fucking know what to say."

"I'm sorry."

"Surely there's something we can do?"

I gulped and closed my eyes. "Look, this is heavy duty fraud we're talking about. The people who tampered with Adrian Dark's diaries are suing Ken Wheeler for millions of pounds' worth of back payments of royalties and other ongoing payments relating to songs they claim that Adrian wrote, and not Ken. But Ken *did* write them."

"If you'd bothered to do your research you'd have known that Ken Wheeler was generally accepted as the writer of those particular songs, wouldn't you? And you'd have asked questions before taking it this far?"

"Yes. Sorry, Sylvia, there's nothing I can say. These bastards have used me to give credence to their fraudulent claim. It's a clumsy attempt at fraud which will probably fail, and me and Charngate could get prosecuted for fraud."

"Prosecuted?"

"As accessories to fraud. Or maybe just sued for damages. I'd definitely be an accessory to fraud, and Charngate Publishing might be named as a corporate co-conspirator."

"But why did you get us into this mess, Sean?"

"Most of these songs were written in the 1970s. Not that many people in the know are still alive to substantiate the claims. The ones who are have probably been bribed to back up Vernon's story. Apparently Ken Wheeler has Alzheimer's, so his memory can't be trusted either. It's a horrible combination of circumstances. It was reasonable for me to assume the diary entries were genuine."

"If you'd really been studying Adrian Dark's life for years, as you told me, you'd have suspected something like this."

"Yes," I admitted. "If I'd been more familiar with his work I probably would have done."

"Oh shit. You know I'm tempted to say that you probably deserve to be sued, but I think even if the litigation was all down to you, our reputation would suffer."

"Yes," I agreed. "It would."

"Bloody hell, Sean, I went out on a limb to help you in this, and now, cancelling everything is going to make me look like an idiot, and it's going to cost us money. You'll have to return the advance. We might have to charge you for all the wasted time."

"I know. How do you think I feel?"

"I don't care how you feel. I just hope I can keep my job after this shit show!"

"I'm sorry."

"You fucking should be, Sean! Don't come back here expecting another chance, because you've blown it big time. We won't forget this. I say, we won't forget this."

"Neither will I."

"Just fuck off, Sean. Go and ruin someone else's career!"

"Sorry," Rob sympathised after I'd cut the call. "Why

didn't you tell her someone just tried to kill you?"

"She'd have wished they'd succeeded."

"Did you really claim that you'd been studying Adrian Dark's music for years?"

"Yes. When you're pitching for a book you stretch the truth a bit. Everybody does it."

"Tell me something, Sean. When you confronted Mairéad about what they did to you, was there a moment when you were tempted to go along with it? Just accept what had happened and take the money?"

I took a deep breath as I watched the scenery out of the car window and felt an incredible weight of misery. "For just a few seconds, while Mairéad was talking, I almost managed to see things from her point of view. She has this way of mesmerising you, of making you think she really knows what she's talking about, *that she's right.*"

"Just a few seconds, right?"

"No longer than that. Shit, what does that make me?"

"Don't apologise for being human, Sean.

The next call I made was to Kate Doyle.

"Sean," she said calmly. "Before you start, I'm sorry, right? I know I said I wouldn't sell a story about Laura but it was too good an opportunity to miss."

"What are you talking about?"

"Isn't that why you're ringing me? I pitched an article to one of the dailies and they bit. I've blown Laura's secret life as Sarah in the Sky. Do you hate me now?"

Shit! I pictured how Laura must be feeling, with everyone knowing about the life she'd done her best to keep secret. But I put the thought out of my mind. If it was done, it was done.

"Speak to me, mate. Even if you just tell me to fuck off."

"Someone just tried to kill me," I told her.

"No shit?"

"Look, Kate, I've got a story for you." I briefly summarised all the details of what I'd found out, of the way Mairéad and Vernon had tried to make use of me.

"Blimey, Sean, I thought you had a trusting nature, but this is off the wall. They've really tried to shaft you, haven't they?"

"But luckily they haven't succeeded. And I'd like to get my own back if I can."

"You mean if some friendly investigative journalist was to make this whole thing public, the attempt to defraud Ken Wheeler and make use of your naivety in the process?"

"That's what I'd like."

"Even if it makes you look like a patsy?"

"Sure, but I'm a patsy who found out in time and turned the tables. That makes me seem a wee bit less foolish."

"Yeah, it does. And courageous. I'll test the water, do the research on the court case, talk to some contacts and get back to you ASAP."

"Thanks, Kate."

"Thank you, mate. Scoops like this are my bread and butter. I'm onto this right now. Talk soon, yeah?"

As I cut the call I knew that after seeing Ken Wheeler's lawyers, I had to talk to Mairéad urgently.

Revenge was going to be sweet.

THIRTY-TWO

For the second time that week I was admiring the huge scarlet letters on the plate glass wall of Landseer's premises in Frome. Indeed the entire feeling of the day was somehow as if I was taking part in a drama that was about to have a strange and unpredictable ending. The prospect of confronting the woman who thought I was already dead was something I was looking forward to.

I had the gut feeling that the attempt on my life had been Vernon's idea, but the fact that Mairéad had told him about my best friend so that they could send the suicide text, surely had to mean that she knew all about it.

I thought back to when she had saved my life, when the gunman had broken into my house, and she had thrown the kettle full of paint in his face. Was it really just serendipity that she'd arrived and she'd reacted as if by instinct? There was another thing too: at the time she had not known if I'd finished the book, and she desperately wanted the book completed and in print, so, at that time, it was important that I stayed alive.

The light from Landseer's highly lit interior spilt out onto the car park across the road from where I was sitting in my car. Everything that had happened in the last few weeks seemed like a blot on my existence, a stain on my life.

Everything about it seemed wrong. Except for Laura. She was the only constant in a weird changing world.

Laura. The pain of falling in love with Laura was ever-present. Now that I was convinced that she was not a killer, it was hard to accept that she was only the interesting, chatty, book loving person I knew for part of the time. At weekends she was someone else entirely, an outspoken, sporty, aggressive woman called Sarah, who made a habit of breaking the law and risking her life, simply to show off to her army of unseen fans on social media.

Why did she do it? Dr Fanshaw had not made any guesses as to why she yearned for accolades from strangers. Was there some deep psychological reason why she wanted to show off? And if she was lying, if she had indeed attacked Roger Bracken and tried to kill him, was it so very bad? After all, if he had raped her mother, maybe the feeling of hatred had become overpowering, and she hadn't been able to resist?

Now that Kate had 'outed' Laura as the outspoken scary Sarah in the Sky, perhaps it was the lesson she needed? If she was cleared of the attack on Roger Bracken, and released, she would be forced to stop acting as Sarah, since the police would be watching her every move.

But I had to put all thoughts of Laura on the back burner. Right now, I had to face the humiliating fact that a woman whom I'd once been in love with had used me as a patsy, and then had no compunction in agreeing to my murder, just because I wouldn't play along.

Now it was my time for payback.

My plan was to try to catch Mairéad alone by following her home. What to do then?

I was going to have to play it by ear.

I answered my mobile, noticing the caller was Kate

Doyle. In mild irritation I thought again of the blue streak in her blond hair, the outspoken vulgarity of her, the coarse insensitive voice, the jarring cockney accent. She had argued forcefully when I'd told her I was going to confront Mairéad, telling me that I would be walking into a trap.

"You're still going to see that Irish bitch?" she barked.

"Yes."

"You know that it's a bloody stupid thing to do?" she snapped coldly.

"Why?"

"She arranged for you to be killed, didn't she?"

"I think that was Vernon."

"But she went along with it. *She told him you were turning them in.* She knew what he was going to do to stop you. Yet now you're gonna wander in there on your own. What the fuck do you think is gonna happen?"

"I don't know yet."

"Which is why you should let the police handle it."

"Sure, Kate, did you not realise I was in the police myself? I know they'd have no hope of catching the goons who tried to kill me. And even if they did catch the men who did it, they'll never link them to Vernon."

"But it's done with. You've settled everything now, spiked their guns, you've fucked up their case, so they got no reason to kill you anymore. Why not just leave it alone?"

"I appreciate your help, Kate—"

"Are you always this fucking stubborn? Are you always this *fucking stupid?*"

She went on for a long time but I wasn't listening. I could almost taste my revenge, yet I wasn't savouring it yet. That would come later.

And then I thought of another possibility. On the very day I'd been planning to go and see Laura at Novelicious, she'd been arrested for the attempted murder of Roger Bracken. She had been picked up driving away from his house, her fingerprints on the murder weapon, and her reason for going to see him was to confront him about her 'recovered memory' of his alleged attack on her mother. The police had disbelieved her claim that he was perfectly all right when she left the house.

But was there some other explanation? After all, I now knew that Vernon Dark had been prepared to arrange my 'suicide' in order to protect his get-rich-quick scheme. But for that scheme to succeed, he also needed the musicians who were around at the time when the songs were written to attest that they were penned by Dark, and not Wheeler. Roger Bracken was one of the few people alive who would have known exactly who wrote which songs, and there was a fair chance that he was being paid to keep quiet about it. Had he become greedy? If Vernon was prepared to arrange my death, he'd think nothing of killing other people, especially if someone else was on the spot to take the blame.

And then, as the sky turned darker still, Mairéad appeared at the side door of Landseer's and leapt gracefully into a new silver Jaguar. The elegant car swooped out of the car park and edged out onto the road.

I pulled out and followed, keeping just the right distance behind so as not to alert her, yet close enough to stop anyone else overtaking me. That wasn't likely, for Mairéad showed no respect for the speed limit, and I had to crest forty to keep up with her. Mairéad had always been like that: impatient, anxious to get in front, to always be in the fast lane of life.

I had pictured the scene ahead a hundred times in my mind. Yet I knew that no one's imagination could possibly cut it.

The last of the daylight had vanished now, and the

twin tail-lights of the Jaguar twinkled like rubies ahead, luring me on as the car snaked along the winding road.

Mairéad, the girl who had been my first real girlfriend, who shared my Irish heritage, who understood me through and through.

The woman who had used my past love for her to play me for a fool, who had nearly succeeded in helping her to commit fraud, where she stood to gain many thousands, if not millions.

Enough to buy a stud farm in Ireland – what I've always wanted to do.

I suddenly remembered how she had always loved horses, telling me about the farm where she grew up, just as I had done.

Bushnell Grange turned out to be a brand new housing development, still apparently with empty apartments for sale, with a grand looking show house at the wide, flower-decorated entrance, the sales office now closed, but lights still burning in the window. I followed the wide track, breathing in the aroma of the perfect flowerbeds on either side, where the neat luxurious new homes in Albatross Drive, Heron's Walk and Sparrow Den led off the main thoroughfare towards the green hills in the distance. Mairéad's home, Number 65, was one of the large detached houses, and I watched as she swooped the big cat of a car onto the pristine white concrete, opening the up-and-over garage door for the car to purr into its lair.

I parked a short way along the road, sat back in the seat, and breathed deeply, psyching myself up for what was about to happen. Then I got out of the car and walked back to her house.

As I stood on the step and rang the bell, I realised that there was probably video surveillance, and she'd have the choice of alerting Vernon that I was still alive even as I stood on her step. Did she live alone, or did she share the house with someone? I had no idea.

The tasteful chimes echoed through the house. The door opened.

"Sean!" Mairéad cried out in delight as she opened the door fully, throwing her arms around me and squeezing me tight. "Thank God! I knew you'd change your mind."

THIRTY-THREE

Changed my mind?

Nothing made sense anymore, and as I followed her, listening to her chattering away, I wondered if I was going mad. It's true she was still beautiful but somehow her beauty was essentially flawed now. Close up I had noticed that she had a network of lines around her mouth, which I used to find sexy but now I found repellent. Even her eyes seemed different; right now they held a cynical glaze, where once there had been a spark of the sheer joy of living.

I followed her into a huge living room, with a white thick-pile carpet and pure white walls, their bare hospital-like sparseness broken up by neutral boring paintings. I thought back to her bold, brash and lively paintings at art school, the style and individuality in her work in those days: the swirling lines, the wild colours. I remembered one of the teachers watching her sketching, and his admiring expression as she formed curves and shapes and the strangest swirling designs. I could see why he was so impressed. Some people have instinctive style, instinctive passion for artistic creations, and Mairéad had had it in spades, that sense of freedom and individuality and a kind of 'wildness' that all gifted artists have. The woman I had known as an art student would never have chosen to live with lifeless, banal paintings like this. I yearned for the past, for her to be the trailblazing talented artist she had once been, not the shallow, greedy, social-climbing criminal who stood before me.

There were other differences, nuanced and vague, but nevertheless illustrative of someone so different from the woman I thought I had known. It was as if the Mairéad I had known in the past was dead and gone for ever, and this chameleon had taken her place.

"I knew you'd see sense in the end." Her smile was warm and genuine as she sat down on the black leather sofa, and I took the too-large armchair opposite, sinking back into the upholstery that felt as if it was six feet deep.

I recognised the upmarket perfume she always wore, reminding me of the outdoor fragrances of trees and fields.

"I haven't had the chance yet to discuss with Vernon how much to offer you, but he can afford to be generous. So." She leaned back, smiling. "What finally changed your mind?"

Think. Take it slowly and carefully.

"Have you spoken to Vernon recently?" I asked her.

"Not since you called to see me last. Boy, didn't he just go off the deep end about you." She laughed to herself. "Shouting and raving and threatening all sorts! But I told him to wait, to give you a chance. He doesn't know you like I do. He'll be over the moon when he finds out you're on our side after all."

"Can I just get it straight?" I asked her. "All you want me to do is keep quiet?"

"That's all. You've written the book and sent it to the publishers and in a matter of weeks it'll be on sale. You've done what we wanted."

"But what about Timothy Reason? He's the man who told me about the fake entries in the diary, and he knows Ken wrote those songs, not Adrian. He's going to be a big problem."

She frowned. "Leave it to Vernon, he'll talk him round."

"And if he can't?"

"Relax. Vernon always finds a way."

"And another thing. Will I have to lie on oath in court?"

"What's the matter? That Catholic guilt eating away at you again, Sean?" Again her silvery laugh, as if she hadn't got a care in the world. "No, you won't have to break *your word to God*," she reassured me, smiling. "Writing the book is all we need, and you've already done that, so when it's published we'll be home and dry. If they call you to appear in court, all you have to swear to is the truth: that you copied the information from the diaries, that you used the entries for the dates of the songs he wrote as the basis for the book. That you saw the diaries, which will have been destroyed by then, and that's what the entries stated."

"Would I have to say that other people had corroborated the entries?"

"You'd have to talk to Vernon about that. But don't worry, there's not many people around who know the truth, and the few who are will be on our side, we've been really careful about that."

"Who are we talking about?"

"Oh, just one or two guys from the old days, mates of the Nightingale Green guys. The good thing is that at the time Ken wrote those songs, he was still nominally in a writing partnership with Adrian, they were actually writing songs together concurrently, so only a handful of people actually know for certain who wrote which song, and they were good friends, they trusted each other. Of those few people, some are dead, and the rest we've sorted out."

"But aren't people going to wonder why didn't Adrian notice himself at the time, that Ken Wheeler was claiming to have written songs that were his?"

"Sure, we were worried about that. But everyone knows how useless Adrian was at the business side of things, he trusted his agent, who's dead now. We're arguing that the agent took bribes from Ken Wheeler to hoodwink his client."

"Complicated."

"What did you expect? People don't just come up to you and shower you with cash, you have to be a bit creative and think hard and fast." She sat back in the chair, a dreamy look on her face. "God, Sean, I don't mind telling you. Setting this thing up has been a logistical nightmare. It had better bloody well be worth it."

"You've bribed people who were around at the time to lie about Adrian Dark writing those six songs?"

"Do you have to be so crude?" She frowned. "Jeez, you wouldn't last five minutes at Landseer's. We say things diplomatically, we smooth things over with a nice little layer of finesse. You'd not believe the things the auction house gets up to – selling paintings we know are fakes, but because they've been authenticated by bent experts they go for millions. The antique furniture whose provenance is dodgy. Everyone's at it, you know that, Sean? The more respectable the organisation, the more corrupt they are, all that matters is that you don't get caught. The beauty of this operation is that knowing who wrote those songs is down to the people who were close to Adrian Dark and Ken Wheeler when they were written, which is basically just the members of Nightingale Green, and their friends plus a few odd hangers on. As I say, most of them are dead now. Rock singers don't always make old bones."

"What about Roger Bracken?"

She frowned. "What about him?"

"He's in a coma and likely to die."

"Do you think I don't know that?"

"He must have been one of the people you had to pay for silence."

"What if he was?"

"So if he dies it makes things easier for you, doesn't it." I watched her face carefully. "Was he asking for more money?"

She stood up. "What are you talking about, Sean? What's got into you? Just fuck off with your questions, you're like a little old lady who's fretting about her shopping list! *It's all done and dusted.* It has nothing to do with you anyway. Why are you asking about Roger Bracken? I heard on the news that Roger Bracken was attacked in his own home by that crazy woman, Vernon's mad-arsed half-sister, Laura Kaplan, and that she's been arrested and charged. What's the matter with you?"

"You remember Laura, from the auction, don't you, Mairéad? She was nice. Kind, friendly and talkative. She didn't seem like a murderer to me."

"I remember just before the auction that you couldn't take your eyes off her."

"I've got to know her well."

"Really?" She looked me up and down. "If you charm your way into her knickers it'll only be the start of your troubles, I can promise you that."

"What do you mean by that?"

"Vernon told me all about her. She's mad. And she's dangerous."

"Is she? And how do you know that?"

She stared at me, the beginnings of doubt entering her features. "Believe me, Sean, I know it."

"Tell me about James Patterson. Remember Patterson? The American guy you paid to pretend he wanted the diaries? Who staged that ridiculous pantomime after the auction."

"Getting Patterson to persuade you to give him the diaries was Vernon's idea. I thought it was a wee bit over the top. But he wanted to make sure you were serious enough about the project to fight for it. Plus he thought that it would make you more determined to finish the book quickly – knowing that someone else was in the game."

"Clever."

"A touch of genius so he said. That's Vernon, he dots all the 'i's, crosses every 't'."

"Good old Vernon. And you told me that you and Hugo, the auctioneer, were an item. When all along it was Vernon you're really with, isn't it?"

She stared at me, and laughed. "You're joking, right? Vernon and I aren't anything but business partners. He already has a partner. A young guy called Philip, who's quite a few years younger than he is. Sure, Sean, there's a thing or two you don't know about our Vernon."

"So tell me."

"It doesn't matter. Sure, I'm not one for tittle-tattle. Vernon lives life on the edge. He's into a lot of dangerous enterprises. He sails pretty close to the wind, and right now he needs big money quickly or, he told me, some of his business colleagues are not going to be best pleased." She mimed cutting her throat.

"Vernon's a gangster, in trouble with other gangsters?"

She nodded. "You'd not believe some of the stuff he's

mixed up in. Makes me shiver to think about it."

I waited for her to talk but she didn't go on. "Of course we have to get rid of the diaries now," I told her.

"Oh Jesus, don't we just. The longer they're around the more danger there is that this whole operation could go tits up, because I copied Adrian's handwriting myself, and I'm no expert. It's a certainty that they'd not stand up to scrutiny. Everything is at a mighty delicate stage. The whole thing is hanging by a thread." She held her hand up, making a fist, the knuckles blanching, hard and white and cold. "But we just have to hang on a wee bit longer and we're home and dry. Eventually it'll come to a court case, and it'll be up to a judge and jury to decide and you just never know what might happen. But a book in print that's based on diaries that once existed, that's a good psychological weapon. And every week that goes by, Ken Wheeler's Alzheimer's makes his testimony less and less credible. Time is on our side." Her lovely sky-blue eyes narrowed dangerously. "But, Sean, you're acting a bit weird, do you know that? There's something else going on here, isn't there?"

"Something else?"

"You follow me home here at eight in the evening, unannounced and uninvited, and you tell me you're going to cooperate with our little scheme. Why didn't you just ring me?"

She got up and went across to the mantelpiece, where she picked up a bottle of whisky and poured from it into a glass. "Would you like a drink? After what you put me through these past couple of days I reckon I need one. God, Sean, if you only knew what a relief it is to know that we can rely on you."

"I'm not drinking."

"Really? From what I remember you never used to

refuse a drink. And I don't mind telling you, Sean, that I've been needing quite a bit of this in the last few days." She turned round and took a long pull from the glass she was holding. "When I had this idea, it seemed so simple, you know? When Vernon found out the actual value of Adrian's estate, it was nowhere near what he was expecting – Adrian had a shitload of debts in those final years, and Netherwold had a load of structural problems. Whoever takes it on is going to find it's a money pit. Sure enough, there's a whole heap of cash by most people's standards, don't get me wrong, but Vernon isn't most people, he needs big money, and he needs it fast – he's in some heavy duty trouble right now, he's been borrowing for years on the strength of his big inheritance, and his creditors took the chance, knowing how ill his dad was. He told me it was a mafia family he's in hock to, I didn't enquire too deeply. But that fact is, there aren't even enough assets to cover the inheritance tax without selling all the paintings and artefacts, it's that bad. Vernon has various rackets on the go in London and Leeds, I don't ask any questions, but he's made some bad mistakes recently and upset some pretty high profile characters – the ones you can't argue with, you know?

"And that was when I hit on this idea. At first I couldn't believe we could pull it off. You know that squiffy, slightly scary feeling when you start something full of ideas, then you think it can't possibly work? Yet the more we looked into it, the more obvious it became. Everything was working for us: Adie was permanently in a mess with his business affairs, plus he had schizophrenia and had long since ceased to earn any money. He was hardly aware of what he was doing businesswise, so neglecting to realise he was owed royalties for years and years was quite credible to anyone who knew him. Even though it was a pretty unique set of circumstances, I still wasn't sure if it was worth the risk. But when I looked into how much money was involved, it was too good an opportunity to miss. But it took a heck of a lot of planning and careful handling."

"And I was useful?"

"Sure. You were a godsend. A more experienced writer would have double-checked facts like the songs he was supposed to have written, they'd have been aware of copyright issues, but luckily you just trusted to the one source. And then when you told me you were onto us, God, I was practically on the floor. I had that awful feeling, deep down in my stomach, you know? That feeling deep down in your gut that tells you everything's over. Because make no mistake, if you'd decided not to cooperate we would have been finished. I mean, when I told him, Vernon was shouting and raving, but even he had to realise that without your cooperation we haven't a snowflake's chance in hell of pulling this thing off, and we'd just have to pull the plug on it. But then I needn't have worried at all, need I?" She came across to me. "But tell me, Sean. Why did you come round here to tell me personally?"

"I wanted to see you again."

"I thought that was it," she said, taking my hand and pulling me to my feet. "It's that old feeling again, isn't it? That feeling between us that will never go away. Well, we're on our own here, and I've got the time if you have. It would be a nice way to cement our newfound partnership."

"What about Hugo?"

"Ah, Hugo's nice, he's grand sure enough, but he's not sexy like you, Sean." Her voice was low and husky as she leaned across to whisper in my ear. "God I'm feeling myself get moist just thinking about making love with you, Sean. Ever since I saw you at Christmas, I've been wanting you in my bed. Don't go worrying about Hugo, he's a lovely trusting guy. He likes you and he'll never suspect a thing."

She moved her mouth down to kiss me, but I held her back at the last moment.

And I thought back to Christmastime, when I'd first met this new, different Mairéad, who was so different from the fiery, gifted young woman I had once been in love with. In a flash I could see what she was going to look like many years from now, with wrinkles on her brow and hunted, calculating eyes that could no longer mask their cruelty. Sharp lines were already etched into her forehead and they made her face hard, inscrutable, like a sheet of granite.

"Was I really the love of your life?" I asked her.

"What's that?"

"You told me at Netherwold on that first evening. That I had been the love of your life."

She looked up at me and gave a quick nervous smile. "If only things were different."

"You mean if I was rich?"

"We'll both be rich enough soon, and then who knows?"

"Do you know something?" I asked her as she put the glass on a table and put her arms around my waist, turning her face towards mine, her breath on my chin, so close I could taste it.

"Shut up, Sean. God, I'm hot for you. Why don't you take your shirt off?"

"When I came here I thought you were in on it. I should have realised that while you might be an evil manipulative bitch who despises me, you're not a killer. Vernon organised the attempt on my life without even telling you, didn't he?"

"Attempt on your life?" She looked up at me, frowning. "What in God's name are you talking about?"

THIRTY-FOUR

"I *saved* your life not long ago, in case you've forgotten."

"I know you did." I stepped away from her, deliberately putting distance between us. "But it was more a matter of luck, wasn't it? You happened to come by at the very moment I was being attacked and sure enough you did help me. But that was before I was getting in your way. And before you knew if I had finished the book and sent it off to the publisher." I paused to look at her. "Just after I talked to you, two men abducted me, knocked me out, poured whisky down my throat through a funnel, then drove my car into the middle of nowhere and piped the exhaust through the window with me inside and the engine ticking over. As I had already told you, I had sent the book to the publishers, so if I'd died then everything in your world would have been hunky dory. But after they'd left me, the engine stalled. And then I woke up. If Roger Bracken has been cutting up rough, I'm guessing that Vernon didn't hesitate to deal with him too."

She just stared at me, disbelieving. "Do you seriously expect me to believe—"

"When I came here tonight I was certain that you knew all about it. Maybe it was petty of me, but I wanted to see your reaction when you first saw me, when you knew that

I was still alive. But you're not that rotten, are you? It was all Vernon's idea to kill me and you didn't even know about it."

After a long while she broke eye contact. Her lower lip trembled. "There has to be some mistake! Vernon wouldn't try to kill you. Nor would he attack Roger Bracken. For God's sake! Jeez, Sean, this was all about seizing an opportunity, not engaging in murder! Vernon couldn't kill anyone!"

"Mairéad, I confronted you about what I'd found out, then less than four hours later someone nearly succeeded in killing me, and took great pains to make it look like suicide, even sending a suicide text from my mobile. You knew my best friend was Robin, because we'd chatted on the phone when you first contacted me. You knew that he would be the one I'd text if I was in trouble. You must have told Vernon that, because otherwise, how did he know? You told Vernon that I was onto you both, didn't you?"

"Of course I did." She stamped her foot in anger. But then she sat down in the armchair, staring straight ahead. "Wait a minute. You tell me you were abducted by those men on the same day that you spoke to me?"

"Yes."

"I phoned Vernon straight after you came to see me. He listened quietly, then told me he'd sort things out. But this? God above, I thought he'd come and talk to you, try to persuade you, offer you money. I can't believe he'd do something like this. But then, in the circles he mixes in, he has all the contacts. God, Sean, I'm so fucking sorry about this. What can I say?"

"Anyway, Mairéad, this is why I came to see you tonight. To tell you what I've done. Yesterday afternoon I withdrew the book from the publishers, telling them that we were likely to be prosecuted for fraud if it went into print. Everything you've said to me tonight has been recorded on my phone in case I need to use it later to cover myself legally. In fact I've also been on an open line to a friend of mine who's a reporter, and I've already told her all the details, so she knows the truth too. I've already gone to see Ken Wheeler's solicitors, made a statement, outlining everything I discovered and telling them that I had been an unwitting accomplice in your plan. And I've given them the diaries, and they've given them to experts to analyse the contents, to find out if they've been tampered with recently, as Tim Reason alleges they have been."

She stared at me as if she had been shot. Then she ran from the room, and I heard the sound of her vomiting. When she came back she was wiping her face with a towel.

She sat in the armchair and stared at me.

"You stupid evil bastard," she managed to say at last, her voice barely more than a whisper. "Do you realise what you've done? Landseer's value their reputation. Any hint of impropriety and I'll be out. I was on a fast track to be a partner. If they find out about this. . ."

"Get Vernon to drop the court case and everything ends."

"Does it now? Christ, do you have any idea what you've done? After starting litigation against him, do you think Ken Wheeler is just going to sit back and do nothing? We've publicly accused him of wilfully stealing money from Adrian Dark for years and years. He could sue us for defamation of character. This was always going to be a high risk strategy, but if it went against us, we were planning to say that we'd acted in good faith. If everyone knows this was a scam from the start, God alone knows what will happen. Besides, you've just told me you've let a journalist into your little psychodrama."

"I guess I'm not quite such a useful idiot now, eh? But think on this: if your scheme had backfired, then no one would have believed I wasn't in on it all along. I'd have been prosecuted for fraud alongside the two of you."

"I saved your life, have you forgotten that?"

"For which I'm grateful. But let's not get ahead of ourselves here. You arrived unexpectedly, and that's what gave me the drop on him. It was pure luck."

"Jesus, Sean, what gives you the right to destroy my life?"

"You gave me the right, when you played me for a fool. And when your friend tried to kill me."

"Revenge is sweet, is it?"

"Revenge is shit as far as I'm concerned."

"*Was I the love of your life?*" she mimicked me. "Do you have any idea how pathetic you sounded just now?"

I shrugged.

"You want the truth? Here it is, but buckle up, because you sure as hell ain't going to like it. Sure it's true. I picked you up from the past, and I was in two minds about it. I'd heard that Jodie had come here to see Adrian in the last weeks of his life, and that reminded me of your existence. Because, Sean, far from being my first true love, I'd completely forgotten about you. I knew you'd still be hot for me, I knew I could play the nostalgia card, and that I could get you back. And I did, didn't I? You weren't faking it when you made your play for me that first night, were you? If I hadn't told you about Hugo you'd have come back to me like a shot, wouldn't you? Like a lamb to the slaughter. And if you'd never set eyes on Laura you'd have made love to me, Hugo or not, I know you would have done, you'd not have been able to resist me.

"But there was more to it, from your point of view wasn't there? I didn't expect winning you back to be as easy as it was. And didn't you just lap it up?" she jeered at me. "You were so grateful to come down here to see me, to work on minimum wages doing a decorating job, and then your delight at the chance to write the book. Don't kid me that I had to persuade you to do it! Do you know something? All those years ago, when we went out together. Sure, you looked good and you were a darned good fuck, but that was all there ever was to it! Christ, didn't you know? I used to laugh at you behind your back. So did all my friends. *Faithful Sean,* we used to call you, *Sean with the puppy-dog eyes.* And you never knew, did you?"

I shook my head.

"And do you know something, Sean? There was a reason we laughed at you. You're too soft for this world. You'll always be one of the little people. One of the grubby little nobodies who never quite makes it – one of the also-rans in life. I could hardly believe it when you agreed to come here at Christmas. I mean, what sort of a pathetic excuse for an existence do you have, that you're prepared to travel halfway across the country to work as a decorator on minimum wages at Christmas time, when most people have a family, friends, some kind of life! And then, when you were so eager to write the book, it was almost pitiful!" She leaned forward, hatred blazing in her eyes. "You're pathetic, Sean, do you know it? You're the farm boy who thought he could hit the big time. You were a useless policeman, you're a shit artist, and as for that book you wrote, I'd not use the fucking pages to wipe my arse with! If Jodie hadn't died she'd have got rid of you by now. How she must have despised you when she was alive. You're just a joke, Sean, a bloody useless joke!"

She ran at me and fought like a madwoman, biting, kicking, scratching me as if she was demented. As she sank her teeth into the back of my hand, I brought my hand up and slapped her face, hard, so that she fell backwards.

She lay there on the floor and then sat up slowly, staring up at me, the red patch on her cheek noticeable now. I saw her eyes narrow with loathing. "I'm going to destroy you."

I got up and walked to the door. "So tell me, Mairéad. Just how are you going to destroy me?"

She didn't answer for a long time, just stared at me.

*

Half an hour later I was nearly back at Number 46, when a police car flashed its lights behind me, and I drew in to the side of the road, wondering what I had done wrong.

"Are you Sean Delaney?" asked the policeman, his torch beam in my face.

"Yes."

"Would you mind getting out of the car, sir?"

"Why what have I done?"

He didn't answer, nor did his colleague until I was standing in the street.

"Mr Delaney I am arresting you on suspicion of the assault and subsequent rape of Miss Mairéad O'Shaughnessy earlier on this evening. You do not have to say anything, but anything you do say. . ."

*

"You admit that you hit Ms O'Shaughnessy?" asked Detective Sergeant Lavinia Hart.

"She'd attacked me. We struggled. I hit her once in the face, just to get her to stop attacking me."

"Once?"

"Yes, once."

"To stop her attacking you?"

"That's what I said."

I cursed the fact that my phone had run out of battery more or less at the start of the time I was recording our conversation, so my account couldn't be corroborated.

The interview room at Harington Row Police Station was dark and airless, and the blond haired elfin-faced policewoman's hazel coloured eyes seemed to radiate hatred. Her colleague, a tall thin man called PC Slack, was not saying much, just doing a lot of staring. Abigail Marwood, sitting beside me, was the duty solicitor summoned by the police. I had never met her before, nor did I have much faith in her. She was very young, with very short dark hair, had a very serious face, and was blinking a lot, as if she was longing to get some sleep. I had the feeling that a more astute solicitor would probably have told me to say 'no comment' to many of the questions I'd been asked.

"Okay, Sean. You've told us that Miss O'Shaughnessy was once your girlfriend."

"Yes, a long time ago." It was humiliating, sitting in the prison-issue paper smock, since they'd taken all my clothes for forensic analysis.

"And is she your girlfriend now?"

"No."

"Yet you tell us she contacted you out of the blue to offer you a decorating job, miles from where you live, and you accepted this."

"Yes."

"Why?"

"I needed the work."

"Was that the only reason?"

"No. I was keen to see Netherwold Hall, where

Mairéad had invited me to an auction, because it was one of the last places my wife visited before she was murdered, and I wanted to find out anything I could about her meetings with Adrian Dark, the owner."

"So you met up with her and rekindled your romance?"

"No, not at all."

"Yet you arrived at her home earlier tonight, you stayed quite a long time and you left after having an argument?"

"Yes."

"What was the argument about?"

I sighed. It was all irrelevant but there was no point refusing to answer. "I had found out that she and Vernon Dark, Adrian Dark's son, had been trying to use me in their effort to sue a songwriter, who they were claiming had wrongly taken millions over the years, which should have been paid to Adrian Dark, because they were claiming Dark wrote songs accredited wrongly to Ken Wheeler. I found this was untrue, so I made a statement to Ken Wheeler's solicitor along those lines. Two days ago, I was abducted and an attempt was made on my life. I believe that Vernon Dark was behind the attack, his attempt to silence me. I wanted to confront Mairéad for trying to trick me like that."

"And she was angry?"

"Yes. That's why she's concocted this story."

"Um," Lavinia Hart went on, sneering with disdain. "She says that you called round to her home tonight uninvited, and forced yourself on her. When she refused to have sex with you, you first of all attacked her, terrorised her. And then you raped her."

"She's lying."

"Your face is scratched, and we've found blood on her body which we're testing for your DNA. She has extensive bruising around her wrists, breasts and thighs, and strangulation bruises on her throat."

"She must have done it herself. I hit her once in the face, no more than that, and then I left."

"You hit her?"

"She was attacking me."

"Why would she injure herself?"

"Because she hates me and wants to pay me back for exposing her fraud. You won't find any of my semen anywhere on her."

"Come on, Sean, you were in the police! You know that only one third of sexual assaults result in the rapist ejaculating into a bodily orifice. We found evidence of trauma to her vagina and perineum."

"Not caused by me. She could have done it to herself."

"Have you any idea of the suffering that a rape victim undergoes?" The male policeman, PC Slack, took up the questioning. He had a rapidly receding hairline and large brown, deeply miserable eyes. "And the number of people who don't even report the crime, because they're afraid of all the legal ramifications? Victims of rape often just want to forget about it, to make it go away."

"Sure, I know that."

"But Ms O'Shaughnessy has gone through with it, made a full and detailed statement."

I nodded.

It was clear that neither of the police officers believed me.

A couple of hours later, my solicitor came to my cell to inform me that I was being charged and would be told when I had to appear in court.

Fortunately, thanks to asking them to phone my ex-boss at the Met, Superintendent Hardy, I was granted bail on the strict conditions that I had no contact of any kind with Mairéad O'Shaughnessy, nor could I go within two miles of where she lived or worked.

THIRTY-FIVE

I had already packed up my painting equipment and few possessions in the car and handed over the keys to 46 Latimer Row to Landseer's head office in Bath. Paul Bradbeer, the rather irritated looking middle-aged man in charge of the estate agency team, invited me into his office, where I recognised Hugo, the friendly auctioneer I had met at Christmas. The man whom Mairéad had told me was her boyfriend.

When Bradbeer left the room, Hugo lost no time in abruptly punching me hard in the guts. I almost sank down to my knees.

"Report me to the police for assault if you like," he snarled through gritted teeth. "I don't care. You bastard! Mairéad did all she could to help you, she'd gone on about what a lovely guy you were, one of her oldest friends from art school! And in return you put your filthy hands on her, and forced her to. . ." He couldn't even say the words.

When he took another swing at me I blocked his arm, grabbed his wrist, and spun him around, twisting the arm up behind his back, forcing it up high so he cried out in pain.

"I didn't hit you back just now. You were lucky!" I told him.

When he went on struggling I applied more pressure. "Look, Hugo, before I do you a permanent injury, listen to what I'm saying! I did nothing wrong. I never touched your girlfriend until she attacked me, and then I just gave her a tap to make her stop. I never touched her inappropriately, and I swear to you here and now that I certainly did *not* have sex with her."

"Then why have the police charged you with rape?" He'd stopped struggling now. "Mairéad has no reason to make up a story like that, and I happen to know that police only press charges when they're pretty certain they can get a conviction. You're going to jail, sonny boy, and that's where you belong."

He'd ratcheted down his anger, and I judged that it was safe to let him go. He turned to face me, grimacing as he shook his arm to alleviate the pain.

"Do you know what she tried to do to me?" I asked him.

"No, and I don't care," he said, coming close to me, his face within an inch of my own. "But I know what you did to her."

"Were you in on it too?" I asked him.

"In on it? What the hell are you talking about?"

"Landseer's are going to be implicated in a big scandal, and it's not going to do your three-hundred-year unblemished reputation any favours. Mairéad and Vernon Dark forged entries in the Adrian Dark diaries sold to me at the Landseer's auction, in order to substantiate a fraudulent claim against songwriter Ken Wheeler over copyright issues and payments over many years. I was unwittingly caught up in their scam and I blew the whistle."

"Don't talk rubbish." Hugo looked as if he was going to hit me again. "Mairéad would never get herself involved in something like that."

"I've ruined her career with Landseer's," I told him. "That's why she hates me so much. You'll find out soon enough."

"Piss off, you lying bastard!"

*

It was midday, and I felt tired out.

What's that ridiculous phrase? *Sticks and stones can break my bones but words will never hurt me.*

If words will never hurt you you're a pretty shallow human being. I was still feeling shocked after all the things Mairéad had said to me, and the utter humiliation I felt at her words was so mind-numbing I tried not to think about it. Had she always despised me? Had I always been the village idiot at art school, the provincial innocent who everybody made fun of? I thought back to all the failures in my life, all the people I had trusted who had let me down. And she had got a point. When she contacted me before Christmas I had been at rock bottom in my life, pathetically grateful to get a bit of decorating work, and then over the moon at the chance to write another book.

I had originally come to Bath to try and find out who had murdered my wife and why. And I was still no closer to the answer.

The girl I had once thought I knew better than anyone had tried to use me to perpetuate a fraud, and I had fallen for it, in the process wasting weeks of time writing a book, and burning my bridges with my publisher. I was charged with rape, which, if I was found guilty, could lead to a custodial sentence, and it was literally my word against hers.

I was in love with Laura Kaplan, but despite writing to her at the prison, telling her that I believed her, that I *really believed* she had not attacked Roger Bracken, she still would not reply to me, despite me apologising for ever doubting her.

For the past couple of hours I'd been feeling strange, shivery, as if all that had happened was finally catching up with me. I was sitting in my car and leaned back in the seat, trying to sleep, but I couldn't. The shivering was getting worse, and my shoulders and neck were aching, plus I had a thumping headache. I felt like I had a temperature.

I made the decision to go back home to Kent, for where else could I go? I was obviously in the early stages of flu, and I wanted to get away from this damned place, with all its associations.

*

By some miracle I managed to successfully drive back home to Whitstable, despite shivering so badly that a couple of times I had pull off the road and rest. Once home, I went straight to bed and fell into a deep dreamless sleep.

Next day, Kate phoned to tell me to look at the *Daily Recorder*. On page two was the story of how Vernon Dark and Mairéad O'Shaughnessy had falsified diary entries in order to support their claim for lost royalty and back catalogue payments from songwriter Ken Wheeler. According to the article an 'unnamed source' had gone along with the scheme in order to lay a trap for them, pretending to write a book based on the diaries, all along planning to lay the secrets bare. Lawyers for Vernon Dark had withdrawn the court case, but it seemed that Ken Wheeler had instructed his lawyers to launch a counter claim against Vernon Dark for libel.

I've never had flu quite like it, and for the next three days my temperature raged, and I could hardly eat, just managing sips of water and dry toast.

*

Laura

"There've been further developments, Miss Kaplan. That's why you've been released without charge."

I was sitting in the back of the cab with my solicitor, Jane Harryman, still stunned and astonished at this unexpected turn of events. The police hadn't even had the grace to apologise or explain what had happened, simply told me I was free to go, and taken me outside to the police station front desk, made me sign for my belongings, and escorted me outside, to where Jane was waiting to take me home to Bath.

"From what I've been able to find out, it seems that Roger Bracken came out of the coma a while ago and he's no longer in a critical condition. He's been able to talk. He told them that you didn't attack him."

The scenery flashed past and I tried to make sense of it all.

"So who did attack him? Did he recognise his attacker?"

"I don't know. We'll find out soon enough."

I was out of this hell. *They believed I was innocent.*

"Then whoever killed him knew that I'd been there and that I'd picked up the table lamp. How could anyone know that?"

"My guess is that just after you left, Roger Bracken phoned someone to tell them what had happened. Whoever it was had a serious grudge against the man, and seized the opportunity to kill him and have a ready-made suspect to take the blame."

"But who would you call in a situation like that?" I

wondered. "It would surely be someone close to you. A relative or a friend."

"Or else someone who needed to know about your visit. Someone connected with what was going on."

And now everything was possible.

Was there still a chance I could have a relationship with Sean? He'd always believed in me, he'd apologised, after all.

What did I have to lose by contacting him?

*

Sean

While I was lying in bed with a raging temperature, I answered the phone, my throat so sore I was barely able to speak.

"Sean?"

"Laura? God, is it really you?"

"What's wrong with your voice?"

"Hell of a sore throat. Must've got flu."

"Well it's good news. I've been released without charge. Roger Bracken recovered enough to tell them the truth."

"So it's over?"

"So my solicitor tells me."

"And can you forgive me?"

There was a long pause. "I've been thinking about it all the time I've been held on remand. I wanted to hate you when you didn't believe me. It would have been so much easier to hate you. But somehow, in spite of everything, I couldn't."

"I've been thinking about you all this time. When you wouldn't let me visit, what could I do?"

"Christ, Sean, my head's been all over the place. I just blamed you. I hated you at the time, but I realised that I was wrong about so many things. I *did* promise you not to go and see him. I shouldn't have done it. You don't really know me. You'd only just discovered that I've been living a double life as a weekend climber, so I can hardly blame you for thinking I could be lying about other things."

"And can we start again? Start again afresh?" I asked her.

"I want to do that. I want that more than anything. Sean, thinking of you was the only thing that kept me going when I was in prison. I thought I could make it alone, just like I've always had to. I thought I could do it, but I can't. The thought of losing you forever was more than I could stand."

I explained to her that I had flu, and that as soon as I was recovered I would come down and see her.

Two days later I was fit enough to travel. I had one more score to settle before seeing Laura again.

Maybe it was stupid to want to confront the bastard who had tried to kill me simply for the crime of not cooperating in his fraudulent scheme. But I wasn't about to let him get away with it.

I was going to get my revenge on bloody Vernon Dark, the evil little shit who, apart from anything else, had done his best to ruin the life of Ken Wheeler, a sick old man he didn't even know.

It was pitch dark as I retraced the route to Netherwold Hall that I had taken only a few weeks previously, which now seemed like a lifetime ago. When I had arrived full of hope, longing to see my first ever girlfriend, and hoping she might still be interested in me. How different everything had been then, when I'd turned up at the Hall, naive and trusting, to enter this new nightmare world of cruelty, death and betrayal.

Luckily the entrance gate wasn't locked, and I drove

up the winding road, stopping in the front drive and parking next to a white Mercedes saloon.

Of course, Vernon Dark was a desperate man, and possibly he was deranged. He might want to kill me now purely because he had lost everything he'd been working towards. Perhaps it was foolish to go alone to see him.

As I got out and passed the other car I felt its bonnet. Warm. Meaning that Vernon had most likely arrived home not long ago. I hardly noticed the racing bicycle that was leaning against a tree, apparently abandoned there.

Instinct is a funny thing, and in the freezing chill of the night, as my exhaled breath clouded up to the sky, I had the strange weird feeling that something was wrong about the big old house, for there was some indefinable difference about the place. It still skulked there on the skyline, the copper verdigrised statues on their plinths in front of the grand porch. And yet there was a change in the place, some indefinable aura I picked up on.

All the lights were on, the windows blazing with yellow brightness against the black of the night sky. When I got closer to the front door I could see that it was already open an inch. There were sounds from inside, the loud sounds of people talking. Yet if there had been a party, surely there'd have been more vehicles parked in the drive?

I edged the door fully open, crossed the step and walked down the hall, getting closer to where the sound was coming from. I stopped outside the double doors leading to the main dining hall, the large room that had been used for the Landseer's auction.

As I moved closer to listen I could hear that the voices weren't live human voices, for they had a tinny, stagey quality. There was background soundtrack, music and effects, audience laughter. There was clearly a television on in the room, some mindless game show, set to high volume.

The door wasn't locked and I entered at a run, ready for anything.

The large plasma television took up a large part of the wall, and the inane contestants in the game show were sitting behind a plinth, gurning and guffawing towards the camera, while a blond woman presenter was capering along behind them, shrieking and giggling.

And below the screen, on the multicolours of the marble tiled floor, Vernon's body was face down, lying in a huge pool of his own blood.

I walked closer, inspecting the body, which was lying on its back. There was no movement, and I could see the liquid dribbling from the edges of the huge gash across his midriff. I bent down to check on him, but his eyes were fixed and frozen, no breath came from his mouth. It was obvious that there was no point in calling an ambulance.

Then I remembered the Jaguar parked outside. I remembered that its bonnet had been warm, meaning whoever had driven it had arrived recently.

Meaning that Vernon had been murdered shortly after he'd arrived home.

Or else?

Perhaps the car belonged to the killer, who might still be here.

I froze, looking round carefully.

Then I saw him. A black-clad figure wearing a balaclava, still holding a large bloodstained knife. I stared at him for a few seconds, expecting him to rush me. Then I saw my chance. I ran hell for leather towards the window, managed to pull up the sash and climb outside and drop to the ground. I rolled over and over, grateful to feel the harsh stabs of gravel, then I picked myself up and ran towards my car, jumped in and roared away.

As I drove down the Yaddlethorpe Road I reflected that I really didn't care who had killed Vernon, or why.

But the killer had seen my face, and knew that I knew what he had done.

According to Mairéad, Vernon was a criminal who had made powerful enemies, so it was likely that it was one of these people who had settled the score tonight, some gangland enemy who had taken a final revenge.

I was already charged with a serious crime, and answering questions as to why I had been present at a murder scene was not something I wanted to face.

I hadn't noticed any CCTV cameras in the house, and I'd been wearing gloves, so wouldn't have left any fingerprints on doors or walls.

So with any luck, no one would ever know I had been there.

Apart from whoever had killed Vernon.

THIRTY-SIX

I spent the rest of the night in a Travelodge. When I slept I was dead to the world, apart from my nightmares where, as always, Jodie appeared, yelling at me, telling me I had got everything wrong, and that her killer was. . .

There it ended, with Jodie aching to tell me the name, indeed *starting to say a name*, and then falling backwards, down and down as if she was falling through an eternity of space to a place where I could never follow her. This dream had become a recurrent nightmare, so much so that I almost dreaded falling asleep.

But the morning dawned, fresh and bright. After all the hell I had been through: barely surviving an attempt on my life, confronting Mairéad and then being held in custody for rape, and finally coming face to face with the killer of Vernon Dark, I wondered if life was going to be a bit calmer for a change.

I thought of the good things in my life. The best of which was the prospect of seeing Laura again. Somehow, I had finally come to terms with what she was. Now, after going to France with Kate, and reading Dr Fanshaw's notes, I was completely satisfied that she did not have any deep dark secrets in her life. With a shudder I realised that if she ever found out that I had gone to such lengths because I was afraid she was a liar, she would never forgive me. Starting a relationship with secrets was never a good idea, but what alternative did I have?

When I arrived at Novelicious the next day, Laura fell into my arms, and I held her tight. In that moment, nothing else seemed to matter.

"Oh God, Sean, it's all been such a bloody awful nightmare," she muttered, breathing hard, pulling me closer. "I was such an idiot to go and see Roger Bracken, such an *idiot*, and yet still you came and rescued me. I never thought I'd be with you here again, like this. Why do we always seem to mess everything up?"

"I don't know," I replied. "But there's something you have to know. Vernon Dark is dead. I found his body last night."

"Dead?" She stared at me in amazement. "What the hell happened?" She led me upstairs to the privacy of her workshop in the attic.

"What a mess," she told me, after I had recounted all that had happened to me recently. "So, when you found Vernon's body, did you call the police?"

"No, I couldn't."

"Why not?"

"They'd have asked too many questions."

"There was nothing on the local morning news about it."

"Bloody hell." I shook my head to try to clear the burgeoning headache. "Well, I suppose some friend of his will eventually call at Netherwold and find the body."

"How could you be sure he was dead?"

"He was motionless, and the amount of blood was massive. Looked as if he'd been stabbed in the stomach a number of times, judging by the state of him."

"And you actually saw the killer?" she asked.

"Yes, just for a few seconds. But he wore some kind of jump suit and a balaclava – I couldn't have given the police a description of him anyway. By not informing the police it does mean that I've impeded the investigation by delaying it, but what else could I do? My real worry is, that he saw me too. But with any luck he won't even know who I am."

"So he was carrying the knife and he took it with him?"

"I suppose so, or perhaps he dropped it, I don't know. All I cared about was getting out alive. For a moment I thought he was going to get rid of me too."

"Poor darling, what a hell of a time you've had," she said, pulling me closer. "Who do you think it was?"

"Goodness knows." A wave of tiredness swept over me as I strained to make sense of the last twenty-four hours. "But Mairéad told me Vernon was mixed with some shady people and had made some powerful enemies. I knew that of course, because he had the connections to arrange for those goons to try to organise my suicide. Mairéad said that he was mixed up in drug deals and owed a lot of money to the kind of people you don't mess around with."

"But if he owed them money, why would they kill him? What would be the point?"

"Hard to say. But criminals like to make examples of people for others. They need to be respected."

My legs were giving way, and I broke away from her, and sank down on the battered old sofa, covering my face with my hands.

"What is it, darling?" Laura asked me, beside me in an instant.

Having been tough and stoical, having reined in my emotions for all this time, holding her close had opened the floodgates. I held her in my arms, the words tumbling out in a frenzy. "It's *everything*. Everything I touch gets fucked. I came down here to try and find out why my wife had been murdered, and also to earn a bit of money at the same time. Like a fool, I leapt at the chance to write the book about Adrian Dark, because I was vain, reckoning on being a sensational writer because I wanted to show off. Then I found that I was being used as a patsy in a scheme to swindle an old man. I'm no closer to solving the mystery of Jodie's death. I met you, I fell in love with you, and I was determined to help you find out what really happened to your mother and get some kind of justice for you. And I haven't even been able to do that. I've completely failed you. And do you know the strangest thing? I have this feeling that the answer to everything is *this close* but that I'm too stupid to see it."

I thought too, cringing inwardly, of how I had betrayed Laura by going to France with Kate, checking up on her theory that Laura might have deliberately killed a man in Paris. But Kate had promised never to sell that particular article, so my secret was safe with her. Right now I didn't care that Laura lived some kind of a double life. None of it mattered to me anymore. All that mattered was that she was here with me now.

"So has something else happened?"

"Yes. When I confronted Mairéad about using me for her scheme, she reacted in a way I hadn't expected. Stupidly I never even saw it coming."

"What happened?"

"After I'd gone, she phoned the police, accused me of raping her. I've been charged, I have to appear in court within days, and I'm out on police bail. That's the reason why I couldn't tell the police about finding Vernon's body."

"I see." She looked into my eyes. "What do you think will happen?"

"Anything. It's my word against hers."

"But surely there has to be some kind of evidence."

I shook my head. "In two-thirds of rape cases, ejaculation doesn't occur. Penetration is the rape, and it's easy enough to simulate that, and also to give yourself a lot of bruises and claim you were also assaulted."

"She hates you that much?"

I nodded. "I'm hoping she might calm down. Drop the charges."

"If you're found guilty, what could happen?"

I shrugged. "It's a serious charge. I could get a prison sentence."

"Well, it's all going to be all right," she said to me gently. "You've got me. I'll help you though everything. Tell me, did you always believe I was innocent, that I didn't hit Roger Bracken with that lamp?"

"Yes," I lied. "I never doubted you."

And then something happened. Our faces were close and the kiss wasn't meant to happen, but it did.

Soon, nothing mattered but feeling our bodies close, my hands caressing her face, smoothing the hair from her eyes, and feeling the raging warmth of my desire growing.

She felt it too, and without a word, she ripped my shirt off, and I pulled off her top, revealing her small pointed breasts beneath the skimpy black bra.

Very soon we were both naked, and then she felt my hardness and kissed me again. She sank backwards onto the sofa, lying there, gripping my penis and guiding me between her thighs until I was pushing inside and then withdrawing, repeating the thrusting again and again as she panted with pleasure, and the points of her nipples pressed hard against my chest. We reached our peaks of pleasure at the same time.

Afterwards we got dressed slowly.

"That's the first time it's ever happened to me properly," she told me. "The first time it's ever felt right. Always before, I've had to stop at the last moment. But with you, everything was wonderful. That means something, Sean. It means that you're right for me. Finally I've found the one man in the world that I can love."

"I think I fell in love with you from the first moment I set eyes on you," I told her. "Anyway, I'm really sorry, but I've got to go back to Whitstable, to sort a few things out, but I'll be back as soon as I can."

After the misery of the last few days I felt my heart swelling with joy.

At last my life had some kind of purpose.

It was only later that I thought back to the significance of what happened on that day. . .

THIRTY-SEVEN

Laura, three days later. . .

"So, Mr Furby, I inherit the lot? The house, the money, all my father's estate, the back catalogue of his music?"

"Yes, Miss Kaplan, it seems that you do."

"I really don't believe it. I can't believe it!"

"Well, I assure you that it's true."

News of my half-brother's death had been all over the papers and TV yesterday and this morning my father's solicitor, Gareth Furby, had called in at Novelicious to see me. Gareth had been administering Adrian Dark's estate, and I'd spoken to him several times on the phone in connection with my inheritance. The only time I had seen him previously was at the auction at Netherwold, gossiping with Vernon about something.

He was a short squat man with a neat moustache, pebble-lensed spectacles, receding black hair and a permanent half-smile that wobbled on his lips, part deference, part good nature. He had only been here a short time, yet he was looking warily at the dust on all the surfaces of the furniture in the office, the empty box of teabags on the table alongside the small mound of spilt sugar that was going hard at the edges where tea had soaked it and dried out. Gareth was too well-bred to make his distaste for sitting on the dusty chair, apparent. I imagined his office would be like the man: ordered, tidy, and clean.

"It's all very unexpected," he went on. "A bit of a bombshell, really. I thought it was best to come straight round her to see you."

"But I'm still confused. How come I inherit everything? Vernon only knew of my existence for a few months, and he didn't even like me."

"It was your father, not Vernon, who left it to you."

"My father?"

"Let me explain. A long-stop beneficiary is also sometimes called a default beneficiary, and it is usually the last remaining relative of the testator, or even a charity if there is no one else. The essence of a default beneficiary, is that the testator never expects it to be required except in the most unlikely or unexpected circumstances, that's why it's buried in the body of the text of a will, not in the main section. One of the situations it's made for is that it's a provision made for if you and all your family – the people you would normally leave it to – are all killed at the same time, for instance in a plane crash. So if all of the people you would have left your money to are also dead, where does your money go? Hence, if there's no one else at all, a charity is often nominated as a default beneficiary.

"But a more usual situation might also be if the person you leave it to dies soon after the original testator. Imagine a situation, say, where two elderly siblings might leave each other their estates. However, being of similar ages, the second sibling might die soon after the first, and so, without a third person or charity to inherit the money, it would be as if both of them had died intestate, and the Rules of

Intestacy would apply, and the nearest relative would have to be traced. If no one could be traced, then the whole of both of the estates would go to the Crown. Hence in a situation of just one person inheriting the bulk of the estate, it's usual to put in a clause such as 'If so and so dies within twenty-eight days of my own death, then my money goes to such-and-such', the such-and-such being the default beneficiary.

"It's my job to think of every eventuality, and as you know Vernon and you are Adrian Dark's only descendants. At the time Adrian made his will, fifteen years ago now, Vernon was going through a bad patch, he was an alcoholic, a drug addict and suffering extreme mental problems, and he had attempted suicide more than once already. Adrian had it in his mind that if his son suddenly inherited a fortune, he might go wild on drink and drug-fuelled binges, as he had done several times already when he got his hands on any money, and by doing so he might go too far and end up dead. Also, at the time, Vernon had a very unpleasant person whom he was planning to marry, so if Vernon died that character would have got the lot on his demise."

"Who was she?"

"Err, that was another thing. It was a 'he'. Vernon has lived a hedonistic lifestyle, an unconventional one certainly. There was the distinct prospect of him having contracted the HIV virus at the time, and back then the drugs weren't so good, and it used to be a death sentence. So, because of this possibility, of him drinking himself to death or dying of AIDS and this man who Adrian hated getting the money, Adrian reckoned that sixty days was a reasonable period for Vernon to survive. He said that if he survived sixty days, then that was fair enough for him to leave it to whoever he might want to. So he put you in his will as the default beneficiary, to inherit his money if Vernon died within sixty days after the death of his father. Now this is longer than the usually permitted period of twenty-eight days, but since it was included in the will and legally stipulated it is perfectly legal. And in the event, had he lived one more day, you wouldn't have got a penny."

"I just never imagined. . . Me? Inheriting Netherwold Hall and all the money."

"I'm afraid much of the contents of the house has had to be sold to pay the IHT, but because you inherit under the same will as Vernon did, there is only one tranche of inheritance tax due. But there's still the house and a substantial amount left over. Not to mention his back catalogue income. The *legitimate* back catalogue income I mean, the royalties and so on from the songs Adrian actually did write. I heard that Vernon had been launching some kind of legal challenge to another songwriter, Ken Wheeler, about the legitimacy of Mr Wheeler's compositions."

"Mr Furby, clearly I have to wait for probate to come through before I can take possession of Netherwold, and I know that can be a lengthy process."

"Some months as a rule. But fortunately the preliminaries have gone through, so it shouldn't take long now."

"But am I allowed to do anything to the place?"

"Do anything?"

"Since you're the executor, and Vernon was the other executor, I imagine that allows you certain discretion to allow various things to be done."

"Well, yes it does."

"When I saw Netherwold Hall on the day of the auction I couldn't help noticing that the roof of the chapel in the grounds was leaking. I noticed that it's starting to cause rot in the floor, and things are just getting worse and worse. Would I be authorised to have the roof repaired, do you think?"

"Yes, yes, certainly. I'm not sure if I could authorise releasing funds from the estate for the work—"

"Oh that doesn't matter at all. I'd be prepared to pay. And would I be allowed on the premises, to supervise the work?"

"In a situation like this I can see no reason why not. Yes, I have no objection at all, Ms Kaplan. I'll let you have a set of keys and you can authorise contractors to start work whenever you want."

*

Detective Constable Cope

I looked at my diagram and concentrated hard.

It was always better when you noted everything down, when you assessed things properly, rather than just go in, guns blazing.

I was in my study, the room where I can concentrate best. Here, I can play my music, read and think and log on to the *White Knights* and *Britain's Dawn* websites and Twitter feeds, and listen to my music. Because you know, lots of stuff is going on right now, all over the world. *They* are causing trouble everywhere, as usual. Distributing drugs to children, luring white girls into prostitution. They are gradually taking our country away from us.

The thought of my own mother ever considering having sex with one of those animals is beyond belief.

My father being cuckolded by Jimi Hendrix? And then, when he'd found out, effectively murdering him?

What the fuck?

How could anyone ever believe utter bollocks like that?

But evil Adrian Dark had wanted to peddle the myth, and some people would have believed it.

It was strange, looking back.

I thought of summer last year when we had been called out to Netherwold Hall by Mr Dark to investigate the kids vandalising the estate. Dark had gone outside the room with one of my colleagues, and on the desk, I had seen his handwritten notes. When I saw the name of my own father there, I did a double take. I started reading the preposterous tale, of road manager Jack Dolman murdering Jimi Hendrix because his wife was pregnant with Hendrix's child. I thought back to the chill of horror that ran through me, made me feel almost physically sick. The bloody man was writing this in a book, he was going to have this shit published! People would read it and believe it. I had already changed my name so that no one connected me with Nightingale Green's roadie, but there was always the chance that someone might find out the truth of my parentage. And then, if they believed that Hendrix had really been my father. . .

I broke out in a sweat again as I thought of the vial of saliva I had posted off a couple of weeks ago to the genealogy company, for detailed DNA analysis, to establish my ethnicity.

Of course I knew that the result would be that I was one hundred per cent Caucasian, how could it be anything else? But it would be handy to have that fact scientifically verified, for my own peace of mind. And if, God forbid, any rumours that Jimi Hendrix might have been my father ever did surface, I had a great way of counteracting them, using the results of this new technology.

The company *ancestry.co.uk* had only started analysing people's DNA since January of this year. The technology was new, but they claimed that they could give you hard and fast facts about your ethnic origin.

What did I have to fear? I knew beyond doubt that my ancestors had all been Caucasian. By all accounts some of the company's results had been surprising. Not only had they estimated people's genetic make-up with a degree of accuracy, but by comparing your DNA information with that of others who'd also had their DNA tested, they claimed they could even find probable first cousins you never knew you had.

Of course Adrian Dark had had to die, to stop him peddling that ridiculous myth of Hendrix being my father.

I had only recently found out that the Irishman, Sean Delaney, had obtained Adrian Dark's diaries and other papers. Was he going to write Adrian Dark's biography? And if he did, was he planning to include the first chapter, written by Adrian Dark, that I had read, where he describes my father murdering Jimi Hendrix and why?

It would have been a big mistake to kill Delaney before he's told me where the notes are. I have to find his computers too, make sure there are no copies of the documents anywhere.

And, of course, I really do not want to kill Sean Delaney if I can avoid it.

Because I had found out all about his police record. Of how he had been hounded out of the force, because he had accidentally killed one of *them.* Trevor Goodbody, the black drug dealer he'd killed, had also been a pimp, who had ponced out sweet little white girls after poisoning them with drugs to make them complicit in his sex games. Sean Delaney had killed him and in my book Delaney deserved a bit of credit for doing that alone. All he has to do is give me the incriminating papers so I can destroy them! It isn't too much to ask, is it, for God's sake?

But if I just demand them, he's not going to hand them over. So I have to use some leverage to get him to tell me where they are, and to force him not to divulge what's in them.

Leverage.

The best plan is to capture someone close to him, then tell him that she's in my power and he has to do what I tell him, or she dies very slowly.

Laura Kaplan.

She is the obvious target, the obvious one to use. When I saw the way he looked at her, the love in his eyes, what's more he even pretended to be engaged to her. Oh yeah. She's the one that he cares about.

THIRTY-EIGHT

Laura

Gareth had let me have the keys in order to 'take a look around the place'. Evidence of the discovery of Vernon's body having been here was still there, crime-scene tape sealing the closed door to the room where his body had been found.

Why does everything always seem to happen at once? This morning an old client rang and told me about a number of first-edition Wakelings that were going for a song in an Edinburgh estate sale.

Nathaniel Wakeling was a poet in the eighteenth century, his work not particularly well known. But he had owned his own printing works, the volumes he produced were filled with original illustrations, and the paper was best quality 'laid' paper, with a latticework pattern and his special 'W' watermark on every page. These particular books had been kept in a collector's library, and apparently were in mint condition, something that is very rare indeed. Ordinarily I wouldn't have been able to afford such wonderful collectors' items, but now that it's only a matter of a few months before I get Adrian's money, I'd be crazy to pass them up wouldn't I, especially as they'll form the basis for my new library, based at Netherwold? I'd buy them by maxing out my credit cards if necessary, knowing that the money was coming in soon.

I have *always* loved Wakeling's work. And these particular volumes were ones I had read about, and that I have *really, really* wanted for years. It was bad timing that just as I was hoping to have time to be alone with Sean, to consolidate our relationship, this had to happen.

But Sean would understand when I explained it to him. Sean would always understand, that was one of the reasons why I loved him. Besides, he'd told me he had a few things to sort out at his home in Whitstable. I could go to Scotland, get the books and come back and it would all be done and dusted within a week.

And then who knows? Now I had inherited Netherwold Hall, what was to stop Sean moving in there with me in time? Sure, it might be moving our relationship too fast, but it's what I want. It's what I want more than anything.

But does Sean want it too?

Jane Harryman had told me that when Roger Bracken recovered, he had told police that it was Vernon who had attacked him, and not me. As Sean had already explained to me, it seemed that Vernon had been suing another songwriter for years of royalties and performance rights for a number of songs that he claimed that his father had written. Roger had phoned Vernon, told him of my visit, saying that I was threatening to stir up trouble for him, and he was determined to keep a low profile and wanted to back out of his arrangement to back up Vernon's legal case in return for money. In fact Roger had actually threatened to tell the authorities that the legal challenge had been a scam from the start. Vernon had driven straight round to see him, then had become so angry that he had flown off the handle and attacked him and left him for dead.

And now Vernon himself was dead.

As I walked through the building, I realised that at last something was going my way. Finally, after all my struggles, I had, miraculously, won out in life.

Life was so wonderful I was almost scared that it would all fall apart. This morning I had enjoyed a long conversation with Sean, telling him about how I had inherited Netherwold. He was coming down to see me in a week's time, after I'd got back from Scotland, hopefully the proud possessor of twelve of the most beautiful volumes of poems that has ever been produced. They would form the centrepiece of the library of rare volumes that I was planning to establish at Netherwold.

The outside chapel was separate from the main building, set back in the woods. I tried all the keys on the large rings that Gareth had given me, and eventually found the one that opened the lock, then eased the door open on its rusty hinges.

Pieter van Dries had claimed that my mother had died and that the band members of Nightingale Green had buried her under the chapel floor, utilising the trench already excavated by British Gas (the utility company that had been founded just the year before), who had been installing a new pipeline there. It was well worth investigating the possibility, even though it was a longshot.

I put down the pickaxe and spade I had been carrying, and examined the floor itself. Large flagstones by the look of it. A few near the entrance looked slightly different from the rest, so I swung the pickaxe point in between two of them, and managed to prise up a corner, then heaved the slab out of the way.

When a fairly large area of earth had been exposed I began to dig.

I was worn out after half an hour, and took a break.

In all it took most of the rest of the day to excavate just a small area. But finally, as I was about to swing the pickaxe below the foot of earth I had already dug out, I glimpsed something yellowy and twig-like. On my hands and knees I carefully cleaned the soil away, and sure enough found that it appeared to be the bones of a human hand.

THIRTY-NINE

Sean

There was just one last place I wanted to visit before leaving the West Country. One last throw of the dice to try to once and for all solve the mystery of my wife's death.

I had been told that Adrian Dark had been buried at St Mary's and All Saints, the twelfth-century parish church of Penton Feverill, and that he'd been well-liked locally. It was strange to think that this was the same sleepy country village where I'd stopped to rescue the drowning dog just before Christmas last year, marking the start of all my troubles.

I parked in the tiny high street, close to the river where I'd encountered the drowning dog and his family. The church was near here, as was the tiny Spar supermarket-cum-post office. I went into the little shop, enjoying the wet-cardboard smell that old-fashioned grocers always seem to have, and bought some bits and pieces for the long journey back to Kent.

It struck me that this lovely old village had been the place where poor little Laura Kaplan had shivered alone on that terrible night of the fifteenth to sixteenth of October

1987, the night of the Great Storm. How terrified she must have been, abandoned, not knowing where on earth she was, scared stiff, searching for her mother in the darkness, with the wind picking up stronger all the time.

When I had first come here it had been almost evening, the light nearly gone, snow showers on the wind, the gloom of winter, in contrast to the sunshine of this summer morning.

Halfway along the road I found the old church and went through the ancient lych gate that led to the large churchyard. Finding the grave was fairly easy, it was a question of looking for the most recent burials. I found it behind the church, at the edge of a large field, with a fine view out over the hills. There was no headstone, just a rudimentary wooden cross with a brass plaque, with just his birth and death details above the mound of risen earth. Of course, I realised, there couldn't be a proper headstone until the soil had settled.

I heard a dog barking in the distance, then coming closer. As I stood there I recognised Roger, the dog whose life I had saved on my first day in Penton Feverill, bounding towards me, in the company of a woman. As he came up to me and I stroked him, and knelt down for him to lick my face, I recognised the lady I had met before.

"It's so nice to see you again," said the woman, whom I remembered from the last time we'd met, beside the river at Christmas. "And this time in more pleasant circumstances, thank goodness. Now that neither of us is in a rush, can I take you to the café for tea and cakes?"

"Sounds good to me," I agreed.

The children weren't with her today, she explained, they were with her husband at home, while she had popped out to look at her mother's grave and take Roger for a walk.

In the cosy surroundings of the timber-beamed parlour of the 'Village Tea Rooms' we settled into an easy friendship. Rebecca Anthony had originally been a research physicist, and still edited academic papers at home, when family obligations permitted. Her round friendly face, pelmet of dark hair and easy-going smile made her easy to like. I told her about all that had happened to me since coming to the West Country.

"So let's get this straight," she began, taking the first bite of her Danish pastry. "Your wife died by falling under an Underground train, but you believe she was murdered, right?"

"Yes."

"And your main reason for coming down here to the West Country was to try and find out if her murder had anything to do with the death of Adrian Dark, which happened just one week before that?"

"Right."

"Now it just so happens that I remember the night Adrian Dark died. It was quite a sensation here in the village, because he was very popular locally, gave a lot to local charities, that kind of thing. The road leading to Netherwold Hall is the Yaddlethorpe Road, as you know, just beyond the crossroads. We heard about his terrible accident, falling down the stairs, on the Sunday morning. Apparently they thought it happened on Saturday, during the night."

"Sure."

"Well it may be something and nothing," she went on, taking another sip of her coffee. "But I was out late walking Roger that night. And I remember seeing a police car going up Yaddlethorpe Hill very late on that Saturday night. I distinctly remember that car, and I remember thinking the only place where the police car could be going was

Netherwold Hall, so I wondered if there was anything wrong up there."

"You mean a police car was on its way to the big house several hours before Adrian Dark's cleaning lady discovered the body?"

"Yes. I gathered next day that his cleaning lady had gone in at about 11am on the Sunday and found the body. So why was a police car going up there the night before, at around midnight?"

"Did you manage to see the driver?"

"Only momentarily. But I did remember something odd. He wasn't in uniform. He was wearing ordinary clothes, and as a rule it's uniformed officers you see in the marked cars, not CID."

"That's true. Did you tell the police about it?"

"Yes, but they had no record of anyone calling them that night, they couldn't understand it. But I heard no more, so I assume they didn't think it was relevant to their investigation of his death."

"It's something you might like to bear in mind also . . ."

"Go on."

"Look, Sean, I'm sure you've thought of this. I don't want to sound patronising."

"I'm in a hell of a mess and I've failed at everything I've tried so far. If you can think of anything, *anything at all,* let's hear it, Rebecca. Please."

"Okay. Well you've been telling me all about Jodie. The type of person she was. Whatever she was involved in during her final days, she must have been aware that it was dangerous."

"Certainly." I drank some of my coffee, my hands shaking with exhaustion so that I spilt some onto the snow-white tablecloth. I still had not fully recovered from the flu that had laid me so low.

"I've been a scientist, as I told you. Well one thing that was drummed into all of us, I'll never forget. We were taught that any work we did had to be recorded, no matter how inconsequential. I'm guessing that Jodie, as a professional person, would have the same attitude. That she would make absolutely sure that there was a record of all that she was doing, just in case the worst happened. Ideally more than one copy."

"Yes, but all her papers, phones and computers were destroyed in a fire the day after she died."

"Umm." She nodded. "But have you thought of any other places where she might have left information, as a failsafe?"

"All those I've been able to think of. What sort of places are you suggesting?"

"I have no idea." Her forehead wrinkled as she frowned in concentration. "Okay, let's take things one step at a time. You've told me she had a flat in South London that she shared with a friend, where she kept most of her work?"

"Yes."

"Okay. The content of that place has gone completely in a fire. She had an office at your home, presumably, and you've searched there?"

"Yes. She didn't keep very much there, because she was working in town most of the time. She lived up there for part of the week, because most of her work was in or around London, and she sometimes did the odd shift as a freelance copy editor at *The Globe* newspaper."

"And you have no other homes, flats or hideaways? Beach hut? Caravan?"

"No, nothing."

"Did she ever speak about places, or people in her life?

Relatives where she stayed, or places where she could store things?"

"No. She had one sister who lives in Australia, and her parents are retired, living in Spain."

"Hmm. It just seems to me that from what you tell me she was a belt-and-braces kind of woman. Presumably she didn't back up her files in the cloud, or on a computer at work, you said she worked part time at *The Globe*?"

"No, I've checked both possibilities."

"Is there anyone she might have sent files of papers to, for safekeeping? Or anyone she could have emailed information to? Other email addresses she could have emailed things to?"

"I've thought of everyone and everything. And I think the information was so sensitive she wouldn't have trusted anyone else not to use it themselves."

"Umm." Rebecca stared at the pure white tablecloth as she tried to concentrate. "So what's left of her now?"

"What do you mean?" I conjured up an image of her lonely grave, at the far side of St Mary's churchyard, on the lonely Kent clifftop.

"Sorry, that was probably a bit of a tactless way of putting it. It's simply that whenever someone dies, a relative gets rid of most of their possessions or takes them over. But ultimately there's always a handful of bits and pieces. No one ever gets rid of *everything.* There are usually keepsakes, papers, ornaments, items of jewellery you can't bear to get rid of. A drawer full. A boxful. Sometimes a whole room full."

"True, but there's hardly anything now. I gave away her clothes, sold her car."

"No SIM cards for phones knocking around?"

"No, nothing apart from her phone that I kept."

"Jewellery? Was there anything she was particularly fond of? "

"She's got a sister in Australia, and she came over for the funeral, and she came back to the house and I just handed over everything."

"Well, Sean, I'm sorry, but that's all I can think of. All I can suggest is that you examine every last item you have that was Jodie's, and there could be something that gives you some information, or leads you to some person who can help."

"Jewellery," I repeated, almost to myself. "Now that you mention it, she did often talk about an old locket that's been in her family for a long time. Her sister was particularly pleased to get it."

When I was sitting in the car again, on a whim I decided to follow up Rebecca's suggestion, however improbable it seemed.

When Jodie's sister Amanda answered the phone she was pleased to hear from me.

"Hi, Sean," she replied.

"Sorry, Amanda, I know it must be about eleven at night, but it's urgent."

"No problem, you know we're late birds."

"Look, could I ask you something about Jodie's jewellery?"

"Sure." She sounded surprised. "What about it?"

"You remember the big locket, the one that you liked so much?"

"Oh yeah, it's been in the family since great-great-grandmother's time, it used to belong to her."

"It's going to sound stupid, but would you mind opening it up and seeing if there anything inside it?"

"Well, I know people used to put in a lock of hair in

lockets, but I don't remember finding any."

"Could you take look?"

"Okay. Are you all right to hang on for a while? I've got to get to the drawer."

"No problem."

She came on the line again.

"Funny thing, there was a little tiny scrap of paper there which I hardly noticed when I looked before."

"Read what it says."

"Sure. Hang on, the writing so tiny I need the magnifying glass. Here we are: *If something happens to me, go to the grave of Matthew Zebadiah Fazakerly at Kensal Green Cemetery, North London. Examine the flower holder.*" She paused.

"Is that all?"

"Yeah. Does it make sense to you? I know Matthew was our four-times great-grandfather. I didn't even know he was buried in London."

"Thanks, Amanda."

I felt a chill run down my spine as I pictured the tiny scrap of paper concealed in the locket on the other side of the world. I thought of Jodie's handwriting: spidery, tiny, cramped.

And I knew that I was finally onto something.

FORTY

Laura

"Look, I came to see you because I read about you in the paper, and I was worried."

Dr Fanshaw looked like a drowned rat, standing at the counter in Novelicious, drenched from the pouring rain outside.

When we were settled in the back office, he sat at the table, nursing a cup of tea.

I had only just come back from Netherwold Hall, where the police had taken charge of the discovery of the skeleton in the chapel. All I had to do now was wait until they could compare DNA from me, to see if I had finally found my mum. All at once everything, finally, was coming together.

"The thing is, I've read about all the trouble you've been in," Dr Fanshaw explained, "and I feel a measure of responsibility about what has happened to you."

"You helped me to remember what happened to me when I was a child."

"Yes, but as I told you at the time you cannot just rely on these things at face value. As you must know, recovered memory, using EMDR – Eye Movement Desensitizing and

Reprocessing – is an incredibly controversial subject, and opinions differ about its efficacy. As a doctor and a scientist, I don't merely accept everything at face value. I question everything and try to analyse things as carefully as I can.

"The thing is, recently another psychiatrist contacted me, wanting to find out about my work. He has studied many, many cases of alleged recovered memories, and his conclusions are, pretty obviously, that some are genuine and some are not. He's also something of an expert on sleep patterns, an area I'm not so familiar with."

"And?" I watched Dr Fanshaw sip his drink and frown even more.

"As you probably know, what is referred to as the Rapid Eye Movement stage of sleeping, is the very lightest form of sleep and it's typically when we dream the most. This has been proved by waking people in the midst of the Rapid Eye Movement phase, and they can often relate their dreams. As you probably know, dreams are produced from the subconscious – in short, a dream is a fantasy played out in your brain while you sleep. Something, essentially, that you have created yourself. An invention, based on things that have been happening in your life."

"So what are you saying, doctor?"

"That I filmed your testimony while you were talking in the trance, and to be honest I never looked too closely at the footage. But Dr Janson is a world-renowned expert on sleeping patterns. He and I have now focussed our attention on your eyelids during the process. It seems that in the early part of the session you were undoubtedly in a hypnotic trance. However, during the later session, when you refer to your mother being attacked by the band members of Nightingale Green, it's very clear that you exhibited signs of rapid eye movement – flickering behind the eyelids. This suggests to both of us, that this could well mean that you moved from being in a deep hypnotic trance to actual sleep, during which it is likely that you manufactured dreams."

"At what point?"

"Precisely at the moment you relate that your mother was being mauled and attacked by those men, and ultimately raped. What I'm saying is, that I cannot in conscience confirm that what you related happened to your mother was *definitely* a recovered memory. I think it's much more likely that during some of the time when you were hypnotised by me, you were in fact dreaming. I feel that I've misled you, and I'm very sorry. It's a big responsibility."

"But how could I have been dreaming when I was talking?"

"People often talk in their sleep. People even stand up and walk while asleep if they're somnambulists."

"Oh God, if this is true, then I've wasted all this time. I thought I definitely had the answer to what happened to my mother, and now you tell me it wasn't a recovered memory at all."

"I'm sorry. I could be wrong anyway. Recovered memory using EDMR is an imprecise science."

"But my mother disappeared on that night. So if she wasn't raped and killed, what did happen to her?"

"No one knows. It's unlikely that she would just abandon her own child, so I agree that the likelihood is that she came to a bad end that day."

"A body has been discovered at Netherwold, under the chapel floor," I told him.

"Really?" He looked up at me. "Then maybe I'm wrong. Maybe you weren't dreaming and it really was a true recovered memory from your childhood. We just don't know. We'll probably never know."

"But what we do know is that my mother came to Netherwold Hall to see my father, who had only recently got married to a woman who presumably knew nothing about me. Maybe he had stopped paying her child maintenance? Maybe my mother was threatening to tell his wife about his other child unless she gave him money, and they had a row, and he killed her?"

*

In the morning, when I was busy packing the car in preparation for my journey to Edinburgh, DC Cope arrived.

"Have I arrived at a difficult time?" he asked.

"Not really," I told the short, dark-haired policeman who had been so kind to me. "It's just that I'm leaving on a business trip. The car's all packed and I'm ready to go."

"Could I have a quick word? It won't take long."

Rain had started lashing down, and I was frustrated at the sudden change in the weather, meaning there'd be inevitable traffic hold-ups.

"Sure. Look, why don't we get in the car and talk there?"

"Thanks."

"I'm sorry to have to tell you, but the bones you found in the chapel at Netherwold aren't human," Cope said as he settled himself in the passenger seat. "Initial reports say they're the remains of some kind of animal."

"Oh." My disappointment ruined the day, making me feel even more miserable, as the rain swept in torrents down the windscreen. "Well, I suppose it was too much to hope for. I thought the bones were too near the surface anyway. If, as we surmised, they buried her near where British Gas were excavating they'd probably have gone a lot deeper."

"Umm."

"Excuse me, but what are you doing?" I asked him as I saw him fumbling with a cloth.

The last thing I saw was something coming towards my face. Then a strong smell of some chemical.

And then nothing…

FORTY-ONE

Sean

I made it to Kensal Green Cemetery late the following day, when daylight was on the run, and drizzle melted from the sky like sulky tears.

It was a beautiful place really, but the fact of it being a necropolis was unnerving and somehow surreal. I'd read that it had been started by George Carden, a Victorian barrister, in an attempt to emulate the beautiful Père Lachaise cemetery in Paris, a wonderful peaceful space, where the sculpture of monuments and peaceful scenery made it a popular tourist attraction.

But there was not quite so much beauty and scenery here, as I stood at the forbidding stone arch at the entrance. It didn't help that the fine morning had degenerated fast into a gloomy afternoon, with everywhere drizzle damp, my breath clouding as I exhaled. And this part of North London was a scruffy, down-at-heel area, a world of long squalid roads of houses, and scruffy tiny shops, with a brackish dirty canal, too much traffic and too little peace.

I had parked in a side street and jogged across and through the gates, and I felt a frisson of excitement as my breaths clouded into the sky. Along the main path, I wondered how the hell I was going to find his grave amongst all these others. Wikipedia had told me it ran to seventy-two acres of grounds. There were ranks of tombs, many beautiful sculptures, and as I walked along I saw that some of them were huge mausoleums. There were finely carved angels depicted as perfectly formed women, and it reminded me of the notion of a link between a sexual climax and death. Indeed there's a French phrase referring to sexual climax as *Le Petit Mort* – the little death.

Luckily I managed to find someone in the office, and he kindly looked along his lists, and drew me a map showing me where to find the grave.

I passed the trees and the undergrowth and the dreary miserable never-ending rows of tombstones and statues, went up to the end, then turned left and along.

Eventually I found the grave of Matthew Zebadiah Fazakerly in a forlorn corner of the cemetery, fortunately hidden from view to some extent. Unlike many of the other graves, this one had been looked after, even though recent grass had begun to grow around and across it.

On examination I found that the empty metal flower urn was in its own circular cut-out in the marble slab that covered the grave in front of the large headstone. At first the urn wouldn't move in its receptacle, but then I saw that it had been duct taped into place, presumably in an attempt to seal out water. Scraping the tape away with a fingernail. I pulled out the urn. Taped to its base was a bundle of some kind, made of tissue, wool or something soft. It was slightly damp on the outside, but it looked as if the tape sealing the flower urn in place had done a good job of keeping out most of the rainwater. I unravelled the bundle, and there, sure enough, were two memory sticks.

When I got back to the car with the precious items in

my pocket, I plugged one of them into the USB port on my laptop and switched on. I opened the drive and clicked on one of the audio files.

A man's voice: presumably that of Adrian Dark. I listened for a while to his account of an early life, his parents, the family home in Dulwich, South London, his early interest in music, his friends and his hobbies.

I scanned the length of the file, and saw that it was very long, two or three hours of talking. The other files on the drive were equally long, and on opening one of them I found it was the same man's voice talking about his start in the music industry.

Clearly I had the entire account of Adrian Dark's life that Jodie had recorded from long sessions together, all ready for her to write up his biography. This indeed was the entire story of the man's life, hours of recordings of him chatting to my dead wife, in preparation for her writing his complete, detailed autobiography, ghost-written by her. She had obviously made several copies of these recordings, but all the others had been lost. I was now glad that I had withdrawn the skimpy biography I had written on his life, based merely on the diaries and the few small notes that Dark had written himself. These files were the basis for a proper, comprehensive account of his life, filling all the gaps not covered by the diaries. Indeed his diaries were obviously only intended to be an adjunct to this main story of his life.

However, the most recent file on this drive was a recording of Jodie's voice, and hearing her talk gave me a shock. As soon as I heard it, goosebumps rose on my arms as the car's chill air seemed electrified by her words from beyond the grave.

*

I sat there in the car for a long time, as the windows misted up with my exhaled air, and I saw that the drizzle had intensified to a full-on downpour.

This was her interview with Adrian Dark:

Jodie: So, Adrian, tell me what happened to you on the fifteenth of October 1987.

Adrian: I got home late, having been out all day. When I arrived, all hell had broken loose. Angela Kaplan had been there all afternoon and had been with the guys, taking the new drug, Ranazak, that was all the rage back then. It was a bit like LSD, but it affected some people very badly, and because of this had fallen out of favour quite quickly. Angela had fallen into a very deep sleep and they were all panicking because she wouldn't wake up, they were scared she had OD'd.

Jodie: Why didn't they call an ambulance?

Adrian: They were terrified of being arrested for using illegal drugs, and possibly facing charges of harming her. The idiots were flapping about like chickens, Roger certain she'd be okay, Rufus panicking that she might go into a coma. I called a private doctor, who came out immediately, but he said she had to go to hospital urgently. Luckily he knew of a private hospital in Yorkshire and arranged for her to be taken there immediately. He assured me her vital signs were okay and that she was fit to travel, but that he'd go with her in the ambulance to be on the safe side.

Jodie: Why all the secrecy?

Adrian: I had only been married a few weeks, my wife had already left me and I was trying to persuade her to come back. And here I was with the mother of my child, who my wife knew nothing about, having been partying at my house, and now she'd had this bad reaction to drugs, that, if they'd been found in the house, might have earnt one or more of us criminal convictions that would have put the block on us ever touring the States, possibly even jail time. You see I'd only recently got a suspended sentence for possession. I would have lost my marriage and risked imprisonment and my career would have gone down the pan. Of course at the time none of us knew that Angela had brought our child, Laura, with her, we assumed she'd come alone, and because she wasn't conscious she couldn't tell us. The child was nowhere around, she must have hidden under furniture in the house as soon as Angela came into the room where they were partying.

Jodie: How did you get her registered in a hospital without her name getting out, and matching up with the woman the police were looking for later on?

Adrian: That was easy. We registered her there under her real name, Vanessa Beale. Vanessa had changed her name to Angela Kaplan a while ago because she was working in the circus, and she thought it sounded more stagey. However she had never done it legally, she'd just started using her new name, and everyone had known her as Angela Kaplan for several years. That was Angela, never finishing things off, just do the first bit of a job and not follow it up. And since she worked for cash, and was outside the social security system, proving her identity wasn't of importance to her. She'd put her name as Angela Kaplan on Laura's birth certificate, but officially her legal name was still Vanessa Beale. Unfortunately we found out a few days later that the partial brain damage was permanent, and Vanessa was in a very bad way for a number of months, and I paid for her treatment all the while.

Jodie: What happened to Vanessa?

Adrian: She's still there. She has the best care possible. Of course if I'd known that Angela had brought our daughter, I would have just played it straight and told the police everything, but I didn't know until later, and by that time it was too late. I only heard that Angela's daughter had been found in the village when the manhunt started, and by then, how could I tell anyone what had happened without incriminating myself? The social services had been doing their best to catch up with Angela in order to take Laura into care for ages, so, even though the police searched for her whereabouts, Angela's disappearance just made things simpler for the authorities.

The morning after the Great Storm provided another shock for everyone. After the previous night's drama, Angela had left in the ambulance, and then we had the storm. Roger was examining the damage to the grounds, and found two of the oldest trees uprooted. Not only that, he found the metal trunk that had been buried under the tree, unearthed. He smashed it open and found the Kendal Treasure.

This posed a problem for me at the time. I had inherited what had once been Kendal Abbey from my father, eight years previously, but it was specifically stated in the will that if the Kendal Treasure was ever found it was to be given back to the Gasconade order of Friars, who were still in existence in southern France.

The guys could have told the Friars anytime they wanted to, so it made sense for us to divide the treasure four ways. It coincided with the end of the line for Nightingale Green: we had been going stale as a band for a while by then, and we all felt trapped, and wanted to do different things with our lives. A big chunk of cash allowed us all to do just that.

Besides, the awful thing that had happened with Angela was deeply troubling, and had upset all of us, for we all felt responsible. To be fair it was no one's fault: it was a new drug, similar to LSD, but since then found to be so potentially dangerous to some people that no one risks using it now. If only we had known then.

I've done some terrible things in my life, and I can't make any excuses.

So, Jodie, those are the secrets of my life. I hope you can understand why I kept them to myself for so long, and why, now I know I haven't got long for this world, that guilt has prompted me to want to tell the truth. When I'm gone I want you to explain everything to my daughter, whom I have included in my will. Tell her that I always felt guilty for putting my legal family's interests ahead of hers. My only excuse can be that my wife knew all about my finances, and I couldn't have explained making payments to support Laura. I had to sacrifice my old family for my new one, something I'm deeply ashamed of. And I hope, with the legacy I have left her, that I have made some kind of amends.

When I'm gone, Jodie, you are welcome to publish this wherever you want to. Laura deserves to know what happened to her mother. And, crucially, she needs to know that her mother never abandoned her.

I've been a bastard in this life, but right now I am trying to put things right, even though it's too late in many ways.

And I would like you to write my biography, if you think anyone will publish it. The diaries, and my own beginning of my autobiography are here, and I want you to have them. My account of what I found out about the death of Jimi Hendrix is a bit unusual, but I hope you'll be able to include that, as I feel it is very important, even if it upsets some people. And I have decided that, after a lot of thought,

I should name the person who killed Jimi Hendrix, rather than leave it anonymous as I did in the rough draft. He was Jack Dolman, and his wife was Alison Dolman. If Alison Dolman's son is unaware of his paternity he might be upset, but I can't help that. Indeed, I can't be sure that Hendrix is the man's father – only Alison Dolman knows the truth, and she died a long time ago, as did Jack. But since she had not become pregnant by her husband in five years, the chances of them conceiving at last were slim.

Whatever, I believe that the truth has to be told. And after all, a lot of people would be very proud to have been fathered by arguably the world's greatest rock guitarist of all time.

By the way, I found that policeman guy, rooting through my papers the other day, I wouldn't trust him, there's something strange about him, so, Jodie, take care.

FORTY-TWO

Laura

"Where are you taking me? Why have you put handcuffs on me?"

He wouldn't answer me, just went on driving, staring ahead, his expression distracted.

"Who are you?"

"I'm Detective Constable Steven John Cope."

"I know that. But I don't understand. Have you arrested me?"

"Laura, I'm tired, I've got a lot on my mind. I have a lot of things to sort out and arrange. You're just one part of this whole mess, but I have to deal with you first."

"Deal with me?"

"Shut up!"

Without warning he hit me in the face, all the while his other hand was on the wheel. I felt tears spring to my eyes as much from the shock of it as from the pain, which was radiating from my mouth. My lips had been rammed hard against my teeth and I could taste blood.

"I'm sorry. But you just went on talking. I couldn't stand it, I have to have peace and quiet to think, you see?"

"Sean will be looking for me."

"No he won't. You told him you were going to Scotland for a week, and I've got rid of your car, so no one is going to miss you."

I said nothing, staring ahead out of the window, wondering what the hell was happening.

Sooner or later we'd have to stop and he'd have to let me out. Then I'd have my opportunity. DC Cope was staring straight ahead, but I could see a deadness in his eyes that I'd never seen before. He was behaving on instinct, just treating me as a nuisance, part of his 'business' to be attended to.

There was blood in my mouth. I didn't want to swallow it, and I couldn't spit it into a tissue because my hands were fastened to the seat behind me.

So I leaned forward and spat into the footwell.

That was when I caught sight of the leaflet for the Aryans Supreme rally on the car floor.

"Y-you belong to the Aryans Supreme?" I asked him.

"We are the natural leaders of the world!" he said angrily, glaring at the road. "Everywhere, there are black and brown people eroding everything they touch. The child-molester gangs in Rotherham, the drug and gang culture in London. It's everywhere in this country. It's everywhere all over the world. Why can't people understand that some races are inferior? Why can't everyone understand that *we are the Master Race?* All the rot in the Western world started when the black people came here. The degeneracy, the breakdown of society. Everyone knows it, but no one will ever admit it."

I didn't reply. He was talking frantically, as if he'd been wound up. There was a maniacal gleam in his eye.

"Did Sean let you read your father's diaries and notes?"

"No."

"Don't lie to me! You've read those lies about Jimi Hendrix being murdered because he impregnated the man's wife! You've read those lies, and you'll tell other people about them, won't you?"

"I don't know what you're talking about."

"You know too much. That's why you have to be silenced."

When we stopped at the next traffic lights, he took a bottle from the back seat and soaked a cloth with it. As I strained to pull myself away, he managed to hold it against my face.

I fought to stop breathing in the vapour, but in the end it was no good. When the next bout of oblivion came it was a relief.

*

I woke up on my own in the dark. My hands were free now, and I was lying on something hard, like soil. There was a musty smell, like very old damp and derelict buildings, with a faint aroma of earth, rot and decay. Beside me was my handbag, and as I rooted through it, I could see that he had left everything apart from my phone, of course. But luckily there was a tiny keyring torch still there. I switched on the light and saw that I was in a small cave-like enclosure. There was a large plastic bottle of water and a couple of packets of sandwiches, and further away, a bucket.

I got to my feet, gingerly walking around, finding the space was very small. At one end of the room was a door, but there was no apparent handle, and however hard I pushed it wasn't moving an inch. The walls seemed to be stone. As I looked at the long rectangular box beside me, I had a suspicion what it was, and what the other boxes were too. I held the torch closer to the top of the thing, to see the words *Lord Henry Alton, born 18 July 1830, died 20 December 1910*, inscribed on a brass plate.

FORTY-THREE

Sean

"So you've done part of it," Robin said, using tweezers to position the staircase correctly against the wall of the model of the big Georgian manor house he was building. He pushed gently as the cyanoacrylate adhesive bonded the surfaces, a tiny bulge of the clear gel glue apparent at one part of the seam. "You know that Adrian Dark told Jodie all those secrets about himself, and about Laura Kaplan's mother, and his role in her disappearance. Adrian died shortly afterwards and so did she. It seems that someone killed them both to stop the secret coming out. And of course before Jodie was able to tell Laura the truth."

Rob's workshop at the vicarage smelt of freshly cut timber and PVA wood glue, and he had been working at his latest project while I was telling him what had happened to me in the West Country. After the long drive I had not slept well when I returned to Whitstable, and today I had a terrible headache and the mortifying awareness that I had failed at everything I had tried to do. I also had an uncomfortable feeling about the future, as if bad things were in the pipeline, and there was nothing I could do to stop them.

To my great frustration, I couldn't get hold of Laura. I had tried to phone her repeatedly to give her the exciting news about her mother, but her mobile number was out of order, and when I reached her friend Barbara at Novelicious, she said that Laura had left for Scotland yesterday, but that she had not heard from her either, nor could she get in touch, which seemed very odd to both of us.

Why was she out of touch? We had arranged to meet up and discuss the future, yet she had gone off without a word, hadn't even phoned, and now would not answer her phone. I had the awful feeling that something was wrong, but I didn't know what it was.

"But who, apart from Laura, would care about the secret of her mother's accident coming out?" I asked Rob. "All that Adrian confesses to, is that Laura's mother was given this dangerous recreational drug by the other members of his band, and she had a catastrophically bad reaction to it, as a result of which she's brain damaged and living in a nursing home. But what kind of a mother goes ahead and takes a party drug when she's supposed to be in charge of her child? Presumably no one forced her to take the drug, and it didn't harm the others. I reckon she was just wildly selfish and irresponsible, and ultimately very unlucky that she reacted as she did. The other secret – that the Kendal Treasure had been discovered, the bit of information that got Jodie interested in the first place – wouldn't matter to anyone either. So if Adrian Dark was murdered, and it wasn't an accident, who killed him and why? And the same for Jodie. Who killed her and why?" I paced around the room, pausing at the window to look out at the village green.

"You know, Sean, I think you're missing something. I

think you're too close to all that's been going on to think clearly." Robin put down the tiny tool he'd been using and looked directly at me. "Think back. Apart from the diaries, was there anything else in that box of papers?"

"Yes. There was the opening chapter of the biography that Adrian Dark was writing himself, that he never got any further with. The remainder, of course I now know is recorded in the audio files that Jodie was going to use."

"He mentions 'his biography' as if he's talking about the part of the biography he wrote, not the diaries. So what did he write about in the part that you have?"

I frowned, trying to remember. "It was one of those dramatic 'beginning chapters' that's supposed to hook you in. You know the kind of thing. A biography starts with some wham-bam-slam shocking event to attract the reader, then if it follows the usual pattern, chapter two is the usual tedious childhood memories presaging the gradual chronological journey culminating in his successful career as a pop star."

"So?"

"It was a rather unconvincing account of finding Jimi Hendrix's body, and his theory that he had been murdered."

"Murdered?" Rob said in surprise. "I've read a lot about the life of Jimi Hendrix, and his unexpected death. And I always understood that the evidence pointed more or less incontrovertibly to the conclusion that he choked to death in his sleep – just a terrible accident."

"Yes, practically all the witnesses at the time agree with that, as did the coroner and the findings of the inquest. In fact the Hendrix family were particularly litigious, so I believe that if there'd been a shred of doubt as to the cause of death, they'd have had it investigated, and they didn't. I was so intrigued that after reading Adrian's chapter I read up on the facts again from three separate sources. Jimi Hendrix died at some time during the night of the seventeenth of September, 1970. He was in bed with his girlfriend, Monica Danneman. She woke up beside him in the night and found she couldn't wake him up, so she phoned a close friend, Eric Burdon, and asked what to do. Burdon, one of Jimi's good friends, flew into a panic. He was miles away, and urged her to call an ambulance. She didn't do so until much later. When the ambulance arrived she wasn't there, and they found his body in the otherwise deserted hotel room, the face covered with vomit, comprised mostly of red wine. I'm not sure if they attempted resuscitation there, or realised it was too late. At any rate, Monica was nowhere in sight, he was alone in the hotel room, and was taken from there to hospital, where he was pronounced dead. The inquest concluded that he had taken nine Vesparax sleeping pills and a quantity of red wine at some time during the evening or night. At some stage he stopped breathing as a result of vomit blocking his airways, and he died. In fact one of his girlfriends stated that he had almost died in a similar way not long before that."

"So he wasn't murdered?" Robin said.

"The police didn't think so at the time. Neither do I. After all, there was a full investigation. However, there was one book written a while ago by a roadie, that stated a similar thing to what Adrian claims – except saying that Jimi Hendrix's manager murdered him, his motive being that Jimi was talking of leaving him and going to someone else, which was incidentally true. But the idea of Mike Jeffrey murdering him doesn't make sense, any more than Adrian's account does. How can you expect to murder someone by holding them down and pouring red wine down their throat until they choke to death? As a method of murder it's a non-starter. If you want to kill someone, the first rule is to make sure you succeed, so pushing him out of a window, arranging a car accident, even doctoring the pills he takes, those methods would have made much more sense."

"So, tell me again, Sean. What is Adrian's account of Jimi's death?"

"He claims a similar thing to the roadie: that he saw someone going into Jimi's room in the night, someone who forcibly made him drink too much red wine in order to choke him to death."

"Dark knew about it and didn't try to stop him?"

"I don't know. I can't remember what he says, but I think it's along the lines of seeing the man leave the room afterwards, then going in and finding Jimi dead. I think it's nonsense, something he made up as a tantalising way to hook people into his book."

"And what was supposed to be the motive?"

"Oh, let's see." I struggled to remember. "Something about jealousy. Yeah, that's it. In the thumb drive file with Dark's confession, he names this alleged 'murderer' as Jack Dolman, who I learned was on the fringes of the music business – a fairly unknown musician. He allegedly murdered Jimi, because Jimi had made his wife pregnant."

"So is it possible that whoever murdered Adrian and Jodie, did so because they were afraid of this theory becoming made public? That Hendrix had fathered a child who was unaware of his true paternity?"

"But who would care about that, after all this time?"

"How about the child that was born? What if he or she didn't want it known that their father might have been Jimi Hendrix?"

"Who would care that much?"

"Someone who was a racist, and grew up assuming he was ethnically pure Caucasian. Someone to whom the idea of being partly of black heritage was something he couldn't bear to face. Who would hate the thought of his friends and associates thinking he was of mixed race. Strikes me that the allegation of the murder of Jimi Hendrix is immaterial to our killer. What he really does care about is the *reason why* he was supposed to have been murdered: the rumour of Hendrix being his father. All along the conundrum is that no one would care about secrets being divulged because it was all so long ago. But this son or daughter of Alison Dolman would be in their late forties now." Robin paused, staring at the interior of the model of the manor house, then back at me. "No one benefitted financially by murdering Adrian and Jodie, so it's fair to assume, as you have done, that they were killed to stop some story coming out. I think you need to try and trace the child born to Alison Dolman, then approach them, with this theory that Jodie uncovered, and see how they react. How can you do that?"

"I know a private detective who's brilliant at hacking into data. Now I have a name I can ask her to look into it."

"I think that is your answer, Sean, I really do. Find whoever it is, and they might be able to help you."

"I will."

When I got back to my house in Whitstable, a text arrived on my phone:

I demand to have the papers written by the late Adrian Dark that are in your possession. Your friend Laura Kaplan is being held and will only be released once these papers are mine. If you refuse to give me them, she will die. Get them and wait for my next instructions. I really don't want to kill you, because you killed that man, so I know you are one of us.

Accompanying the text was a photograph of Laura,

lying somewhere asleep. Laid out on her chest was *The Times* newspaper, with today's date.

I texted back:

Okay. I have what you want: the handwritten notes made by Adrian Dark, you can have them. No copies exist, and you can trust me not to share anything I've read with anyone else. Tell me where to meet you.

I thought long and hard, wondering what the hell to do now.

You killed that man so I know you are one of us.

What the hell was that about?

FORTY-FOUR

I phoned Jeanette, the private detective I knew, told her of all the facts concerning Jack and Alison Dolman that Jodie had learned from Adrian, and asked if she could trace any children of this couple, and any details of what had become of them.

I explained that it was possibly a matter of life and death and that I'd pay anything she wanted for fast results. She said she would get right onto it, but could not promise immediate success.

After that, I set out for the West Country once more, realising that Laura's kidnapper would most likely be holding her somewhere in the local area.

The more I thought about it, the more it seemed that Rob's theory had to be correct. Adrian Dark and my wife Jodie could have been murdered to stop anyone finding out about Adrian's bizarre claim of Jimi Hendrix fathering a child with Alison Dolman. Now it seemed that this person had kidnapped Laura in order to force me to give him the handwritten papers of the first chapter of the autobiography. But that would not be enough for him. He would know that I might have made copies. More importantly, he could not allow anyone who had read the story to go on living, in case they told anyone. They had to die, just as everyone had died so far.

His plan was obviously to lure me into the open, get me to give him the papers and any copies, so that he could then kill me. And since Laura knew who he was, he would probably kill her too. However, he had to keep her alive for long enough to get me to agree to his demands.

I arrived in Bath in the early afternoon, wondering what to do, and checking my phone for the fiftieth time to see if another text had arrived.

As I sat there in Morrison's car park, just outside town, I gazed out at the yellow bath-stone buildings wondering what the hell I could do to find Laura.

The woman I was in love with was imprisoned somewhere, scared, not knowing what was happening to her, or why.

When the tension had built up so much that I wanted to scream, my mobile rang. Thank God! It was Jeanette, my detective friend.

"Sean, I've had a bit of luck. . ."

*

Detective Constable Cope

Everything is over.

It's been over for me for quite a long time now, ever since that night last year when I was called to Netherwold Hall and quite by chance began reading Adrian Dark's memoirs. I should have known then that trying to keep something secret is tantamount to impossible, without radical, root-and-branch destruction.

Everything had seemed fine back then: Adrian and Jodie, the journalist woman, were out of the picture, and I had found no apparent records of the lies Adrian had written anywhere at all, the whole problem had been solved, once and for all.

Or so I had thought.

But now?

I now knew that Sean Delaney had bought Adrian Dark's diaries, and was writing a biography based on these. What I had not known until recently, when I'd been chatting to Laura Kaplan, was that in the same box as the diaries Delaney had bought were handwritten pages of his autobiography.

The opening chapter, the papers that I had read by chance all that time ago!

So Delaney was privy to the secret, perhaps he was even including it in his bloody book, for God's sake! I can't trust him. I can only hope that his book hasn't been completed yet, and I'm in time to stop it. Even if Delaney does bring me the original papers, he'll have made copies, electronic copies that are probably even now stored in the cloud. If my secret wasn't out already, it soon will be. And then what will happen?

Some sensationalist rock historian would query the story about Hendrix's apparent murder, and the reason behind it. And it would get into the newspapers, and, sooner or later, people would link his name to Alice Dolman and Jack Dolman, and then they'd find out that I had changed my name. All my friends and contacts all over the world would know, or would doubt and suspect, and wonder if indeed my father was a black man!

I drank more whisky, and felt the soothing comforting feeling, the tears falling as I sobbed.

I thought of my mother and father. My mother and my *real father*, Jack Dolman, for that was the truth. I had his eyes and his hair, didn't I? That's what everyone used to say when I was a child. I remember some loud unpleasant man talking to Mum and looking down at me, and declaring, "Blimey, he's the living spit of Jack. No chance blaming this one on the milkman!" And then his nasty rancid laugh, as Mum smiled nervously. I hadn't known what he had meant, and Mum had just told me he was a 'silly man', and to take no notice. Now I blessed him with all my heart, now I wanted to thank him.

My schooldays, the loneliness of no one wanting to play with me. The black boy in the class, who everyone liked. Then the other black boy, Delroy, who had gone out with Mary, my first sweetheart. At thirteen, I had come upon them behind the old gymnasium at school. She had her skirt pushed down below her knees, and Delroy had his hands all over her, his black filthy body inside hers, thrusting and pushing, and in that moment I wanted to smash his head into a bloody pulp.

But I hadn't done so. I despise myself now, when I think back to that time. I had run away, scared that they might have seen me. And I cried on my own for an hour. I couldn't stop thinking about Mary, whom I had longed to talk to, to be with, the very idea of holding her hand had filled me with a kind of dread wonder. And yet that evil black bastard had just done those unspeakable things to her. . . I wanted to kill him. I fantasised about killing him, making Mary watch me as I choked him to death, and then hitting his head over and over again with a hammer, until the skull split into a bloody pulp of blood and bone.

However, years later I heard that Mary had had a child with Delroy. At that time the boy had been a teenager. I had traced him. And one dark night I had found him in a back alley and stabbed him to death.

The army was the only time I had ever been happy.

The army had been my family. It taught me to be tough and fit, how to use weapons and how to kill people. Then, falling in love with Jane, who'd insisted I left the army after my five-year stint and take another job. Joining the police had been hard, I had never really enjoyed it. And Jane had left me in the end, just like everyone had left me, and by then the army didn't want me back. All the recruitment posters had blacks on them now, the army was ultra PC, the blacks were there, they were *everywhere*. Even some of my senior officers in the police were blacks! Where would it end?

I stopped brooding and brought my thoughts back to the present. And that was the moment when I switched on the computer and noticed the email from *ancestry.co.uk*, saying that the results had come in for my DNA test. With a glow of relief I realised that at last I would have the confirmation that the ridiculous story about Jimi Hendrix being my father was untrue.

I clicked open the email and downloaded the results. Then scan-read them.

Then I read them again more slowly, unable to believe what was there on the pages. I printed them off, stared at them for a long time before believing they could possibly be true.

All my life I had believed that my parents were both pure Caucasian people.

And now?

Fuck!

I picked up the biro on the desk and, venting all my fury, stabbed it deep into the back of my left hand, wallowing in the agony, relishing the pain, watching the blubbering welling up of blood, knowing that nothing in the world mattered any more now.

And then I realised that my whole life had been a sham.

According to their results I was 50 per cent Afro-Caribbean. Not only that, but in the list of 'probable first cousins' were two black women in the United States.

And so, my worst nightmare had been confirmed. I had been living a lie. The account that Adrian Dark had written was true: Hendrix had indeed been my father. Whether my legal father, Jack Dolman, had murdered Hendrix I had no idea, but as far as I was concerned it didn't matter anyway.

Because now everything, for me, was over. There was nothing left.

I cried for a long time, cried until there were no more tears inside me.

Now that my life was going to end there was a kind of peace to it, a feeling of calmness that I had never expected. Of course Laura would die, imprisoned in the mausoleum as she was, with no way out, no one knowing where she was. But why should I care? She was just one of life's casualties, and she always would be: a crazy mixed-up lady, who was better off out of it. She would die, and did it really matter? For her friend Barbara was one of the blacks, and Laura was probably one of those girls who would go with black men for sex. And there would be a peculiar kind of justice when Laura Kaplan disappeared forever. Sean Delaney, the Irishman who loved her, would spend the rest of his life not knowing what happened to her, and blaming himself for not saving her.

Serve the bastard right for destroying me, for destroying everything I stand for, for his bloody wife stirring up all that trouble.

How to do it?

Shit.

I opened the drawer and took out my most prized possession: the Glock 9mm automatic pistol that I had bought illegally, and had never dared to use. The same type of weapon I had become familiar with in my service career.

You read about putting the gun in your mouth closing your lips onto the barrel and then. . . Or pressing the muzzle against your forehead. . . Oh God, what if it doesn't kill me, and I have to lie here paralysed?

No.

That's why they tell you you have to put it in your mouth, clutch the barrel between your teeth and tilt the muzzle onto the roof of your palate, then squeeze the trigger. . .

Oh Shit, oh shit, oh shit, this is it.

This is fucking it!

This is. . .

FORTY-FIVE

"Jack Dolman's son was named Jonathan, and he was born on the fourth of March 1971," Jeanette told me. "When he was eighteen, he changed his name to Cope and joined the army, the Parachute Regiment, where he served with distinction, getting several commendations. In 1996 he got married, left the army and joined the police force as a constable, then, two years later, joining the CID, serving since then as a detective constable."

DC Cope. The kind detective constable who had been so solicitous over Laura's plight. She would have trusted him, just like people always trust police officers. Just like Adrian Dark must have trusted him on the night he died.

So now it all slotted into place. I remembered how we had been assigned to another officer when we first went to the Lido Road Police Station, but that Cope had taken over, keen to be the one to help us. How Laura had told me that at first he'd been unhelpful, yet the second time we'd met him, he'd been suddenly extremely sympathetic to Laura's enquiries.

Whereas in fact Cope already knew all about Adrian Dark's affairs, because somehow he had learnt of the first handwritten chapter of Dark's biography, in which he asserted that Cope's father had been Jimi Hendrix, a rumour that he was determined to destroy at all costs. Rebecca, my new friend from Penton Feverill, had told me that she'd seen a police car going up the hill leading to Netherwold Hall on the night that Adrian Dark had died. . .

He had come to Netherwold Hall on that Saturday evening and caught Adrian Dark off-guard, pushing him down the long flight of stairs. Late at night, Dark would have been reluctant to let a stranger into his house, but a policeman? Everyone trusts a policeman. Whether or not he had died in the fall was anyone's guess, but if he'd been unconscious at the bottom, would an investigation reveal that his neck had been broken by anything other than the fall? Cope had belonged to the elite Parachute Regiment: men who are trained to kill with their bare hands.

And then, learning that Jodie had been working with him, he had decided to silence her too, since she was certain to have known the dread secret in his autobiography.

But it didn't end there. Cope had found out that Dark's partial biography had been sold in the auction, with a view to it being published. When he discovered this, he knew that he had to get hold of it, and eliminate anyone who had read it. So, discovering that I had bought it, he had broken into the house I was staying in and tried to find it, panicking when I turned up, and being prepared to kill me if necessary.

And now? Vernon Dark must have told someone that he had read the start of his father's autobiography, and Cope had come to hear about it. Which was presumably why he'd been murdered.

*

It had now been several hours since Cope had phoned me. Why hadn't he called back?

Should I go to the police, and report Laura as missing?

What would be the point? Cope was in the police force, he'd probably hear about it, and would be in a position to stifle any investigation into her whereabouts.

My only hope of rescuing Laura lay in getting to Cope first and neutralising him. Fortunately, my detective friend Jeanette had been able to give me an address for Detective Constable Steven John Cope.

Half an hour later I was parked outside Cope's house to the south of town.

It was mid-afternoon, and I was tired out after the long drive, and was suffering an overdose of adrenalin. I had finally found the answers I had been seeking for so long, but now all that mattered was rescuing Laura from a desperate killer. Everything was finally adding up, just at the time when my life was spinning out of control.

I parked around the corner to the neat row of terraced tiny houses. Cope's house was at the end. I walked around the side and along a narrow alley. There was a gate leading into the back garden – the catch smashed fairly easily.

Once in the back garden it was easy to find the back door of the house. There were no lights on anywhere, nor could I see anyone through the windows.

Finding a big stone in the back garden I smashed the glass in the upper panel of the door, then reached inside to turn the key that was in the lock, and opened it.

As I went into the kitchen I was aware of a new and different smell – something I had been familiar with a lot time ago: the faint astringent aroma of burnt gunpowder. Plus something else, something coppery and metallic, something like hell on earth, a smell to make you vomit.

I went upstairs, half expecting what I was going to find. I kicked open the door to the first room, and there he was, the gun still in his hand, the muzzle half-in and half-out of his mouth. Behind what had once been his head was a spread of multi-coloured fluids and bloody fragments on the white wall.

On the desk there was no note. Just assorted scrappy papers, the open laptop, the magazine of an organisation, *The Friends of Friendless Churches*, some handwritten lists on lined paper.

And on the walls were posters for Aryans Supreme, and a magazine of the same name was on the table. I scanned the contents, and, as the name implied, it was a publication to promote an organisation who had secret meetings around the country, and in Europe, advocating the supremacy of the Caucasians, with articles about supposed 'rape gangs' composed solely of black members, who operated with the supposed 'tacit approval' of the police, who were apparently 'too scared of being accused of racism' to act appropriately. There were articles by self-styled scientists, who offered supposed facts suggesting that the brains of black people were intrinsically inferior to those of white people.

Belonging to this organisation would clearly be inappropriate for a serving police officer, so his membership must have been kept a closely guarded secret. Of course the organisation was borderline illegal anyway, so most of the members would want their connection kept confidential, so for obvious reasons there'd be no public meetings or rallies, and members would communicate via secret meetings, telephone, or possibly the dark web. The website addresses in the magazine articles didn't look normal to me.

There were also articles from various provincial papers referring to the murders of black teenagers: one in Bristol a few months ago, another in Brixton, London, which had not been solved, but which it was assumed were gang related.

I thought of DC Cope's dark skin, his dark eyes. What must have gone through his mind, when the possibility was raised that his father might have been a black man? Fear? Panic? The feeling that his whole life had been a colossal joke? More than likely there was denial. Denial and hatred for the purveyors of such falsehoods. If that's what they were.

And then the other piece of the puzzle fell into place.

I don't want to kill you because you're one of us.

One of us? Even if my shooting of Trevor Goodbody had been forgotten by most people, within police circles it was still widely known about. Cope would have read that I had killed a black man, an evil drug-dealing black man, and in his warped mind that would have put us on the same side. So he would have been reluctant to kill me if there was any way to avoid doing so.

Then I caught sight of the printed pages from the company, *ancestry.co.uk*. It was the summary of their estimation of his ethnicity, based on his DNA sample.

It seemed that, according to the expert scientists, Steven John Cope was in part ethnically Afro-Caribbean.

Ironically, if Adrian Dark's theory that Jimi Hendrix had been murdered rather than died accidentally had been made public, no one nowadays would care very much, or even bother to question it. Likewise Adrian's assertion that Jimi had had an affair with Cope's mother, resulting in his conception. No one would notice or even care, and since Cope had changed his name, it was a chance in a million that anyone would make the connection.

But in Cope's mind it mattered. A mind-set of years and years of undiluted hatred and bitterness is hard to fathom, but the idea of being ethnically descended from the race you have hated all your life must have been horrifying.

Denial was the only way he could possibly face it, and the idea of anyone else being privy to the lie was more than he could stand.

And now that he had discovered that it was not a lie was why he had given up on everything and taken the only way out.

And my Laura was somewhere imprisoned, possibly dead, possibly dying, and I had literally no idea where she could be.

I closed my eyes, trying to think. Then I had an idea.

Taking a tissue from my pocket to cover my hand, I probed his pocket and then, sure enough, I found a car key on a fob.

I ran downstairs, out through the kitchen back door, into the garden, and into the front of the house and the main road. There were about six cars parked there, but when I pressed the key fob for his car, the hazard lights of the nearest vehicle, a grey Audi, flashed twice, and I heard the familiar beep-beep of an unlocking car door.

Inside his car, I turned on the ignition and managed to work out how to switch on his satnav. I wrote down the postcodes of his last three recent destinations, all of them for today, then got out, locked the car again, and ran back into the house to carefully put the key back into his pocket.

Back in my own car, I keyed the most recent postcode into my own satnav and set off, furious when I ended up at the police station where Cope had been based. Panicking now, I entered the second most recent destination and drove there.

It was a small village on the outskirts of Bath, and, it appeared that when I heard the satnav's upmarket female voice declaring *You have reached your destination*, I was in what appeared to be a recently established industrial estate.

Furious and getting scared now, I tried the third satnav destination, but this was in the centre of Bath, indeed it seemed to be the car park of Waitrose.

Think! Think!

Cope had been to three destinations this morning. Since he'd sent the text to me at 9am, it was reasonable to suppose he had recently been to see Laura, indeed the time and date of the photo he had sent me was on it. Laura wasn't at the Waitrose car park, and she sure and certain wasn't at the police station.

So that left the last destination, the industrial estate, so I drove back there.

I looked around at the alleys and the huge metal buildings. I could only assume she was being held in one of these heavily-locked warehouses or factories. How the hell was I going to find her?

Getting out of the Land Rover I looked around, scanning the horizon. Was she locked in one of these impenetrable buildings, secured with chain link fencing, and very efficient security? There were even warnings of guard dogs. I looked along the different side roads, beginning to panic now, wondering whether it was time to just give up and call the police and hope that they could do something I could not.

It was at the third side-road that I saw the derelict building. Then I remembered the small magazine on Cope's desk, the membership magazine entitled *The Friends of Friendless Churches*, featuring this particular derelict church on its front cover.

Close up the old structure looked to be on the point of collapse. It had been a Victorian church, but the roof had collapsed into the interior, leaving the place open to the sky. One wall had partially collapsed too. As I got closer I could see that it was surrounded by a small churchyard, but the gravestones were at all angles, stones in some cases having been lifted clear of the ground.

Think.

If Cope had a key to get into the church, and had tried to imprison Laura there, she'd have had no difficulty in simply climbing up to the roof to escape.

Unless she was tied up. Or locked inside an enclosed room.

As I got closer to the weed-encrusted, half-rotten wooden door, I could see that it wasn't even closed properly, and I pushed it with my shoulder. With a squeaking heave, it swung inwards, allowing me into the strange ravaged interior: rotting wooden pews still either side of the central broken-tiled walkway, leading to the upper dais, where an altar might once have stood. Light poured down from the huge gaps in the roof, and I could see that birds had made a nest in the upper rafters. Sure enough, a crow flew through the roof and perched there for a moment, as if daring me to come any closer.

The place was obviously empty. Yet this was where Cope had driven his car this morning, presumably, just before he had sent the text to me about having kidnapped Laura.

I walked around every part of the building twice, peering into every nook and cranny. I even called her name out loud.

But the sound just echoed back at me.

And then I saw something glinting in the last of the sunlight, just under a ray of sunlight from the hole in the roof.

FORTY-SIX

I bent down and saw that it was bright metal, like gold. Something like a bracelet, with the fastening broken. I don't normally remember jewellery, but now I had the distinct memory of seeing this particular item, with the skull and crossbones design I could just make out on one of the links, as falling down across the white glove Laura had worn when I had first met her at Netherwold Hall, when she was examining the rare books.

She was here somewhere.

I stared along the church interior once again, tried the tiny vestry, even opened the cupboard in the corner, but with no luck.

"Laura! Laura!" I called out again and again.

Then I heard it. A muffled thumping sound, very close.

"I'm here! I'll find you!"

I concentrated hard, moved slowly, trying to get closer to the sound. Eventually I was standing in the centre of the aisle, below the dais. In front of me was the huge marble slab of a tomb, set into the floor, with a named inscription faded with age on the metal plaque in its centre. Closer inspection showed a tiny relatively clean section of stone, just beside the edge of the white marble slab. I knelt down and put my ear to it. The thumping was louder here. In the corner of the church I could see a stumpy club hammer, and I raced across to get it.

Hammering the edge of the marble slab shifted it fractionally, just enough to open up a tiny gap.

"Sean?"

I could see Laura's face below me.

"I'll have you out in no time."

I found a discarded scaffold pole nearby, and pushed the end into the open gap, using it to lever the marbled slab aside. When I'd moved it to expose a six-inch gap, I could see Laura staring up from below, about eight feet down. Clearly she wouldn't possibly have been able to dislodge the stone herself from below.

When it was open wide enough, I could see her properly. I found a scaffold board and fed it down into the hole, then used it to climb down into the crypt. Laura was very weak and tired, but she managed to use the board to climb up, and I followed.

She was filthy and bedraggled, and I hugged her close, glorying in the pure joy of finding her alive, and cheating Cope of his desire to let her die. I was really glad that he was dead. If he'd been alive, I would have taken great pleasure in killing him myself.

Laura began to cry, great heaving waves of hysteria as she leaned against me, with my arms around her.

"Hush now, you're safe," I told her.

"But he might be here! He might come back. It was the policeman, DC Cope."

"I know that. He won't come back. It's over."

"How do you know?"

"He's dead."

She couldn't stop crying.

"I've got some news, by the way," I told her. "Your mum is alive. She's ill, she's been ill for years, but she's still alive."

"Alive?" She broke away from me, staring into my face. "How?"

"It's a long story."

"Where is she?"

"In a hospital in Yorkshire," I said. "I'll take you to see her as soon as I can."

"How did you find me?"

I told her all about Steven Cope, and how Jeanette Pierrepoint had managed to trace his whereabouts so that I could tackle him, and Laura asked about the address, interested to know where he had lived. Then I took her home, and helped her climb up to her attic flat above the shop.

"Look, I'm sorry," I told her, "but I need to get back to Whitstable as soon as I can. I found Cope's body and didn't report it. The longer I stay around here, the more danger there is that the police might try and link me to Cope's death. The sooner I get away from here the better."

"Do you think anyone's discovered his body yet?"

"Depends if anyone's reported him missing. But I broke into the place. I broke the law by not reporting the death. I'm already on police bail, accused of rape, so if the police arrested me now I'd have some difficult questions to answer."

"You get off. Goodnight, my darling. I'll see you soon."

FORTY-SEVEN

It was hard to believe that things were finally sorting themselves out in my life. During the next few weeks, I was lucky enough to get some more portrait commissions around the country, so I spent my time travelling around to these jobs, and staying in Whitstable as much as I could, and also visiting Laura in Bath whenever possible. It was a hectic life, but I was loving it. The more I got to know Laura, the more I found myself relaxing in her company, feeling I was getting to know her more and more. I thought back to the nightmare times when I was afraid that she might be a cold-blooded killer. How easy it would have been back then to give up on our relationship.

There was one cloud on my horizon, of course, and the charge of rape hanging over my head was something that woke me up in the dead of night, leaving me in a cold sweat.

But as always seems to happen in life, the things we worry about are rarely as bad as we fear. And the events we cannot possibly envisage pop out of nowhere and ravage everything. Which is what happened to me.

The aftermath of DC Cope's death had been predictably messy. When he didn't turn up for work and wasn't answering calls, his police colleagues broke into his house, two days after I had been there. His horrific suicide made front page news in all the local papers, even making the nationals. In his flat they found all the information on several racist organisations, including the Aryans Supreme, and his internet history, under a false email name, linked him with far right racist groups all over the world. The specialist police unit would be weeks going through all his material. There was no mention of his house having been broken into.

They had also checked Cope's work record, and found that on the night that Adrian Dark died he was on duty, but there was no record of where he actually was, in fact he was out of contact for several hours, claiming that his mobile battery was dead. The coroner had reopened the investigation into Adrian's death in the light of this information, and the indications were that they might easily conclude that he had been murdered, and Cope posthumously charged with the crime.

And oddly enough the team investigating Vernon Dark's murder were delighted that a bloodstained knife was found in Cope's flat, and the bloodstains were a match to Vernon's DNA. Investigations were ongoing, but the likelihood was that Cope would be posthumously charged with the murder of Vernon Dark too: apparently Vernon, in addition to being a petty criminal, was also known to be a blackmailer, and it was a reasonable assumption to make that he might have discovered the truth about Cope's paternity from reading his father's notes for his biography and was attempting to blackmail him with this knowledge, thus supplying a motive for his murder.

More disturbingly, at Cope's flat police found a number of cuttings from newspaper articles about the recent stabbing of a black drug dealer in Bristol that had been attributed to intergang warfare, and another similar murder of a black man in Brixton, London. A valuable WWII dagger issued to Gestapo officers was found with bloodstains on the blade, which forensically matched up to the two murdered black men. In the press DC Cope was being described as the 'Beast of Bath', for the killing rampage that police had only just realised was down to one man.

As for Jodie's murder, the main reason why I had come down to the West Country in the first place, the CCTV footage of the crowd on the Underground platform was traced, and it turned out that a man answering Cope's description had been present at the time she fell in front of the train, but proving he did it was a tall order, and while I did not have high hopes that her murderer would ever be found officially, his culpability for her death had been proved to my own satisfaction. Although I had found Jodie's killer, he wasn't facing any conventional punishment, but he was dead, so justice was served.

*

Several months later the dreaded time had come for my own legal drama. I was standing up in the dock in court, heart thudding in my ears. I was waiting for the start of the case against me for the charge of raping Mairéad O'Shaughnessy. There was a long delay, and as I looked across to the public gallery, my heart gave a lift as I saw Laura sitting there patiently, giving me a smile of encouragement.

I tried to see Mairéad in the public gallery, but it seemed she wasn't there, and then I realised that of course, she would be in an anteroom, waiting to be called to give evidence. It all seemed unbelievable, surreal. And then, just as finally we expected the judge to begin proceedings, a clerk came across to the judge and had a whispered word with him.

The judge addressed the court, announcing that the case had been dismissed and that I was free to go. Hugo, who I had seen in the public gallery, glared at me, as did DS Lavinia Hart, the copper who had charged me, and her glare of hatred proved whose story she believed. My barrister went over to chat with her prosecutorial colleague and when she came back, she was smiling.

"It's all over, Mr Delaney," she told me, putting her hand on my arm. "Ms O'Shaughnessy has dropped all charges. The police have no choice but to dismiss the case."

"Great." I felt a huge wave of relief wash over me. "Why do you think she changed her mind?"

My barrister Emily DuPont, a grey-haired, tall, and dignified lady whom I'd grown to like very much, gave a guarded smile. "It's one thing lying to sympathetic police officers and lawyers, but being cross examined by expert barristers in court is no picnic. Even if you're telling the absolute truth, a wily lawyer can tie you up in knots – I certainly planned to do so. Between you and me, I'd guess that the fact that Ms O'Shaughnessy had tried to involve you in an attempted fraud, and you'd refused, was something I was going to bring up as a motive for her false accusation. And I suspect it is something she definitely didn't want attention drawn to. What's more, I had a word with that songwriter you told me about – Ken Wheeler, and he had been prepared to appear in court if necessary to help our case."

As I was leaving the court, Hugo caught up with me in the corridor. "So you got away with it?" he asked, catching up with me.

"Mairéad was lying," I told him tiredly. "She probably didn't want to lie on oath."

"You know Mairéad has had a mental breakdown?" he

snapped at me, grabbing my lapels and trying to shake me. "She had trouble with prescription drugs not long ago, she had to go into rehab. Well it's happened again, she's started using, and God knows what's going to happen now. It's all your fault."

"Believe that if it makes you feel better."

"I ought to. . ." He was pulling me closer to him, now we were locked together, face to face.

I thought of telling him how Mairéad had come on to me that night, how she had been prepared to have sex with me, and how upset she'd become when I not only turned her down, but informed her that I wasn't helping her with the scam. But what was the point of upsetting him further? Bedsides, he'd never believe me.

"Now then," DS Hart said, taking Hugo's arm and gently disengaging him from me. "This is a court of law. No fighting, please, gentlemen."

She glared at me. "And, Mr Delaney, if you're planning to stay around here, I advise you to take care. We'll be watching you."

I nodded. "I guess I can't blame you for hating me. If I thought someone was a rapist I'd hate him myself."

"Don't get clever with me, Mr Delaney."

I returned her glare but she didn't back down.

"As I say, we'll be watching you."

Laura came up beside me and took my hand, confronting my enemies, and I found that I didn't care that they hated me.

So what should have been a time of celebration was tainted with bad memories. However, after all the stress of the past months it was good to know that I was finally off the hook.

With all the media attention I had been getting, some

of my portraits had been shown on television and social media; the publicity had earnt me a couple more promising commissions, and I was due to go to Birmingham next week to take up the first one, a retired industrialist who thought my style was, 'Absolutely wonderful, lad'. And to my surprise, Sylvia from Charngate Publishing had phoned me, full of apologies and understanding, asking if I'd be willing to undertake a book about my experiences concerning the 'Beast of Bath', as DC Cope had been christened, and the circumstances surrounding his crimes and subsequent arrest. Even though there was now no reason not to publish the book about Adrian Dark, Sylvia didn't mention it, and neither did I. It was Dark's wretched memoirs and diaries that had caused my wife's death, and I wanted nothing more to do with them.

And it had been a rocky road for Laura and me but we had finally won through and found a wee bit of happiness, or so I hoped. We were, at long last, a couple. I still felt the same about her as when I had first set eyes on her at the auction, all those months ago. We had talked for hours about the abuse she had suffered as a child, the evil things that had been perpetrated at that accursed place Harper's Dyke. As an aside, it turned out that only the month before, Ashley Donaldson, one of the most prolific sex attackers at the children's home, had died in jail.

Soon after we got together I took her up to the grim dark red-brick building in a village just north of Bradford, West Yorkshire. The Hargreaves Hospital was where her mother Angela had a nice neat little room of her own. She was an elderly lady now, smart and clean, able to walk, talk and eat, and seemed ostensibly normal, but she was unable to hold a real conversation, or even maintain eye contact for very long. As Laura looked at her it was amazing to see the spark of joy in Angela's eyes, as something in her fogged and troubled mind seemed to realise who the woman in front of her was.

I left them together, holding hands and gazing into each other's eyes, while I walked along the hospital corridor. Although the walls and ceilings were painted a bright clinical white, and there were thick dark carpets underfoot, there was such an air of misery permeating the place that I couldn't wait to leave. That evening, Laura told me that she had spoken to her mother, and found that she had a lot of moments of clarity. At one point she had looked into Laura's eyes and told her that Adrian Dark was not her father – she had just pretended that he had been, because she had had several frantic nights of sex with him and he was a rock star and rich, unlike her real father, who had been a waster.

Was it true? No one knows, and Laura didn't really care. The absurdity of life had meant that she had inherited all of Adrian Dark's worldly goods by a twist of fate, and she probably wasn't even related to him!

Would it have been better for Angela to have died all those years ago, rather than survive in this nightmare world of confusion and negativity?

I honestly didn't know.

I was in love with Laura and everything should have been fine between us, but the fact that she had inherited Netherwold Hall was, to me, a big problem. She had a successful business, and now she owned a mansion. And what did I have? A tiny house in Whitstable, a car and a precarious career that had only recently shown a spark of success. Even though I spent a lot of time in Bath, I did miss my life in Whitstable, and was not prepared to up sticks and move into Netherwold Hall, as Laura had suggested, and

Laura didn't want to live in Kent – especially as her shop and business was in Bath.

I wanted to keep my independence, was that so very bad? I loved her, no doubt about that, and I knew that she loved me, and as far as I was concerned that was key. Even so, Laura was urging me to move out of Whitstable. "After all," she pointed out reasonably, "there's lots of room in this house, you could have one of the upper rooms with all that natural light for a studio, you don't need to live in Kent, you're travelling all over the country painting people's portraits anyway. I'm already planning to move my bookbinding workshop into Netherwold, you could have a studio there and we'd be truly together all the time."

And a few weeks after that we had got engaged. Laura had arranged this big party at Netherwold Hall to announce our engagement, but I was not so keen. Remembering all the videos of her exploits climbing buildings, I still found it hard to reconcile the wild show-off climber and dicer-with-death Sarah in the Sky with the Laura whom I loved. She'd long since closed her website and Twitter and Facebook accounts, and Dr Fanshaw said that she had finally been cured of her Dissociative Identity Disorder, and no longer felt the need to escape into the life of her alter, Sarah.

I had come back from Whitstable to attend the party at six in the evening, and I was already late. Lots of people had been invited to Netherwold Hall, and outside caterers had been engaged to host the event. I was uncomfortably aware that my best clothes – an ill-fitting suit and stiff-collared shirt, didn't quite cut it as any kind of lord of the manor, and the very idea repelled me anyway. I didn't know many of the guests: Barbara and her friends and a host of various people I'd never met before, and to be honest I was wary of meeting them. Who were they anyway, I wondered?

Laura had told me that she didn't have many friends. Why was she throwing a party, showing off like this? This extrovert was someone I found difficult to relate to. I knew that marriage to the quiet, shy Laura was what I wanted above anything else.

Wasn't it?

For a fleeting moment I thought of my wedding day to Jodie. A cold rainy morning at a register office. Just me and Rob and Jodie and her sister, with the staff acting as witnesses, no fuss, no bother, just a brief business arrangement. But afterwards I had walked out of that place feeling that I'd done the right thing, that everything was going to be okay, that this leap in the dark was going to be the best decision I had ever made in my life. I thought of Jodie's lonely grave on the Isle of Skye, the view out from the clifftop over the sea where she had wanted to be buried, to be close to her ancestors. I longed to go up there now, to tell her about all that had happened, and of how I had found her killer, that I had finally done something right, I had played a part in killing a monster, so that the world was a better place.

And inside Netherwold Hall were all those people whom I really didn't want to meet.

But it was just a party, right?

For weeks now I had been working on a special portrait of Laura, and now it was beside me in the front seat of the car, and I was going to present it to her today, and I hoped she would approve.

It was going to be a happy day, the day that would cement my newfound happiness.

So why did I feel as if something wasn't right?

Crazy though it was, there was some tiny thing about the night that I'd found Vernon's body that was still niggling at me. I had thought and thought, racked my brains over what it was, but there was some tiny impossible-to-access detail that was skulking at the edge of my memory, a fragment that I couldn't catch.

Falling in love is supposed to be wonderful and magical. Yet the reality was that it made me miserable for much of the time, and I remembered how it had been with Jodie and me: violent rows and passionate reconciliations. Lots of our relationship spent apart, but an unspoken understanding of each other's moods and temperaments.

But I pulled myself together and parked the old Land Rover in Netherwold's grand front drive, next to a brand new Porsche, wondering if I would somehow be able to square the circle of being Laura's partner, when she was so rich, and I was not. I looked at the portrait on the passenger seat beside me, her lovely face gazing back at me, the whimsical expression that I'd captured in her eyes, the up-tilt to her mouth that had made me love her at first sight, even though I hadn't realised it at the time.

Sitting outside Netherwold Hall, I was feeling those cold-feet nerves everyone must experience before such a commitment as marriage. And I was just about to get out of the car was when I got the phone call that changed my life.

I answered my mobile without even looking to see who it was.

"Sean, mate?"

I recognised the harsh vitriolic tones of Kate Doyle.

"What do you want?"

I would never forgive her for selling the story about Laura to the *Daily Record*, when she had promised me she wouldn't do so. Kate belonged to the part of my life I was ashamed of, the period when I doubted Laura and had spied into her past life, something I could never ever tell her about. Emil Hervé's fall to his death was a subject that I would never ever talk to her about.

But Kate had helped me by publicising my part in Vernon's failed scam, so I guess I owed her something.

"I got some news," Kate went on. "And I reckon you're gonna hate me."

"News?"

"Sorry, mate, but you're not gonna like it." She paused. "Fuck it. There ain't no easy way to tell you this. You know that old lady in Paris, in the flat above the balcony where Emil Hervé and Laura were climbing, before he fell and was killed?"

"Yes? The witness who'd had a stroke?"

I thought back to that previous lifetime, the nightmare period when I was afraid for Laura's sanity, and had gone to Paris with Kate to investigate what had happened there.

"That's her. Well just now I got a call from her son, to tell me she's recovered. And guess what, she's remembered seeing Emil fall."

A shiver ran up my spine and I had the urge to swallow down the bile that had gathered in my mouth. "So?"

"*She saw Laura push him.* She saw Laura Kaplan kissing him one moment, then deliberately breaking out of their clinch, stepping back a bit. And then she saw Laura deliberately push him to his death. She says it definitely wasn't an accident. His clothes were in disarray, it looked as if they were going to have sex, but she had changed her mind. The lady heard him say something like, '*D'accord, d'accord, je comprends, nous arrêtons*'. That means, *okay, okay, I understand, we'll stop*. Seems that the poor bugger was terrified, he was struggling with her. She literally heard him *begging for his life.* But in spite of that, Laura deliberately pushed him to his death. *She deliberately pushed him to his death.* It was no accident, she's absolutely categorical about it."

FORTY-EIGHT

I couldn't swallow. I felt my throat close up as if I was going to choke. "How can she be certain?"

"I dunno, but she is," Kate went on. "She doesn't want to go to the police and stir up all that trouble again, she just wants to try and forget all about it. Not long after she saw the murder she had the stroke, and she reckons the shock of seeing that had something to do with it."

"Who else has she told? Why is she lying?" I demanded frantically.

"Fuck it Sean, *she's not lying!* Why would she lie? Why do you think I'm telling you this, mate? Believe me, I don't wanna to spoil your relationship with Laura, why would I want to do that? Believe it or not, I *like you*, Sean, that's why I'm warning you. That's why I'm telling you this, because you have to know. Laura, your girlfriend, *has deliberately murdered someone*. There ain't no way out of it. You've gotta know. And if she's murdered once, then—"

"I don't believe you! *Fuck off, you bitch!*" I yelled as I cut the call.

I didn't believe her. I couldn't believe her. There had to be some other explanation.

No, I didn't believe her.

And yet.

The tiny but forensically clear whisper in my ear told me the excruciating truth that I had known deep inside for all this time and had tried to deny to myself.

And then I had the cold hard twist in my guts, felt the wave of pure misery wash over me and the blur of the beginning of tears, so that everything swam in front of my eyes. After a short time I managed to control myself. I tried to look at things from all directions. I remembered the transcript of Dr Fanshaw's assessment of her mental condition, her confession to having attacked the boy at school, and almost blinded him, the confession of letting the perverted social worker who had been attacking her, die like a dog of a heart attack because she didn't fetch help – which I had made excuses for. . .

But it had to be untrue. Fanshaw was an experienced psychiatrist. When Laura had asked him if he thought she was capable of murder when acting as her alter, he had assured her that her descriptions of her murderous attacks on others were merely her imagination, and that she could not have done anything as Sarah, that she would not have done when she was shy law-abiding Laura.

Shy law-abiding Laura. . .

I don't know if it was the shock of the news, but that was the moment when something kicked into my head. It was the missing section of my memory of the conversation I had had with Laura about finding Vernon's body.

"Did he take the knife with him?" she had asked me.

I had answered that he had done without even thinking.

But how had Laura known that he had been holding the knife when I had encountered him?

A lucky guess?

Maybe.

Or something else.

I drove back to Bath, feeling physically sick, and nursing the overwhelming hope against hope that there had to be some explanation for it all. I was heading for her bookshop, Novelicious. It was an hour after I had been supposed to be at Laura's party, and I was ignoring the texts from her:

Sean where are you? Darling, everyone's waiting for you? When are you coming?

Not caring about the consequences, I parked outside her shop and went round the back of the premises and broke open the back door, going upstairs, straight to Laura's office.

I logged on to her laptop, relieved that she didn't bother with a password. Then clicked on her internet icon, heart hammering wildly as I opened up her history. I scrolled down, clicking on the websites she had viewed all that time ago, which she hadn't deleted. Back, back and back I went.

And there it was.

There the fuck it was.

Just two days before Vernon had been murdered, were the searches for 'default beneficiary', 'longstop beneficiary' and 'wills'. Adrian Dark's will had been a complicated legal document, but the part of it where it said 'and if my son, Vernon Dark, should die before 60 days elapses after my own death, then the beneficiary shall be my only other living relative. . .'

Reading that section of the will would have been complex to a layman, a fragment of a long boring document that most people wouldn't even look at, which was why she had checked up on it. And he had been killed on the fifty-ninth day after Adrian had died.

On the same day there was a search for 'All Covered

up', a shop in Bristol that specialised in selling balaclavas and dark tracksuits.

I just sat there. Then I looked again at my phone, noting the sixth text from Laura, asking me where I was.

The dagger found in Cope's flat. I remembered in the aftermath of me rescuing her from the mausoleum, driving back to her flat, and her asking me for Cope's address – I had wondered why she had wanted to know. But of course after I had left her it would have been easy for her to drive round there and plant the knife that same evening: a way of ensuring that she got a ready-made culprit for the murder she needed to get away with.

The murder of Vernon Dark, that meant she inherited Netherwold Hall and her father's money and back catalogue.

I thought back to when I had first seen her at the auction, and been mildly curious about the strange woman with the six fingers. Then I remembered when I had first seen her at Novelicious, the impish smile, the way she had leapt down from the ladder and fallen into my arms, and all I had wanted to do was to hold her there, keep her safe, protect her from the world and love her forever. The wave of sorrow I felt was so great that I couldn't move for a long time.

And I thought about how essentially lonely Laura had been, how she'd whispered to me how much she loved me, and that she would never love anyone else again, and that all she ever wanted in her life was to live with me. And it had been what I wanted too. I still loved her. I couldn't stop loving her.

Oh God, how I wanted it . . . Still wanted it. . .

For a fleeting second I was tempted. She was a killer, but I could ignore that, couldn't I? The old man at Harper's Dyke had deserved to die. But Emil Hervé had not, he'd simply been in the wrong place at the wrong time. Vernon was a bastard who had tried to have me killed.

But were there others? What about the hypnosis session with Fanshaw, where Laura related nearly blinding the boy at school who had tried to kiss her? And then, years later, climbing the electricity pylon with a boy and him falling to his death, and everyone assuming it was an accident, when Fanshaw told her it had indeed been an accident. Yet under hypnosis, Laura had admitted to killing him when she was Sarah, only Fanshaw was convinced she had been lying.

But love could conquer everything, couldn't it? I could simply shut it from my mind, pretend none of those things had happened. . .

Couldn't I?

I went back downstairs for the last time and got into the car. My phone was ringing now, and I had the urge to throw the damned thing out of the window. But I switched it off, pulled myself together, and started the engine.

The journey back to Whitstable was going to be hard. All around me I could still smell Laura's perfume, I guess that I would smell it until the day I died, and it would evoke all the horror, fear and torment I was going through now and would be going through for days, weeks, perhaps years.

I stopped beside a field, and got out of the car, taking the portrait of Laura I had spent so many hours painting. I held it up in the air, tears pouring down my cheeks, and then threw it into the sky, as hard and as fast as I could, then watched it flying through the air, caught on the wind, cartwheeling and spinning, eventually disappearing into some trees in the distance. I got back into the car and started on my journey back to Kent.

And tomorrow or the next day I was going to have to

face up to Laura and tell her that I knew the truth.

One day.

But not today.

I just had to get through the next few hours.

And keep on breathing.

Read on for the first chapter of the second Sean Delaney Mystery: *The Irish Goodbye*

***

THE IRISH GOODBYE

ONE

The screaming whine of the burglar alarm rang out. And all the lights in the castle flickered into life, flooding the darkness with dazzling white.

"Hey, you! Stop! I've got a gun!"

I heard the yelling as I ran away, leaving the painting I'd planned to steal on the wall and abandoning my own forgery on the flagstone floor. I got a sudden image of the shotgun's business end before the roar of the explosion. Then the ratchet clatter of the pump-action reload.

I made it down the wide staircase, through the hallway, then past the door and into the echoing high-ceilinged kitchen.

As I ran for my life, again I heard the roar of the shotgun behind me. Felt the hot warmth on my arm. Caught a glimpse of the blood rapidly pulsing down over my right hand.

Gunfire again.

But this time it went wide, and I ran on, careering through the kitchen, dripping blood onto the flagstones. I made it to the outside door and climbed out and onto the clifftop, where I dared to breathe and paused to bleed. I held on to the hope that my pursuer was still inside the castle, hopefully having lost my track.

The next gunshot, closer now, proved me wrong.

The moonlight made everything almost as bright as day. And the night air was cold and fresh, the salty ozone a welcome relief after the oppressive old-stone-and-furniture-polish aroma of the castle's interior. I ran on and reached the cliff edge, where I braced myself for the long agonising climb down the sheer rock face, remembering the rain-slicked craggy handholds that had ripped apart my fingertips on the way up.

In just a few weeks I had become a forger, a liar and a thief, the kind of person I normally despised. I had scammed my way into this grisly world, and now there was no way out. I had broken into a castle to steal a valuable painting, *The Dwarf of Sienna*, by Johannes Bartolomew, and pretty soon I was likely to be locked up for years with no prospect of bail.

And I had been shot, possibly badly injured, and my sliver of opportunity to escape depended on using my injured arm for an agonising climb down the cliff to the rocks below.

How had I come to betray every principle I had once held dear?

It was all because I had fallen in love with Anna.

*

Three weeks earlier

"My father was murdered!"

The girl with the green hair was barely recognisable as the gawky twelve-year-old child I remembered from fifteen years ago. The ugly duckling had changed into a lovely swan, and I couldn't take my eyes off her. With her fashionable black skirt and discreetly glamorous make-up, Anna Wilde was attracting more than her share of disapproving glances from the other mourners at this ghastly funeral. Miss Green Hair backed away from the lectern and rapped her scarlet-painted nails on the top of the plain pine coffin, causing it to rock with embarrassment on its rickety trestles.

"And the police won't do anything about it!" she went on, face flushed, her voice rising with anger. "That man killed him and they're covering it up!"

Her finger was pointing towards us, the congregation of po-faced mourners. I was at the back, tucked out of sight, and had been counting the seconds until I could escape from the stultifying gloom of this ancient Sussex church, with its acres of carved stone, shiny bum-crushing pews and its cloying aroma of old stone and damp earth.

But now that I'd seen Anna, I wanted to stay.

More than anything in the world.

The vicar, who had stepped aside just now to allow James Wilde's daughter to deliver the expected eulogy, moved quickly, accompanied by a graceful woman whose long dark hair swung loose around a lived-in face that looked like trouble had been a long-time guest. The pair took Anna's arms and she tried to shrug them off. Then, as she objected noisily, they managed to frogmarch her from the dais, out along beside the rows of sour faces and horrified glares.

I thought back to three months ago. The phone call from the man who was now in the coffin had been late at night, and out of the blue. Why, oh why, hadn't I taken it more seriously?

Sean, you've gotta help me, I'm in real trouble. I heard that you've been in the police, so you might have some idea of what to do. I've got myself into a terrible mess, and I'm bloody scared, man! I just don't know where to turn. . . Help me, mate, for God's sake help me!

It had been recorded on my answerphone at home in my studio at Whitstable, Kent: my one-time boss, James Wilde. Clearly drunk, over-the-top, voice slurred, making no sense, as had happened many times all those years ago, though in those days it was usually a more prosaic emergency than this one. I had rung back several times subsequently, but there was never any reply, so in the end I gave up, assuming it was just a drunken outburst. Then, again out of the blue, a couple of days ago I heard about his funeral, and knew nothing about how, when or why he had died, apart from the briefest summary in the newspaper report of an accidental drug overdose.

I longed to stand up and tell everyone that James Wilde had been a chancer, a libertine, a liar, and was a hopeless alcoholic. But all I'd gleaned from the vicar so far were pompous stuffy tributes and insincere platitudes that glossed over his failings and said nothing about his real virtues. James's faults were legion, but he'd also been a larger-than-life character who was widely acknowledged as a talented artist. And the warmth of his personality could light up a room.

When I had first left art school in 2001, I had joined his studio and learnt much of the complicated skills required for restoring and cleaning valuable paintings, and stayed for six of the happiest months of my life. He introduced me to the music of his generation: Crosby Stills and Nash, Fairport Convention and Bob Dylan, and I always remember the folk and rock numbers of the 1970s he loved so much, crashing through the studio as we worked, while hearing the opening riffs of The Eagles' 'Hotel California' always takes me right back to those happy days. He taught me that restoring paintings was all about technique, skills and knowhow and a billion trade secrets, whereas creative art was all about hard work, observation and making your craft as natural as breathing.

My first suspicion about his morals was when a man came into the studio with an ancient canvas that appeared to date back to the seventeenth century, as did the wooden stretcher to which it was fitted. It had been covered with a background colour, known as a 'ground' – and this ground was cracked all over with artificially grafted 'age lines'. The customer maintained the fiction that he wanted it 'restored' and 'cleaned', going on to explain that the invisible painting was in fact a lesser known Vandervelde painting of a number of sailing ships in harbour, and he proceeded to give us a collection of photographs of similar works by Willem Vandervelde the Younger, portraying precisely this kind of scene, with large galleons ranging down to tiny schooners. He told us that the details, and in particular the artist's signature, had been 'lost', and perhaps we could bring them back into focus somehow?

Of course James knew exactly what to do to recreate the 'lost' masterpiece, and together we did the job, utilising many of the tricks that the celebrated artist and forger Eric Hebborn had passed on to him when they'd worked together for a brief period in the 1970s, long before I was born.

This had been my first introduction into the world of art forgery, and though it seemed to be well-paid work, I had never wanted to get involved with such illegal activities on a regular basis, and after helping James by rediscovering the 'lost' work by Vandervelde, I much preferred to stick to our legitimate employment of restoring, cleaning and repairing old paintings. However, to say that this was the reason I left would not be true.

Why did I leave him?

That's a question that I never like to answer, or even to think about.

Because bisexuality is a bit of mystery to me.

Printed in Great Britain
by Amazon

86342754R00226